**Also availab**
**anc**

**Goddess with a Blade**

*Goddess with a Blade*
*Blade to the Keep*
*Blade on the Hunt*
*At Blade's Edge*
*Wrath of the Goddess*
*Blood and Blade*
*Bad Blood*

**Diablo Lake**

*Moon Struck*
*Protected*
*Awakened*

**Cascadia Wolves**

*Reluctant Mate* (prequel)
*Pack Enforcer*
*Wolves' Triad*
*Wolf Unbound*
*Alpha's Challenge*
*Bonded Pair*
*Twice Bitten*

**de La Vega Cats**

*Trinity*
*Revelation*
*Beneath the Skin*

*Giving Chase*
*Taking Chase*
*Chased*
*Making Chase*

**Petal, Georgia**

*Once and Again*
*Lost in You*
*Count on Me*

**Cherchez Wolves**

*Wolf's Ascension*
*Sworn to the Wolf*

**The Hurley Boys**

*The Best Kind of Trouble*
*Broken Open*
*Back to You*

**Whiskey Sharp**

*Unraveled*
*Jagged*
*Torn*
*Cake* (novella)
*Sugar* (novella)

*Second Chances*
*Believe*

*Bad Blood* contains descriptions of violence, blood, stalking, threats of violence, a great deal of foul language and death.

# BAD BLOOD

LAUREN DANE

If you purchased this book without a cover you should be aware that this book is stolen property. It was reported as "unsold and destroyed" to the publisher, and neither the author nor the publisher has received any payment for this "stripped book."

Recycling programs for this product may not exist in your area.

ISBN-13: 978-1-335-49083-4

Bad Blood



For questions and comments about the quality of this book, please contact us at CustomerService@Harlequin.com.

Carina Press
22 Adelaide St. West, 41st Floor
Toronto, Ontario M5H 4E3, Canada
www.CarinaPress.com

**Printed in U.S.A.**

This one is for Ray.
Who always believes in me.

Dear wonderful readers,

Hello there! I'm so glad to see you back for another installment in Rowan's story. When we last saw Rowan and her ever-growing cohort of allies, they'd finally vanquished a very powerful faerie who'd been at the head of a conspiracy that had cost the lives of many innocents, including some of Rowan's loved ones.

It's just a few weeks later as *Bad Blood* starts with Rowan getting pulled into a whole new mess. *Bad Blood* will be the start of a new two-book story arc where you'll get to know more about Darius and the Las Vegas Trick of Dust Devils, along with Genevieve Aubert and the Conclave of witches. The stakes are, as usual, quite high as we get drawn into another shadowy corner of the supernatural world.

I'll be back in 2024 with *Blood and Magic*, the conclusion to this mini story line.

Read Hard!

*Lauren*

# *Chapter One*

Genevieve Aubert made a cutting motion with her hands, pulling them apart, and as she did, she pushed her intent to end the magical working she'd just performed. To seal it off so nothing could leak out and harm an unsuspecting passerby.

With an internal pop, the outside world reasserted itself all around her in the kitchen of a rickety house in Long Beach, California.

"Well?"

"Always so patient," Genevieve murmured to her friend and partner on their current investigation, Rowan Summerwaite.

Three young people had gone missing, two of them witches. Which brought the total of missing witches—that the Conclave knew about—over the last six months to one hundred and ninety two.

"I'm not done yet. Their presence is strong here in the kitchen. I'd say they were all here recently. Within the last week. To be as specific as I can as I know you'll ask," she said quickly before Rowan could speak. "It's been four days since they've been here. Give or take twelve hours."

She walked through the living room and headed into

the first of three bedrooms before throwing open her internal shields to view the space through her magical sight.

Where there'd been bright ribbons of life energy clinging to surfaces and furniture in the other rooms, in the bedroom she stood in there was…nothing. No errant wisps of magic that had settled from the two witches who lived there. No life energy.

Continuing to use her othersight, Genevieve walked the short hall to the other bedrooms, finding the same psychic emptiness.

When she'd finished, she repeated the cutting motion to end the spell. The details of the magical world all around them settled into the background as her day-to-day perspective snapped back into place.

"Their imprint…" She paused, thinking on the right way to describe it to Rowan. "All living beings leave some flotsam just from their presence in a place. Life energy. Witches in particular leave another sort of evidence behind, an imprint of their magical power. Like spiderwebs in a corner. That's been erased—magically—from the bedrooms and bathrooms, but not from the common living areas." She waved a hand around the television room attached to the kitchen and dining area. "They spent a lot of time together in this part of the house. At least one of the witches has done some spellwork in the kitchen. There's no magic here that is unhealthy. Nothing violent. But once you step into that back hallway where the bedrooms are it's as if someone has used bleach, or another such cleanser. Magically, that is."

Rowan's gaze sharpened. "Why would their imprint whatsits be gone from the bedrooms but not the kitchen and common areas? I get that you can customize a working and all, but why choose those spaces and not others?"

"I don't know. It could be they were taken at night so all three were sleeping. Or early in the morning when one was showering and the other two sleeping or getting ready for work in their bedrooms. Or perhaps there was something magical that could have identified the perpetrators."

Rowan wandered around the area, looking in drawers and on shelves. She pulled out books and peered behind photo frames. "All the missing witches, at least the ones that have been reported, they've been healing or green witches, right? Hang on a sec, I want to text David to add some filters to the searches we're running."

David was Rowan's valet and the manager of U.S. operations of the Hunter Corp., the organization responsible for enforcing the Treaty that protected humans from supernatural beings. He'd only agreed to stay back in Las Vegas because it was daylight and because their guard was far more than adequate. He was very protective of his boss—who was equally protective of the young man she considered a son—but also intelligent and good at his job, so he'd handled the details best handled back at the newly opened Hunter Corp. chapterhouse.

"Check the connection we can find between the humans and witches who've gone missing together," Genevieve said. "I assume you're filtering out the disappearances connected to the Blood Front and the black market siphon spells."

Rowan nodded shortly. "First thing I asked him to do in the text. He's most likely already thought of that. He's pretty smart that way."

Just three weeks prior, Rowan, Genevieve, and Clive, the Vampire Scion of North America—and Rowan's husband—managed to work their way to the top of a conspiracy that had involved scores of missing witches. Witches who'd been drained of their magic to power a Faerie who'd been cast out of his realm.

They'd left a trail of dead, responsible parties. Some loved ones had been lost and Genevieve had been working with the Conclave Senate, the governing body of magical practitioners worldwide, to address internal leaks that had led to the deaths of so many they should have been protecting.

Instead of the disappearances finally coming to a halt after they'd vanquished a nearly immortal being, seven new missing witches had been reported over ten days. All recent disappearances, which meant they couldn't be tied to the prior business with the Blood Front because they'd only recently destroyed it by killing off said nearly immortal being.

Which meant there was more going on. Whether it was a whole new problem or something connected was something they'd have to figure out.

Just that morning, Genevieve had left Las Vegas for what was supposed to be no more than a few hours of meetings with other witches in the Conclave Senate on the topic of the internal leaks within their ranks.

By the time the plane had touched down at the Burbank airport, the report of the missing witches had been delivered to her inbox, changing the trajectory of her whole day. Two hours after that, she'd met up with Rowan, who'd traveled from Las Vegas, and they'd driven to the rental house the three missing people had shared.

"I've got some contacts inside the local police department," Rowan said from where she'd crouched to look through a drawer. "The family of the human called it in. Cops checked here, found nothing amiss. The guy works at a bicycle shop about half an hour commute away. One of the witches works at a garden center nursery type thing and the other does dog grooming. Let's pop by their jobs to see what's what after this."

Genevieve moved to stand at the doorway of the central bedroom and finally, at the edge of her vision she caught sight of...something. A splinter of magic she wanted to pluck and examine.

Inside her head, the voices within her, the spells, teachers, all that energy rose at once, clamoring for dominance and attention. She was over seven centuries old, and she'd been learning different types of magical practice since she was a child. Each layer she learned, each new discipline, each new teacher had become her armor, but sometimes when she performed a working the combined knowledge and energy got so loud, so painful and overwhelming it took discipline and steel to wrestle it back. Mostly they comforted her. Reminded her of her strength. But it could be overwhelming so she'd come up with various ways over the years to quiet the voices so she could perform the magic.

The back door swung open, and it was clear who was coming inside long before he entered the room.

Sage and salt. His scent. That tang that was uniquely Darius rose and fell like the tide. That magic—his magic—left bits and pieces of itself on her. In her. Made itself at home within Genevieve's essential magical talent.

He was an ancient being. A sense of very deep time emanated from his bones. Throbbed like a pulse. Against that, her magic seemed softer, younger, though many of the traditions she used for various workings were as ancient or older than he.

His general expression was inscrutable though menacing. Sometimes outright menacing. At times when she allowed herself to look deeply into his dark brown eyes, it felt as if she saw forever reflected within. When he used his magical energy, his pupils were ringed by amber fire. His hair lay in twisted coils, dreadlocks he often had tied back, exposing the harsh beauty of his features. Regal. Otherworldly in its perfection. High cheekbones and a sharp nose. His medium brown skin had a bronze cast when the light hit him just right. His lips drew her attention time and again, the fullness of his lower one a temptation she'd not felt the like of in so very long.

His very slight smile as he approached told her he'd caught her staring.

How could she do anything but stare?

Though he was wearing designer trousers and a thin, navy blue cashmere sweater instead of his more usual motorcycle boots and jeans, he still emanated a wild power. A strength and threat of danger impossible to miss.

He'd come for her. Because he'd sensed she was overwhelmed by the inner voices. The knowledge of that stunned her, even as she was finally allowing herself to believe that he would always do so.

Darius touched her elbow and a pulse of Dust Devil magic rolled through her until she could think clearly once more. Not that the voices died, but they subsided.

It hadn't been the first time he'd done such a thing, or the first time using Dust Devil magics had created a similar sort of harmony within her.

Dust Devils were beings of chaos magic. A long-ago branch of the wild hunt. In an unexpected turn of events a few months prior, Genevieve had become the priestess to the local trick—what they called groups of Devils.

Being their priestess had amplified her talent exponentially. Every few days she discovered something else, a new ability or an ease with a magical working that had been far more difficult before. In turn, she'd become what Darius likened to a conduit for the Trick. Her magic enabled them to access more—and retain longer—the power they gathered as they rode their motorcycles up and down the Las Vegas Strip. All that excess emotion was a banquet.

Genevieve was too old to pretend away the fact that something deep and potentially life-altering was developing between her and Darius. It was more than romance. More than sexual—though there were a great many romantic and sexual feelings between them—it was an acknowledgment of a connection. A soul connection.

She might not pretend it was just casual, but it still terrified her to have such depth of feeling for Darius. Worried that she was weakening herself to rely on someone else.

Yet, every day she let him into her life a little more, and despite all the fear, it had been a good choice. At the very least one she had no plans to give up.

"Thank you," she said. Despite the rules about putting oneself in the debt of another, Genevieve wanted him to know what it meant to her that he came when she needed him to.

He leaned very close to whisper in her ear. "It is my pleasure to help."

Shivers ran from the place on her neck where his breath had brushed straight to her nipples. The man was a menace. A delicious, delightful, wickedly sexy menace.

"There is something here," she murmured loud enough for Rowan to hear and understand what was happening.

"Faint. If I can tease it back into existence there should be evidence of the witches who made the working."

"That's handy," Rowan said as she stepped out of the hallway. "I'll wait in the kitchen." Rowan was the human vessel to a goddess. The magic and power she gave off could be blinding. And so bright it often obscured things that lived in shadows and places in between.

Darius did not retreat as far. His personal magic tasted of hers, was bound with hers. It was distracting for other reasons if she spent too much time pondering *that*. So she put aside the wonder at their connection and focused on her job while he kept watch on the area around them. Letting her fall into the world of her magic without worry.

Once her othersight was open, Genevieve bent to examine that little fleck of magic. Committed it to memory. The feel of it. The flavor. It was brittle, as if the burst when the spell detonated pulled the juice away, leaving it a husk. A dried-up leaf at the end of autumn.

Somewhere inside, the voices rose, but only a few. Just the ones who knew the song she began to sing in a language that hadn't been spoken in a thousand years, calling her magic to fill those veins within that desiccated spell fragment, reanimate it enough for Genevieve to get a good look at just exactly what it was.

She coaxed and soothed, drew gently but firmly, slowly rebuilding the fragment enough to finally get a good look at it, cataloging all the elements she could before that little wisp finally brightened and then popped from existence.

"Are we done here?" she asked Rowan. "I don't recognize the caster of the working used. But there are elements of it that feel familiar. I will need to go to the

Conclave building to confer with my assistant so that we can begin a search. I'll figure it out in the end."

Rowan nodded. "I have my own car. You go handle witch business at witch central. I'll do some poking around at their jobs to see what I can find out. I'll check in with you after that and if you don't need me here, I'll meet you back in Las Vegas."

"Fine. Do be careful or your husband will complain, and I will never hear the end of it," Genevieve told her. As Rowan was frequently involved in very dangerous activities, it bore repeating on a regular basis. On top of that, the Vampire she was married to was an arrogant apex predator whose loyalty and focus, above all else, belonged to his wife.

"He's a pussycat." Then Rowan laughed. "Just kidding. I'm always careful. It's been three weeks since someone has tried to kill me. I probably shouldn't have said that out loud to jinx it. Update me or David when you can."

After Rowan left, Genevieve turned back to set a series of spelltraps. If anyone came home, or walked through the house, it would trigger and notify her after embedding a tracker into whoever was there.

"And wherever did you learn that?" Darius purred at her.

Proud he'd noticed and was impressed, she barely resisted preening. "I trained under a battle mage for many years. Better than fingerprints any day."

# *Chapter Two*

Normally, Genevieve would have given Darius the grand tour of the Conclave building. It was one of her favorite places on the planet. A Beaux Arts masterpiece chock-full of magic and witches. The archives took up several floors, lined with some of the oldest records and spellwork they'd managed to gather and hold on to, even during purges, burnings, and other types of persecution they'd fled from over their history.

But that day wasn't about tours. She had a series of meetings to attend with a bunch of witches who loved to use rules of order as a way to battle with one another. Every meeting that could have ended in an hour could last three or four times longer, depending on who attended and who chaired.

Witches loved rules so much they enshrined everything with them.

"Just up this stairway," she told Darius.

He kept one hand free, but the other rested at her elbow. Not restricting, guiding. "This is beautiful," he said quietly.

She smiled his way. "Thank you. Next time I come, I'll give you the grand tour. There are extensive gardens for ingredients for various types of spellwork just out there."

Genevieve pointed once they reached the wide gallery at the top of the curved stairs. "Madame is here today to gather some starts for the house and to visit with her son, Bastien. Samaya, her oldest child, is my right hand here at the Conclave."

Lorraine, or Madame, as most people called her, was Genevieve's assistant and house manager. She kept Genevieve fed, rested, paid attention to things like bills and the marketing, and guarded her against anyone or anything who'd attempt to harm or steal time they did not deserve. She was one of a long familial line who'd served the Auberts for generations.

Though she scared most everyone, she'd decided to treat Darius like he was hers to take care of as well. He allowed it. Perhaps he was afraid of her like everyone else. Whatever the reason, Genevieve found it incredibly sweet and ridiculously sexy that he was so kind.

It also meant that her close inner circle within the Conclave Senate were those she could trust without hesitation. Given the real sensitive nature of what they were looking into, it mattered.

In addition—or perhaps, related—Genevieve and her team had opened a deeper investigation into the leaks within their organization. The horror of the full extent of betrayal from within the Conclave continued to reveal itself bit by bit. They'd discovered witches working with Vampires and an ancient Faerie. Those witches had sold the locations and identities of their fellow practitioners. Fellow practitioners who'd been kidnapped, drained, and killed. For profit. For power.

It ran counter to everything they stood for. For some it had shattered their ideal of community and coven. At their core, they were supposed to protect one another against violence and mistreatment from the outside world.

They all knew what it meant to be the target of the mob. The inquisitors and the holy men who'd arrested, tortured, drowned, and hanged had thinned their numbers and left them constantly looking over their shoulders simply for existing. The Conclave made them safer together. Created community in far-flung places and safety in numbers. Taught their young how to use their gifts, trained in control.

For centuries Genevieve had bounced around the globe. She'd learned and taught and when called upon, she'd fought for her people. Like her father had done for nearly a millennia. Like her cousins. They were Aubert. It was their lineage to defend.

She had great power. Unique talent and familial and political connections. Nearly two years prior, Rowan came to her for help on a case. Turns out that case had connections to the magical world and Genevieve had taken it as a sign. One she'd been subconsciously waiting for. A sign to grow a community around herself that included friends. A sign to take up the mantle that belonged to her family and be more active within the Senate, build its defenses, sharpen its offensive capabilities.

It was time for her to ascend to the level she'd been born to.

She made introductions as they went through to her offices and once she and Darius were alone, she said, "I'd reiterate that I'll be in meetings for the next few hours and as you're not a member of the Senate, the chambers are off-limits to you. You can go off to do whatever you like, but we both know you already do whatever it is you like. So. Please make yourself comfortable here. Samaya will be with me, but her assistant, Rabia, will be at the desk. Let her know if she can send for anything. If you do decide to stretch your legs, just remember to take the keycard I gave you."

He took her in as he stood, stretching to his full height as he stalked to where she stood. "I'm not going anywhere until you do."

Stubborn chaos demigod.

"Very well. I will return when we have breaks."

He placed a staying hand at her elbow a moment. "Even here in this place full of witch magic, if you speak my name into the air, I will come. Nothing can stop me should I wish to enter your Senate chamber. In defense of you, I can go where I like," he told her and some wild part of her deep down thrilled at his declaration. The experience of being defended the way he'd done wasn't something she'd experienced before. It was delightful and addictive.

She nodded. Because she'd called his name twice now and he'd come without delay. It meant something to her that she could trust his promises.

Samaya briefed her as they headed to one of the meeting rooms. "This morning while you were at the missing witches' house, I was informed of a rumor regarding a group of witches who have been organizing outside the Senate. Pushing to loosen rules regarding how we interact with humans. The Sansburys are apparently involved."

Tristan Sansbury was Genevieve's ex-husband. He and his family were powerful and venerated despite being a bunch of assholes. Genevieve wasn't surprised to hear they were involved.

"Anyone else?" Genevieve asked.

"The Salazars and Clares," Samaya said with a sigh.

The Clares were another family that liked to prattle on endlessly about the *old* ways and traditions while pushing for fewer rules about how witches were allowed to use their magic. Always in the context of using magic to manipulate or coerce humans.

It was all so much bullshit. Their oldest law, the most important one was that magical practitioners did not use their gifts to harm others outside extreme situations like self-defense. *That* was traditional. *An it harm none, do what thou wilt.* That was their rede. Their guiding principles.

Witches, be they Genetic witches like Genevieve and her familial line, who were something other than human with life spans similar to Vampires, or Conclave/Independent witches who were humans possessing some magical gifts, had a responsibility to use their talents with care and thought.

In the end, after all the politicking was done, the problem they currently faced boiled down to petty bigotries. Witches like the Sansburys, Salazars, and Clares thought humans were beneath them and therefore it didn't matter how they were treated.

Sadly, such beliefs weren't unique. Acting on them? Well, that was connected with some of the disappearances. Witches within the Senate had been the ones who'd leaked the location of many of their fellows, now missing and dead, to the Vampires.

Was this attempt at rule changes connected? Or was it straight-up capitalism with a twist of xenophobia? "Let's dig in on this. Figure out exactly what's going on. Then we can know how to address it," Genevieve said quietly.

"Speaking of rule changes," Samaya said. "A family is seeking revision. They run a business that provides entertainment acts for casinos, lodges, and cruise ships. I've sent it to you, Gaius, and Zara. Read it over and we can discuss next steps afterward."

Gaius and Zara were the other two witches working on the investigation Genevieve was heading up.

"*Bon*," Genevieve said. "While this is in process, let's put together a dossier on this family and their businesses. Who are they?"

"The Procella family. I'll look into them more deeply as you've asked. Bas would likely know, so when he's done with my mother, I'll talk with him to see what he has to say."

Bastien had a great deal of magical talent with green things. His mother was the same. But he was ridiculously charming and so pretty it was difficult not to stare at him just for the pleasure of it. People shared private things with him all the time. Brought him bits of gossip. Unloaded their own secrets. He'd told Genevieve once it was a gift and a curse.

"Good idea," Genevieve said. "I don't know much more about them than they're Americans. I sat on a committee once with one of them. Hugo, I think." She curled her lip. Hugo had been odd in a creepy way. Some European witches had a real issue with Americans. Elitism and snobbery went hand in hand with older Genetic witches sometimes.

Rowan had barely touched down in Las Vegas when her phone began pinging and dinging. "For fuck's sake," she grumbled, tucking it away to grab her bag and deplane.

A car waited for her several feet away and her valet—who also happened to be the manager of U.S. operations of Hunter Corp.—leaned against the driver's side pretending to casually wait, but she knew he kept watch on his entire field of vision. As she'd trained him to do.

He had short, very well-cut dark blond hair he ran a hand through before straightening to his roughly five ten or eleven. At his wrist, the Mido Ocean Star she'd given him as a congratulations for his promotion to head of all U.S. operations. Sunglasses with green lenses that echoed with the green in his tie. Perfectly knotted. The vest went with the navy trousers and the suit jacket she had no doubt existed somewhere. Dark brown oxfords she knew were specially treated on the soles so he would be able to run and fight in them if necessary, completed the whole look.

"Thanks for coming to get me," she told him as she approached. "I haven't read any of my texts or listened to a single voice mail. Give me the bullet points on the way to the office. I'm driving so move yourself to the passenger side." She flapped a hand at him.

He knew better than to argue and soon enough they were headed away from the private airfield toward the building she'd just established as the United States Motherhouse of Hunter Corp.

"Okay. Go," she said.

"About ninety minutes ago the Nation sent a response to our hiring announcement. It's pretty much what you'd expect. They're not prepared to endorse such a plan in its current state, but they *invite* discussion via workgroups and studies. There's a two-page addendum with their asks bullet pointed. I'd say only about one in every fifteen is realistic. Obviously they know you're going to see this for what it is. The big surprise is that there's a new player."

"Really now? Do tell," Rowan said.

"On the letterhead they refer to themselves as Vampire lords."

Rowan guffawed. "Stop!"

"I'm absolutely serious. I've never heard of any of them, though you probably will have. Vanessa is gathering information on them now, so you'll have dossiers shortly." Vanessa was their new tech and intel whiz. She'd come to them after the person who'd held the job before her, Carey, had been murdered as part of a complicated knot of a conspiracy that had led them to some wicked powerful Vampires, sorcerers, witches, and a Faerie caught on this side of the veil.

Rowan missed Carey so much it had been difficult to let herself like Vanessa, but as the weeks had passed, the tiny purple-haired woman covered in colorful tattoos had begun to grow on them all.

Carey hadn't been the only loss. After two years of relentless violence that had left dozens of Hunters in the field severely injured or dead, Hunter Corp. had changed the way it did things. On multiple levels.

Most of those changes were no one's business but Hunter Corp.'s.

But there were a few things they'd wanted to include the Vampires and Conclave in. Chiefly, the special teams HC was in the process of creating. They'd already established one with Genevieve and Rowan to deal with any cases having to do with magic. And they were in the process of hiring one and possibly two Vampires within the next day or so.

Which is why they'd notified both the Conclave and the Vampire Nation of what they were planning, inviting feedback several weeks prior. *Not asking permission.*

"I've never heard of a Vampire lord. That sounds like

some made-up bullshit. But it's on the letterhead of the Vampire Nation, which says whatever it was or wasn't in the past, they're being tolerated now." Rowan frowned.

She'd expected time-wasting dramatics. They were Vampires after all. The most extra of all beings. Mainly because they were next best thing to immortal and anything happening quickly was anathema. It was a knee-jerk response she often thought was genetic by that point. Add to it that it was easy to get bored, so everything had twenty layers over it to provide entertainment. Still annoying, but she knew it came with the territory.

"Additionally, the Nation's response was only sent to London and Paris. They had no idea we weren't included until someone from Susan's office called to speak with you about it."

"Someone woke up wearing their petty pants. Theo must be pouting. This screams, *pay attention to me*." Theo was the First. As in the first Vampire. Ever. Beyond ancient, and ridiculously powerful. He ran the Vampire Nation. He was sometimes homicidally unstable. Other times hyper focused and disciplined. Always intelligent. Not just an apex predator, but one of the most deadly beings in existence, period.

And he was Rowan's foster father. He loved her and her attention, and sometimes threw little tantrums until she gave it to him. Tiresome. But it kept him from murderous rampages across Europe, where his keep lay, and if she was totally honest, she loved him too and didn't want him to fall into the lure of the yawning loss of sanity that lay below the knife's edge he walked.

She still feared him. For good reason. In any case, it was all very complicated, but that was family for you.

David read off a few names and she grunted. "I recognize a few of those names. I'll be interested to see those files Vanessa is putting together. These lords are important enough to have Scion-level access to Theo. But only if he allowed it, which he so clearly has. I'll contact the other partners so we can draft a plan. Until then we say nothing if we're approached by anyone other than Hunter Corp."

Once back at the office, Rowan wrote up her notes from the workplaces of the three missing people in Long Beach, forwarding a copy to Genevieve. All three were liked at their job by bosses and coworkers alike. None had any history of no-shows. They had friends who noticed their absence. But the three also liked to drive out to Palm Springs on a whim so many assumed that's what had happened.

David came into Rowan's office with a large mug of coffee and a croissant the size of a salad plate. "Susan is coordinating with the other partners and will text the details. She said she figured you wouldn't be too bothered, and she was right. She said she trusted your response to be the correct one and that the Nation wasn't worth trying to have a meeting across multiple continents."

Pride warmed her. Susan was Rowan's former trainer within Hunter Corp. That she had such confidence in Rowan's skills pleased her. "Okay, good. We are all too busy for this bullshit. Anyway, this," she held up the Nation response, "was not written by Nadir."

As annoying as the situation was, it was an ideal training moment. David, as her valet, had completed enough training that he was an integral part of her investigations. She needed to include him as often as possible instead of giving in to her need to control everything herself.

"It wasn't?"

As one of the Five, Theo's personal security team, Nadir was the only one who ever spoke in public. She was called the Voice, and sort of like the Pope, was the First's official representative to the Vampires he governed and to other supernaturals worldwide.

"She's a thousand years old. An absolutely brilliant negotiator and diplomat. That," Rowan pointed at the paper, "is ham-handed and full of *look at me* type language. Chaotic because it's so obviously written by committee. It's too long. And the insults are clunky and petty in a way she'd consider beneath her. To be honest, David, I don't know what's going on. Once we figure out who they are, we'll have a better chance at figuring out what they're up to and why they were allowed into this process to try to mess it up. Goddess only knows if we'll have this handled by the time we have to leave for Prague."

"I have a sinking feeling that this Joint Tribunal will be full of drama and threat behavior. Please do not go anywhere alone this time. Set a record for times in a row someone *doesn't* try to kill you at some event you're compelled to attend because you are attempting to do the right thing," David finished, slightly flushed with emotion.

The Joint Tribunal was essentially a quarterly work group between Hunter Corp. and the two major governing bodies in the supernatural world, the Vampires and witches. A year and a half prior, Rowan had been at one when a super-powerful magic-using Vampire with delusions of godhood had ambushed her, leaving her barely clinging to life and in need of a great deal of very powerful Vampire blood.

And that hadn't even been the only dramatic thing that happened over the three-day meeting. Rowan had been challenged to a duel. Theo had executed someone.

She'd punched several people and there'd been a tsunami of Vampiric posturing. And the beginnings of the conspiracy within Hunter Corp. had been exposed. She'd nearly been blown up by a fucking purse bomb when she'd rooted out the Hunters who were the traitors.

Rowan waved a hand at all those good times. "Hopefully we can avoid duels to the death and ambushes. I can't say there won't be blood and maybe tears. I only have so much patience with them."

David choked on his tea.

"I have patience! I can wait years for things because the amount of time I can hold a murderous grudge is forever. Speaking of my petty streak. Find out the time of sunrise in Germany tonight. Let's send our reply five minutes before that."

Surprise and then admiration danced over David's features as he realized what she'd be doing and the big fuck you it sent to reply right when the Vampires she'd be addressing would be sucked into daytime rest before they could mount any sort of reaction.

They thought they could fuck around and now they were going to find out.

Rowan wrote an email with her thoughts on the Nation's response, and sent it to all the relevant parties before she did anything official. Celesse in Paris, France. Susan in London, England. And their two newest Hunters promoted to full partner, Adaeze in Kano, Nigeria, and Ant from St. Petersburg, Russia. The earlier trouble within Hunter Corp. had been exacerbated by some partners acting unilaterally. They made choices *together* when dealing with important matters now.

After a series of emails back and forth, they decided to

issue their response from London instead of Las Vegas. It separated it from Rowan and said it came from Hunter Corp. officially.

Vampires were all about appearances. On the other hand, her foster father—the most powerful Vampire on the planet—would pout at losing that access he totally thought he had a right to because of their relationship. But that also underlined that this was not a Theo and Rowan issue, but a Nation and Hunter Corp. problem.

*We do what we want. We don't need permission.*

They had to play a game anyway so they might as well give as good as they got.

# *Chapter Three*

As Genevieve walked through the halls of the Conclave building, she let her power unfurl like royal raiment. A cape of warm, heady energy that pushed out from her body.

That day Genevieve had chosen all white, from the slim trousers to the double-breasted cape-sleeved blazer and sleeveless blouse. The only color came from her scarlet, sky-high pumps and the rubies strewn across a diamond pin tucked into her hair. Darius had given her the antique beauty that morning before they'd left Las Vegas.

She wasn't entirely certain how, but wearing it had added to her power. Had marked her in a way that said to everyone she'd ascended to a new level. It suited the rubies she wore at her ears and wrists. It said power in another way. It said money and influence. She was rich in spells, rich in magic, rich in talent and connections and in this place bound by centuries of hierarchy and tradition, it was the most valuable type of currency.

*See me.* Not a request. Not a question. At seven hundred years old and a Genetic witch, she'd earned her place in the upper-echelon leadership of the body that governed practitioners—magic users—worldwide.

Each component was a piece of armor. Combining not

to *say* power, but to radiate it like a pulse. They were all predators of a type in this wing of the Senate. She wanted their continued support of her investigation. Wanted their certainty she would succeed.

Needed to show those who may have used her in the past that she was far beyond their reach now and should they ever attempt to repeat their prior ill treatment, she would crush them.

At the head of the table stood the leader of the Conclave. Konrad Aubert was a thousand years old but appeared to be in his late thirties. Though he currently wore a suit, he seemed equally at ease dressed in gleaming, bespelled armor. Lush caramel-colored hair swept back from a brutally handsome face and brown eyes that missed absolutely nothing.

Those eyes currently held open approval of her little display of strength.

Before she could reach her father though, another man stopped, blocking her path.

"Genevieve?"

She looked him over and though he was vaguely familiar, she couldn't place him. "Yes?"

He beamed at her and then bowed. "I'm Hugo Procella. We met several years ago. I've wanted to set up a time to speak with you to regarding some issues my family would like addressed."

Ah.

Samaya stepped to her side and slightly shielded Genevieve with her body. "Mr. Procella, your request has been submitted through official channels. If you'd like to take a meeting with Senator Aubert, you may contact her office."

He didn't even look at Samaya much less bother to

thank her. Genevieve took that knowledge and tucked it away. How someone treated those in service for one reason or another said everything about that person.

"Perhaps you'd allow me to take you to dinner while you're here. Or in Las Vegas. My family has a house there you'd enjoy," Hugo said.

"I'm afraid that's not possible," Genevieve told him and stepped to move around him.

Hugo followed, continuing to block her progress. "I assure you, it's not just about business."

This entire situation made her grumpy and uncomfortable. Embarrassed for this witch who didn't want to understand what was going on.

"You're blocking my path, Mr. Procella. I've given you my answer. You have submitted the proper paperwork and when I have a moment, I'll look at it."

"But you haven't given me your private number so I can call you," he said, trying at flirtation.

Genevieve reared back slightly but it was Zara who'd approached this time, pausing at the opposite side from Samaya, both forming a defensive line.

"It's time for you to move along," Samaya said, her tone gone entirely cool and flat.

"This has nothing to do with you," Hugo said, his eyes never leaving Genevieve.

"Your rudeness does not go unnoticed," Genevieve said, giving him nothing but no. "You've been told what will—and won't—happen. If you haven't been told something, you may assume the answer is no on that as well."

He ducked his head a little. Artfully playing at remorse. She knew her lip was curled and made no effort to smooth her expression.

"Have dinner with me. Without business talk. You and I, Genevieve, we would make a fine couple."

"No, thank you. I'm involved with someone." At that, she gathered up her magic and pulled it around Samaya, Zara, and herself. It created a sort of energy buffer that would give a painful electrical zap if one got too close.

It backed him up immediately. Samaya sent a look to the guard at the door and then back to Hugo Procella.

When he saw the guards approach, he seemed to pull all that weird energy he'd been spilling back into himself. "I do like a challenge," he said before leaving.

"What a creep," Samaya muttered.

Genevieve noted her father coming toward them, concern on his face.

Samaya and Zara moved to the table to take their seats.

"What was that all about?" he asked Genevieve.

She gave him a brief rundown on the situation and the gossip about Clare, Sansbury, and Salazar working together to demolish the rules protecting humans and the possible connection to whatever the Procella family might want. She hesitated over telling him about the way Hugo had come on to her, but held it back because it felt strange to say so when she'd handled it herself.

They spoke briefly about her working with Hunter Corp. She'd taken the biggest issue between the Conclave and Hunter Corp. off the table when she'd assigned herself to Hunter Corp. as a liaison. She would not draw a salary from HC, so her motives would never be in question on that front. It had eased objections the way she'd hoped it would though some still were opposed because they didn't like depending on outside actors or anything new of any type.

"I had not imagined Hunter Corp. to be such an ally,

but I can see the reasons for it. You have my support in the direction you're attempting to take the Conclave in," he told her quietly, but not so softly others wouldn't hear.

She lowered her chin slightly in thanks. He should, of course, support what she was doing. He'd been a warrior the entirety of his life. Few understood the way he had, the real danger to them if they did not pay attention to their enemies within. Konrad Aubert was a warlock. A warrior who used magic as a weapon in defense and protection of his people. Lore said he'd fought his first battle at just twelve. Accurate or not—and to be sure, the world a thousand years before held plenty of twelve-year-olds on battlefields—he'd been a fighter for centuries.

Witches needed to operate at high security because someone was always trying to kill them.

Three bells sounded to officially open the meeting. The Recorder would take minutes while Konrad would chair.

Unlike the general Senate meetings, committee meetings like this one were far less prone to endless peacocking and delay via the hefty tome of rules they operated by.

And yet, she found herself repressing a curled lip of distaste at the sight of her ex-husband. Tristan had seated himself at her right. Gaius was on Samaya's right, looking very smart in a charcoal-toned suit, his dark blond hair cut expertly to frame his handsome face.

"I was attempting to explain to Tristan that he was in Samaya's place," Gaius told Genevieve.

Genevieve remained standing, towering over Tristan. She repeated what Gaius had just told her. "That's Samaya's seat."

"I'm a Senator. She's an assistant," Tristan said.

"You're not on this committee. You're a guest. Guests sit there." She pointed.

It wouldn't do to argue with him. He *wanted* engagement. Wanted to force her to interact. Outside of those moments when it was absolutely unavoidable, she never gave him one single extra syllable.

"There's someone in your office," he burst out, exasperated, but he did give the chair to Samaya, who rolled her eyes behind his back.

Darius was no secret. There were rampant rumors about her in the paranormal world since she'd become the priestess for the Trick. The Sansburys liked to consider themselves royalty of the Conclave like it was still seventeenth-century Europe instead of the modern world. They had power and influence. But theirs wasn't the only type anymore.

Genevieve amused herself imagining Tristan trying to get anything from Darius.

"You knew this?" He left the end of the sentence hanging, clearly expecting to be informed of who it was. And if Darius hadn't told him, she had no plans to.

"Did you need something from my office?" she asked, knowing full well he was desperately trying to engage her and get details.

"I merely wanted to be certain there hadn't been a security breach," Tristan said, trying hard for earnest. And failing.

Rowan would have said something like *as if*, but Genevieve sent Tristan a bland smile that said absolutely nothing at all. It was more than he deserved. He most certainly had no business whatsoever in her office, especially since his family was apparently stirring trouble.

"Who is it?" Tristan asked right as a single bell rang.

No more side talking. It was all business from then on out or she'd get a dressing-down from her father in front of everyone.

Genevieve turned and settled in her seat. At her left, Samaya, a spritely blonde with a pixie cut wearing a herringbone suit that flattered her pale skin and blue eyes. At her right Zara, long and lean, her hair close cropped to expose the lines of her face, including the tiny gold ring in her nose. Deep brown skin, utterly perfect posture, and a coral-toned jumpsuit completed the look.

Genevieve knew they made a picture. Optics, they called it. Another piece of the armor.

Konrad opened the meeting and handed it to Genevieve and she laid out all that had been done in the aftermath of so many kidnappings and deaths of their fellow witches.

"To date, one hundred and ninety two witches have been reported missing. The most recent two as of earlier today." The number staggered her. It grew weekly. So many grieving families and friends. So many communities trying to get through the loss of one of their own.

And now this troubling rise in humans who were going missing in the same area the witches had. Was there a connection? It seemed far more than mere coincidence.

Genevieve concluded, "The picture changes regularly due to all the information coming in. Each step leads to another. Our investigation is ongoing. There are still leaks within the Conclave."

"It would be easier not to talk to your back," Tristan said. "You have no proof there are more leaks."

"Good god, man, do shut up," a Senator from across the table said.

"I didn't ask your opinion either," Tristan said.

"I am chairing this meeting. You do not have the power to challenge the topic or who speaks on it," Genevieve said. "I've asked you several questions you continue to avoid answering. So now let us revoke that question and you can close your mouth."

Ever predictable, at her back she heard his intake of breath as he was about to say something and she tapped her thumb against her other fingers in a shut-up motion. Her magic pushed slightly, closing his mouth and preventing him from uttering a word.

Well. That was new. She hadn't even meant to use magic but it had obeyed her wish to shut Tristan up regardless.

There was a pause as the room digested that. As they witnessed the leap in her power level that marked her as the second-most-powerful being in the room. Genevieve didn't want to pull too much from the Trick, but the magic had been easy, not even a minor dip into her energy reserves.

That satisfied her a great deal.

Konrad looked to her, pride in his features. Unhidden, which left her a little off-balance. She smiled at him for a flash before she went back to speaking.

"You can either leave or remain and obey the rules of the meeting and the laws of basic civility. There are no other options." With that said, Genevieve flicked her fingers and let Tristan speak.

"What I meant," Tristan said carefully, "was those witches were caught. They were punished. We must move on. To continue this folly where we have hundreds of missing witches and more weekly is intrusive. This cannot be our entire identity."

"More of a comment than a question," Zara said. "Are

you suggesting we abandon pursuing justice and closure for the loved ones of these missing witches? Because... it's disruptive?"

Tristan said, "It *is* disruptive. Senators feel as if they're under a magnifying glass. Every aspect of their lives under scrutiny. There's no evidence there are any more guilty parties left. It is difficult enough to go on after the tumult of the last months. There is no need to rehash or invent new villains."

"Your viewpoints have been recorded. Moving to the next item," Genevieve said and gave an overview of where they were at. Tristan wasn't the only Senator who thought they were doing too much, so she was as transparent as possible while protecting the integrity of their investigation.

For a while, he made noise at her back, squirming and sighing, but he managed not to speak. She'd forgotten how petulant he could be when he didn't get his way.

It went fairly quickly after that and she finished up, satisfied she'd done all she could. She'd eased some minds and hopefully that would result in more support.

"I'll keep this committee updated. If you have any legitimate concerns or questions, please don't hesitate to contact one of us or our offices." Genevieve waited for the three bells to sound and shot to her feet, neatly avoiding Tristan as she did. She'd been neatly avoiding men she loathed for centuries now. It was second nature.

Darius opened her office door to admit her as the light from the windows at his back lit him like a holy statue.

The beauty of him caught her up, stealing her breath and coordination for a few moments.

On her way past, he pressed a courtly kiss to her temple. The heat it left raced over her skin, as sensuous and intimate as most other sexual acts she'd experienced.

She hummed her pleasure and then did once more when she noted the low table in an adjoining conversation area, full of food.

"Madame Lorraine delivered a meal less than five minutes ago. She repeated her threats of violence should you not eat what she has sent for you to eat," he told her, amusement in his tone. "There's a male witch in the hall who keeps looking over here. Shall I wave, or throw a knife through his left eye?" Not so much amusement that time.

Cutting off that direct line of sight, Genevieve stepped to the door and closed it without giving Tristan a glance. "I know which of those I'd prefer, but we'll do neither instead. Come, share a meal with me."

He bowed his head slightly.

"Dust Devils are very good at body disposal. For future reference," he said as he placed a linen napkin over her pants before seating himself across from her.

"I will endeavor to keep that in mind," she told him with a smile. "Thank you," she said of the cloth on her lap.

"You look like an angel of vengeance today," he said with a slight shrug. "A stain from the food would mute that."

That and he just…took care of her. It was as wonderful as it was confounding. She wasn't used to it, and he was…well, so scary and gruff most of the time but to her he was this. Gentler. Softer. So very sexy.

"Tell me who the male was who attempted to come in until he noticed I was here. The one out in the hall just now. He demanded to know who I was. I told him you weren't in and therefore he needed to leave."

Demanded? And he was walking without a limp? "I'm sure he took that well," she said.

"I closed the door in his face. He didn't knock or try to come in again. He took nothing. Left nothing. I would not have allowed it."

"I'm sorry to have missed that," Genevieve said as she tried not to snicker and failed. "That's Tristan Sansbury. Another Senator. He's a fool." She would have waved a hand, but she was busy eating the garlicky chicken and rice Lorraine had outdone herself with.

"What's he to you?"

There were times over the last weeks, since she'd become a priestess to a Trick of Dust Devils, where she'd been confronted with just exactly how *other* Darius was. He was in her business constantly. He'd declared she needed a guard with her at all times and most of those times it was Darius who'd filled that job. He opened her doors and pulled her chair out, took the lids off things, and carried heavy items. He didn't so much glare at other males who gave her attention that was of an intimate nature, it was more like he let the other men see just a part of what he truly was. Either way, there was a marking of territory that was…timeless in the sense of very powerful beings at the top of the food chain.

There was simply no way to avoid that he considered her not only his priestess, but his woman.

As she, too, was an apex predator. She understood that to expect human behavior from a being as old and powerful as Darius would be fruitless. It would never be who he was, and it was important to her on a cellular level that he never feel like he couldn't be truly himself around her.

"We were married once. For five years." She added the last to underline how little time she'd given to Tristan. Theirs was no great love dashed upon the rocks of an unkind world. "It was...a bad choice on my part. I was ill prepared for his idea of marriage. He was ill prepared to be a partner. I moved to dissolve it." Tristan's family, having netted themselves an Aubert, had made noises about fighting the divorce until Konrad's solicitor had stepped in and there'd been no further issues.

"Should have chosen knives," he muttered, bringing a startled laugh to her lips.

"He loves being aggrieved more than most anything else in the world. He's just made an ass of himself in my meeting and will be looking for more attention to ease the sting." She made a decision to share a little more. "He and his family are connected to some of the conspirators we've found so far. We haven't gone public with all of them yet. Zara and Gaius are building evidence on them all. We don't want to move until we've got enough to bury them."

Darius nodded.

"I used my magic on him earlier," she said quickly, telling him of the incident. "I can do such things easily, but it was a spontaneous thing, barely any intention and he was at my back. I didn't even have to concentrate," she added. Proud. There were wards in place that limited most use of magic against other witches and despite being a peacock, Tristan was no weakling. She'd proved herself his superior.

He smiled very slightly. "You are growing in power. This is pleasing. It serves the Trick but keeps you safer at the same time." The barely there smile faded into a frown. "You did this in front of others?"

"News will have traveled across the globe by the time lunch is over. The all-Senate meeting starts after our break, so I expect there won't be a single empty seat left. Gawkers will rush in. It serves me," she said, answering his unasked question. "I've ascended a level of power. That will definitely raise my profile here and also, remind everyone that to take me on is to fail miserably."

"Then I most definitely approve." He tipped his chin at her. "We will look at this Tristan creature. If he is a threat to our priestess, we must know. If we find information connected to this case of yours, we will share."

She knew she didn't have to tell him to be careful not to be detected. Chances were very high that he was better at investigations of such matters than she was.

Genevieve kept his gaze. Not something she did with most other beings. Vampires wanted to try to roll you and other witches and shape-shifters took it as a challenge. Which it was most often. But sometimes it was just nice to look someone in the eyes and connect, person to person. No agenda.

"I'm certain you have some sources I can't even imagine. So I'll say thank you and warn you his sire isn't as useless as he is. He knows how to use his political and magical power. Though doubtless not against a Dust Devil." And wouldn't that be fun?

He didn't smile. But he thought about it. She just knew that part.

It was more than enough.

"We have powers and abilities these Sansburys cannot defy or defend against. We cannot be challenged in your defense." Darius didn't wave his words away as a way to soften the threat. He served them to her so she could know what they were about. What they'd be willing to do in her honor.

The fluttering of tenderness and a wave of vulnerability left her uncomfortable and off-balance and yet thrilled.

Neither of them spoke for long minutes. Simply eating and enjoying their companionable silence.

"Will Tristan take his grievance into this next meeting? Attempt to assuage the sting of your new power by manipulating the process?" he asked at last.

"Undoubtedly he will be bringing his feelings into the all-Senate. My meeting was small. I was the chair. It took hours, but it ran orderly without procedural dueling." Genevieve shrugged. "Witches do so love rules and processes. And we love to use them to show off and punish one another most of all. I make it a point to never get involved in most procedural battles. The more one does, the more time gets wasted. I speak when my voice is necessary. Otherwise, I let it flow around me."

"You don't make enemies as easily that way." Approving.

"If I make an enemy, I prefer to do it on purpose. Like offense. I am old enough to see the benefits of listening more than I speak. Of shepherding my power—political and magical—for times when they're needed. And, when it's necessary, using it however the situation calls for. Reputation is best kept with occasional reminders."

"This is a decidedly old-world way of thinking," he said, his voice a rumble in her bones.

Genevieve laughed a moment. "When I was fourteen, I was sent to learn in the household of an important noble in Venice. The noble was a widow, and my teacher was her chief strategist."

Darius said nothing. Simply gave her all his attention.

"Strategy is its own type of magic. It's intuitive. It involves a certain amount of fate or luck. A great deal of patience. Charm. Intelligence. One begins to cultivate sources and other types of support in as many places as possible. There's a deep, old magic in the confidence you can find in yourself when you enter any sort of negotiation or diplomacy. My teacher gave me many tools but the most important was patience.

"In some cases, getting what you want takes years in the making. Especially when you're dealing with creatures who are powerful and nearly immortal. Problems usually develop over time. Fixing them takes twice as long."

"And dealing with nearly immortal beings means anything that feels sudden or new is automatically distrusted," he murmured.

"Yes. Precisely."

"How long were you in Venice?" he asked.

"Twenty years until the widow, who was a Vampire, had to relocate as rumors of her not aging had begun to circulate. I went back to them three more times. All after I'd become a Senator. I learned battle magics from her sergeant at arms while she was in Norway."

"I'd have thought your father would have taught you."

"Konrad arranged for me to study with Rebecca. The widow I spoke of. She had been loyal to him during the crusades. We didn't really live together for him to teach me things."

Darius's brow furrowed but he withheld comment.

Genevieve said, "I'm seven hundred years old. You know better than I that the world was far different then. He was a warlock. Frequently on a battlefield or organizing an uprising. In a world where travel took months at a time, there were years I didn't see him." Though he had sent her things. Polished stones from Spain, spells from a shaman in the Netherlands. Viking rune stones she still used.

He wasn't around, but he hadn't forgotten her.

He did smile then and it transformed his face, bringing her breath a little short. "And you are a warrior as well. In your own, equally powerful way."

To say she was wildly flattered would have been an understatement.

"Your people need that strength of leadership to get through the storm." He looked at her long enough that understanding lodged in her gut that he was saying something deeper.

This trouble wasn't over and there was more ahead to unveil that would shake their world.

He touched her wrist. A brief slide of the pad of his index finger over the delicate bones there. He searched her features a moment, as if memorizing them. "Earlier, while we were at the home of the missing witches, your power rose quick and sharp. The presence of your...facets increased."

"Facets?" she asked.

Her wrist remained cradled in his hand, his fingers curled around her, the heat of his skin sending delicious tingles through her skin.

"You call them voices," he murmured.

"But why do you call them facets?" It was important somehow, that she ask.

"What comes when you call your magic—that swell of power that tastes and feels of many things—isn't from the outside. Not a voice from another. These perspectives and feelings are all yours, Genevieve. They are facets of your power. You call yourself a Lattice Witch, yes? One who can take multiple disciplines and weave them to create unique spellcraft?"

She nodded.

"Facets, elements, steps, whatever of those terms you connect with the strongest."

"You've given me something to think about. I had not considered it from this perspective." The knowledge weighed against her shoulders but in a portentous manner rather than a curse. It would need investigating.

"Then I am doubly glad I brought it up. What I intended to say was that when these facets of yours got in the way, I've been able to lend you some assistance."

As if the voices had been soothed. Or settled in some way. "I had assumed your magic lent some calming energy. It helps. There are times when it gets very loud and it becomes difficult to hold the thread of my working," she said.

Darius moved so that he cupped her jaw on the left side of her face. "Here?"

Genevieve stared into his gaze as she registered his skin against hers as he pulled her hand up to replace his.

"Hold as I was."

Fascinated, she watched as his gaze blurred even as his dark brown eyes went midnight with a flare of amber at the pupil. Her pulse thundered as he leaned close and cupped her palm as he blew a long breath against her throat just below her ear.

He spoke, his words lyrical and loaded with magic that soaked into her skin and…for want of a better term, created a buffer between the facets or voices or whatever it was, and the part of her brain that connected with her magic. It lowered the volume and in doing so, her pulse calmed.

Though he was the reason she remained breathless. He was so near, his lips at her throat, his magic sliding into her, seducing her own.

Her magic liked him a very great deal.

"When you need such assistance in the future and I'm not at your side, simply hold your jaw as I showed you."

The addition of another tool to deal with the times when all the threads of her power tangled and threatened to drown her brought relief so sharp it nearly hurt. "This is very helpful," she said.

"You have the ability to do this yourself by using the magic of the Trick. I will help you learn. In the meantime, I've created what one of our newest Devils calls a hack. The spell is there just under your skin. Your hand there triggers it."

There was so much to learn about not only the kinds of workings she could perform using the salt magic the Trick had unlocked for her. Not the least of which was just what sort of magic Darius wielded and how.

"Will you tell me about your magic?" she asked as she opened her eyes after taking a deep, centering breath. He stepped back but the heat of him, the scent of his magic still hung in the air.

"Depends on what you ask," he said. But with that ghost of a smile that he only seemed to use with her.

"You should know I quite like a challenge," she told him seriously.

"You say that as if I would run away."

Samaya knocked on her door, so Genevieve reluctantly gathered her things.

"All right. Thank you. I'm optimistic we will be done

by ten at the latest so rather than spend the night here in Los Angeles, let's go back to Las Vegas. I would remind you that I'm perfectly safe here within these walls and that if you wanted to go and do whatever, I'll call you when I'm done, but I know that would be useless."

"Perfectly safe is always a lie, Genevieve. But you're close with me here."

## *Chapter Four*

Clive strolled through the outer doors to his office and knew immediately he wasn't going to like whatever his assistant, Alice, had to tell him.

"Scion Stewart." She tipped her chin down in deference. "I've just put some tea in your office so you're right on time. I believe we may want to have a brief meeting before you begin your evening."

A chill crept down his spine, but he followed her into his office, hung up his suit jacket, and settled behind his desk while she took her usual place across from him.

"Don't waste time with any preamble. Tell me."

"The Nation has forwarded the response to Hunter Corp." She handed over a sheet of paper.

He scanned it and read it twice more before placing it on the center of his desk blotter. Running a palm down a tie that didn't need straightening, he allowed a sigh.

Rowan would most definitely not be pleased. And it was probably the reason his wife hadn't been at home when he'd woken for the day.

A quick check of their bond and he was satisfied she wasn't in pain, incandescent with rage, or sad. A plus.

"No response from Hunter Corp. as of yet?" he asked Alice.

"Not that's been routed to us. I know someone within the Nation who would alert me should such a thing happen though."

Rowan liked to call Alice a Vampire Mary Poppins because she was so accomplished at so many things. She seemed to know everyone. Was adept at fighting as well as the sort of management and diplomacy it took to manage a Scion.

Of course she had a source at the Nation offices. He allowed a satisfied smile. "Well done, Alice." He pointed at the paper. "This is nothing but trouble. Tahar has allowed the powerful within his territory far too much leeway on this." One of the five Scions worldwide, the Vampire charged with the governance of those in Africa and the Middle East was very old and powerful and had the attention of the First if for no other reason than Tahar posed a legitimate threat should he choose to.

"I expect however Rowan and Hunter Corp. decide to reply will be an absolute delight. She's quite clever. Those bigoted old arseholes in Tahar's territory are in for it." Alice laughed.

Clive wished very much that if this nonsense had to happen, it was happening six months from then. Rowan had enough on her shoulders, the grief at the loss of those she'd loved so much still a cloak around her. It wasn't going to make her easier for the Nation to manipulate and amuse itself with. No. This Rowan, the one who'd had her wrath, had eradicated those directly responsible. And now she was in absolutely no mood for nonsense and games.

"There'll be blood," he murmured.

Alice took a deep breath. "We must endeavor to be sure it's not hers."

He needed to give Alice a raise.

"I expect someone from Nadir's office will be in contact at some point. Right now these pompous Vampire lords will be feeling rather smug. But eventually Hunter Corp. will respond."

Clive knew his wife wasn't going to give the Nation whatever it was this response was meant to elicit. To do so would be admitting weakness.

Rowan was many things. Weak wasn't in their number.

His wife was about to deliver a master-class-level lesson and if she weren't already struggling through so much, he'd look forward to watching them all bleed for it.

Alice briefed him on some other urgent issues and left to go back to her desk.

Clive sat awhile and considered contacting Nadir via her direct line and decided against it. She knew his position. He'd already submitted his commentary regarding the Hunter Corp. mixed-team plans. He didn't support it wholesale. There were things that needed to be addressed and he bulleted them with proposals regarding how the Nation could negotiate a better outcome. And now, none of that would happen. This ridiculousness would result in pushing her and by extension Hunter Corp. further away.

Clive would bet Nadir and those who did know Rowan weren't even close to celebrating. They knew what was coming.

The only person he needed to contact for sure was his wife. He considered calling her rather than texting, but in the end, he was fairly certain she'd ignore a call from any Vampire at that moment so a text—which she might also ignore—would be more likely to at least be scanned.

Good evening, darling Hunter. Meet me for dinner later? 10? Do take care of yourself.

If he could coax her into dinner, at least know if she'd eaten. And if he got her face-to-face, he'd be able to charm her and perhaps blunt the severity of the argument they'd be having.

There'd be consequences of all types now that the Vampires had chosen the way they had to make their first move. They'd only managed to push her harder toward doing whatever it was she wanted to do. Only now, she'd be petty. And most likely violent.

Mmmm. He smiled, thinking of the way Rowan looked when she was worked up. Magnificent. As long as he wasn't the target.

Three hours later his screen lit with her return text.

That's what you choose to text me?

It'd been a risk that failed. He'd known it when she hadn't replied within thirty minutes.

He decided to call her instead and to his surprise, she answered.

"What?" she barked.

"I'm pleased to hear you did, indeed, take care of yourself this evening and are alive and well. As for the rest, shall we save this for when we're together? Over some carbohydrates and some wine?" he asked, keeping his tone smooth.

She was silent for so long he sighed. "Rowan, I don't wish to disagree with you over the phone or via text message. Nuance and subtlety are lost without facial expression."

She made a rude sound he was sure came with a middle finger on the hand that wasn't holding her phone. "I bet you can guess exactly what my expression is right now."

Clive very nearly laughed because he knew *exactly* what sort of face she was making. Annoyed. Frustrated. Disgusted by the attempts at delaying Hunter Corp.'s new teams. She'd leave him wary and at full attention in case she leaned toward violence, but she'd draw him in anyway. Because he found his Hunter irresistible in this guise. Even while he protected his bollocks.

But he didn't want to derail his very reasonable request to have this discussion. *In person* where the chances of a great deal of misunderstandings cropping up were lower. And he wasn't above knowing—and using—the fact she could be swayed with some sensual chat and persuasion.

"Of course I can. I know my wife very well. Have dinner with me at home. We can talk about this in private. Just an hour from your day," he coaxed.

She snarled. "I arrived home ten minutes ago," she said and disconnected.

"Alice, please contact Elisabeth to let her know I'm on my way and I'll require a dinner for Rowan and myself," he said as he paused at her desk on his way out.

"You should perhaps bring something along. You sent her flowers recently, so how about chocolates?" Alice went to a cabinet in her office and pulled out a deep brown box he knew held Fran's caramels, a favorite with his Hunter.

Another reason he appreciated Alice so very much. "Thank you," Clive told her as he took the box. "I'll be back after my dinner. Give me two hours."

"I have the first aid kit ready just in case," she called out as he left.

It didn't take very much time to get from *Die Mitte*, the Vampire Nation–owned casino, hotel, and the Scion's current headquarters in North America to the home he and Rowan had moved into the month before.

Grumpy wife inside or not, the sight of the gates opening and the lit windows of their house just beyond brought him a deep sense of satisfaction. They were making a safe harbor for themselves. Complete with a dog and staff.

He'd walked in through their front door, held by Betchamp, his butler and co-house manager, when Hunter Corp.'s official response to the Nation came through.

"Where is she?" Clive asked, sliding his phone away. He'd read it after he was with Rowan.

"Elisabeth will serve dinner in fifteen minutes. Ms. Rowan is in the pool with Star and David," Betchamp said.

Clive thanked him and, after dropping off his things, he headed out to the backyard, following the sounds of barking, splashing, and a lot of laughter. Enough that it warmed his heart, welcoming him home more deeply than the sight of the lights in the windows.

And there she was, his finest thing, swimming, tossing a ball as Star jumped into the air to catch it before she landed in the water with a splash. She paddled over to Rowan, dropped the ball off, and scampered out of the pool to do it again, this time on David's side.

"Elisabeth says dinner will be ready in fifteen minutes," Clive called out.

Rowan tossed—threw—the ball to him but his reaction time was faster than she'd assumed because he caught it easily. And then realized his error when Star barreled into him after it, soaking his suit.

Clive couldn't even be mad because the dog began to kiss his chin, clearly pleased to see him. And because it was a clever way to poke at him and he found it incredibly alluring when his wife was devious.

"Oops," Rowan said as she got out, water cascading down her skin, silver in the moonlight. "I'm going to clean up and I'll meet you at the table in fifteen minutes." She sauntered past him, the ghost of a curve to her lips.

Somehow, he ended up totally wet and stinking of dog but the dog in question was dry and clean. Fluffy as she barked and then trotted past him into the house.

This is what became of your life when a magic dog chose to be your spouse's familiar.

"I need to change as well," he told her as he followed in Rowan's wake.

"We're not having shower sex so forget it. I'm hungry and pissed off and not in a *hey-let's-work-it-out-on-one-another* way." She shut the door in his face, and growling, he moved into his closet to get rid of his wet clothing.

By the time he sat across from Rowan at their dining table, he'd cleaned up, changed his clothes, and read the Hunter Corp. response.

Elisabeth poured him a glass of wine and put a basket of bread out with fresh butter. As Rowan dived in, Elisabeth gave him a look that told him to let his wife get some food into herself before he started in.

It would be safer, certainly. A hangry Rowan was a dangerous creature. More dangerous than usual in any case.

"I made some short ribs and roasted potatoes. Tomato

and cucumber salad because I know how much you enjoy it, Rowan."

Rowan smiled, pleased, a slight bread high already leveling off her outward anger. "Thanks, Elisabeth."

Clive knew for certain his cook, housekeeper, and co-house manager couldn't have put this meal together in the short time since he'd left his office. She'd clearly been cooking for hours given how tender the meat was. Having her and Betchamp there with them in Las Vegas had been surprisingly smooth. And had definitely eased their lives. The house was expertly run, and Clive had two allies making sure his wife was fed, watered, and rested.

David joined them, filling his plate like Clive wasn't about to have a private conversation with Rowan. Who gave Clive a narrow-eyed look daring him to say a single word about it.

In for a penny.

"As I just read your reply to the Nation's response, I assume that's why you're vexed?" he asked.

"I'm past vexed." The calm manner she said it didn't fool Clive one bit.

"Sending a response like that to the Nation after the sun has risen certainly indicates such a thing, yes."

"It was sent five minutes *before* sunrise. After spending hours going back and forth with the other partners to decide on wording, that's when it was approved to go. Contrary to Vampire belief, the world doesn't revolve around them. Things take time. Time I could have spent continuing to hunt down the people responsible for this mess. By the way, I was in Long Beach earlier today at yet another missing persons situation, so Vampires picked the wrong day to declare themselves lords who think they are the boss of me. Furthermore? If I want to find a spell that causes that response to end up tattooed on Theo's balls, I'll do it whenever time of day I please. The Nation doesn't own me or pay the bills at Hunter Corp."

Well. He'd have to pretend he didn't hear that heretical rant regarding the First. He tried very hard not to listen or remember anything Rowan said about her foster father when she was angry at him. The First loved his daughter very much. In a twisted way that had left scars inside and out. Things were...complicated and had left Rowan with very strong feelings about Nation attempts to control her in any way.

"I rather find the response to have been gracious and measured," David said with a shrug before he speared a potato and popped it into his mouth, the little shit stirrer.

"Right? I could have said so many things. The options really were endless, and I'll never stop being bitter that Susan and Celesse vetoed the best ones," Rowan said. "You'll note the absence of the term *numbnuts*. Because I'm fucking gracious."

Clive pulled up the response on his phone and read, "Hunter Corp. will continue interviews for these positions and expects to have the first teams up and operational within sixty days."

"See?" Rowan put some more asparagus on her plate before she pointed her fork at him for emphasis. "Gracious. I didn't say, hey fuck you for wasting my time when my friends got killed because of Nation and Conclave treachery. I do what I want, so suck it."

"Hunter, I do think sending something telling them you're hiring who you want and not addressing a single point in their first response is telling them you do what you want and to suck it," Clive said. "And then waited until after sunrise to send it."

"I heard you the first time. Goddess you're annoying." She flipped him off. "It's not a secret or some clue you had to figure out. We all know when it was sent. That was the actual point. Like the way the Nation response was only sent to London and Paris." She sent him a smile full of teeth and he was glad of his training that kept him from rearing back.

These bloody idiots.

Clive shook his head. "I didn't know that," he admitted. "I'll send Nadir's office my opinion of such a reckless and petty delivery. She'll see it when she wakes for the evening."

"They're all ancient Vampires. They'll be up a while yet, certainly long enough to read our reply." She cackled. "I know you all don't really dream, but I hope they think of me all day long."

"Taunting Nadir seems ill advised," he said. Though there were others involved in this mess, Nadir was the Voice and as such had responsibilities far beyond her personal feelings. "Though you must know she supports efforts to come to a compromise between the Nation and Hunter Corp., she's walking a line here in her official capacity. She'll hold to the demands of her position."

"Are you telling me she'll do whatever Theo tells her to do and she'll never show any indication of how she really feels even if she disagrees with him? Uh, yeah I remember," Rowan told him, voice thick with the emotion of the memories of some of the darker sides of her father's Vampires looking the other way, or worse, when he'd disciplined—a polite word for what had happened—Rowan.

Clive took her hand a moment.

"I apologize. My wording was clumsy."

"I got you, Scion." Rowan smirked at him, and she returned to the subject. "I see what's going on. Very little about that response says Nadir. I mean, she's got a certain way of negotiating and I saw parts of her there. But on the whole, that response reads like it was written by committee. *Vampire lords*, really." She rolled her eyes, and he barely resisted a laugh because she was right. "Doesn't look like these bellends were active until this month. I'm going to imagine they got access via Scions who then opened the door."

Clive raised a brow, needing to tread carefully. He didn't want to evade her attempts to get answers but his position and his relationship with his wife relied on each making the other do their respective jobs. He needed to know how much she'd figured out already so he could do what he could to help her get the answers she deserved.

"They're being treated as senior advisors. The Scions are involved, obviously, and the advisors are handpicked and forwarded via our offices."

Her sour expression was accompanied by a rude hand gesture.

"That's a new one. Or, rather an old one made new again," he said, admiring her ability to pull rude gestures from across time and geography to find the perfect one for any given situation.

"You deserve even worse, Clive. I told you not to treat me like I was ignorant. Senior advisors with enough access and power to get in the middle of Nadir's process? Who? If this was such a regular occurrence, why did I never see it or learn about it? He doesn't consider them as important as Scions or I'd have known. I'd have met one or he'd have taught me about their purpose."

Clever. Clive simply devoured her with his gaze. His brilliant wife. Her brain as sharp and dangerous as her blade. She was a bulldog, stubborn, vicious when necessary and once her jaws locked on, woe be to her enemies.

"So," she continued as if he'd answered by his silence, "they're recent. As such, they'd need to be, as you said, pushed forward. We've had some hours after your response to look into these self-titled lords. I know in whose territory they're located, so it's no big mystery which Scions brought them to the party. Tahar and Takahiro for sure. Warren has enough trouble in his territory, so I don't think he's inviting any more. Paola's territory is far too stable. Her Vamps are all old loners. They don't go on killing sprees and Hunters don't need to get involved. None appear to be from North America. There are a few I can't find. Yet. I will though. It's all a matter of time."

She was, as always, astute about Vampire politics.

"You are correct that none of it is coming from North America," he allowed.

"We'd be in an ER, not sharing a meal if you had done this behind my back. However." She paused as she ate a while. "I guess the *we're at war on your behalf* portion of the program is over and it's back to business as usual. Fine. I'm not a Vampire. Hunter Corp. is not the Nation. We're doing what we do, and we're done seeking input over it. I'm hiring for these mixed teams. Tomorrow, actually, as we've got three potential Vampire candidates back for second-round interviews."

"Which Vampires?" he demanded.

"If you won't be part of the process, you can't have access to those details. It's not complicated. I'm not dick measuring or fang comparing or showing my feathers. You keep trying to suck us in to this ridiculousness, but we won't allow that now any more than we would have a year ago."

Clive held a hand up. "If I know the basics, I can help. You don't have to say names. Just whether they're Nation affiliated or rogues." They had people who could hack into Hunter Corp. just as Hunter Corp. had people who'd broken into Nation systems, so he didn't need names. He didn't *want* names at that point because if he did, he'd have to be truthful if asked by the First.

"Two of them are rogues," she told him. Meaning one was affiliated. "I'm telling Clive this information, not the Nation."

He nodded, accepting her terms. Grateful she was sharing at all.

"Look, we don't need to hire problems. That's not our goal. We're very aware of the fine line we need to walk with these teams. We received forty-three applications from Vampires. We interviewed six and only three made it to this last round.

"As you can infer from the numbers, we were very particular about who made it to the interview stage. We've run deep background checks. Each has been interviewed in person. None have human or Vampire criminal records. Both in their application materials and to me personally their reasons for leaving the Nation were given and I'm satisfied with them."

"You know the issue of rogues within the Nation will complicate matters." Rogues were generally ignored as long as they didn't break laws or endanger anyone. They didn't tithe like Nation-affiliated Vamps did, but they didn't use any of the services provided to members either.

But Vampires were hierarchical. They respected fear and power, and rogues made an end run around organized power structures. As Vampires were already suspicious of Hunters, adding rogues into the mix was going to be an issue.

Rowan pointed her fork at him for emphasis. "*I* provided plenty of notice as to what I was planning. *I* explained why I needed to avoid delay and get this done to deal with the problem we're facing right now. *I* made it very clear that should any delay tactics be used I would simply do things without your input. If Vampires were so set on Affiliated Vampires being on Hunter teams, you had a process to say so. Instead, you played to type and decided on games. This is what is colloquially known as fucking around and finding out." She shrugged and Clive didn't have the energy to argue. Especially when her points were correct, and he didn't want to be cornered into having to admit that to her out loud.

They finished dinner. "Walk me to the car, darling?" Though she gave him a hard side eye, she rose as he did and took up at his side on the way outside.

Rowan said when they stood out front, "I'll figure it out. We both know that for a certainty. So if you have the ear of any of them, you should let them know they have a closing window of time to jump ship. Otherwise, I'm coming for them. Maybe not this year because we've got far too many things as it is on our calendar. But I won't forget. This is personal." Rowan cocked her head. "Tell them, Clive."

"I have. And I will continue doing so." He risked his health leaning down to kiss her, but fortunately she believed his promise and stepped into his embrace, opening her lips on a sigh.

"This is for Carey and Thena and all the protected who have been targeted and harmed. I'll burn their mansions, *pied-à-terres*, villas, and penthouses to the ground for this. Not as Hunter Corp. As the Vessel. Understand? I will consider them the same as the Blood Front fuckheads who ordered the hits."

He hummed his pleasure as he pulled her close again. "You know what it does to me when you're a vicious bitch." That she was so savage in the face of a threat by predators most people had no idea existed but would run screaming into the night if they were confronted with was part of the core of the woman he was endlessly fascinated by.

He'd tell them. Some of them would listen. Others would have to learn the hard way and since he already thought Tahar needed to police his territory better, Clive really looked forward to watching the slow-motion car crash that was about to happen to him. The other Scion, Takahiro, wasn't a true believer in this bizarre response to Hunter Corp, but he did, as Rowan rightly guessed, have pressure from some of the most powerful Vampires in his territory and had felt duty bound to put them forward to the First. He'd still get his ass kicked by Clive's very pissed-off wife, but he'd probably survive without permanent damage.

"I adore you," he told her before giving her one last kiss. "I'll see you in a few hours. Are you in for the night?"

She nodded and he felt ever so much better that he knew she'd be safe until he returned. That's when he saw the box of chocolates on his passenger seat. "Ah! Wait a moment." He reached in and produced them for her with a slight bow. "To help you remember not all Vampires are the ones whose houses you want to burn to the ground."

She smirked. "Thanks, Scion. I'll save you one. Maybe two."

# Chapter Five

It was about an hour after Clive had returned home for the night. They'd worked in the companionable quiet of their sitting room after enjoying a snack.

Over and over she'd opened up the file David had pulled together for the final round of Vampire interviews they'd be conducting later that afternoon. Rowan read through all the documentation of each of the three multiple times. She kept going back to the beginning and looking through it all over again, but the fourth time she'd made it all the way through, she tossed a folder to the table with a sigh.

Clive's attention flicked to her. "Are you well?"

Rowan pressed the heel of her palm to the center of her chest, just below the hollow of her throat. "There's something," she muttered.

He didn't panic but he did shift his work aside so he could turn to her completely, taking her in carefully.

That he didn't touch her, didn't interrupt her was her own personal miracle. He was there. He'd burn things down to help. But he was waiting for her to tell him.

"There's something I'm supposed to know," she said at last. Rowan pointed at the papers she'd been reading over and over. "In there." She held up a hand. "They're personnel packets for each of the Vampires we're interviewing tomorrow so you don't need to go through them."

He narrowed his eyes at her, and she held her ground.

"You're far better off with plausible deniability unless we have no other choice," she added, and Clive heaved a sigh but relaxed slightly. Because she was right.

"Fine. For now. Is this related to your dreams? Prophecy in some way?" he asked.

"Yes. I think so. The dreams are images, and this is… you know how some days you just have a feeling about something. Turning right down a road a few blocks after your usual, or you grab a sweater on a perfectly warm day and a storm blows in and the temperature drops. I've had feelings before. Anxiety over something that seemed out of the blue."

Rowan hadn't ever really been human. Born to the vassal to the First and an acolyte to the goddess Brigid, her very existence had been against the law. And then as she grew, Rowan began to manifest magical gifts, enough that it became clear she was the first physical Vessel of Brigid in centuries. Part of her connection with Brigid was the gifts that increased in intensity and power and in number over the years.

And more than just the passage of time, it seemed she came into new gifts after tumultuous events in her life. Nearly being killed was the main offender. Not her favorite. But together with massive infusions of ancient Vampire blood on more than one occasion to save her from certain death, these events had unlocked an affinity or talent or something like that with prophecy and foresight to go along with superior speed and skill on the battlefield and her increasing ability to emotionally soothe and calm others in times of need.

She was working on understanding it all better. There was no manual. It was very much by the seat of her pants. But Rowan's connection to Brigid, her sense of being able to let go and trust she'd find her way, grew stronger and deeper each day.

"All right. I approve. If it warns you early, that keeps you safer," he added before she could ask. "So, you've got a, let's call it a *knowing* there's something in these documents that will lead you to something important."

On surer ground now that she had words to define it, she rolled her head and shook out her shoulders to release the tension she'd been holding. "Yes, yes, that's…it's not the Vampires themselves, but something or someone connected to them. Maybe a place?"

"Surely you can't hire someone if they're connected to this, Rowan." Frustration laced his tone.

So nosy! "Really? This right now?"

"Yes! You're having some sort of premonition about one of the Vampires you want to hire. Of course, I'm curious as to who, though I do trust you when you say they've been vetted."

She sighed out a breath. "It's not that kind of thing. It's not *about* him. The idea of hiring him isn't the thing I need to pay attention to or worry about. I'm not… I don't know how to do this, much less find the right words to communicate it. I'm stumbling along the best I can."

Heat banked low in her belly as She made Her presence known. Brigid burned through Rowan, bright and steady. I am here. We are one.

Clive's mouth flattened against, she knew, all the things he wanted to say to get her to reveal who she was hiring. He was being her husband right then, even though the Scion was always right there too.

Because of that, she found some patience. "I promise you if I thought for even a moment it was about him, I wouldn't make the offer. Or I'd wait. It just feels..." Rowan pressed her hand over that same spot on her chest. "It's good that I hire him. And I think I'm supposed to." A flare of power in her chest left her a little dizzy. But surer that yes, indeed she was supposed to hire him. "I'll see him again later this afternoon and if there's even a twinge, I won't make an offer. I don't need to shoot myself in the face to get back at the Nation."

He growled a little. "Fine. So what do you plan to do? How can I help?"

"Do not make me sorry I did this," she told him as she narrowed her gaze at him.

He laughed and then tried to sober up. "I apologize, darling. I do find it so delightful when you're so wary and feral. I'm terribly worried you'll hurt me, but also hoping quite fervently you will."

Snort laughing, she flipped him off before leaning close to kiss him thoroughly. Rowan held up the part of the file dealing with Aron, her top candidate for the job and the one she had that *knowing* about.

"I need another set of eyes on this. I can ask another Hunter. But I thought perhaps you might have some insight. Something I'm missing but you'll see."

His amusement wisped away, replaced by a flash of tenderness and then he pulled all his smug around him to make her feel better. "You know I'm dying to see that."

Rowan nodded. "I do. I'm trusting you as my husband. If you have an issue, you tell me to my face. You don't take this to the Nation unless you truly believe it's necessary they know."

He paused, thinking it over, and then nodded. "I can agree to that."

She handed the file over and left the room, prowling to the kitchen for a slice of citrus cake before everyone else ate it all. And also to resist standing over Clive as he read. She trusted his word but knew herself. She'd want to see every expression, every pause and change in breath and then demand to know what he meant.

Clive did his best to put aside being Scion because what Rowan needed was for him to be her spouse. He'd probably never admit it, but the Vampire she was about to hire was a fantastic candidate. Clearly qualified.

He knew who Aron Jimenez was, of course. Clive had a file on all the powerful and high-profile rogue Vampires in his territory. There were a few dozen. Americans did love their rebellion so it was no surprise that Vampires of that same bent would be attracted to the place. Mostly they didn't make trouble and he left them alone unless that changed.

He didn't rule his territory anything like his predecessor had. And once the Vampires of North America had figured that out, they'd reacted accordingly. Most of them kept themselves on the right side of Nation law and attention. Those who didn't want to do so had been executed or had left.

When Rowan returned, he attempted not to show his astonishment that she'd managed not to poke at him the whole time, demanding to know what he thought and why. She placed a slice of cake near his cup of tea and sat across from him.

"To start, I cannot argue that he's not a very strong candidate. No problems with the Nation. And, just between us, cheeky to have broken into Nation databases. Clever as well."

Her delighted laugh brought his smile.

"If you provided me with information when I requested it instead of playing games, I wouldn't have to resort to other methods. But needs must and all that. Don't be such tight-asses with information if you don't want me getting it in other ways."

"Theft. You mean theft," he said.

"Well, yes, of course I mean theft," she said. "Because you didn't give it to me when I asked. So, that's okay."

That brought a belly laugh. "I do adore you," he managed to say once he'd gotten his breath back. "Your defense of your actions is always entertaining."

"I don't need to defend myself." She raised a shoulder.

"So long as we're both on the same page," he teased. "This is a rather detailed dossier. I plan to bring some of these ideas to Alice to apply to our own hiring process. I didn't see anything that leapt out at me. He's not a baby but also not an ancient. Powerful enough to hold his own and prevent a challenge from most other Vampires. His Maker lives in the same region, which indicates a level of self-control that will serve him well as a Hunter. But also that he's not out to create trouble for Nation Vampires. Perhaps it's about a Vampire who can challenge him? Another who is more powerful. One who lives in close proximity? A former employer or a client he had to deliver unhappy news to. An ex-lover or someone who still resides in the line he left who resents him. Vampires live a long time. It could be many things."

"You gather drama and petty beef like dust in a dark corner." She shook her head.

"Or it could be the Vampire you anger to the point of

violence when you hire Aron." He shouldn't have said it, but he worried for her on the best of days.

"That could be it too." She shrugged. "I think I have to ride this one out. Do the interviews as we'd planned and trust whatever it is will come to me. I'll know when I know, I think."

Star had been napping under Rowan's desk and at that, she snapped her head up and barked before returning to her sleep.

"I think that's a yes. It's really too bad I don't have any way of calling Carl up for a chat to see what he thinks."

Carl was Rowan's very own sage. Kooky, as she called him. He wore outlandish outfits and gave her prophecy in his own meandering way that she claimed drove her to violence, but Clive rather believed she enjoyed figuring out.

"Do you feel there's danger in this path?" he asked, trusting she'd tell him the truth.

"Yes, in a big-picture way. Things had been sort of blurry since we killed off Guy the Faerie. Not calm as much as maybe everyone on all sides was taking a breather. I think that's over." Rowan pressed her hand against her chest again and he wondered if she even knew she was doing it. Wondered, too, just what that meant.

"But I don't think hiring Aron is the dangerous thing. Well, not the dangerous thing in this context. Yes, of course I know the Nation will flip their shit when we do this. But that's a whole 'nother type of trouble." His wife, the target of multiple—nearly successful—attempts on her life, said this all so breezily it set his teeth on edge.

"I do hate that you have so many possible avenues of danger in your life. I'm delighted to be nearby just in case someone or something comes at you." He pinched the bridge of his nose and attempted to find his composure.

"Me too. But you're a Scion and I'm a Vessel, a Hunter, and generally bitchy. So loads of beings have some sort of issue with me. It comes with the territory. Now. I ended up telling you about one of the Vampires I'm hiring even though I said I wouldn't. Which means you'll need to be extra Vampirey and avoid answering truthfully if Theo asks you."

"One step at a time, darling," he told her. Clive would protect her. He'd choose her over the Nation and the First and he hoped he'd never have to do so. She was his country. His queen. His everything.

"I know you want to ask questions about Aron. Ask them fast and don't be ridiculous or I'll rescind my offer."

A declaration of love. Clive gave her a heated look and she sent him a raised eyebrow.

He said, "I read through that material. He's an excellent candidate. I'm disappointed he was driven away from the Nation because I'm certain he'd be an asset. Now Hunter Corp. will count his skills as their own and the Nation has lost a chance to place one of our own within your number to keep an eye on you on our behalf. Fools."

Rowan snickered. "Honestly, I can't believe they missed that. But I'm not in the *help the Vampire Nation spy on Hunter Corp.* game. All those years of life and they managed to build a big bank account and closets full of haute couture and yet not a moment spent on being smart. Works for me, I guess."

"And the other Vampire you believe you might hire?"

"Katya. Her family is affiliated. Pays their tithe. She was born, not Made. They're average in most ways that matter to the Nation. She's fantastic, but you're all so obsessed with designer labels you forget about *quality.* In any case, they're so average the Nation will complain but mainly just for form. She fills a space. Her skills are appreciated by Hunter Corp. and she's not going to spy for you."

"Clever." She'd given him several clues. Enough that he could most likely figure out who she meant. But his deliberate ignorance would serve both Rowan and Clive. He didn't need to know.

"Instead of more questions I'll give you some advice you can take or leave. Tomorrow in your interview you should know not only why he left, but why he wants to be a Hunter knowing just how much trouble it will bring down on his head. He's a rogue, but not a hermit. He's active enough in Las Vegas in the Vampire community that they'll notice he's working with you, and they won't all react positively. Why take that risk?"

Surprise rode her features as she blushed. The smile she gave him was so open and sweet it stole his breath.

"It's my final question to all candidates who get to a final interview. It's a shitty job. People are always trying to fuck you up in some way. The benefits are good though, if you live and all. You didn't have to use your question opportunity up to help me," she said. He'd moved her by taking her side and he regretted not telling her up front that he'd supported her with this latest Nation nonsense.

He cupped her cheek briefly. "I'd give my life to help you. Now, before anyone catches us being so bloody tender toward one another, we should fuck."

She shot to her feet and peeked at the clock. "Forty-eight minutes until sunrise. Wow me."

Feeling rather smugly sure he'd do just that, he took her hand and dragged her into his room.

# *Chapter Six*

By midday, Rowan found herself feeling very satisfied, indeed. After a late breakfast they'd turned into a work meeting, she and Genevieve had headed into the Hunter Corp. offices. In the hours after that, she'd managed to finish several hours' worth of research and meetings before the sun went down and they held second-round interviews of two of the three Vampires she'd told Clive about earlier that morning.

Everything she'd heard and felt had underlined her prior conviction that while Katya was ready to take on a spot at Hunter Corp., the other Vampire needed more seasoning before Rowan would be comfortable sending him out into the field and trusting him to serve as able backup. She wanted to talk it over with Susan first, but Rowan felt like a Hunter Corp. training program would help him to develop those skills and some loyalty to them as well.

This step was good for the overall effectiveness of Hunter Corp. But it also created a bridge, a new type of connection and relationship with other paranormal groups. A connection different than what they'd already had or tried. Something organic that had the potential to change relations between them all for the better.

Rowan hadn't mentioned the *knowing* to David or Genevieve. It felt like she needed to do this herself. Not let anyone else's perception get in her way, though of course Brigid burned bright within Rowan, which was guidance, but of the type it had felt right to follow.

That knowing had led her to exactly that moment where she was wrapping up with Aron. She'd worked with him briefly when she'd first landed in Las Vegas and had trouble with the Vampires not being reined in by Clive's predecessor. Since then, she'd gotten intel from him a handful of times. He was steady. Had excellent discipline and control over his blood hunger.

He'd scored high marks with blades, hand to hand, and guns. A big plus was that he had his own sophisticated intelligence network spanning over the western and southwestern United States.

She liked him. Brigid seemed to as well given the warm weight in Rowan's belly. It definitely wasn't that she shouldn't hire him. No, she knew for certain Aron wasn't the problem.

David had asked his last few questions and left the room. As with the other two candidates, Rowan wanted to speak privately when she asked her final question. She felt they'd all be more frank if it was just her.

"You have to understand this is going to piss off the Nation when I hire you. And we both know I'm going to hire you. So what's driving you to do this?"

Once that had all been said, that frantic beat at the back of her mind calmed.

He leaned back a bit and thought a while before he answered. "For the last seventy-five years I've been getting past what happened in the thirty years before that. I came to Vegas after I left my Maker's line in 1947. Not much here back then, especially by today's standards. Still, more than enough for me to make a living if I had the courage to." He shrugged.

Rowan understood what it meant to have someone else in control of every aspect of one's life. Understood the brutal reality of Vampiric society. He'd been little more than a child when he'd been Made—illegally—at barely sixteen.

"Those three decades are no longer a weight on my chest. I can defend myself. I've trained and hardened. Learned. I see trouble. I see imbalance and it feels like I need to be right here to do something about it," he told her.

Still not quite saying what Rowan needed to hear. There was something *just right there*. Just outside her vision, a whisper she couldn't quite understand.

She allowed her vision to blur a moment, reaching out, touching the papers in front of where she sat. Waiting for something to pop.

Aron watched her carefully before speaking. "What's bothering you?"

"That's a very long story." She laughed, rueful. "There's something at the back of my mind. Telling me I need to pay attention to something about you. Not *you*. It's not about you. But connected somehow."

He cocked his head. One of those Vampiric movements. Humans did something similar, but this was something very much other. He moved like a predator, though to his credit, not like *she* was prey. Smart.

"Is there something I can do to help?" he asked at last.

Rowan looked down at the papers, wondering about his neighborhood, but the moment she thought it, she knew that wasn't it. She asked him about his clients but that wasn't it either.

"Your Maker. Tell me about him," Rowan said and relief, nearly painful, shot through her.

That was a good direction.

Though she and Clive had discussed Elmer just before sunrise and Clive had said Aron's Maker was old and well connected, there was nothing in the data she'd culled about Aron's Maker to indicate he'd been the subject of Hunter Corp.'s official attention.

"As I explained, he was abusive. It's not an unusual story really. I think I stayed hoping things would change, or that I would maybe? I left after I finally worked up the courage to do so. I haven't had direct contact with him since I left, understand. But especially once he ended up here in Vegas, I'd be a fool not to keep an eye on him. Make sure he stayed out of my way."

Rowan had kept tabs on Theo after she'd escaped the Keep, too. It paid to know where anyone who had the reason or the ability to curtail your freedom was at any given time. Another point in the pro column of hiring him.

"Smart," she said. "That way he can't sneak up on you from behind."

Aron pointed at her. "Exactly. He arrived here back in 1984. I knew the moment he stepped foot on the pavement. I sent an official communication reminding him I wanted nothing to do with him and to leave me alone. I wasn't that worried. Not by that point. I had established a life here. Connections and roots. Las Vegas is my city in a way it won't ever be his." Aron waved a hand. "Backing up a little. At first, I had concerns. He had been possessive of me and I wasn't convinced he hadn't shown up to attempt to win me back. Or take me back."

Rowan blew out a quiet breath. She knew that fear.

"The truth is mundane really," Aron continued. "In the time I was with him, I wasn't the first, or the last young human he Made. Certainly, after I left, he continued the practice. Some look a lot like me, others totally different. So, what I believe is that it's not about me. He wanted my youth and my beauty and what wasn't given he took by force and manipulation. When I left, he found more youth and beauty. There's always more."

The wider world was a buffet for powerful beings like Vampires. Truth was, yes, there would always be more youth and beauty lining up to be abused. Some because they don't know any different. Some because they craved it. Some because they had no other options and being Made created a family. A place to belong.

Aron paused as he thought his words over. Sadly, the story he told wasn't that unique. Most older Vampires had bullshit power trip behavior as their daily exercise.

"You asked why I want to be a Hunter. Since I left Elmer's line, I've helped dozens of Vampires escape bad situations. Here in Vegas, I've helped two of Elmer's Made with cash and contacts to start over far away. I'd like to continue that work. I think as a Hunter I could do even more."

It was a violation of the Treaty for Vampires to hold any of their line against their will. They could file an official complaint to be freed from their line or petition their Maker to be severed and freed. Sometimes Vampires had to pay to buy their freedom. It was a better system than it was before the Treaty, but it was rife with manipulation and abuse. Vampires considered their Made as much theirs as the rugs on the floor and the cars in the garage.

Rowan didn't trust easily. But as she heard Aron speak

about the things that mattered to him, she accepted that he would be part of her life—an important part—from then on. He'd be as solid as David or Genevieve. Friendship would grow from it.

The *knowing* had been about more than one thing. She'd thought it had nothing to do with Aron, but she'd been wrong. She'd been meant to hear these details for multiple reasons. Not just as a warning, but this glimpse into the heart of what drove him as an individual.

"There will be people who say I'm hiring Vampires to tweak the noses of the Vampire Nation. And I do love to tweak noses, don't get me wrong. But my aim is to do a better job protecting those within our mandate. Be the shield between them and beings like your Maker. You know the world of rogues and those Affiliated Vampires whose voices go unheard. I think maybe they're long overdue to be included in that mandate."

"He's got influential friends," Aron said, returning to the subject of his Maker. "Old Nation family-type influence. Someone or more than one person has protected him over the centuries. It's why the last Vampire of his I helped leave refused to file an official complaint. If they stay quiet, he lets them go and that's all they want. So many of them have stunted development. The ones who get Made so young by predators like Elmer end up ensnared in an imbalanced system. They have little power or influence. They don't continue an education. They freeze, emotionally and mentally."

This Elmer was a sleazebag. But Clive and Aron both had said he was influential so he was good at being a dick. He definitely needed some looking at.

"These illegal Makings happened here? In North America?" she asked.

"Yes. But Scion Stewart wasn't in charge at that time. Jacques was, and he was close to my Maker."

Friends with that douchelord Jacques? Well, that only underlined how terrible this Elmer was. "You have no reason to believe this, given your history with the Vampire Nation, but Scion Stewart doesn't tolerate such lawbreaking," she murmured, offhandedly as her gut burned with rightness. "When I find Vampires in breach of the Treaty, I usually touch base with the Scion's office. I don't do that in all cases and I'm sure you can imagine the scenarios I mean. But unless I need to execute a motherfucker on the spot, I try to work with the Nation. Yes, we enforce the Treaty. And part of that is making Vampires uphold their own rules. We have enough asses to kick as it is. Let them break a toe."

He nodded. "All right."

"The first two weeks is training and testing. You'll be screened by a witch and read by an ancient Vampire. There's a great deal of paperwork you'll need to fill out. David has a packet for you and he'll walk you through everything should you decide to accept our offer," she said, needing to move forward.

His wary expression shifted into pleasure. "I do. I accept. I can start right now. I mean, if you need me to."

Yes. She needed him to. That much seemed to ring through her veins. He'd be valuable on the investigation of his Maker and that was starting as soon as possible and it behooved her to get him hired and cleared to work as immediately as safely possible.

But it wasn't going to happen on that schedule. Safely as possible took time. That was the first thing. But also, putting Elmer on her to-do list had to wait until she returned from the Joint Tribunal.

"Let's get you completely cleared security clearance wise first. Then you train. And learn about Hunter Corp.'s processes. There's a regular workgroup meeting between all the bodies governed by the Treaty. It's taking place next week. It's an endless schedule of meeting after meeting with annoying formal shit thrown in so I have to get dressed up and stop getting things done to slink around being clever and obeying hierarchical rules. Also work, if I'm being honest, but annoying. All that is to say I've got too much to manage between now and then. By the time I return, you'll have finished the preliminaries and be ready to start in the field."

He nodded. "All right, then. I'm still happy to accept."

Rowan called David in to start the process before she headed off to track Vanessa down.

Vanessa had been hired to deal with their tech stuff after Carey had been killed. She'd proved to be efficient and clever from day one and Rowan had thrown off enough grief—though it was always there, lurking, ready to jump out at any moment—to begin to like the other woman.

"You created this background on Elmer Marsc. He's Aron's Maker. It was helpful but I want to know *everything* you can find out about him."

Vanessa, whose hair was currently yellow and orange, began to clack away at her keyboard. "Gotcha. I assume this is an as-soon-as-possible type situation?"

"Do what you can as you can. We've got other priorities that are more pressing. Does that work?"

Vanessa nodded. "Yep."

"Appreciate it," Rowan called out as she left.

She went to her office, called, and made an offer of employment to Katya, who would begin training once

Rowan returned from Prague. She'd be read at some point before Genevieve and Clive, along with Rowan, left.

Then she sent a text to Clive so he'd see it when he got out of the call he'd gone into with Nadir.

I need an ancient to read my new Vampire employees. One of them tonight if possible. I could find such a Vampire quickly, but you'll be shirty if I don't ask you. Plus you're very handsome and obviously the best at such things. Let me know.

It would be better if she hired someone outside the Scion's office. Politically better for Clive and far less annoying for Rowan. But he would absolutely get in a snit if she didn't ask him. She was a rug too. Or a car. He loved her, which made her worth more than that to him, obviously, but Rowan had known he was an old-school, Scion-level Vampire when she'd gone and married him so it seemed rather unfair to expect him to act like anyone else.

The witch read was way simpler. She headed across the bright and open common workspace in the center of their floor to Genevieve's office.

The witch turned from her screen to smile up at her.

"Do you have some time?" Rowan asked.

Ten minutes later they'd settled in a corner booth at a nearby dessert shop where everything smelled like cotton candy and cherries. Genevieve had cast whatever spell it was that enabled them to chat without being overheard.

They'd had breakfast earlier but that had been in a conference room doing some work. Also, she and Genevieve had the same tendency to burn through calories through their jobs and needed to refuel or be useless.

And who didn't like ice cream? Or pancakes. Or Mexican food. Whatever. It had become a little ritual in their friendship that Rowan liked a lot.

Once they'd ordered, Rowan didn't waste time. She caught Genevieve up on the salient points that she'd hired Aron and needed him to be read as soon as feasible. Katya would come in to handle all her paperwork and when she did that David would be sure to schedule the rest.

Rowan wouldn't share everything at all times with Genevieve. After all, they each had their own loyalties to balance. Still, they had trust between them, and Rowan knew her friend shared with the same sort of freedom.

Genevieve would do the working when they returned after their sundaes. David would be finishing up right around then anyway.

Her phone buzzed with a call from Alice so she picked up quickly.

"Clive got your text. He's still in a meeting so he wanted me to contact you to say he'll do the job and not to have anyone else do it first. He can accommodate you in an hour at your offices."

Neither of them said exactly what it was he'd agreed to, and Rowan didn't want that to change. "I'll see him there. Thank you."

"Vampire screen has been handled." Their treats came and Rowan dug into the strawberry cheesecake ice cream that was her current favorite. "Will it be too hard on Aron to be read by you and Clive in one night?" She had no idea, but she didn't want to go injuring the guy before he'd even been an employee twelve hours.

"It's fine. I assume you have questions, and you want me to watch as he answers?"

"Is that your usual process? I've had a few people read magically but it was different each time. A few of those times were during or after a battle so it got bloody. I assume that's not the case this time."

Genevieve's pretty laugh seemed to dance in the air between them. "What do you want from the read? That's the first question. I can examine him for any sort of spells or geas."

A geas was a magical chain that kept an individual from speaking or communicating regarding a certain subject. Theo had a geas on him for centuries regarding one of his old side pieces who then tried—and very nearly succeeded—to kill Rowan. He'd been big mad and lots of blood had been spilled. In the end, Rowan killed Enyo and now that the bitch was dead, dead, dead, the world was better off.

"Yes. I don't think he does, but you're a far better judge of such things and I can't take the risk without being sure. Can you read intent? Like is he for real or hiding something?"

"If he opens to me, I'll know if he's genuine or not. If I have to fight him, it's harder to tell. Especially with good liars and true believers. Vampires are quite often one or the other. If I'm fighting to get past whatever blocks and it's muddied, I'm trying to figure out if they're being evasive or just trying to keep me out because they don't like being examined that closely," Genevieve said and then really truly clapped her hands with delight after a huge bite of her birthday cake sundae.

"How do you manage to still be so delicate and pretty

and Frenchly perfect when you do stuff like that?" Rowan muttered.

Genevieve laughed. "The answer is that I am seven centuries old. I've been all sorts of people over that time. Being Genevieve is my most attractive trait. My favorite outfit. I feel comfortable in it, yes?"

Rowan did understand that and hoped to have that level of self-acceptance someday. Not as hard as it might seem when one looked like Genevieve and had the sort of power she had. But still.

"So. I'm going to ask about Darius. You can not answer if that's what you want. I'm dying to know, though," Rowan added.

"We're taking it slow. On one hand, I feel safe saying we're both attracted to the other. Deep, sensual attraction," Genevieve added like Rowan couldn't have figured that part out when Darius and Genevieve seemed to eye-fuck one another every time they were together.

"And you're good with that?" Not a judgment at all, just a question. Rowan would support her friend in any case.

"It's been a very long time since someone has moved me the way he does. It's a lot to process. Perhaps if I wasn't so sure we were...*together*, which I am, I'd be less okay with this part. He's got a full-time guard on me. He came to the Senate meeting to protect me."

"Where is your guard today? I didn't see anyone in the office."

"Marco's out there somewhere. He's my main guard. Though Darius quite often shows up to *relieve him*. In other words, take over." Genevieve waved a hand. "I've invited him to come into the building. He can work in my office or one of the conference rooms. Or I can let him know when I need to leave. But they all ignore me when I say things like that, so I say it anyway for politeness' sake, but know they'll do whatever they want in the end. Or whatever Darius tells them to do."

"When I came to your house when you first moved in, that was the first time I'd seen a Dust Devil in shorts. I'm dying to learn more about what they're all like," Rowan admitted.

"They're everything I assumed and nothing like I thought they'd be all at the same time," Genevieve said.

"What does the Senate think of your ascension to priestess to a Trick of chaos demigods?"

"There's talk, of course. We do love gossip so much." She laughed. "Most of the reception I've received has been positive. They see it as an alliance with a great power. It raises my profile in that way. Others, well, there's always mutterings about purity and the like. But of late, those mutterings are louder and more pronounced. They see me serving as a priestess as being robbed of something. Of me being sullied by it and since I'm highly ranked it bears on their reputation as well. I don't care at all what they think. But there's an element of bigotry to it I will not abide."

"Nor should you. I get it from the other side of the situation. Clive is the Genevieve in my story. He's a golden boy. Powerful. From a very highly ranked, extraordinarily connected family. A Scion who would have been expected to marry someone of his rank. But they got a human who ran away from their leader's Keep and then made a career out of killing Vampires."

"They got a unique power in the world. A Vessel to a goddess. A full partner in Hunter Corp. A foster daughter of their king. You have brought Clive's position up, not down. We both know how they are. He's collected a priceless treasure. They may not like that you kill Vampires for a living. But they certainly like a power like yourself being connected to one of their powers," Genevieve said.

Correctly.

"Clive says a lot of those things too." Rowan grinned. "Still, all those someones of his rank? Man, they are so fucking heated up that I snatched their perfect Scion up and tied him to my bed." She laughed at that a bit. "What does Konrad think?"

"He's of the mind that it makes me, and thereby the Aubert line, stronger. More influential. After all, who else's family has a priestess serving a Trick of chaos demigods? He wants to host some sort of family gathering over the winter holidays to celebrate and also introduce the Auberts to the Dust Devils and vice versa. He's got an estate large enough to host such a thing, so as long as I don't have to plan it, I'm in support. I want the Dust Devils to be treated with the respect and honor they deserve."

"You're very sweet on them," Rowan said, pleased her friend was so happy.

"I really am," Genevieve admitted. "They're all so lovely to me I just can't tolerate any of my family not being equally lovely. We're all a bunch of black sheep anyway. I think it will be fine."

They finished up eating and headed back to the office. Rowan didn't want Clive arriving while she was still away. He'd be nosier and bossier without her around to keep him in line.

# *Chapter Seven*

When they'd arrived back at the chapterhouse, Genevieve and Aron got down to their magical business, David had gone to deal with other administrative stuff, and Rowan had gone to her office, where she could have a few minutes to think about everything she needed to be doing over the next week.

They'd have to leave for Prague in a few days. She wanted to poke around in Elmer Marsc's life before they did. David was coordinating with the other chapterhouses to compile all the data they'd need for various meetings. The official itinerary had been decided upon a week prior and she'd already put together notes for everything she was responsible for. They were in the process of hiring or transferring in all the support they'd need. Now that she was responsible for a far larger territory and had consolidated most major administrative positions to be run from Las Vegas, her tiny three-person staff from the old days wouldn't do at all.

Which meant more interviews that whole week while David helped settle all the transfers from various Motherhouses across the globe, including his new assistant, Vihan, who was starting in two days' time. Rowan and David both had worked with him in London. He'd helped manage Susan's office and though Rowan's friend was affectionately miffed they'd recruited her employee, he came with only the highest of recommendations from everyone he worked with.

It annoyed her that she had to leave the country right as everything was coming together but that was simply how things worked in her world and everyone working for Hunter Corp. knew it. They might as well be starting while she was on a whole different continent.

Clive arrived just minutes later. Their bond sizzling and shimmering the closer he got. Rowan didn't wait to be told he'd arrived. She simply headed downstairs, pausing near the stairwell to watch her man stroll in.

That night he wore a black suit with a deep gray shirt. No tie, though she knew he'd probably started off his work night with one. He looked stylish and handsome. And very dangerous.

Though she hadn't announced herself, he barely glanced at Malin as he headed to Rowan, taking her hands in his, lifting them both to his mouth to brush a kiss over her knuckles. A year ago, she'd never have allowed such a public display.

She wasn't the same woman she'd been a year ago.

The flash in his gaze sent heat racing through her. He knew exactly what he was doing. How lucky was she?

Still, she was the boss and all, so she gave him one last moment and stepped back. He kept one of her hands, and after calling out her thanks to Malin, Rowan led Clive upstairs and into her office, closing the door at her back.

"Thank you," she said. "He's in with Genevieve right now. When that's finished, she'll bring him here. He knows a Nation Vampire is reading him, but I didn't say it was you."

"One does like to keep one's hand in the game, so to speak," he said.

"And you get to be nosy."

He smiled. "Curiosity is an important trait, darling. What would you like me to read for?"

She and Clive had basically the same type of conversation she'd had with Genevieve, only emphasizing all the Vampy stuff rather than magic.

"Before he comes in, I need to tell you something about his Maker. Aron wasn't even seventeen when he was Made. And that was 1917 so I understand things are different now than they were then, but I also have intel that hasn't stopped him. Looks like there have been at least two Makings of underage humans since then. I'm going to be looking very closely at Elmer Marsc. I thought you should know."

"I assume this hasn't been reported officially to anyone within the Nation?"

"Who would they have gone to? Part of it happened during Jacques's term as Scion, and from what I'm told, they were close. We both know Jacques never gave a shit about humans anyway, so if Elmer was a buddy and sent Jacques money or women or whatever struck his fancy, Jacques wouldn't have done a thing to stop underage Making. There was no profit for him in it."

Clive adjusted his cuffs as he considered what she'd said.

"Will your source be willing to speak to me about it? Make an official report?" he asked carefully.

"Maybe. And don't get mad," she added at his expression. "You know how this goes. Why should any of them trust the Scion? Not you, obviously you're not Jacques, but the office. The power structure that has created this very problem. I've already started putting together a dossier on Elmer. I'll find him and if he's doing anything I don't like, he'll know."

"And will *I* know? This is a Vampire-shaped problem."

"With a sword-shaped solution, so back up there," she said, pointing at him with her pen. "I'm going to look at him and see what I can find. *Me*. Hunter person. I'll forward whatever I discover that connects to you."

"The Vampires who've been wronged deserve to have the Nation solve their problems. Having Hunter Corp. do it estranges the Nation from those who need us most."

"I agree they need you. I agree it will do them good—the Nation as a whole—to be able to count on you. But that's not going to happen overnight. I've already told Aron you would never tolerate such violations of the Treaty and I told him that because I believe it to be true. I *want* the Nation to be better at dealing with those who are at the very bottom of your hierarchy. I'm happy to push in that direction but I too have a duty to protect people. So I'm doing that. And then, when the time is right, I'll include you and help bridge that gap because I have my own work to do."

He growled a sigh but didn't argue. Because she was right. She was sad to be right because it hurt Clive too. He was a Vampire with all the annoying things that came with it. But he was a good leader who truly cared about those Vampires he was sworn to protect, and she wanted to help him continue that.

She changed the subject. "Did you have a meeting about me today? Are all the fragile Vampires all ascared of the big bad Hunter?"

He gave her a put-upon sigh but the smile lurking around his mouth told on him. "Not a Scion meeting. I spoke with Nadir to relay my opinion of several aspects of the official response. From what I understand, I wasn't the only Scion who called out the way the response was only sent to London and Paris. Nor was I alone in pointing out our behavior was pushing our allies away."

She harrumphed. "Did you tell her I was hiring Vampires during your call?"

"No. That's your business to share. But you did alert them it was coming so I doubt anyone will be surprised when you announce. Though I'm certain the aftermath will be quite diverting."

She barked a laugh. "I'm working on that. We don't make press releases when we hire Hunters. I may as well put a neon target on their backs, for Goddess's sake. I told the Nation we were hiring and that's what is happening. I don't plan to keep Vampires up to date on personnel matters within Hunter Corp. and that's not even because I'm being petty or difficult. *However*, I need to extend official protection to the Vampires we hire. Easiest way to do that is official contact between us and the Nation. So I'll notify Nadir's office and she'll tell the Scions. I don't like it, but I think it's the best way given the options I have."

Rowan looked up to catch her spouse pinching the bridge of his nose and tossed a paper clip at his head. "Stop! You're going to wrinkle all that suave British handsome and you won't be my trophy husband anymore."

If anything could give Clive wrinkles it was his wife's penchant for finding trouble anywhere and everywhere. Still it was a relief she saw the need to inform the Nation and the reason why.

And it was a great relief she'd turned to him to read her new employee.

"What do you think of Aron?" she asked.

If she began to develop a mind reading gift he'd riot. She was canny enough as it was.

"Because you obviously looked into him yourself when you went into work today. Especially after I asked you for help," she said, answering his semi-panicked unspoken worry.

"My impressions remain the same as they were when I looked at your dossier." Which had been far more detailed than his own. He needed to speak with Patience and Seth, his top lieutenants, urge them to pay closer attention to all the Vampires in his territory, especially the rogues. Not to take on trouble, they had plenty already. But rogues still had the same powers and thus posed similar problems as affiliated Vampires. It was simply good sense. And perhaps if they felt looked after in some way, less would choose to eschew the Nation and declare themselves rogues to start with.

"Shall I keep it private that you did the read on him?" Rowan asked. "You know it's better if I tell Nadir it was done. Like I said, I don't want war with the Nation, and it'll underline that Hunter Corp. is doing its best to screen out all troublesome candidates. But there's no need to say it was you."

"I've no doubt you're right about that. I considered the point of anonymity, but I believe if it's known, at least to Nadir—who will guess anyway—it only strengthens your case here. You're not trying to hurt the Vampire Nation. You even let a Scion in to part of your screening process. It's a win."

"That's very savvy, Scion. Thanks."

If only she took all his suggestions so easily.

David brought in a pot of tea, Prince of Wales, one of Clive's favorites, and let them know Aron was ready for him.

She didn't tell him to behave or be nice or ask if she could stay. She trusted that he would never abuse his position—as her husband and as Scion—and that meant everything to him.

"Give me a moment with him. I'll introduce you two and leave. I've got to deal with some other stuff anyway." She went to the door, but paused a moment to drop a kiss at his temple. It was absently affectionate and therefore he was glad to be sitting or he might have gone a little weak at the knees. This feral creature who'd started off their relationship with so little trust now came to him freely to touch or comfort. Goddess willing, he wanted to continue this sort of coming together. Wanted to be worthy of her.

Rowan was admittedly relieved when Aron approached and neither he nor Genevieve appeared to be upset in any way. Though she had a gut feeling that told her Aron was exactly what she thought he was, trust but verify would be her motto.

"Are you ready for the Vampiric part of the screening?" Rowan asked him. "Genevieve assures me there's no danger in being read by two different beings in a short span of time. The process is confidential. Nothing he or Genevieve learn will go any further unless it poses harm to someone."

"I've never met the Scion. It will be my honor to be read by him." Aron dipped his chin slightly.

"Figured you'd guess," she said with a smile.

"There are many powerful beings here in this building just now." He nodded in Rowan's and then Genevieve's direction. "But the Scion's power signature, well, there's nothing else I've ever felt the like of. Even from his predecessor."

Clive would love that.

"All right, then. Genevieve, I'll be with you in a moment. I'm just going to introduce Aron to Clive," Rowan said.

"Young David has some tea in process for us, he says. And Lorraine has been by to bring food she'd prepared and ordered me—and you—to eat." Genevieve nodded to Aron. "It was a pleasure, Vampire."

Aron's features had gone a little softer as Genevieve seemed to float away in her flowy, flowery dress, her hair done up in some sort of complicated braid. Roses and lavender hung in the air in her wake.

"Yeah, I get it." Rowan winked and then indicated he follow her into her office, where Clive rose, tall, suave, handsome as fuck, haughty, aristocratic, and undoubtedly powerful. Usually her Scion toned himself down, which meant this was a display. A pretty hot one.

"Scion Clive Stewart, this is Aron Jimenez."

Aron kept his direct gaze from Clive's and tipped his chin in a measure of respect. Not as deeply as a Nation Vampire would have, but more than enough to show respect of the Vampire and his office.

Finally Clive eased it back and held out his hand. Aron grasped his forearm instead. As warriors. But when the clasp ended, Aron turned his hand, wrist up. Showing respect. This was a Vampire who understood the world he stood outside of.

Clive nodded, satisfied and even a little pleased.

Rowan left them to it and headed to Genevieve's office only to nearly walk into the door when she caught sight of Darius reclining in one of the chairs, a teacup cradled in his hand. He was turned, facing Genevieve, nearly all his attention—certainly he knew Rowan had approached—on the witch. Genevieve leaned against the desk, a smile on her lips as she sipped her tea.

"I didn't know you weren't alone. My pardon," Rowan said. She didn't know how to address any Dust Devils much less the one in charge. They were all so unearthly in the way they held themselves, in the sheer wall of energy that seemed to swirl about their bodies like the twisted winds named after them.

She generally treated beings that ancient and full of power with wary respect. The same way she handled Theo. You never knew when something you thought was innocuous would end up pushing a button for something with enough power to level cities.

Genevieve regarded Rowan and gave a lazy wave of her wrist, sending her bracelets jingling and clacking where beads or stones met. "I made Darius come inside to have tea with me. He's my guard for the evening and there's simply no reason to be out there when I'm in here."

"She lured me with Madam Lorraine's cooking. If I could steal her from Genevieve to cook me such delights I would," Darius said in a dry tone.

Genevieve noted Rowan's surprise at Darius's humor. He must feel comfortable around Rowan to reveal that part of himself, which pleased her because if he liked Rowan, Rowan would relax around him, and they could like one another. And since Rowan was her close friend, one Genevieve spent a great deal of time with, she wanted them both to be at ease.

And she found herself wanting Rowan to loosen up and get to know Darius. Her friend was funny and though sarcastic and blunt, truly loyal and courageous. Such bright fire for someone who'd only been alive the blink of time's eye.

"Anything we speak of here will not leave these walls without your permission," Genevieve said. "Fill a plate and let's talk of Aron."

Rowan did, pouring herself a cup of tea and settling at the chair nearest the desk.

"He was open to be read. I sensed no lurking spells. No compulsions or geas. I'm no lie detector, but my power says he is genuine in what he portrays himself to be. He spoke some of his life when he was with a Maker." Genevieve sniffed, vastly agitated by the way Vampires could be toward those they should protect instead of victimize and use up.

"He's got a strong moral core. He believes what he says he does. He's not coy. His past doesn't weaken him. Rather it gave him focus and direction. A cause. He doesn't hate all Vampires. But he does loathe his Maker and those like him."

Rowan said, "Can't say as I blame him on that. It's my perception that he's taken what happened to him, and more importantly, how he got through it and out the other side, and crafted a life for himself where he can help others who, like himself, got tangled up and may not know how to get free. Vampire or not. He just feels to me like a being who seeks meaning in what he does."

"I concur with that."

"You'd be comfortable working with him? Having

him at your back if we were in the field or in some sort of confrontation?" Rowan asked.

"Yes," she said without having to think on it overlong. The Vampire had read clean to her. Not pure. He had burrs and snags, bitterness and anger here and there. Most beings did, especially ones over a hundred years. But his driving force was one she admired. It was genuine.

More than all that, there was a sense of purpose. As if he was meant to be there. Needed to be.

Rowan nodded and then finished up her tea. "Clive is done. Please thank Lorraine. These little lemon butter cookie things are so good I could eat two dozen in one sitting. It was nice to see you again, Darius. Please be welcome here any time. Genevieve, your skills are much appreciated."

Genevieve walked out with Rowan. "I am left with one certainty. He's supposed to be here right now."

Rowan sucked in a breath. "I need to talk with you tomorrow about a few things. For the moment, yes, I agree."

Once Clive had given her the thumbs-up on Aron, she'd sent her new Vampire Hunter home for the night. She'd promised dirty sexual favors—the best kind—to her spouse in payment for his services, and he'd gone back to his office.

Quickly, while it was still dark at the Keep, Rowan created a script about hiring Aron and sent it off to Nadir's office.

# *Chapter Eight*

Rowan sat up from a deep sleep at the sound of a knock on her door. "Yes?" she called out.

Elisabeth came in, holding a tray, David at her back, a smile on his face.

Rowan wanted to say something, but every part of her that had been conscious snapped off at the same time, yanking her back into a sleep that did not want to let go.

Sensation seemed to slowly resettle as her consciousness sharpened, burning off that depth of sleep Rowan had come to associate with prophecy dreams.

She floated until the scent of book leather and expensive whiskey wrapped around her attention and tugged.

When her eyes opened, she met those of her expensive Vampire whose power smelled of smoke and peat.

"There's a new smell," she muttered, willing herself to focus on him. "Is it dark? How long was I out? Shouldn't you be at daytime rest?" Star had draped herself over Rowan's thighs and she moved to the side, but didn't leave the bed, keeping contact with Rowan's body.

"That is a great many questions for someone who passed out," he said. "The sun has only just set." He kissed her forehead and then her mouth as she tipped her face up. "David said you had work all morning long.

You were supposed to brunch with Genevieve but that got rescheduled. You and David had lunch and then you came in to take a nap. Told him you had a headache."

Rowan touched her temple. Yes. It was coming back now. When she'd woken up first thing, Genevieve had canceled due to Conclave business. So Rowan had worked on a proposal for the Joint Tribunal and made several calls to the evening side of the world where Vampires were awake.

She'd decided to lie down awhile before Genevieve was due to come over for tea and gossip. Her head had throbbed, the pain of it had sapped her energy, and finally she'd given in and come into her bedroom to see if she could sleep it away.

Clive continued to examine her features carefully. "That was just two hours ago. The sun went down about forty-five minutes past, and I've been here since trying to get your lazy rear end to wake up. I've answered your questions. My turn now," he said as he helped her to sit with the pillows fluffed at her back. Hating so much that she'd worried him yet again, Rowan didn't insult him by pretending away or calling out the anxiety wafting from him. Instead, she took one of his hands and kissed it in thanks for being there.

"What new smell do you mean?" he asked while she was still loopy with loving him.

"I think perhaps it's more that I can detect it now, rather than being *new*." She tested the words and they felt right.

Rowan thanked him when he handed her a mug but she didn't sip right away. He gave her a severe look. "Don't be suspicious. David did whatever it is you do to take a perfectly lovely coffee and ruin it with heaps of sugar and cream."

Pleased by the sight of her viciously handsome Vampire, she leaned in to sniff the steam. It was still warm, so she didn't waste time, taking several sips while waking up bit by bit while considering his question about the scent. It kept her from panicking about the way she'd just...passed out, powerless over the dream.

"You all have unique power and scent signatures. For some time, I've been able to scent ancient Vampires," she admitted. They smelled of almonds and being able to detect it was something about half the population could do though most of them didn't pay any attention. If they were very lucky, they'd never have to.

She hadn't been so lucky. She'd learned early on to use all her senses when surrounded by predators. Which was why she'd managed to stay alive despite the life she led.

Rowan continued, "The last two years or so I've been able to detect some Vampires at the very edge of a thousand or so. They're a little more bitter. Like the charcoal after a fire in a firepit. But those scents are about age. You. Well, you smell like money and power. I don't think other Vampires your age all carry that scent." She considered. "Your father. Yes. I noticed it but figured it was his den or study or whatever his man room of business and expensive liquor is called."

His exasperated smile was affectionate.

And he didn't deny what she'd said. Huh.

"So a Stewart-line type thing and each of you has your own spin on the original." Rowan stretched up to sniff him and then pressed a kiss to his throat before settling back against the pillows. "Can you smell each other? How come I didn't know about this until right now? Why didn't Theo tell me? Or someone?" Maybe in Hunter Corp. data there was something about individual-family-line Vampire scents and she'd just never seen it. Maybe Theo would have told her if she hadn't run away at sixteen.

"Isn't this fun?" Clive said but clearly, he was being sarcastic, so she made a face.

"I'm very fun. A fun factory." She gave him the finger.

"There's my wife," he murmured, and she pretended not to hear the relief in his tone. "Rowan, what happened?" he asked softly before kissing her forehead.

"Lots going on right now. I had this…knowing thing yesterday as you know. Then there were interviews and weird stuff going on with the witches. Genevieve was going to tell me some more about that and I was going to tell her about the knowing thing so I guess I can add this dream too. Anyway. I don't know just yet what it means. Just that it's got to be connected somehow to something or other that's in my way."

"My greatest concern is that according to David and Elisabeth you seem to have been pulled back into this dream involuntarily. And for you not to remember the hours before you went to nap…you have a very sharp memory, darling Hunter."

"I remembered after you told me. I don't think the dream itself was a cause of my memory loss. My system was out of balance, and it took me a bit to find my way back to consciousness. But, in honesty, no, I've never been pulled back into a dream like I was today. Not that I've had a lot of practice yet, this is a relatively new development slash gift from Brigid. I think the knock on the door pulled me from the dream, but the dream wasn't done. That's the best way I can put how it felt."

"Tell me, then, about the dream."

Genevieve had given Rowan some basic lessons on how to center herself to open her magic. Her magic was where the dreams came from because her magic came from Brigid.

She set the mug aside and controlled her breathing, creating a focus that unlocked her memory of the dream. It was too much, and her lungs seemed to seize up, refusing to work, refusing to expand. The deluge of images threatened to drown her all while she was unable to draw breath.

Pins and needles began to prickle across her chest and her vision blurred at the edges.

But she was forged of stronger stuff, and long-learned patience and courage clicked into place. Rowan remembered herself. Remembered she was in her home, her husband within arm's reach. These were images she was meant to have. Meant to interpret somehow and they were not supposed to harm her.

Warmth pooled in her belly and Rowan let the panic go. Truly opened herself to whatever energy it was that was the conduit for the dreams. She found a way to take the raw power of it and create images that made sense to her brain.

The first few times were too fast, leaving her nauseous and dizzy. But each time she got a better grasp and after a bit, she figured a way to rewind and slow the images down.

Words rose to her lips after she swallowed back the need to throw up. "Poker chips and a building wave. High winds. A storm. Houses on a shoreline," she said, and he handed her the notebook she kept in the top drawer of her nightstand so she could write it all down.

"Do you know what any of it means?" he asked, brushing her hair back from her face. He was about two minutes away from ordering her to eat something. She could see it building in the tension of his shoulders.

"Not yet. I'll have David get with Vanessa to start running some searches with those keywords. I don't think it'll be literal, that's too easy and straightforward." Rowan was still learning the prophecy stuff. It started off confusing but eventually she figured it out before it was too late.

She wanted to improve, figure things out before the very last minute when it was life-and-death. She'd consult every source possible and see what shook loose.

"I do think the storm imagery is about trouble coming. But we knew that. I'll also see if Genevieve might have any ideas. She has such a deep knowledge of so many types of magical traditions, something that seems like one thing might easily be something totally opposite."

"Perfect. As she's here, set up at our dining room table watching movies on her laptop with David as they waited for you to wake up. Once at the table, you can eat something."

Not even two minutes.

She got out of bed and after a quick brush of her teeth and a tidied braid of her hair, she headed out to see her friends and devour a large plate of whatever wonderfulness Elisabeth had created.

Genevieve gave Rowan a careful look before closing the computer and setting it aside.

Elisabeth pointed to a chair, which Clive held out for her. So many people bossing her about. She must be still recovering from that dream because normally all that being told what to do would make her want to punch someone. Mainly she wanted food.

Elisabeth warned, "Before you overwhelm Rowan with all your questions, let her get some food into herself." A plate was slid in front of her. "Pork with mushrooms and roasted vegetables."

"Damn right it is," Rowan said as she happily tucked in. A tall glass of water was placed nearby, along with a basket of warm bread. "This is amazing."

Beaming, Elisabeth made a shooing motion at the others to eat as well. Star yipped and trotted over to her bowls to scarf down whatever her dinner was.

"They don't get pork and mushrooms? What did they do to you?" Rowan teased Elisabeth.

"We ate while you took your sweet time sleeping the day away," Genevieve said. "Though it would be terribly rude of me not to have some bread." She took a bite and made a sigh of pleasure. "Now, it's time to overwhelm you with questions, Rowan. What happened?"

"I meant to tell you about this over brunch today," Rowan admitted. She didn't want Genevieve to think she'd been hiding something from her, or worse, that she didn't trust her friend. That Genevieve's pretty features seemed to ease made Rowan glad she'd said it.

Once she'd explained the *knowing* she'd had that was somehow connected to Aron and most likely Elmer Marsc, Rowan gave them the basics of her dream.

Genevieve cocked her head. "Darius mentioned a coming storm only the day before yesterday. Not a direct warning to you or I would have shared. I'm not sure what the rules are when it comes to you and things outside the Trick."

Rowan blamed being hungry when she sought to reassure Genevieve, but really it was that part of her that was also growing, that need to protect and console that always seemed to burn bright exactly when it was needed. So much was changing in the witch's life. So many allegiances and loyalties to weigh. Her friend must be so alone in ways most would never see much less understand. But Rowan did. "This priestess thing is new and you're trying to find your place within the Trick and that whole world. It's necessary for you to consider whatever you share and with whom. I trust you, Genevieve, to tell me if I need to know."

Genevieve nodded once and then smiled briefly. "That you dreamed of a storm as well just two days later isn't a coincidence. And isn't that fascinating?"

It certainly was. Did the Devils have a gift of prophecy or was Darius one of those handful of Dust Devils with magic? Already the fear about the dream had faded and Rowan wanted to know more about half a dozen things she'd discovered that day.

"Fascinating? I rather find my wife simply losing consciousness far from fascinating," Clive said. He'd brought his chair closer to hers than he normally did. Close enough that he could touch her easily.

He brushed a hand over hers and then tucked her braid back. Normally, she'd put a stop to this overprotective business because he was already prone to being in her face all the time about everything she did. With reason, she supposed. But. But, she'd scared him. He'd have woken up to news she'd been unconscious. While he was at daytime rest. While he couldn't have done anything.

So she let him fuss because they both needed the reassurance.

Genevieve tipped her chin, acknowledging the emotion beneath Clive's sarcasm. "Rowan's gifts from her Goddess are growing. Her prophetic path and mine are aligning. This could lead to both of us being more powerful. We create a mirror and double our energy."

Wow, really? Like a Transformer? Cool.

"Which keeps everyone safer," David added and that reminded Rowan not to act so flip right then when Clive was still petting her.

"I don't like not being really good at it yet," Rowan admitted. "But I'm learning with each episode. The techniques you taught me to deal with the images from a dream so I could manage to make sense and catalog them helped a lot today," she told Genevieve. She didn't need to go into how it felt like she was drowning, suffocating as the images flashed through her brain at dizzying speed. The important part was she'd managed it. They all needed to know she'd be all right because she was too stubborn not to be.

Rowan continued, "This happened here at home. Even if I'd been alone, I would have woken up when I was supposed to." She looked directly at Clive. "I'm okay. Just now with added fortune-telling dreams."

"Is it safe for you to travel to Prague? Should you hold off?" he asked.

"I'm no medical expert—or expert of any type—on prophecy. But I don't think Star would let me go anywhere if it was dangerous to do so. And I've traveled since my first dream with no ill effects. I think this is just another thing to add to our plus column. Another weapon. Another shield."

His eyes told her he hated the idea of putting her in any danger. There was guilt there. Panic at losing her.

Because she knew that fear for him, she leaned in to kiss him quickly.

"I promise. If there's a problem, I'm not going to put myself at risk unless I have no option otherwise and I need to intervene."

"Spoken like a woman who grew up understanding how a nonspecific oath can get you into trouble," Clive told her, but there was a little less unhappiness on his features.

She was at a table with a near five-hundred-year-old Scion-level Vampire and a seven-hundred-and-change-year-old Genetic witch whose family line was apparently the Who's Who of the magical world. One didn't make promises or oaths or anything of the sort without thinking very carefully with beings as powerful and dangerous as Clive and Genevieve. Both seemed driven to protect her, so that made Rowan even more careful to not box herself in.

Rowan sent him a smug smile and he kissed her temple. She loved when he did that. It was so tender, and it made her feel precious but not in a gross way.

"I accept your promise," Clive said by way of following up.

"As do I." Genevieve nodded and then added as she put her phone away, "Now that you're awake, I need to return to my home. Just for a few minutes but there are papers I need to sign, and they were sent there. Then I will come back, and we will discuss many things."

"That sounded mildly threatening," David said.

Genevieve sent him a beautiful smile. "Did it?" She stood and in a flurry of jangling bracelets and floral-scented air, left, calling out her goodbyes to Betchamp and Elisabeth.

It was a good thing he was as near immortal because otherwise, the fear would have taken yet more years off his life. Loving Rowan wasn't for the fainthearted. His wife seemed to consistently draw powerful beings who wanted to kill her. And now Rowan was having these spells and knowings settling in with enough force to knock her unconscious. It filled him with fear even as pride won out. She was like no other being on the planet and part of that was her courage and outright hostility to being told what to do.

Not once when she'd been unconscious had their bond weakened. She'd been there. Steady. Strong. Vibrant. So, he'd taken a few calls and sat at her side, occasionally ordering her to wake up. Rowan being Rowan, she'd ignored those orders for forty-five minutes.

Genevieve had been correct. These prophetic gifts Rowan was manifesting would make her safer. There was a period of time as she struggled through to figure out how to interpret whatever she'd seen, but his wife wasn't friends with failure, so she'd find a way soon enough. And then she'd have another strong weapon in her arsenal.

But those forty-five minutes when she was beyond his reach would take a lot longer to leave his memory. Though she was strong through their bond, he could do nothing but sit at her side. His finest gift, and when it came to this sort of thing, *he could not protect her.* No matter that it was his greatest desire.

And there was the no small matter of the development of a significant gift.

"People will find out, eventually," Clive said as he kept an eye on her while she steadily cleaned her plate. Her appetite was strong. To see her eating with some gusto made him feel better.

"The prophecy stuff you mean?" she asked and when he nodded, she shrugged. "Eventually people will figure it out somehow. I'll slip up and mention it to the wrong person, or be overheard, or someone else who knows will do so. It's a big planet, but our paranormal world is small enough. Everyone is in everyone else's pockets."

"Darling, it's also the fact that you're not just some random shopkeeper in London, or a solicitor, whatever. You are Rowan Summerwaite. Vessel, Hunter, mated to the Scion of North America. Raised by the First. Our world is crawling with those who are fascinated by any or all your myriad strengths and miracles."

He quite disliked it when she discounted just how incredible she was.

She shot him a smile. A secret flash of appreciation and affection and he soaked it in.

"It all adds up to those in our world are too in my business for me to be able to keep this prophecy stuff secret. What's a secret weapon, however, is whatever information I get from these dreams and knowings and goddess knows what else I might start doing."

He frowned at that last bit. "Let us hope dreams and knowings will be enough. You will inform me as soon as possible if not immediately if anything else happens." Not a request. He didn't care that David, Elisabeth, and Betchamp were around.

Rowan gave him a look, he knew, considering insulting him or arguing in some way. But the line of her mouth softened.

"As for the rest? I think it's a fair approach and an excellent example for the paranormal community of your strength and cunning."

"If it scares off even a third of those who might have made a run at me, it's a win. I wish they all respected me and didn't act like dicks, but sometimes you gotta use terror as an example." Rowan shrugged.

"I most certainly agree with that. If they fear you, they will avoid crossing you. It makes my job easier as well. If my Vampires are convinced you're too much to take on, some will choose to find another way to deal with a need or a problem that doesn't include breaking the Treaty."

David picked up his phone when it chimed at him, but it was the soft intake of breath and the shift of his attention to Clive that sent a chill down Clive's spine. David seemed to be giving Clive a few seconds to be the one to tell Rowan about whatever it was before he did.

# *Chapter Nine*

Sage, salt, copper, and the slightest thread of ozone greeted Genevieve when she stepped from the car she'd parked in her garage. Darius pulled his motorcycle next to her and she didn't stop herself from taking in the way he moved as he swung one long leg over the seat to saunter over to where she stood on the driveway.

Motes of power floated freely, sticking to her hair like snowflakes. Slowly melting into her. It had been that way since the first time she'd been to the house she now called hers. So much power it seemed to fall from the sky, swirl around her like autumn leaves or springtime cherry blossoms.

Three houses ringed a large cul-de-sac with drought-resistant plants in their front yards. All sat back from the street and sidewalk and the scale of the curve they all stood in was large enough that while they were neighbors, there was plenty of space between each property.

There were other noises rising in the air all around them, but her attention snagged on Darius. Nothing else was as interesting. He stepped close enough that the width of his shoulders haloed the light around him.

She'd noticed that. Light seemed to have different rules when it came to Darius. Sometimes it seemed to flirt over his features, at turns fierce and shadowy or bronzed and sensual. Always intense. There was a sense of deep time that emanated from him that humbled her. Fascinated her. His magic was vast and ageless and seemed as integral a part of him as Genevieve's own was.

But his was elemental in a wholly unique way. It seemed endless and without form. A huge, churning sea of power and magic that called to her. He was the moon, drawing her, swelling all around until she was drunk with him.

Glorious.

"Already our ground feels different—better—with you here. Your magic has…flavored ours. I can taste you." He sucked in a deep breath and held it for a moment before exhaling.

His magic seemed to come to life, swirling around hers as he exhaled. Glittering onyx shards, slivers of gold, and mists of silver caressed the air, landed on her skin, leaving a tingling in its wake.

Right then, the earth at her feet, the sand and sage and that vein of salt all surged up, pleased to greet her. That welcome had filled an empty spot and had soothed the voices inside. Had settled that anxious need she'd had for the last two decades to float around.

The moon hung overhead, heavy and fecund. Even the time was magic as it passed, weaving between them something deeper. Achingly intimate.

Darius looked at this ethereal witch and yet another part he'd thought frozen over forever thawed. Sparked to life once more. It had happened more than once since she'd walked into their bar the month before.

Moonlight silvered over her, highlighting her beauty

and that bright spark she carried within, Her facets like the glittering center of a precious gem.

He hadn't *wanted* so deeply in thousands of years.

Each breath he took was full of her as the night settled all around them. He held his elbow out and she wrapped her hand around it; the heat of her sent a wave of pleasure through him.

"That's new," he said as they reached her front door and noted the explosion of blooms on the giant bougainvillea on either side of her porch.

"Oh. Yes, yes, it is." She smiled and he turned to face her.

She was so close he could scent her skin and the myriad flavors of the magic that ran through her cells. Spicy. Alluring. Sweet. A little bitter here and there. All her.

Genevieve tipped her head back to look at him better, her lips slightly open, and there was nothing else he could do but lower his head to capture her mouth with his own.

She only looked soft and fragile. The moment he met her lips and the kiss had begun there was no hesitation. She lifted her arms and wrapped them around his neck as they both stepped closer, body to body.

He hissed at the contact. Little arcs of electricity zipped between them, the storm of his power rising to greet hers, not quieting, but calming. Containing itself to keep her close. His awareness of all the levels of his othersight—his magical ability to see the world around him in myriad ways—seemed to expand outward, farther and farther. Her power seemed to amplify his, boosting his sensitivity, stealing his breath.

Her taste was tangerine and allspice. Her tongue stroked his and she made a small sound in the back of her throat he'd kill to seduce from her again. Against him, her body was lithe but strong, the fire of her existence warm and bright as the sun.

He'd wanted this. Had thought over and over about the moment their slow dance became something deeper. His mistake was in underestimating his attraction to his pretty witch. Thought perhaps she was an itch to scratch and some fascinating company in his life.

But her kiss, those arms wrapped around his neck as she gave as good as she got, their power coating one another until it rendered him drunk, told him this craving for her had dug its claws in. The way he wanted his hands or mouth on her every moment of the day had come to live in him and had no plans to move.

It was bigger than he'd assumed, but far too late to do anything but continue forward to see what else this witch had in store for his life.

His hands had come to rest at her hips, and for long moments the image of holding her like that as he slid deep into her body over and over sent shivers racing over his skin. With a shudder at the effort it took, he forced himself to break the kiss before he slid his palms down to grab her ass and haul her to the bedroom.

They paused for long moments, both breathing a little harder than usual.

"There'll be more of that," he said. Not a question. A statement because the heat between them was only the tip of his attraction to their priestess.

"I'm pleased to hear it," she said, her lips quirking up into a smile.

"I smeared your lipstick," he told her, using the pad of his thumb to swipe the side of her mouth.

"I know." She stepped to a mirror in her front entry and reapplied a pretty pink shade to lips swollen from his kiss and quirked into a smile. There was something so secret and special between them right there, in that bubble of time. Things had changed after the kiss. They'd drawn closer. She wasn't wary or afraid at all, so he set aside that worry that she'd be discomfited by what he was. The feral quality he and all the rest of the Devils possessed scared a lot of people. Usually that was great because it kept them out of Devil business. But if he'd have seen fear in her eyes—fear of him—it would have sliced to the bone.

He stepped to her side, grabbing a tissue from the table fronting the mirror she'd just used so he could erase the evidence they'd been kissing. The outward evidence. Inside everything had changed and there was no wiping that away.

Lorraine called out from the center of the house and as one, he and Genevieve headed to her.

Darius had developed a tender spot for Madame Lorraine. Gruff, cranky, and no small bit tyrannical, she ran Genevieve's house and her life with confidence, force, and deep love.

In a French so old it had taken him a few days to remember how to speak it, Lorraine pointed at the large envelope on the nearby table. She nodded her head at Darius in greeting and he bent over her hand to kiss it.

From the corner of his gaze, he noted Genevieve's soft smile as she turned to the papers she needed to sign.

"Have you eaten?" Lorraine demanded as she poked a finger into his ribs like he wasn't a being that scared people off from feet away.

Before he could answer, she took his hand and pulled him to the kitchen island and ordered him to sit.

Guess he was eating.

"Is all well?" he asked Genevieve, who was still examining the paperwork.

"No. What I do know," she said, laying the small stack back on the table, "is that I'm not going to sign anything before more research."

Lorraine put a sandwich wrap in front of him, along with some sort of pickled vegetable salad. Genevieve told her she'd eaten only an hour before at Rowan's. And she got a death stare and a plate with a smaller version of his wrap and the pickle.

Guess she was eating too.

She pulled out a pipe and lit it, taking several slow, deep hits, blowing the funky fragrant smoke out in a long stream. He'd noticed the difference since she'd taken on the position of their priestess. She needed to smoke less. Got lost in those facets of hers less. It pleased him that the Trick had done her a measure of good because she'd most certainly done it for them. Since she'd joined them, her magic had created a veritable daily feast for the Devils. So much energy flowed now that she'd opened the taps.

"Can you talk about it with me? Whatever is bothering you?" he asked, wanting very much for her to share.

"Two days ago when I was at the Conclave for meetings, it came to my attention that there were rumors of some families working together to force the Senate to relax rules regarding magic use and humans. This proposal is to allow magic use for entertainment purposes at a casino owned by a prominent family within the Conclave. Normally, I don't much care when it comes to magic shows or illusionist acts." She shrugged one shoulder. "But this is asking to use coercive magic in situations where humans might refuse otherwise. Card tricks on stage aren't misuse of magical talent. But."

He waited, not speaking. Just listening.

"This feels connected to those rumors. And I oppose

any move that chips away at our laws restricting our talent to make someone do something they would not do otherwise. If there's no consent, I don't support it outside situations of self-defense. I don't know any of these witches well but for one unpleasant encounter before my first meeting the day before yesterday. I can remedy my information deficit on the rest by asking trusted sources." She shook her head.

"You are no youngling, Genevieve. You understand there are things you know because there's concrete proof in front of you, and things you know because on some level, your magic is saying to stop and look closer. Don't sign anything until you're satisfied you looked closely enough. If this family does not like your delay, they can speak to me about it."

Her laugh exploded from her, showering the whole space with joy that was uniquely hers. "Oh if I could, Darius. What a delight that would be."

"They will be frightened enough of Genevieve," Lorraine said. "She only looks soft and pretty. Inside she is a warrior."

"On the outside too," Darius murmured. "The beauty is what they get caught up in, but the ferocity is on the surface as well. In shadows and dips, in the shift of her gaze, and the confidence of her walk in sky-high heels."

"You two will turn my head and spoil me. I shall have a rather high opinion of myself and then what?" Genevieve teased.

"Then you will have finally taken the lesson of your worth," Lorraine said shortly.

Genevieve moved from his side to Lorraine, taking the other woman into her arms, embracing one another for long moments.

* * *

"I am entirely certain I could not survive without you. Thank you," Genevieve said softly in Lorraine's ear.

A pang then that brought tears she managed to hold back. Because she *would* have to survive someday. Even Lorraine, as long-lived as she was, wouldn't see more than a hundred and twenty or thirty years. She would die and Genevieve's heart, the part that belonged to this beautiful woman who held Genevieve's life together so well, this witch who'd mothered her even as her own never had, would break. There were many cracks in her heart where she'd borne the loss of others of Lorraine's line who'd been with her over the centuries. She would survive because that was what she did. And it was better to have loved the people who passed from this world over and over through her long lifetime, than to turn remote and cold, treating those who served in her household as if they were just the jobs they did.

Lorraine, and before her Serah, and before her there was Britta, Helene, and Margaux, who'd been the first.

"Pardon," she said breaking the embrace, "I was wool-gathering."

"Now you can sit down and finish eating. I did not make it for you to waste." Lorraine narrowed her eyes and pointed, but the shine there was of affection and concern.

Darius grinned at her for one moment.

"*Magnifique*," she whispered as his grin transformed his face. Another side of him. Easier. Open. This man she could see at her side at night as well as the day. She could tell her secrets to this man. It set her heart pounding before she could blow out a breath and get herself under control once more.

"Now whose head is getting turned?" he teased.

She made a face at him before turning back to her plate. Lorraine's wooden spoon was nearby and she was quite fast with it when she was displeased.

"You were accosted by someone other than Tristan at the Senate?" Darius asked and Lorraine's attention homed in on the words.

She told them both an abbreviated version of that bizarre scene with Hugo Procella.

Darius grunted. "Can I throw a knife in *his* eye at least?"

Her phone rang. At that time of night it was most likely bad.

Samaya said, "Are you with Rowan right now?"

"No. Why?" Worry had her shooting to her feet.

"Just open your email and call me back when you're done reading what I sent you. No one is in immediate danger." Samaya disconnected and Genevieve looked to Darius, who'd gone very still.

Waiting to do whatever it was she needed.

"That sounds ominous," Genevieve said as she opened the attachment Samaya had forwarded. She read it twice and called Samaya back.

# *Chapter Ten*

Clive had been about to simply ask David what was going on when his phone signaled an incoming document. As he read it his spine straightened, his focus getting tighter and tighter as he finished the attached note from Alice. Bloody fucking hell.

His very observant wife demanded, "Is everyone going to look at their phone without telling me what the fuck is happening or what?"

Clive drew a deep breath and quickly glanced to David before he locked onto Rowan once more. "I think perhaps you should read this and then we can discuss. I don't want to color your perception."

"Just fucking great. So bad no one wants to tell me about it? Vampires are assholes," she muttered as she brought her phone out as it too started to make noise. She snarled and began to read her screen.

Elisabeth added some more food to Rowan's plate and after a distracted but genuine thank-you, Rowan continued to read while she ate.

She was silent so long Clive nearly interrupted.

Finally, she looked up, put her fork down, and dabbed her mouth with her napkin before setting it aside as well.

"Did you know about this?" she asked him, deadly calm.

"No. I only learned of it right here. Alice has friends who forwarded this to her, and she sent this to me and said she was calling to verify with human staff. Rowan, I don't think Nadir knows either. When we spoke yesterday, she'd have said." Clive looked at his watch and calculated the time difference. "It's nearly sunrise at the Keep. Chances are she's only just found out this was sent. We may not hear from her until sunset there tonight." Which caused concern because when the sun finally went down at the Keep and Nadir got to work, it would be morning there in Las Vegas. He'd be at daytime rest and unable to intervene if necessary.

Rowan asked in a flat voice, "Is Theo in on this?"

Clive very carefully answered. "As I've said, I had no idea this was going to happen and given all I know I don't believe this is an official Nation response. Which means Nadir doesn't know. If she doesn't, he most certainly won't." He paused. "The First has taken a hands-off approach with these Vampires. For reasons I'm sure make a great deal of sense to him, but I cannot possibly intuit." It had been, Clive believed, a way for the First to keep Rowan's attention. Play a game with her. Not malicious, but careless. So careless it was cruel. She would feel manipulated. Controlled. And deep down in places she told herself and everyone else had healed, she was bleeding that he hadn't just chosen her.

She allowed a stroke of her wrist and a touch of the ring she wore that said she was his.

He said, "Rowan, this is…you and I both know this is far beyond what *anyone* within the governance structure of the Vampire Nation supports. If they've sent this without the knowledge and express permission of the Voice there's only one way this ends." Scion or not, none of them could protect any Vampire in their territories if and when the First passed a sentence down against them. Tahar would be likely working on his arguments to keep his life and his territories. He and Takahiro had better hope Nadir took pity on them in how she framed this to the First. And that they knew nothing of it. If they had…

Honestly. Fucking Vampires were the most extra of beings on the planet. After rolling her eyes and making a jerk-off motion, Rowan said, "They declare any Hunters who are Vampires or who worked for Hunter Corp. in any other capacity outlaws to be arrested and executed true-dead immediately. Then these fucking shitlords further declare that by hiring them, Hunter Corp. is in violation of the Treaty. Which would then itself be null and void. This arrives on Nation letterhead, issued by Vampires who were part of the process as of two days ago."

Clive's deep sigh amused her far more than the proclamation. "I still find myself absolutely astounded," he said. "I'll repeat there is no way I believe this is an official statement. Nadir doesn't work this way. You said so yourself."

"I'm far more convinced this isn't her because this is amateurish as fuck. She's not an amateur. If she wanted anyone executed, she'd do it and then announce afterward."

Clive raised a brow but then nodded, accepting her point.

"Did Nadir tell the Scions about the hire?" she asked.

"Yes. It was a professional communication from her office to each Scion. A simple notification but she emphasized you had shared voluntarily and that no action on our part was expected or tolerated."

Rowan snorted. "Or is it even related to a leak from a Scion to one of these Vampires? They knew up front that I was going to hire Vampires. I said so. And I said it again after the first response from the shitlords. I think that's what I'm going with because I can't respect myself if I called them Vampire lords. It's too ridiculous in this day and age and I will not abide it." Amused, she shook her fist at the heavens in jest.

"Equally possible," Clive allowed with an amused expression. "I'd prefer the latter, to be frank, to the reality of a Scion giving this information to your shitlords."

Rowan waved a hand. "Let's put aside this execution order for a moment. Do Vampires think we didn't have this all looked over by legal scholars? Multiple Treaty experts and our attorneys all say we have the right to hire whoever we want. And I bet the Nation did too and was told the same because obviously. I do hope the Nation realizes I'm not throwing myself on this grenade to save you this time."

Growling, she said to David, "Get in contact with the other partners. See what they all think. We need to figure out how to respond to this."

After a few clarifying questions, David shoved two cookies in his face before grabbing his things and heading off to organize her world just the way she liked it best.

Rowan took a deep breath, closing her eyes as she breathed out slowly. In again, held it and blew it out.

Just a few feet away Clive was on his phone. Probably to Alice. His tone was terse, but not formal.

When Rowan opened her eyes Genevieve texted, We should talk. Senate just received something from Vampires.

Rowan texted back, Will be in touch in a bit.

She told Clive, "Confetti."

He flinched slightly, not taking her meaning, and that's when she realized she'd said what she had.

"Oh, well look at that. There was confetti in my dream. I thought maybe it was part of the sea spray from the storm, but just now I think it was confetti, not that I know what confetti might mean. Like you know." She mimicked tossing confetti into the air and then gave him a cross look. "I mean really. I have entirely enough on my plate just now and you Vampires can't just chill out for a day?" She waved a hand at his phone, which continued to light up with texts. "We've already made our hiring decisions. Part one handled. But part two? Once I get up from this table I'm headed into a conference with the other partners. You'll understand our reaction to this threat to assassinate Hunters will be severe.

"Depending on how you handle this, Hunter Corp. continues to be open to hearing your concerns. A face-to-face meeting or two during the Joint Tribunal would be best or the old Vamps will misread everything on a screen. However, if the Nation doesn't handle this correctly, we might not attend anyway."

Without using their other senses to translate someone else's intent—their pulse rate, sweat, humans could rarely lie without their body chemistry putting out an acrid scent—they assumed someone was mocking or insulting because they didn't understand current technology and didn't bother to educate themselves.

"That's madness, Rowan. If Hunter Corp. drops out of the Joint Tribunal just four days shy of the first workgroup meetings, you'll create a bigger schism," Clive said.

"*We'll create*? Who. The. Fuck. Do. You. Think. You're.

Talking. To." She shook her head and made a slashing motion with her hand when he began to speak. "This entire situation is of your making. We were prepared to ignore what most would have taken offense at. I assured the rest of the partners this was just Vampiric showboating, and here we are with execution orders. You all love games so much, play them with each other and leave the rest of us alone. If you don't, you get what you fucking get, Scion."

Her phone joined his, reminding her with each vibration that she had work to do.

David interrupted. "We've got a conference scheduled shortly from the chapterhouse. London, Las Vegas, Paris, Kano, and Moscow."

"Okay." She stood but before she could take her own plate to the sink, Elisabeth clucked at her and snatched it from Rowan's hands.

"I expect you've got a long hard night ahead of you both. Alice will take care of Scion Stewart and I know our David will be sure Rowan drinks her tea and has some fruit later. I've packed up a basket for you to take along," Elisabeth said.

Rowan thanked her and once she turned back to the kitchen, talking with David about something or other, Clive stood, looking reluctant.

"Go to work," she told him. He was concerned for her and that was sweet. But he had to be Scary Scion Stewart and stop worrying about her. "I'm getting on a call in less than half an hour so I need to get moving." She blew out a breath. "I'm fine," she said quietly. "You should be more worried about those shitlords who just went around the tenth-most-powerful Vampire in the Nation. I don't need to do shit because whatever she has planned will be way worse."

He hated to leave. Yes, she was fine, but for how long? And what if she lost consciousness again? What if after he was gone, she began to believe he had any part of this foolish gambit? Or that regardless, Vampires were all now the enemy? She'd taken so many terrible blows, suffered so many losses.

As if he'd spoken aloud, Rowan put her hand on his forearm and then slid it down to tangle their fingers together. "We're good," she said. Echoing their conversation from the night before.

"I implore you to remain safe. Wherever you are. Remember to eat, and drink water. Shall I come pick you up on my way home?" he asked.

"Let's hold that in reserve. I don't know where I'll be yet. You be careful too. These Vamps are working overtime to start a skirmish. To what end who knows? You all have plans within plans within plans. But some of those plans might be to strike out at the Scion of North America. Then I'd have to go berserker. Yadda yadda yadda, rivers of blood, drinking from the skulls of my enemies and all that. I really have a tight schedule so don't get hurt."

They were a pair. Both strong and yet worried for the other. But he healed a hell of a lot faster. The idea of a world without her fire was unthinkable. If he did think about it, it brought him to a place where he could do nothing but worry. In the end, it would break them if he ever tried to cage her.

# *Chapter Eleven*

When Rowan arrived at the office, Genevieve was there. Malin, the receptionist, handed Rowan honest-to-goodness handwritten phone messages and said coffee had been made in preparation for her arrival.

Maybe this one wasn't employed by a serial killer to spy on her like the last one had been.

"The Conclave has been made aware of the response to Hunter Corp. by the Nation," Genevieve said when Rowan and David came down the hallway.

Rowan sighed. "They sent it directly to you, or to the Senate?" Every single aspect of this communication had been shaped to cause offense.

"They sent it to the Senate Information Office and it was forwarded to all the Senators from there. My assistant sent it to me."

Rowan took a sip of coffee before she could do something other than snarl. They didn't even send it to all the Motherhouses, but they sent a copy to the Conclave? "This whole thing is mystifying. Not that they'd play games—that was expected—but this threat to execute Hunters? We've been getting along reasonably well of late."

"Except for all those Vampires trying to kill you for years," Genevieve said.

"If I recall correctly, so have a lot of witches. Plenty of humans too," Rowan replied. "But you know how this goes. Only trying to kill me an eighth of the time *is* successful diplomacy with Vampires. And look, if they're not afraid of me—and they will be by the time this is done—they sure as fuck should be terrified of Nadir. There's no place they're going to be able to hide from her." She saw the blueberry muffins with that brown sugar stuff on top and considered it. She'd had a slice of cake not too long ago, but it did seem like a rule to have something with a cup of coffee, and she was very polite and liked to adhere to baked-goods-based etiquette.

After balancing a muffin and her mug, they headed toward the conference room on the third floor.

"I'll be interested to sit back and watch how you handle this. Obviously the Conclave is not going to threaten to execute witches who are employed by Hunter Corp. Even if we disagreed with it that would not be our way. As the liaison between the witches and the Hunters, I'm on your side. I hope the Nation understands what happens when practitioners work with Hunters against them. That's how the Treaty came out to start with." Genevieve went on a bit in French, calling the Nation the fools they were.

"I'm sorry we didn't get a chance to catch up. Care to share anything right now?" Rowan asked quietly when David left the room with Vanessa to do something troubleshootish about the call they were about to get on.

"Most of it is personal. It can wait."

"Things with Dust Devils are well?" Rowan asked. Genevieve wanted to talk about it, to share this thing going on in her life and Rowan wanted to be sure her friend understood she wanted to hear about it. Cared about the things Genevieve was experiencing.

Genevieve nodded. "I know. It seems incongruous, but they really do seem pleased to help. To make me happy." Rowan's friend gave that Gallic sniff that meant three things at once. "I bought wallpaper some years ago. It's quite ridiculously sumptuous in blacks and deep greens shot with gold." She blushed. "Even I am embarrassed to admit how much it cost. Still, I have always imagined it hanging in my bedroom. I've wanted a lush, sensual place full of textures and fabrics that soothed and cocooned. I returned home from a two-day Senate meeting to find Lorraine had led a group of Devils to a storage facility in Los Angeles where many of the things I've collected over time—for my eventual home—had been gathered. They'd hung that wallpaper, set up my bed. All the things I'd been setting aside for centuries and they're now in my house and I find it's rather as lovely as I'd hoped it would be. And just a few days ago, a group of them showed up and let her boss them around for hours while helping build some containers and then they filled them and some big pots placed wherever Lorraine felt would grow best. And the magic there? The herbs and flowers and other things they'd planted that day have all grown and matured. Rosemary now hangs in the air along with the sage and sand. They flirted with her and complimented her cooking and if for nothing else I'd love them for making her happy."

"I'm glad to hear they're such a big part of making that house into your home. Home is a relationship as much as a place," Rowan said.

"Yes! That's it exactly. More than that, being here right now with all of you is important." Genevieve paused. "Even this stunt from the Nation. I cannot help but think…it feels like it should be happening."

Rowan nodded. Agreeing. "I've been waiting for the other shoe to drop. There's more coming." And then she had to explain the saying to Genevieve.

The smile on Genevieve's face rendered Rowan's friend even more beautiful. Soft and pleased with her whatever it was with the Dust Devil. She looked to the doorway and said quickly while they were alone, "Darius kissed me earlier. Under the moon. He touches me like I'm his and I don't stop him. This is altogether new, and I've been alive long enough that I try to resist this giddiness. I know I should hold back until I understand better what it is that drives me toward him."

"Aside from the face? The body? The intelligence and power? The way he looks at you like he wants to spread you on a piece of toast and take a bite?"

That had her friend laughing and waving a hand, the jingling and clacking had become part of the whole Genevieve package in Rowan's mind. "I am ever so pleased you are my friend. You do know just what to say when I need to hear it. There's simply no one else now that I've met him."

"I understand." And she did. Rowan was herself in an unlikely relationship with a powerful, ancient being who did whatever the hell he wanted and what he'd wanted was her.

"That you do comforts me. I can look at you and your Vampire and understand a relationship, a working, happy one, is possible between two very different beings."

Shortly after, David came back in, and Genevieve headed to her office to deal with something she said she'd received earlier that night. He'd also supplied her with a refreshed cup of coffee she suspected was decaf, but as he'd replaced the muffin she'd demolished with a fresh one, she didn't say anything but thank you and settled herself in camera view as the meeting started.

Clive told Alice on his way into his office, "Please connect me to Nadir at the earliest." The sun would be rising soon up in the Wetterstein where the Keep was located, and Nadir made her home at the side of the First. But she was old enough she'd be awake and aware for a few hours more.

"She's called twice. I have her direct number so once you're ready, I'll put you through." Alice's features, normally so calm, had tightened around her eyes. She knew what this situation could blow up into.

He'd only barely taken his seat when Nadir's call came through. "We need to keep this brief. I just received a message that Rowan will be calling in five minutes," she said immediately.

"Good luck with that," Clive replied. She'd need it. They all would.

"After I stanch this bloody wound with Hunter Corp. I need to deal with these creatures Tahar and Takahiro invited in and set free. Tell me what the temperature is with her?"

"She expected the worst of us, time wasting and other silliness. And we gave it to her. The first response annoyed her, but as I said, she was expecting it and was prepared to move on, understanding it would come up in some guise at the Joint Tribunal. Now it's far worse and it's not just Rowan who is angry. All of Hunter Corp. has had it. What does he know?" Clive asked of the First.

"I'll brief him after sundown. He'll prefer things to already be handled and then, I imagine, he'll contact Rowan directly. Andros is on the wing."

The air left Clive's lungs in a surprised rush. Andros, one of the First's Five, was silent death. A combination assassin and spy. That he had gone to deal with these lords wasn't a good sign for the fools.

As for the direct call from the First, Clive would need to monitor his wife's emotional state, so she was in the right frame of mind when her father contacted her. It made Clive angry that he had to, that the world rested so squarely on Rowan's shoulders when it came to the First's possible cataclysmic moods.

His anger didn't matter. So he put it away.

"This means the Nation has declared them outlaws?" Clive asked carefully. It wasn't against Vampiric law to hate humans.

The real Vampire issue was that they'd spoken with authority they did not have. They represented themselves as speaking for the entire Nation and that was their crime. And that was a thing that may have signed their arrest warrant.

Clive bloody hoped so. Xenophobic Vampires were one thing. Threatening Hunter Corp. pretending to be the Nation was another entirely.

"They have been called to appear before the First by sundown. I will hear their perspective and go from there." No doubt, if Clive had been there, the anger in her words would have sliced him to the bone.

"All right. There needs to be a meeting of the Scions. I'll have Alice coordinate with the others and your office."

"Agreed. Were I a Scion, I'd consider uniting with the others to force some sense into my brethren." Nadir paused and continued. "My human staff knows to share everything pertinent with you if you need to contact me during daylight hours." She paused again before saying, "I've been alive twice your lifetime and there have been worse moments. Moments where I knew there was no way to avoid bloodshed and death. This is *not* one of them. These Vampires have crossed so many lines they have done my work for me."

In other words, Nadir was going to end every single hope and dream of these lords even sooner thanks to their utter lack of control. Clive wasn't sure he hoped Rowan got to the Vampires who threatened her people before the First did. Rowan would love the closure of ending them herself, but their leader would create punishments that would make the offending Vampires hurt for a very long time.

"I must go. Rowan is calling," Nadir said and disconnected.

And after the ground the First had won by protecting Rowan the way he had after Carey had been killed, Clive was very worried his wife would never open herself up to her father again. And the First would deserve it because while he was not behind this recent communication, he'd allowed the interference to start with.

Entirely preventable.

Alice came in with several file folders and a cup of tea. "Paola would like a call from you on this matter. Warren sent along his assurance that where you fall on this issue, he is at your side. He'll be in contact after sunset. I expect a lot of business will be happening right as half of you are waking up and the other half are going to daytime rest."

"Block my schedule off for ninety minutes at ten thirty. I'm about to see if I can entice my spouse to eat a meal with me. She won't be going home so early though. Please arrange with the chef to create enough food for a dozen humans. I'll take it over to her office with me." His wife was food motivated during times of high stress, so it was a way to check in with her and be sure she was taking care of herself.

His chef, a notoriously temperamental, very old Vampire who'd cooked for Clive's grandfather, Malcolm, had taken a deep liking to Rowan. He loved cooking for her. Never missed an opportunity and often sent Clive home with different things he thought would please her.

Rowan never understood why she inspired such devotion, but it was clear to Clive. She saw them. Those Vampires in service who put themselves into their work. She paused and appreciated it, complimented them on it, even in her gruff way. The Vampire elite might have negative feelings about the Hunter, but he rarely saw a situation where a cook or servant, an administrative assistant or whoever, didn't leave an interaction with his wife without liking her even just a bit more than they had before they met her. Not all Vampires of course, some of them were dead after meeting her.

Rowan wanted to smile at the sight of Nadir's face on the screen. A Vampire that old being so comfortable with modern technology wasn't that common, but Nadir herself wasn't that common.

Which was good because Rowan wanted to see her face as they spoke. Wanted to get the full story she'd pick up. Clive insisted Nadir had no physical tells and Rowan didn't bother to correct him. Nadir's eyes narrowed ever-so-slightly when she was confused. Sometimes her right hand would twitch when she got very angry. And when she lied, there was sometimes the tiniest of lifts of her left shoulder.

Clive had tells too. A slight tip of his head to the left. When he was being deceptive or evasive, he tapped his forefinger against his thumb. Exhausted by her nonsense, he pinched the bridge of his nose, but that wasn't really a secret.

Rowan got right to the point. "Hunter Corp. will not be issuing a public reply to this latest communication. It is beneath contempt. I am, however, calling you directly to register our response officially to the Nation. Wasting time is one thing. Putting an execution order out on Hunters violates the Treaty in three different ways. As with any other threat to the life or health of a Hunter by a Vampire, we will respond to protect our own. These Vampires have been put on our red list." As in Hunters could consider killing any of these shitlords on sight as self-defense.

Nadir opened her mouth and then shook her head. She tried again. "These self-titled lords are nothing. Bored Vampires sitting around saying the same things they have for millennia. Reacting to all the recent events that have cast the Nation in an unfavorable light. It's not illegal to hate humans or Hunters."

Recent events that were their own damned fault.

Rowan said after reminding herself not to let any of this be personal and failing, "You know I don't give a raggedy fuck about second sons and their useless children sitting around in private clubs complaining in nasal tones about the cattle. Keeps them off the streets. That's not what this is about and I'm far too impatient with Vampire games just now to play. Even with you, Nadir. These Vampires used official Nation channels to issue a death threat. Fix that or we will not attend the Joint Tribunal."

Nadir didn't bother to hide her wince. "I am aware of the problem this creates between the Nation and Hunter Corp. and will rectify it."

"I'm watching closely and keeping very loose plans next week. And those Vampires who openly threatened Hunters have declared themselves enemies and will be dealt with. They'd better keep their heads down because we already know where two of them live. There's a lot of hours between now and sunset. Who knows what could happen?"

Nadir said, "Can you hold off on anything for twenty-four hours? It's sunrise here, which means I'll—and your father—be at rest until sunset in twelve hours."

The mention of Theo sent a flash of hurt through Rowan. This stunt weakened her politically. She had to act or risk losing the faith of those she was responsible for. And he hadn't done a thing to stop it. He knew the personal toll the last six weeks had taken and he'd just let her take the hit. Without even a warning. At best he forgot, but it was more likely he got a kick out of messing with her. Not maliciously, but he was a narcissist, and his amusement would have been his focus, not her feelings.

She couldn't change him and expecting him to be something he simply was not created to be would never work. Worse, it would only end up with more pain.

"This never should have happened. You and I both know it. That first response was a slap in the face. These dudes with visions of *lord* grandeur are suddenly up in business they do not have the experience to understand. They've inserted themselves into the process no one invited them to, and they were allowed to remain. In the forty-eight hours since, you could have ameliorated the damage. You did not."

Nadir opened her mouth to speak but closed it again. Rowan waited and ordered herself to rebuild her damned defenses or she was playing into the plans of her enemies.

"Mistakes were made," Nadir allowed. "Politics within the Nation are never as simple as they might seem, which is a fact you're intimately familiar with. You are correct that they never should have been allowed to remain in the process. I made that call and now I will address it. I would not wish for this enmity between us. Not between the Nation and Hunter Corp. and not between you and me."

"I'll give you twenty-four hours." They'd need every last minute and they had no one to blame but themselves. "*Unless* they come for me or mine and that means all of Hunter Corp. In which case, they will be killed true."

Nadir inclined her chin slightly in acknowledgment and thanks. "I will take your offer of twenty-four hours with appreciation of the opportunity to repair this breach."

"I'll speak with you again then." She disconnected. It didn't feel entirely safe to depend on anyone within the Nation, so she'd hold back with everyone but her spouse—who'd never allow such a thing anyway—and hope to be proven wrong.

Then she spoke to David, "I need those dossiers. We run this hunt and unless the Nation handles it, these fuckers will die. Maybe even regardless. Special teams hold until we identify our targets. Loop Adaeze in. Her territory most likely contains at least one of these assholes." Kano was the second-largest city in Nigeria and in Tahar's territory. Chances were, more than one of the "lords" lived there. Adaeze had been a field Hunter for twenty years and had only recently taken on full-partner status within Hunter Corp. They needed to expand leadership roles so that a wider array of territories were represented. That was how Antony had been promoted. Russia was a gigantic territory and Ant knew it better than anyone else with his skill and experience. There were several others in the process at some level be it interviews or contract negotiation.

Sometimes in the chaos of all the death and loss it was hard to remember that there were good things. Good people who wanted to help. Just months before Rowan'd been convinced she was going to have to leave Hunter Corp. behind and now she was at the helm, guiding it through the shallows, back out into safe waters. And that felt…right.

A lot of the rest of her life was out of sync and full of violence and drama, but in this she had no doubts.

What she wanted to do so much, so much her skin itched, was to call Theo and tell him off. Yell at him for putting her in such a position. Demand an apology for the way he just played with her like she was a doll, or a piece on a game board instead of the daughter he claimed to treasure so much.

How many times in her life would she feel like little more than an object for someone else's amusement? And how many more of those times would it be Theo who'd yet again done it?

The darkened screen of her phone taunted her to slide her finger along it, wake it up, and tap the number of the phone in his sitting room. He'd be there, taking tea, slowing down. Sunrise wouldn't affect him for at least a few more hours. Though he'd be stuck in his light-tight chambers until the sun fell so he'd have to sit in his fucked-up behavior until then.

He'd set this in motion. If he'd let these shitlords have a personal audience so they could have whined at him and then fed them before sending them on their way none of this would be happening. He'd wanted her attention and instead of getting it like any normal being would, he only thought of himself. Displaying her at will to fit whatever grand play he had running in his imagination.

It made her feel small. Invisible except for the mask she'd had to wear, one he'd designed. For long moments she was alone again, as she'd been before Clive. Before people who loved her and saw her. Understood her.

She wanted to slap his face for making her feel this way again. Wanted to take him by the shoulders and shake him. Goddess, she wanted him to know what it felt like to be so utterly adrift with no one to help guide her to shore.

But she couldn't. Because though he was better than he'd been in months, Theo still walked too close to the edge of his sanity for her comfort. To call him and yell at him would feel good for the merest of breaths and then it would be horror. She couldn't risk being the thing that pushed him over the edge into that dark, violent place that resulted in so much death and pain. He might harm those she cared about as retribution. Especially those who lived and worked in the Keep. He'd regret hurting them. After he regained his sanity once more. Maybe he'd apologize, but they'd still be maimed or dead. Or he'd lose his control in a place where their world would finally be exposed uncontrovertibly.

It remained her responsibility to keep him in check for everyone's sake. Even if it took pieces of her every time she had to put what she wanted or needed to the side. It seemed to be only her voice that was able to reach him when he began to wander. It seemed blasphemous to throw that away for a quick jolt of satisfaction for finally telling him just exactly what his sanity cost her.

She wasn't adrift anymore but if she hadn't been for

long years of her life, Rowan wouldn't be who she was that day. She would always want to protect people and that was easier done when she accepted what was possible and let the fuck go of what never would be.

Clive sat straight in his chair as he focused on his bond with Rowan, not liking the anguish thrumming through it.

Not danger or physical pain. But a throb, like a toothache.

He quickly made arrangements to have the food delivered and set up at the Motherhouse and after a few words telling Alice where he was off to, he made his way to his wife, needing to see with his own eyes just what had upset her so.

No one stopped him, though it was clear there was anxiety about his presence that felt more related to what the Nation had done than him personally. He didn't much like even a small cooling of the friendliness he'd earned after a lot of time for the Hunter Corp. people to see—and trust—his intentions. He didn't much like that it made a difference to him either. Before Rowan, he quite honestly wouldn't have noticed one way or the other.

Her door was closed but he knew she was inside. Knew she must have felt him approach the building. He tapped twice and upon a muffled come in, he opened and after one look at her expression, he stepped in quickly, closed the door at his back, and simply walked to her to draw her into a hug.

"You're here," she said, her face pressed into his neck.

"Of course I am. What's wrong, love?" he asked.

At that she began to cry, confusing him further. He wanted to fix it right then at that moment. He drew her to the couch and then settled her in his lap. She snuggled closer, burrowing herself against him. That she did so rather than resist his efforts was a victory and a heartbreak.

He simply rubbed her back in wide, lazy circles, letting the tears rage through her.

After a while, the storm of her emotion eased back. He handed her his handkerchief to dry her tears.

She rolled her eyes and snorted and the grip on his heart lessened. "You always have handkerchiefs. It's so perfect and gentlemanly."

"Shall I tell you a secret?" he asked before kissing her forehead.

"I was going to make a rude crack. But I find myself very much wanting you to tell me a secret," she said as she refolded the snowy white square.

"I always wear one should you have need. It pleases me to know it's in my pocket just in case."

She turned so she leaned back against the arm of the couch, lying across him, her ass still in his lap. Her face was tipped up, neck exposed with so much trust he'd never quite get over it.

"It pleases you to take care of me," she said, understanding him so well.

"It pleases me to take care of you," he agreed. "You, the partner I never thought to want because I had no idea any creature such as you could exist. That I should be so blessed by the universe that you are mine means it is my job to deserve you. If I'm to be getting husband credit here, note I also arranged for a late dinner to be set up in one of your conference rooms. Alice and David coordinated."

Tears sprang to her eyes. "You called me love. You

came for me. You bring handkerchiefs just in case I need one. And we know how often someone had to scrub blood out of most of the ones you give me. And you feed me." She sniffled and her bottom lip wobbled slightly.

He cupped her cheek. "What's wrong?"

"I gave this speech earlier about remaining brutally impersonal when it came to dealing with the Nation over this threat situation. Partly to protect myself," she said quickly, "but also because strategically it was best. And as I was talking to Nadir I just got so mad and sad and then really mad that I was sad. It was a whole thing and honestly I don't have time for whole things, Clive!"

He kissed her quickly.

"And then after the call I just sat here thinking about it all and I wanted to call him and yell at him for creating this whole mess to start with. Destabilizing my leadership with my colleagues! Why? Because he's a meddlesome old man who wants to fuck around when he isn't getting as much attention as he thinks he's entitled to."

Clive wasn't surprised she'd hit that point. This was pure manipulation on her father's part.

"But I can't," she said, and her voice broke. "You know why I can't say any of that. Why I need to get my shit back under control so I can absolutely be stern but utterly controlled when I deal with him. Because he'll have to admit he was wrong, and he hates that, so my best bet is to let all his rage at being wrong fall on the heads of these Vampire lords. Otherwise he goes nuclear and I don't want that either. As utterly fucked-up as it makes me, I don't want him to hurt himself," she whispered.

He took a deep breath, thinking carefully on how to respond. Not to protect himself from the First, but to care for Rowan's heart.

"You're right," he said. "We both wish you did not have to bear such a weight on your shoulders. And we both know such wishes mean nothing when it comes to what is. What you are fated to be whether that is fair or not. I only know this is your gift and your curse. You hold him to the world because you are in it and at last he can be in your life once more. I cannot take this responsibility from you. But I will always help you bear it. And if that means a cry when you really just want to do violence, or a trip somewhere, an orgasm, anything I can do for you, darling Hunter, I will because you are mine."

"If the smell of garlic wasn't making my stomach growl and there weren't a bunch of people congregated around who'd hear you rutting upon me, I'd totally take you for a ride right now," she teased. After a slow kiss she touched her forehead to his. "Thank you. For the food and the handkerchiefs and the way you must have rushed over here when you felt me through the bond."

"I love you," he said simply.

"David's hovering out there," she murmured, standing, and setting herself to rights.

"He knows I'm here and we haven't come out. He's afraid we're fighting or fucking," Clive teased because she needed him to. "Let's go eat."

"Tell me about whatever Nadir said first," she told him, blocking their exit.

"There's my bride," he teased, dropping to brush his lips against hers. He gave a brief overview and she blew out a breath at the news regarding Andros.

"Andros taught me how to track. He's scary good at it. But many of these shitlords have addresses. I'm putting together a list now. Getting eyes on scene."

"Rowan."

"Again with the saying of my name that way. What? I can't lay the framework to execute every one of these fuckos who threatened Hunters? Because I can and I will. If the Nation refuses to handle this, you can't cry about it when I step in." Clive noted the zeal in her eyes. These Vampires had created a far larger problem than they'd ever imagined. Fools.

"You'll give Nadir her time. Andros is no empty threat, you know it."

"We'll see. One way or another it'll be dealt with. I know who all these Vampires are now and one by one, Hunters will locate their homes. We'll find them and handle them if the Nation doesn't."

After their meal, Clive needed to get back to the office to keep an eye on everything that was going on just then. So she walked him to the car and wrapped her arms around him. "Thank you. I'll see you when you get home. Be careful."

He gave her an exceptionally haughty look and she fanned herself with a hand.

"You be careful as well. I don't think these Vampires will move. I think they're all talk, as it happens. But pay attention anyway. I see your car here and I take it David will accompany you home so yes, I'll see you there. Go to sleep if you need to."

"Foolish Vampire. You need to pleasure me. So if I'm napping, wake me up."

## *Chapter Twelve*

"Hugo Procella had an actual Journie Main handbag delivered to your office as a gift for you," Samaya told Genevieve as she came into the kitchen of her home in Las Vegas.

Naturally, Darius was in the kitchen at the same time and his attention lasered in on her immediately.

"Why would he do such a thing?" Such an extravagant gift was totally inappropriate, though Hugo Procella seemed not to care about what was appropriate when it came to whatever he wanted to do.

"Those bags cost twenty grand," Darius said and then smiled at Genevieve's surprised expression. "We sometimes run luxury goods when the opportunity comes along, and the money is right. But they're not a casual gift for a friend."

"I'd say not. That's a *hey I want to put my wiener in you so here's an expensive incentive because I'm too lazy to work for it by getting to know you* present. After that weird way he creeped on you at the meeting the other day, this is way out of bounds," Samaya said, pausing to hug her mother.

"He called the office for you yesterday and I took the message myself. No, I didn't give it to you because it would have been a waste of your time. I informed him you were very busy and would respond to the rule change proposal when you could. Obviously he didn't like that answer hence the bag showing up as if that would change your mind."

"Where is the bag?" Genevieve's skin crawled at the thought of it.

"I called his office to let him know you couldn't accept it. A few hours later he showed up to argue with me in person. I finally had to threaten to call security to get him to stop. I made him take the bag with him and said I'd throw it in the incinerator if he left it. So I jumped in my car and headed here. Made it here in time for Mom's meatballs and egg noodles so that's always a plus."

"Stay over tonight," Lorraine said. "The room next to mine is clean and the bed is made." As if Lorraine would ever allow anything else but a prepared room?

"And, Gen? He didn't lose his temper outwardly, but his eyes told a whole different story. He hated being told no," Samaya added.

"I need to deal with that proposal so he can be gone from my life," Genevieve said.

"You don't have to do anything," Darius said flatly. "Or, say no and be done with it."

"I figured you'd ask to take over and handle it," Genevieve told him quietly as Lorraine left to show Samaya her room for the night.

He licked his lips and didn't speak for a few moments. "I want to," he admitted. "But that's not what *you* need. Not at this point."

She cocked her head and found herself far closer to him than she'd realized. The heat of his body seemed to buffet and then wrap around her.

As much as the way he was protective gave her a thrill, the way he so clearly understood she needed to address the demands of her position in the Senate on her own terms made her weak in the knees.

It wasn't a handbag so expensive it would have embarrassed Genevieve to carry it that was the way to her heart. It was this. A partner who paid attention to what she needed, and didn't want.

"Don't mistake this for me saying I won't step in," he said, his voice a rumble against her skin. "If this goes left, if he continues to pursue you after you said no, I can't stay out of it. I won't. I will protect you." He cupped her cheek. "Understand that part. But I see your strength and I respect it."

What could she say to that? This man who was used to always being in charge who stepped aside so she could handle things on her own was irresistible. A combination of things she'd accepted she'd never find in one person.

"Thank you." They weren't supposed to thank one another. It created implied debt and powerful beings hated being in debt. But it was important to her to say it. It was okay to have debt between them.

Lorraine and Samaya returned and Darius kissed her forehead before stepping away and getting back to chopping things on Madame's command.

"I want to know what these families are up to," Genevieve said at last. "The Procellas want this change and I want to examine why. I'm going to enlist Rowan. Samaya, you can get in contact with Sergio, the grandfather—not Hugo—and let him know I'd like to speak with him further on their proposal. Let me connect with Rowan first."

Darius considered it and then nodded. "She's a good choice. Sees what people try to hide from view. And she's got an amazing ability to break her enemies. I respect that."

Genevieve would have to share that with her friend, who'd be thrilled to hear such a compliment.

Rowan picked up on the second ring. "Hi there, how's things?"

"I need your help." Genevieve went over the situation and her suspicions.

"Hell yes, I'm down. I love to spy on people and I'm going to be honest and admit I want to know more about the witches living in my territory who aren't the good kind like you."

Of course she did. Smiling to herself, Genevieve let Rowan know she'd get the specifics to her once she had them.

The following morning, Darius had shown up at Hunter Corp. with Genevieve and they all headed over to the meeting being held at the Vegas home of the Procella family Rowan had already started building a file on.

It had become obvious to her that there were paras in her city she didn't understand well enough. Good or bad, she needed to know the basics to better do her job, so she'd jumped at the chance to not only help a friend, but be nosy while getting paid for it.

When the gates had opened and they'd come up the drive, the mansion beyond had Rowan guffawing. If there was a single flourish in the world that hadn't been somehow affixed to the giant carcass of ostentatious excess she wasn't sure she could find it.

Ornate scrollwork crawled over columns and around doors and windows. Several luxury cars were parked to the side of the main front steps leading to the massive front doors, also covered in carvings and doodads.

"It's like a five-year-old's dress-up box exploded," she murmured to Genevieve. "I thought Vampires had excess down, but this? This is quite a challenge to their dominance, I'll give you that."

Genevieve grunted softly.

Genevieve's call the night before asking for assistance had presented an opportunity not just to be nosy, but also because it was a good opportunity for Rowan to be able to help Genevieve instead of the other way around.

The double doors slid open to reveal two uniformed staff and a tall woman in a perfectly tailored suit standing perfectly in between them.

The perfection was a mask, like so many things, Rowan thought. Perfect Suit's gaze went to Rowan twice. So quickly if she'd been most anyone else, they'd have missed it.

But Rowan wasn't most anyone else and something about this scene bugged her. As if it was all just one or two degrees off in either direction.

"Ms. Aubert, please come in." Perfect Suit indicated the foyer just beyond with a sweep of her hand. "I'm Mr. Procella Senior's aide, Lotte."

Genevieve nodded and stepped into the house. Rowan really didn't like it that she hadn't gone first. Silly, because Genevieve was absolutely capable of handling herself.

And then the uniforms began to close the doors with Rowan standing on the porch.

Genevieve said something. Not words. A sound with feeling. A sound with full-on pissed-off offense and a blast of magic blew the doors all the way open, slamming back to the walls hard enough to knock things down deeper in the house.

At Rowan's back, she heard the car door open, and boots hit the gravel. Darius had gotten out and a throb of deep, endless magic rose. Waiting to be aimed.

Though normally, Rowan would have stepped out of the line of fire and let the Dust Devil at it, Genevieve was in the house and until she was safely at Rowan's side, Rowan didn't want to start a battle.

So she reached for sarcasm because that was her type of magic. Stepping closer to the door, she made eye contact with Genevieve to be sure they were on the same page and then she shifted her attention to Perfect Suit. "I have a lot to learn about the differences in rules of courtesy and civility between my world and yours, Lotte. In mine, we only slam doors in people's faces if we *mean* to offend them." Rowan sent Lotte a sunny smile with lots of teeth. That translated fairly well, and the other woman narrowed her left eye and like an idiot she'd handed Rowan one of her tells. "Which makes me wonder why you'd want to offend someone like me and whatever you think you'd get out of it."

"And your guest as well, of course. I'd assumed she would wait for you outside as is *common*. She can sit in the kitchen," Lotte said to Genevieve, pretending as if Rowan wasn't right there.

Common? Well look at Perfect Suit turning her bitchy up to eleven like Rowan didn't exist at a perpetual fifty.

Genevieve went very still and then turned, sauntering out to where Rowan had just been about to saunter in.

"Is it common for you to be rude to invited visitors to this home? You're proud enough to proclaim such an embarrassing thing? Inform Mr. Procella Senior that should he still wish to discuss this matter, he can contact my office to make another appointment. Please also inform him that *you* are to have nothing to do with any communication between his family and me or my offices. I find you intolerable."

With that, Genevieve managed a turn that was a flounce with just the right amount of aggressive dismissal. Damn, Rowan's friend was really good at this stuff.

She tucked her arm around Rowan's left, providing a united front as they descended the steps leading to the car.

Rowan wanted to ask if they should make another try to get inside or what Genevieve wanted, but she didn't want to be overheard and risk weakening Genevieve's actions so she followed along, waiting for any indication to do otherwise.

They were almost to the car when a man appearing to be in his mid-thirties or so stepped from the house, hailing them both.

"I'm with you. Lead and we'll figure it out," Rowan murmured.

"It's Hugo," Genevieve said before they turned as a unit and Rowan went into a stance that kept her at readiness should she need to defend herself or Genevieve.

"Genevieve, it's lovely to see you. Ms. Summerwaite, I'm Hugo Procella. You're here to meet with my grandfather. Please, let me apologize for what just happened."

He was handsome as such things went. Probably five ten or so. Dark brown hair in a tousle that took a trim every two weeks. Suntanned, like he'd just returned from somewhere tropical rather than just being outside in this part of the world. Clad in a very well-made pair of trousers, designer loafers, and a button-down of the quality and styling Clive normally wore, he didn't scream money, but there was a whispered chorus. She bet he had a huge section in his closet for thousand-dollar sunglasses and a boat he only took out once a year. Not a perfect suit like Lotte, but certainly a uniform just the same.

Currently his rather unremarkable brown eyes were trying very hard to appear remorseful for what was surely not novel behavior. A house like the one beyond had at least a dozen staff. They were employed by rich and powerful people. The visitors here would also be rich and powerful people. Rowan imagined *their* reception was far more welcoming. No, for Senior's aide to have treated Rowan the way she had, the ease of her condescension told Rowan the house beyond was full of demeaning talk about humans and other beings who weren't Genetic witches.

The Procella family, at least the one who controlled the door, had a very high opinion of itself and a very low one of everyone else. Rowan could work with that. People didn't look at what they thought was beneath them. She could do plenty of damage from below.

Genevieve looked at him, sliding her hand up to cup her neck a moment, and the magic in the air changed. Hugo noticed too, his eyes widening slightly, but said nothing. Not removing his gaze from Genevieve's face in a way that sent a slow wash of unease through Rowan.

Footsteps at her back as Darius moved from the driver's side around to the passenger rear door. Waiting.

And still, Hugo's attention remained on Genevieve.

How the fuck it was this witch in front of them had no outward inkling he'd even taken notice of Darius when the power in the air was undeniable, Rowan wasn't sure.

She didn't trust it. It made Hugo impossibly stupid or impossibly arrogant. Both were dangerous to Hugo's health when he was already on a shit list for the creepy way he'd latched onto Genevieve.

"Will you please come inside? Let us treat you with the hospitality and respect you are due." He looked to Rowan. "Both of you. I know who you are, Ms. Summerwaite. We are honored to have you here." He bowed but not nearly enough for the level of insult.

Didn't really feel that way. But Rowan kept that to herself. For the moment. One never knew when a little verbal taking to task would be necessary, so it paid to be ready.

"If you were honored, and you know who Ms. Summerwaite is, why has your staff acted in such a manner?" Genevieve asked, a razor draped in cashmere. "The entire Conclave looks bad when our members show this side of themselves to honored guests."

The tightening around Hugo's eyes told Rowan he was about to lie, and he was mad about it. "I believe it was a misunderstanding. Not all the information was conveyed to Lotte."

"Calling it a misunderstanding is an attempt to evade responsibility. That indicates personal weakness. Is this how your household responds to all visitors?" Genevieve sniffed, disappointed, and Hugo's polite mask slipped for just a moment, leaving his frustrated anger on display.

A breath later that smile was back in place, along with big *look-at-me-I'm-innocent* eyes. Hugo said, "My grandfather is very traditional and slow to adopt newer ways. He means no malice."

Again this fool thought Genevieve wouldn't notice that he evaded answering and taking responsibility? His grandfather was a small-minded bigot and trying to pass it off as being traditional. A common enough tactic.

Lying to a Senator, also common.

"I'm seven hundred and fifty-four years old. Yet, I understand basic courtesy. I understood it long before your grandfather was born. It's merely another excuse."

"We have gotten off on the wrong foot," Hugo said. "I'm sure Ms. Summerwaite wouldn't want to be the cause of trouble between us." The way he said *us* indicated he meant far more than witches in general.

Rowan said nothing. Gave no indication of how she felt about that, but Genevieve wagered in her head Rowan was punching him square in his throat.

This had gone on long enough. Genevieve drew up to her full height, and in her towering heels she loomed over Hugo Procella, looking down her nose at him. For a moment her mouth twisted as she caught a glimpse of the darker heart of this witch. "I grow tired of you speaking apologies out of one side of your face and then doing nothing but putting the blame onto others. These two things are mutually exclusive. Your family is asking for permission to do something that takes a great deal of discipline and control. So far, I've seen neither from a single one of you." Genevieve flicked her wrist, but her bracelets did not sing for him. "I would speak with Rowan privately. You may wait wherever it is *common*," Genevieve said.

He bowed slightly but the little tremor that ran through his muscles reminded Genevieve of an eager pet, one desperate to jump all over someone. "Of course. I will await your response." He retreated to the house. A blast of cold slid down her spine.

Darius stood, holding the door open for Genevieve and Rowan to slide into the back seat.

He circled slowly and got back in behind the wheel. Stoic and very still. But the annoyance seemed to flow from him anyway and she understood he allowed that. Like he'd made noise when he'd gotten out of the car. She'd been out with him enough to know he made no sound unless he wanted to.

He reached forward and toggled a switch of some sort and the windows opaqued so they couldn't be spied upon from the house. There were other ways to listen in, so Genevieve clapped her hands together three times and sang under her breath. Her magic leapt into place, dancing with the magic of the Trick, and clicked around the car creating a barrier no one could hear through.

"Those windows? I want them. Is that a spell?" Rowan leaned into the front seat and then seemed to realize she was demanding answers from the leader of a Trick of Dust Devils. Despite the seriousness of the situation, it amused Genevieve to see when Rowan's curiosity overpowered her wariness.

"One of our businesses creates custom builds of vehicles, planes, and helicopters. The windows have a thin sheet at the center of each. The switch activates the microcircuitry in them, and the reaction creates opacity," he told her.

Rowan breathed out an excited huff. "I'd very much like to talk to you about these builds for Hunter Corp. at some point, which is not now obviously." She looked back to Genevieve, who wore a smirk.

He fished a business card—a fucking business card—from a pocket and handed it her way.

"Agent of Chaos Productions?" Rowan laughed. "I

see what you did here," she told him as she settled back next to Genevieve.

"Before anything else, I apologize for that scene," Genevieve told her. "I've been alive a long time and across cultural shifts that quite frankly astonish me daily. These are Conclave witches. Born with more privilege than most will ever dream of. The access they have to the halls of governance is unparalleled. To have invited me to their home and treated anyone in my party—no matter who—in such a manner is a violation of our deepest laws of welcome and sanctuary."

"I'm not offended," Rowan said and then put a finger up to forestall Genevieve's reply. "Certainly the *behavior* was offensive. But I'd only be offended if any of those fuckos was actually better than I am. And they aren't. Magic or not, no one in that building is my superior in any way. What does bother me though, isn't what happened to me, but that they have done this to you through your entourage. That's a different level of disrespect. That's an attack on your position and it occurred while you acted in your professional capacity. I don't like that one bit. What are they up to? If they think to come at you, we need to be sure you're protected."

Darius grunted his agreement.

"I'm touched that you should worry for me," Genevieve allowed. She was. That they both wanted to protect her humbled her. Left her grateful. "It's not…there's a move by those, as I said, who want to be freed to use their magic on humans for their own gain in ways that are coercive. Generally, I use my power to be sure such things don't happen, but I can't deny there are those within the Conclave who feel any exposure to humans or compassion on their behalf is lowering. I don't know if the situations are directly connected. I don't know if the Procellas are part of this group of families but I find it difficult to imagine they are not. Coincidence can only hold up so long before it becomes impossible not to draw a conclusion."

"You're an old, powerful Genetic witch. The head of your family line is like, the king or whatever. You're strong but you still work to make things better for others who aren't as strong. These are all things weak people despise because they're too spineless and selfish to do the same. So they want to denigrate compassion because where's the profit in that for them? It's the idea of you, Genevieve. So perfect and strong and wasting it all on those who don't deserve you like they do." Rowan shrugged one shoulder.

"Just so," Genevieve replied after a long pause. "As a result, I'm not inclined to go into that house where you and, by extension, I were treated so poorly. It teaches a bad lesson I think. And Hugo makes my skin crawl."

"He must be in that foyer positively dying for you to come inside. He looked at you weird. With the rich-lady purse being spurned and his failed attempt to get you to go out with him, you'd think he'd get the message. But I don't think he has," Rowan said.

Darius didn't turn around when he said, "His energy was sharply focused on you, Genevieve. Do not meet with him alone. This is Devil ground. There will be no successful attempts to use magic to sway or coerce you here, but that is above and beyond whether or not you should deal with them right now."

"He could have been interested in my power, you know." Genevieve had been used by those who thought to control her and therefore her magic.

"Of course he was!" Rowan said. "Lady ma'am, aside from being drop-dead gorgeous, rich, fashionable, and well connected, you're a supernova of magical power. That's part of your appeal."

And yet, it occurred to Genevieve that Rowan had just as difficult a time with people being attracted to her for her power, like it wasn't part of why she was so magnetic to start with. Like it wasn't as much of *her* appeal as her hair.

Darius listened to their conversation while he continued to keep an eye on the situation outside. No one could see in, but he didn't need his eyes to sense the world around the car. If the witches in that house or anywhere nearby used magic to spy on them, he'd know. At the approach of anything larger than a housecat, he'd know.

"There is an eagerness about these witches that unsettles me," Darius said, pretending his unease didn't also have to do with the way the witch had watched Genevieve like she was a precious jewel he had to possess.

"Yes! That exactly," Rowan said, and Darius fought a smile. Genevieve's friend was a power only now just waking to her full potential, but she had a youth to her, a zest for everything he'd seen her do. Ferocity in defense of her friends. Loyalty he rarely saw the likes of. That the Vessel included Genevieve in the company of those she considered under her protection and care pleased not only Darius, but the entire Trick who'd been watching Rowan at a bemused distance for the years she'd been in Las Vegas.

"I could refuse to sign the permission. If I did that, others would follow suit." Genevieve paused. "But then

I don't have a way to find out what the hell is going on. And there is something here."

"They can meet you at Fleur," Rowan said of the Vampire-owned-and-run restaurant in the heart of Las Vegas. "They'll have to know it's a Vampire run place, so they'll need to debase themselves to attend." She snorted a laugh that had him liking her even more. "Arrange the meet for, let's say six? They don't open for dinner until eight. They'll feel better because it's still daylight and therefore the Vampires will be away. But there are things just as scary as Vampires that don't need to worry about sunlight. They can make their little pitch to you. I'll be there and it'll irritate them. Lucky me!" She laughed and Genevieve joined in.

"It's a great deal of fun to watch you deliberately wear people down until you break them," Genevieve said.

"Is that what we're doing?" Rowan asked. "No judgment. Just have to know going in the angle I need to take. Hugo there looks like he lives deep under the thumb of Grandpa or maybe Dad. I'll do some poking around, so I know the right buttons to push."

Darius would attend himself and set a perimeter Marco would be in charge of. Nothing would happen to Genevieve.

"What they're asking for isn't even unique. I just need to understand why. Your eyes miss nothing. You will pick up details I will have missed."

"Which is part of the reason why they wanted to keep her outside, or in the kitchen, which is most likely half a house away from where the meeting would have taken place," Darius said.

Genevieve's indrawn breath told him she hadn't considered that until he mentioned it.

"Okay, we'll make it happen," Rowan said quickly enough Darius knew she'd been aware. Most likely it hadn't been the first time in the Vessel's life where others had tried to keep her out of the way, ignorant of whatever silliness they would try to get away with outside her notice.

"I should go to the door to relay this information," Darius said. "David is still on overwatch and the two of you most assuredly can defend yourselves just fine should something happen." He wanted to keep himself between Hugo Procella and Genevieve as often as possible.

"You're no messenger," Genevieve said, affront in her tone that he could think such a thing of himself.

It filled in some ragged, empty canyon in his soul that she understood his power. Was proud of it.

"But, I *am* a being they can't dream of touching." He loosed the hold he kept on his power slightly. Just a little bit to underline what he was.

"They'll regret it should they try. And not just because of what the Trick would do. All right. Rowan will coordinate the place and you'll give them the message and then we will leave and go eat something."

Two minutes later he got out of the car and reached in to clear the windows once again so they could watch what was going on. Genevieve liked to know what was happening, he had come to realize.

By the time he'd reached the top step, he'd unleashed more of his power, letting his eyes go black. They'd most likely pass out if he showed them his true form with no filter at all so he—reluctantly—kept it low enough to make a point but not outright injure any of them.

He noted the woman in the navy blue suit stood there just behind Hugo Procella. The two uniformed staff to either side were not the same butlers as before, rather they'd been replaced with beefy security guards. Darius made a point to look directly at the holstered handgun each wore—bullets would do nothing but anger him—and then back to Procella.

Procella couldn't retain eye contact with Darius for longer than two seconds. Lucky for him because Darius didn't like this witch at all and would take any excuse he could to leave him bleeding.

"Where is Genevieve?" Procella asked, looking around Darius's body and making an annoyed sound when he saw they were still in the car. "I should like for her to speak to me herself."

As if this creature was worthy of Genevieve's attention. "Your preferences are irrelevant," Darius said and without missing a beat, he continued. "If you wish to take *Ms. Aubert's* time for another meeting your office will need to contact hers. Ms. Aubert will decide the place. Ms. Summerwaite will be attending. There will be no repeat of your earlier behavior." None of those sentences were questions or requests. Darius told him what would happen and then he waited for their reply. Letting them see, letting them feel the sharpest edge of the energy within him. He drew away their fear, the taste of it crisp and spicy. He could continue to stand there for hours and never weaken the slightest. This was Devil ground. All the life energy within its boundaries could be tapped into. Especially now that Genevieve was their priestess and her magic had turned the taps on full.

These witches thought to hold themselves above other paranormals when their very existence could be erased by him and the rest of the Trick in a finger snap. They needed to understand their place in the scheme of things.

The security guards were big, but Darius was *eternal*. His magic was bigger than their brains could even grasp, and because of his connection to Genevieve, it was even greater. More potent. Easier to call and quicker to replenish.

He let them see that in his gaze and when he drew back a little, noting the beads of sweat on their foreheads, the tang of their panic on his tongue, Darius knew they'd understood the message.

They had no further comment because they were terrified.

Darius turned his back and stalked to the car.

## *Chapter Thirteen*

Rowan had only walked into her office when a call from Nadir came through.

"Again, I appreciate the time you gave me to address this monumental cockup," Nadir said right away.

"We don't need to be at war over this if it's handled correctly. But we'll need to speak about some healthy boundaries after we're done."

"I've called a meeting with all the Scions. As you know, Clive and Paola are at daytime rest, so we'll have it shortly after sunset in your time zone. Andros is attempting to meet with some of the Vampires responsible for this. They've decided to run. We both know that's a vain attempt on their part," Nadir told her. "I've spoken with your father. He's…unsettled by this and bids you not to think ill of him because of the actions of others. They will be handled. I say that on my own and also delivering his words to you."

How the fuck was Theo going to be unsettled by shit he set in motion to start with? He was intimately familiar with the stuff Vampires did. He'd done it all at least three times himself at some point or another.

No. She wasn't going back to that place she'd been the night before.

"Well. I hear your words," Rowan said at last.

"Will you continue to hold off on irrevocable action as we contain and eliminate the problem?" Nadir asked.

"Irrevocable as in I can't kill anyone true dead?"

"Rowan."

Why was everyone doing that lately? Just saying her name like that instead of a lengthier reply?

"Here's what I'll say," Rowan began. "Hunter Corp. has already dealt with our response to this. If any of these Vampires moves toward *anyone* under our protection, we will act immediately and irrevocably, as you say. None of us are in Andros's league, but we know who these Vampires are and more importantly, where they are. They can run, but not forever. If the Nation addresses these individuals as they should be handled, we will have no need to move independently."

"In other words, please don't kill anyone because I have it handled and you know very well I do not lie," Nadir said, slightly exasperated, and Rowan didn't care because this whole thing was totally exasperating for her so they could suffer too.

"All right. I'll await your contact after the Scion meeting," Rowan said and disconnected.

David cruised in with someone else at his side.

"Vihan," Rowan said, standing and holding her hand out to clasp his. "David said you'd be arriving this week. What a time, huh? Bet you're wondering why you thought leaving England to come here would be such a fun idea."

He wore an outfit that was a version of the one David had on. Suit trousers, nice shirt. No tie but she'd lay odds it was in his office with the suit jacket so he could jazz himself up when necessary. Though, he didn't need much help because Vihan was a version of David. Handsome.

Stylish in a classic sense but with an edge. In Vihan's case it was the French blue color of the shirt, which warmed his brown skin and highlighted lush dark brown hair, and the trendy shoes.

"I probably shouldn't admit a bit of excitement only makes me more pleased I made the choice," Vihan said.

"We got him settled at his town house," David explained. "He's only across a courtyard from Vanessa."

Ah. That was a secure complex. Rowan knew because she'd seen to it herself when Vanessa had wanted to move in there. It had been warded, and the town houses would be wired with a top-of-the-line security system that included bells and whistles when it came to dealing with threats of a paranormal nature.

It was close enough to Rowan's house and the chapterhouse that someone could be there within minutes if necessary.

"I made the arrangements with Alice regarding Fleur. Ms. Aubert just went into a call with Samaya," David said as he and Vihan stepped inside and closed the door.

Rowan sighed heavily. "Just tell me."

David nudged Vihan to a chair and then crossed to open Rowan's door at a knock.

"Am I interrupting?" Genevieve asked.

"You're right on time, as it happens," David told her. "Come inside. You're going to want to hear this."

Rowan wanted to hide under her desk from whatever was coming next.

Vihan said, "One of my specialties is data. Gathering. Application. I'm working with Vanessa on future probability as well. I started this project three weeks ago when I was hired here. We looked at missing persons. Originally it was connected to the witches who'd been kidnapped, but we factored in others like Vampires and humans due to the Blood Front connection. Especially after Rowan brought that possible connection to our attention when she was in Long Beach a few days ago. The result of our enhanced search filters is that we're seeing a spike in missing persons cases for humans associated with magic users."

Rowan waited, knowing he'd tell her what the connection was.

Vihan looked to David, who gave an encouraging nod. "Skip the next few steps and just tell her the end point," David told him.

"They're all residents of cities or suburbs around those cities with high paranormal populations. Specifically, Vampires and Conclave witches. Seattle, Southern California, Portland, Oregon, New York City, and Nashville have the highest numbers of missing."

David interjected. "Not so much cities that had high populations but rather those weighted with only one main paranormal group. Chicago has been largely unaffected and we know they're dominated by shifters and witches. Same with New Orleans being so dominated by magical practitioners." There were Vampires in the city, but there were far higher numbers of witches of all disciplines and shifters.

"All in the United States?" Rowan asked.

"The data was limited to the U.S. at first, but soon enough I started to see patterns and I needed to enlarge my data pool. Numbers are collected differently in various locations so it's taken me a bit to get the filters right. It's still very heavily weighted to North and South America with similar missing in Buenos Aires and Sao Paulo. But there's a spike in London and another in Krakow

I'm looking at. I'll know more in a day or two," Vihan told them.

"If we had some access to the Conclave records we'd be able to refine this all tighter. We've got some access into the Nation," David looked to Rowan quickly, "so we're able to add that to our information. But the Conclave records are a lot harder to access." He didn't bother hiding they were hacking in. Rowan had told him not to bother. They'd get the information however they needed to. If they asked and were stonewalled, they'd simply find their own way. It made things easier to be up-front with Genevieve and ask first.

"I'll connect you with Samaya. You can work through her to get the information and put you in touch with Asta, the Archivist. I'm not helping you break into Conclave records. But we'll get you what you need," Genevieve said.

"Vihan is putting together a report. All fairly preliminary because we're still gathering data and filtering to get more specific information. Then we can start making some educated guesses," David told Rowan.

"Appreciate the briefing. I'm sure David has already told you this, but don't hesitate to reach out if you have questions, need help, have concerns, whatever. And when you get homesick. I missed London so much when I first moved here. David knows all the places to get good Indian food and fish and chips with mushy peas. Or you can come to dinner at my house since I'm the only non-English person living there." Rowan smiled in a way she hoped was reassuring instead of slightly manic.

"Ta. Everyone's been very cordial so far."

At least a third of her staff at the new chapterhouse slash Motherhouse in the United States were relocating from London as they reorganized with an emphasis on fieldwork and support instead of the monstrously top-heavy executive system of the past. Many of them had worked with David or Rowan in the past or had come with the highest of recommendations from people Rowan trusted.

Now she was responsible for them. Like some weird, slightly murderous den mother. Slightly probably wasn't the right word, but whatever. She used to have three employees and within two weeks there'd be a dozen in Las Vegas. And since they'd gone and made her in charge of all of the United States and Canada, there would be smaller headquarters—chapterhouses—located in places Hunters could use as a home base for their territory, or to bunk out of while they were on a Hunt out of their normal area. Each of those generally already had a staff and some even had a space they just needed to update and staff properly.

There were a lot of annoying details, but they were important, so she did her best to pay attention and make good choices.

"I'll keep you apprised and remind you there's a dinner at ten tonight. Clive sent a note right before he went down for the day," David said as he paused at the doorway.

She'd sure want to know what the hell happened at the Scion meeting so why argue? "All right. Thanks. Can you please work with Elisabeth? Set up a welcome dinner for all the new staff for when we return from Prague? Everyone should be moved here and at least partially settled by then."

"Wait, David," Genevieve said. "My call with Samaya. The Procellas called and very civilly asked to take a meeting with me. Samaya says it wasn't Hugo, but a different Procella, Antonia, who's Hugo's older sister."

She shot a look to Rowan. "We'll speak about that in a moment."

Rowan swallowed back her questions and indicated Genevieve continue.

"They wanted to meet today but I'm not inclined to give them what they want. Tomorrow at six? Darius says he can have coverage."

"The sun will have set or just be setting right around then. There's no way Clive will keep his nose out of it. Though he won't ruin our operation. He's meddlesome, but he opens a lot of doors too." Rowan knew her husband. She would have to tell him up front. Then he'd insist on being there. Or showing up. They'd have to negotiate. But that would be fun for everyone so she couldn't really complain.

"I think Darius would prefer after sunset," Genevieve murmured. Louder to David she said, "Will you please work with Samaya to get everything into place? She'll handle the communication with the Procellas. They're terrible so you aren't missing anything."

David left to handle a dozen things.

"I hope I'm not putting too much on his shoulders," she told Genevieve.

"He's very good at this. And you trust him to be, which pleases him. And now he has his own David who appears to be as efficient and intelligent. You're helping him fly. Letting him find out just how good he is at this."

Rowan sent a relieved look Genevieve's way. "I understand they wanted permission to use some form of coercion magic in…stage acts? Magic acts? They're in the cruise and casino entertainment business, I remember that much. But do they function as a talent agency?

I'm just trying to understand a wider picture so we can figure out just what is going on."

"When they asked for the first meeting Samaya put together a little bit of background for me but by our phone call just a few minutes ago she had more. She's fantastic about finding out things from other people. I'm grateful she's spying for me instead of against me." Genevieve sent a quick smile to Rowan before continuing. "Their business is entertainment based. They appear to provide performing acts to various venues, cruise ships, casinos, nightclubs, that sort of thing. Nearly entirely specific to the paranormal world, but some of the cruise ship stuff is weighted heavily toward humans. That's where they're seeking the permission for. Magic acts for these cruise ships. But that's just one part. They also have private casinos and card rooms in locations across the country. Las Vegas, New Orleans, Atlantic City, Branson are the ones I can remember, but she's sending the information to David. Most of it. I'm sure you understand why it's not everything."

"I do. And I appreciate all you can share," Rowan reassured. "I have questions, but I'll save them until the end."

"All the arms of that main family business report to—and the business is helmed by—Sergio Procella. Patriarch. His second-in-command is his only child, Alfonso. Alfonso is Hugo and Antonia's father. Antonia works directly for her father. She's *his* second-in-command and reportedly knows the business at every level. Hugo is listed as working in development. Samaya's gossip says Hugo is ambitious and not entirely lazy, but entitled and has difficulties listening or seeking out other perspectives."

"Antonia does a bang-up job and puts in the work but

baby brother sucks up to Grandpa who'd rather a male grandchild who thinks like him take over anyway?"

Genevieve raised an eyebrow a moment. "Astute. Antonia and her father, Alfonso, appear to back a certain type of governance and leadership, while Hugo, their grandfather Sergio, and some assorted relations are that charming *traditional*, which honestly means they think Genetic witches are not just different from humans, but better than them. Better than Vampires who need blood and are imprisoned by the sun. It's all very boring and unimaginative as most bigotries are."

"You'd think basically immortal beings would have better imaginations. Or spend their time doing something useful or fun."

"I find myself similarly frustrated. Here we have an actual threat to witches. Not silly fantasies about genetic superiority. And they'd rather pretend away the threat to continue pursuit of this phantom other who will absorb their own guilt and responsibility and become the example. If not for them, we would be better off. It's an old tale. But there's a resurgence of purity nonsense going on now. The way you were treated, that disdain and derision for every being outside their narrow classification, is absolutely connected to that. At least in part."

They took a brief pause when Malin showed up with tea and some sort of citrus-based cookies dusted in powdered sugar.

"Here." Rowan handed over a large linen napkin and when Genevieve's confusion must have shown, her friend draped hers across her chest and lap. "Those cookies are amazing but sugar and little crumbs will get everywhere."

That Genevieve could understand, and she followed suit before trying one of the delightful but messy treats.

Rowan said, "So Antonia, oldest kid but they sent Hugo to us? If a Vampire had done that I'd say Grandpa was making a point. And since Perfect Suit Lotte is his assistant, again, that underlines a deliberate choice to use her as his outward face. His viewpoint is public at least in the magic world. But witches have subtle but super-important differences with the way they send messages sometimes so I could be wrong."

"You're correct. Though there are elements of this that don't fit so neatly within that explanation."

"Like why if they need your support and you'd agreed to come to the guy's house instead of making him come to the Conclave building, they'd antagonize you? Because that's what I want to know. Can they just go around you and get a majority of signatures? Get their exemption that way?"

"There's already a predisposition against coercive magics. Especially in the oldest and most powerful families. They'd excuse it without doubt if the coercion was self-defense. But for entertainment use when audiences paid to then be manipulated? Without knowing exactly how they're being manipulated, but definitely for financial enrichment for the Procella family. That gets near the line many of us don't cross," Genevieve said.

"What about divination though?" Rowan asked. "I know there's an allowance for tarot and other types of readings. Even witches who have no talent for it but have intuition and give readings that are sometimes utter bullshit."

"I'd thought of the same. But as you say even that is regulated. There are laws against manipulating for personal enrichment above the basic cost of the reading. It's complicated, but it's fairly weighted to protect the other party. What the Procellas want is to be able to take a human who might say no if given the choice, to say yes, in a hypnotism or other type of audience participation scenario. And the wording is far too open-ended."

"Gramps and Hugo want this change so why are they not just sucking it up to get your signature instead of offending you?"

"I don't know the answer to that. I've never had personal dealings with the Procellas. They're members of the Senate as are all Genetic witches, but they're not in leadership. They have their businesses, and these private clubs are absolutely illegal from a human perspective but not ours. We don't really care about breaking human law as long as no one is being harmed and they do nothing to expose our existence."

"Let's see what we can see tomorrow night, then. We have far more questions than answers so hopefully we can flip that around after that. There's got to be a reason they're doing things this way. Even if the reason was they're just being assholes."

## Chapter Fourteen

Rowan looked up at David's tap on her door.

"Just received this from Nadir's office," he told her, laying the paper on her desk. As much as she liked to mock Vampires for being out of touch when it came to technology, Rowan found it much easier for her brain to retain things when they were on paper. So important communication was something David most often printed out for her rather than making her read it from a screen.

Yes, she was spoiled and yes, she knew it.

"The recent communication regarding Hunter Corp. employees was sent without the knowledge or permission of, nor does it reflect the views of, the Vampire Nation. These Vampires have violated the hospitality shown them by the First and his offices and will be disciplined for this breach. The Vampire Nation sincerely apologizes for any negative feelings created by this extraordinary breach of our rules," Rowan read and then glanced up at David.

He shrugged. "I'm rather impressed. Not a fauxpology of the *I'm sorry you feel that way*, but a genuine apology for what happened."

"I'm even more impressed because after the last interactions with Nadir I'm convinced she argued against allowing these shitlords into the process and was overruled. She had to then go to Theo to tell him about this mess all while knowing she advised against it for that very reason. And Theo will be mad about these Vampires going around Nadir. Partly because of how I might feel, but way more because he will be personally offended. He let these lords in because it was a fun way for him to take up my time. He didn't think about how they would make Hunter Corp. feel. He wanted to use them to poke at me. But what happened was they used him. They might have gone around Nadir because she was in charge. But he will see it as them going around him." Rowan blew out a breath. "At the very least these Vampires will be spending some time in Theo's dungeon. At worst, they'll spend a long time there and then he'll execute them."

"Would you like me to set up a call with Nadir? It's not sunrise there just yet," David asked.

She looked at the time and then shook her head. "Yes, but not for today. She'll have enough to manage right now, so I'll let her do that. Tomorrow morning when we get here, we'll do a status update and I'll know what the next step should be and then we'll connect with her."

She had enough to do before leaving for Prague. She didn't need to do Nadir's job on top of her own.

"Now that we've heard back from Nadir, would you like me to speak with Aron to let him know what's going on?" David asked.

"Oh, yes, please. Good idea." She'd made a brief call to him when the threat had first been delivered. She wanted him to remain vigilant. She'd promised to let him know when they found out anything new.

"I'm headed home at half past nine or so. Do you need a ride?" Rowan asked.

"Vanessa and I are taking the others out for dinner

and drinks, maybe a nightclub or two as a welcome to Las Vegas," David said.

They were all so young and vibrant. Like Carey had been. It was good that David had a social life with friends his age who also understood his weird life. A small part of her, the panic-stricken part, worried that he'd end up like Carey had. She repressed it, knowing it would hurt her and David both if she gave over to it. "Oh good. Have fun. Don't argue when a guard shadows you all night. Just be sure they get bathroom breaks and stay hydrated. Our new employees and the guard," she added quickly with a grin.

"I don't understand it," she told Clive when he arrived home later that night to have dinner with her. "What do these lords get by antagonizing Nadir other than a ticket to torture town?"

"It's absolute recklessness. I don't like it one bit."

"It doesn't comfort me that you're similarly confused by this." Rowan looked his way. "I was hoping you'd have some inside information that would give at least some context. What on earth are Takahiro and Tahar even thinking?"

"I think, were I in their place, I'd be doing little more than panicked location of these Vampires who'd exposed me to the outrage of the First and the Voice." Just the way Nadir had sounded on that phone conference earlier still sent a cold chill down his spine.

"I thought they were told to present themselves to Theo at sunset?"

"They were. From what I understand, most of them did not."

Rowan's eyes widened so comically Clive nearly laughed.

"Yes, I was as surprised by that fact as you seem to be. I can't imagine why they think they can run. Or what they want out of it," Clive told her.

"And that's the thing, Clive. What are these lords up to? They can't really care if I hire a Vampire. Sure, sure, you all get riled up whenever we ask for something because you hate being told what to do. And I get that, I really do. It's not…it's not enough for me to believe whatever they say they're up to. This whole thing leaves me certain there's something I'm not seeing because there's some sort of agenda at work here and it's not some douchelords getting shirty because I didn't heel like a dog."

"What does Hunter Corp. think of this?" he asked.

"The same as I do. We've all been at this a minute or two so of course we can see right through this. I can't very well demand Nadir tell me what's happening behind the scenes, but I can't believe she doesn't see the same thing too."

He paused. Weighing responsibilities and loyalties. "She had to get in between the First and the Scions. He apparently wanted to pay Tahar and Takahiro personal visits over this situation."

She blew out a breath. "See, the thing is." She licked her lips and after he shifted to sit next to her at the table, took her hand, and kissed her knuckles. He hated that she was ragged when it came to her father. Hated that she had so much on her shoulders, and it didn't matter that he hated it. Clive hated that as well.

So he did what he could, which was to be there and listen.

"Part of me wants to give him credit. Like oh my dad is trying to protect me, wow, that's amazing. But it's not." She pushed her plate aside and turned to face him directly. "He's the reason for this mess. I said that to you yesterday and I won't go over it again. So him threatening to run off and punch some kids who were mean to me? That's not it. He's pissed because his little game backfired and he looks bad. His wanting to go and interrogate a Scion isn't about me at all. So I regret that Nadir had to do it. I've been there. But she's done it for a hell of a lot longer. And I admit I know he'd ease back if I called him. Which would make things easier for everyone else."

"Not for you."

Her spine bent a little as she leaned into him for a moment, nuzzling her face into the crook of his neck.

"Not for me, no. And right now, I'm okay with making this one thing about me and what I want. I don't want to talk to him. I know it's selfish and petty but I'm a petty bitch and we all know that."

Clive snorted a laugh. "Darling, you make the most beautiful and powerful petty bitch I've ever known." He kissed her forehead before sitting back and pushing her plate to her once more. "But you're not selfish. Please finish your meal. You've barely touched it."

She frowned but picked up her fork and began to eat.

"If you needed to step in with him, you would. It's who you are. You consistently put others ahead of yourself and yes, we are in a position where we need to do that regularly. But in this particular instance, you don't have to call him or text him or any of that. The situation is being addressed by Nadir. At this particular moment in time nothing is on fire so let's luxuriate in it while we can."

Rowan frowned a moment. "I don't like this Vampire lord thing. I'm at the information-gathering stage and who knows? Theo might kill them all true before I get a chance to ask them what they're doing in person. Not an entirely terrible result. It would free up some time I need to spend on Elmer, don't think I've forgotten about that creep. Can't do any of that until after the Joint Tribunal. More Vampire time-wasting bullshit. Oh, my Goddess, the fucking years of my life I've wasted on your manipulations."

Clive withheld the smile threatening to make an appearance. "Darling, you're getting yourself worked up only moments after letting go of the last problem. The Joint Tribunal is very useful. We'll be able to resolve several problems with the face-to-face time we get there. Without the enforced regular meetings, you know we'd be at one another's throats far more often."

"If you all just refrained from killing humans—oh shit I forgot to tell you about that."

Her plate was finally empty so he took it and the rest of the dishes into the kitchen before returning to the table, leaning a hip against the chair he'd been sitting in.

"Tell me," he ordered. Then they could get past whatever it was and then he could get her naked. Nothing relaxed her quicker than sex. Thank goddess.

"Don't cross your arms and look all haughty at me, Scion. I won't be having any of that."

"Liar," he purred. She loved it when he *looked haughty* at her.

"Hmpfh." And then she told him about the missing humans and the connection to cities with both Vampires and witches.

He made a note to himself and then hauled his dangerous wife to her feet and against his body in an easy movement. "We've dealt with all our business to-do list items and now I have something else entirely for us to take a meeting over."

He gave her a hard and fast kiss and she spun out of his reach, heading toward their rooms.

"You think you're going to have sex with me?" she asked when he kept following her into her closet.

"Rowan." He smirked and backed her up against the built-in drawers. "*I know it.* It's all I can think about." Though she could have moved easily, she remained, the belligerence of her tone belied by the naked desire on her face.

A quick movement and he'd pulled her shirt up and over her head. Her skin called to him, begged to be touched and kissed, so he gave in, lowering his lips to the hollow of her throat in a kiss that pulled her taste into his system.

So beautiful and dangerous. Tame only for him, and wasn't that a gift beyond compare?

"I'm not entirely sure we've had sex in here yet," he said as he kissed and licked across the line of her collarbone from shoulder to shoulder.

"We had sex in here over the weekend," she said, amused.

"Clearly I need to endeavor to make this time more memorable." Her bra wasn't hard to slip away from her body and he stood back a moment, just looking at her. "You are my finest thing."

Rowan went hot all over at the words and the way he looked at her, mesmerized. That she had power of an altogether different sort over this being still amazed her. This was how he saw her. Rowan. His mate. Beautiful and strong and his.

He more than any other creature on the planet had the

key to the most vulnerable heart of her and while she wanted to punch his smug, gorgeous face regularly, that was a passing thing. What always remained was a sense of wonder that what she'd found with this unlikeliest of partners was its own sort of magic.

Her earlier upset washed away with each brush of his lips. The way his fingers dug into her hips to haul her close as his cologne and the spice of his power combined to tickle her senses, winding through her, leaving her drunk.

Only with him could it be like this. So raw and essential, bared to her soul with him. Her heart pounded so hard she heard it in her breath, knew, too, that he most certainly could. He feasted on her flush, the heat of her from the blood rushing to near the surface of her skin was a siren song.

Exultation rocketed through her when she was the one to wrench that moan of longing from him as she writhed in his arms. He flicked his tongue over her nipple and followed with the scrape of his incisors. Hard enough to sting but he didn't break the skin.

He sucked it into his mouth, drawing the blood closer still and she arched into him, sending through their bond that he could take that final step. Break the skin and take her blood.

He paused, the tension in his muscles a fine hum around his frame.

"Yes," she answered his unspoken question, loving him more that he never took blood from her without her permission. There'd never been permission before him. It had only been a taking.

Clive managed to flip the experience into something

else. He groaned as he licked over her aching nipple and then the edge of his incisor, so very sharp, broke the skin.

Instead of pain, she was flooded with pleasure. Through the bond that seemed to strengthen every day, that brilliant ribbon that connected their…souls…hearts, was a rush of his emotions. He prized her taste. Tenderness at the way she trusted him. Pride. Greed. Loyalty and so very much desire.

Added to the general Vampire chemistry that teased toe-curling desire through her cells, and he was a walking talking sex bomb.

Each pull of her nipple seemed to correspond with a throb of her clit. Her very skilled spouse had nearly five hundred years to hone his technique and he hadn't wasted a moment.

"Thank Goddess for all that rutting you got up to before I came along," she gasped out as he shoved her pants down, one-handed. She managed to get one leg loose, and he was back, his trousers kicked away, cock free and delightfully hard.

He was suave as fuck, which is why it still surprised her in the best way when he had the easy strength to band an arm around her waist and lift her. Rowan managed to get one of her legs up higher around his waist and wrapped it to hold herself in place.

Those bare seconds before the head of his cock nudged into her felt like honey, the anticipation slow and sticky and delicious. Then he was pressing up into her pussy and pulling her body toward him at the same time.

Some of her shoes toppled from their slots at his first few strokes. He spun them to the bench in the center of the space and sat, all while continuing to fuck into her body. It wasn't fast. It was relentless.

Rowan got her knees against the cushion of the bench so she could shift slightly, taking him even deeper.

"Yes," he snarled before pulling her down to kiss. The copper of Rowan's blood altered slightly when he'd taken it, she realized as she tasted herself.

That need to have her drove him as the heat of her body drove him on. She rose above him, hair half unbound. Like a phoenix. She'd remade herself from blood and ashes and it was magnificent to be in her orbit.

Her blood, just a small sip, zapped through him still, little jolts of her power meeting his. Sparking and changing into something…more. The bite of her nails into his shoulders demanded pleasure, and good, sweet fuck, how could anyone merit a creature such as his Rowan?

He found her clit easily and slid a fingertip around it, already so slick and swollen, keeping time with his thrusts.

Each swirl brought her closer, pulled her inner walls tighter around his cock, the hot and wet of her drove him. He wanted to come but she would go first. "A gentleman doesn't come until his partner does," he managed to say.

She laughed, letting her head fall back. She arched with that movement, grinding herself against him. Over and over as a haze of need misted his vision, telescoped on her. Her orgasm came in a hot rush he was helpless to do anything but respond to.

Their bond created a feedback loop of pleasure, his and hers, flowing easily back and forth, so effortlessly it was difficult to tell where he ended and she began.

She climbed off him carefully, laughing when she wobbled. "My knees are rubbery," she told him as he held her by her waist until she was balanced again.

"One does try to earn one's keep," he told her before pulling her to him for a kiss.

"You do okay," she teased.

He helped her change into at-home wear. Soft lounge pants and a thin, long-sleeved shirt. By help, he reached out to kiss or caress whatever part of her body he could and then she pulled him out to their sitting room.

"Back to business," she warned, and they moved to the sitting room couch. Not the actual bedchamber, but still part of their intimate space. It felt right to talk there instead of his office or even the dining room. Things were tense and the reminder that they were both on the same side was important. The place was another talisman, a protection of their marriage and inner life.

"I'm going to give you an update on my hiring plans." She didn't want it to be a secret really, and telling him was different than having to inform the Nation even though it wasn't their fucking business. Clive nodded and turned slightly to face her better. She got up quickly, grabbed the carafe of blood wine and a glass, placing them at his elbow.

"Is this your way of saying I need to be intoxicated to hear whatever it is?" he teased—mostly—as he poured himself a glass.

"You already know most of it. I've given you plenty of clues. I made an offer of employment to another Vampire. The Affiliated one, Katya Mabery. She officially accepted and she'll start after we return from Prague. Would you read her for me?"

Satisfaction warmed him. He got to nose around in her business and help her at the same time. She knew how much it would please him and though she did need a Vampire to do a read on her new employee, she didn't need him in particular.

"Yes, of course. Before or after Prague?"

Rowan smiled at him and leaned close enough to kiss him. "Before if you can fit it in. Otherwise, it can wait until we return. Thanks."

"I could pretend that it's all altruism, but we both know different." He sent her a cheeky grin, delighting in her laugh and quick kiss. "I'll make myself available to you tomorrow after sunset. Does that work?"

"Yes. Aron has already started some of the training. I wanted him read immediately so I could bring him into the investigation into Elmer. But then Vampires went and fucked up my schedule with all this shitlord business."

"Will you also announce this hire to Nadir as you did with Aron?"

"No. I'm done with that. I went the extra mile and got a death threat for my effort."

He winced. She wasn't wrong. But. "You know that wasn't from Nadir."

"What I *know* is that she told you all or your offices or whatever and the information made it to these lords. If she'd been thinking about protection, she would have handled this differently. But here we are."

"She had to inform us somehow. I… I don't think it's correct that it was her being unsafe. I simply don't think she expected this whole thing. And who could have? She threatened us all about that. Demanded Tahar and Takahiro admit it if they were involved. Reminded them Andros would certainly be able to find out in unpleasant ways if they chose to play these games."

"Do *you* think they are?" Rowan asked.

Clive had thought about that on and off since this entire mess started. "Tahar has been Scion for two thousand years. That's…a long time to pretend to be loyal and then turn on the First."

Rowan waved a hand. "It wouldn't be the first time a follower of an important leader changed their mind or allegiance. There've been Scion uprisings before. During Tahar's time more than once."

Clive inclined his chin a moment, taking her point. "I don't know that I believe either of them are treasonous. I'm also not saying I'd be shocked necessarily if one or both were, but it's a dangerous proposition and as you mentioned the previous uprisings, they all end the same. They're going to risk everything for what? Being angry at Hunter Corp. for hiring a Vampire or two? Both men have been Scions long enough that I'd like to think they're smarter than that."

"There are entirely too many things going on in my world that do not make sense. I don't like it."

"Quite so. I'm in agreement with that. As to your other new hire, the Maberys are who they appear to be. What?" He gave her an exasperated look when she squawked. "You knew I'd look after you told me about her and Aron. So I did." And, as Rowan had predicted, Clive agreed that the Nation wouldn't really make an issue out of trying to punish the Maberys to stop Katya from taking the job at Hunter Corp. Or rather, *he* wouldn't make an issue of it and, since North America was where their family lived and they were his Vampires, if Clive didn't make an issue of it, the others most likely wouldn't.

Rowan gave him a close look and then went back to speaking. "I know she doesn't have any complaints lodged against her. She's never been even suspected of wrongdoing. No one else in the line either. Her family runs a business that makes liners for boats and marine craft stuff. Plenty to keep them all in whatever people who make boat liners wear and where they live. Nothing in our records either."

He gave her a look. "How do you know she doesn't have any complaints lodged against her with the Nation?" Clive realized she employed people far better at hacking into the Nation databases than he'd originally assumed.

Rowan rolled her eyes at him. "We already went over this. I'm crafty because you leave me no other option. The information is out there. It just takes a way to open the door to wherever it's been gathered. This petty bullshit doesn't serve you at all. I'll still find out and you get nothing because you let your ego blind you whereas if you'd participated you could have influenced the process. You are all so stupid for this. I mean, great for me and all, but whatever."

"You still made sure they weren't facing any disciplinary action from the Nation." He sent her a raised brow.

"Sure I did because I'm smart. I don't need problems. I just need Vampires on my team to deal with Vampire-shaped problems. Like I checked out all our other hires. Well, let me amend that a little. Genevieve and Zara aren't employees in that sense. But I did a background run on them both. I don't need problems," she repeated. "I need solutions. These will be Hunters who are out in the field with the authority to investigate and in some cases apprehend and maybe or execute. I need people with control."

She'd probably never admit this to him but the back-and-forth they did in these situations really helped her work things out in her head. He had a way of debating, never being cruel, but not holding back. It enabled her to work through ideas, refining some, rejecting others. If she couldn't argue convincingly, she most likely wouldn't do whatever it was.

Rowan stretched and then settled against him, contented after that bout of spectacular closet sex.

"I hear you'll be taking a meeting at Fleur tomorrow." It pleased him immeasurably that she would make use of his resources that way. She knew it because it rushed through their bond.

"That was next up on my things-to-tell-Clive list. I figured Alice would run it by you though."

"She did. I'm happy to know you'll be in my space where you'll be safer. I assume you'll want surveillance."

"You can try. I'm not sure your cameras will work against whatever privacy spell they might use. Genevieve has one she just flicks out there with this snazzy little thing." Rowan tucked all her fingers back but her middle and pointer and imitated that wrist movement. "Anyway. Fleur seemed like a moderately neutral place outwardly but with plenty of opportunity to spy and take the lead over these dumbass witches."

"Alice says the chef is staying late and then he'll come in immediately after sundown so he can send out your favorite appetizers during the meeting." Clive shook his head with a smile. "The chefs at *Die Mitte* and Fleur all dance to your tune. My theory is they love to watch you eat as much as I do."

She blushed, ducking her head a little so her hair covered her features. "They must really love me these days since it feels like I eat pretty much all day long." Rowan changed the subject. "These witches, the Procellas? They're as fucking ridiculous as any Vampire I've had to deal with. Though," she admitted with some chagrin, "I'm not as good at dealing with them as I am with Vampires. I need to learn more. I do know the Procellas and their way of seeing the world is the polar opposite of Genevieve's. She's old and powerful and rich and all that, but I've never seen her act like a sanctimonious ass. This mansion, Goddess, I didn't even get inside because, duh, impure. But it was just as ostentatious as you'd imagine. Took three fucking people to answer the door and not a one had a bit of manners. I just know there's about forty pounds of excess gold on a lot of furniture. The old man probably snaps his fingers to get someone's attention and tips a dollar after running servers off their feet at a restaurant. Their staff did have great uniforms though. Like Dior-type great. Smart and elegant. I guess if I had enough money to pay three people to answer my door, I'd want them looking good doing it. Anyway. This creepy-ass Hugo guy nearly slobbered all over Genevieve and that was gross. Seriously, the way he put his attention on her made my skin crawl. Darius wasn't pleased about that part, let me tell you! But that's another reason I'm glad we can use Fleur. I would have argued against meeting at weirdo mansion for sure. They were so rude and she'd been doing them a favor by going there."

"To spy on them," Clive teased.

"To figure out the answer to yet another situation where we're trying to figure out just exactly what the Kentucky fried fuck is happening. Because that mess today was so amateurish. And for what? Why antagonize someone you need?"

"Why indeed? It seems the question we can apply to multiple situations as you mentioned earlier. Still, if anyone can keep you out of trouble or at the very least protect your back should trouble come, it's Genevieve. When I'm not there, naturally," he added and gave her a smug look.

"Naturally," she said, tone dry.

"As it happens, I too have a meeting at Fleur right after sunset. I'd rather thought I'd be unable to accommodate them but now it looks as if our schedules align," he said lazily, just to rile her up. Goddess help her, she loved it.

"What a coincidence," she said with a snicker.

"Isn't it just? We can ride over to your offices together afterward if you like, so that I can read Katya."

"We'll see. I don't know what I'll be doing right before that so I may have to rush over to Fleur instead of coordinating with David."

He just patted her thigh, which was his way of saying he'd do whatever he liked and if he really wanted to drive her to her office, he'd make that happen so she should just give in.

Normally she'd poke at him over it. She couldn't let him steamroll her very often or he'd be in her business all day every day. But she liked their little work sessions, and she knew he secretly loved it when she shared gossipy tidbits.

"Darius is not terrible," she told Clive. "He drove us to the meeting today and was the guard. Do not make that face at me! David was on overwatch." Rowan pointed a finger at him. "Also, I don't know Darius's whole story but he's powerful enough to level a city block and absolutely motivated to protect Genevieve—and by extension, me—at all costs. Speaking of protection. The car he drove had these windows." She told him all about the opaque thing and that she'd ordered an installation of at first three vehicles and then three more in the following months, working around their schedule, which apparently was incredibly busy but because he had smooshy feelings for Genevieve, he fit them in.

"Not terrible. Such high praise," Clive said.

"It is! There are so many truly terrible beings we have to deal with regularly. Anyway, he's still spooky as fuck, but he's warming up to me, I can tell. Plus, he's on Genevieve's side, which is my side by extension."

"Goddess help me, but that made sense," Clive teased, pulling her into a hug.

# *Chapter Fifteen*

Darius found himself on the patio just outside her bedroom and he wasn't sure why and that was total bullshit. He knew why. Because he couldn't be anywhere else. Because she called to him and he didn't want to ignore it anymore.

The sheer curtain panels wafted in the breeze through the open doors. He caught her scent easily and then she was there, her dark hair free in a fall of lush curls. The curve of her lips as she opened the screen and beckoned him inside was a smile just for him.

Face bare of makeup she looked even younger than usual as she indicated he sit wherever.

"Lorraine is long asleep," Genevieve told him. "But she made some tea for me to drink and brought two glasses so she must have had a feeling about an early morning visitor."

"I knew I liked her," he murmured before turning his attention to Genevieve again. There were lit candles all through the space bathing her in tawny liquid gold as she padded around, feet bare. The deep blue silk pajamas she wore fluttered around her, caressing and accentuating the lines of the body beneath the fabric.

His palms tingled as he thought about sliding his

hands over her curves while his lips felt the phantom of her skin right at the juncture of her jaw and her throat.

She chose the chair across from his and tucked her feet up under herself before smiling over at him, leaning on her elbow to get a little closer. "What brings you to my lair tonight?" she asked, delight in her eyes.

Truth was, Darius could make up a dozen reasons to be there without admitting his craving for this witch. He'd been many, many things over the many years he'd been in existence, but never had he been a liar. And if he didn't lie to others, why do it to himself?

He was there because she was all he thought about every moment he wasn't doing something else. And even then. Even then the song of her power, of her magic and energy and yes, her gorgeous fucking face, haunted him in the background.

"Lair?" He leaned closer to her, placing his elbows on his knees. "That sounds dangerous."

"Or adventurous." She fluttered her lashes and a lightness only she seemed to bring bubbled through his belly and chest.

It had been centuries since he'd been teased this way. He wanted more.

"I came because you were here, and I wanted to see you."

"Oh. Well." Her pleased smile stole his breath a beat or two. "I'm glad you did. I was thinking about you and there you were. As if I'd conjured you," she said. "Normally I might say to a human or someone like Rowan, *tell me about yourself.* But I find that question harder and harder to answer the older I get. I imagine for you it might be the same. I like to ask more specific questions. Or you can tell me random facts. I'd like that too."

"You first. Why did you come to Las Vegas?" he asked.

"First it was because of Rowan. I'd come here to see her during a previous investigation. *Investigation.* Isn't that a fun word? I love it. And then I liked it. Not the heat. But the simplicity of everything. It's clean. It's spare but not desolate. So much magic." Her gaze flicked to his. "And then there were the Devils and…you. I wanted roots. Wanted to pause to choose to live a different way. I'd wandered for a long time before that. There's purpose here. That's why I stayed."

He liked it. Liked knowing little things about her, though what she'd just shared wasn't little at all.

"I came to Las Vegas three years ago. Marco is someone I've known for a few thousand years. I came out here and those things you spoke of were true for me. But also there was peace. There's a great deal of background noise in the world. All those emotions just flowing like a churning sea. It's beautiful and savage at the same time. I hadn't planned on staying until I'd been here three days. My first sunrise here. We'd been out on a ride and we stopped right there in the middle of the road and just watched as the sky began to gray, then blue, purple with crowns of orange and gold and then boom." His magic had exploded into life, digging itself into the metaphorical dirt and he'd agreed. "Out here in the desert the human noise fades so it's just the roar of that churning power. Soothing. I never left."

"Where were you before you came here?" she asked next after nudging a tall glass of mango iced tea toward him.

"In the few decades before I came here I was in Brussels. Or, rather just outside the city itself." He paused. "Before that though I stuck to North Africa mainly. You are old enough to know how the names for places change over time." The physical place itself had changed too. More desert, less green. "It pleases me that the Nile still flows. I used to fish in it. Back when I was…before I became a Devil."

"I'm so very curious, but feel free to not answer anything you don't wish to. How does one become a Dust Devil?" she asked.

He sipped the tea, appreciating the peppery bite of the mango. "We all come by it in a unique way. In my case, something terrible happened to my family. It drove me." He stopped speaking as he searched for the right words about how he'd felt over four thousand years before. "I lost myself in vengeance and then in loneliness. I went to one of my wife's family members. She was a witch. There was a ritual. Then after a time I was offered a choice by another Devil. I accepted."

"I'm sorry for whatever happened to your family," she said with a brief touch of his hand.

"It was a very long time ago."

"Memory doesn't work that way. Long time ago or not, it happened, and it clearly affected you and the course of the rest of your life deeply. Such moments in our lives are hard to overcome, but they don't simply dissolve once we're past them."

"You sound like you speak from experience." He wanted her to share but knew bringing those old pains to the surface wasn't an easy process. Darius found himself not wanting her to experience even the tiniest bit of discomfort.

"I was little more than a small child when I was sent to my first teaching. My father believed it was necessary and important for all Auberts to learn not only how to use the magic they'd been born with, the magic that was easy to use, but to learn every manner of practice possible and master it.

"My first tutor was what today is a cliché of a witch. She lived in a shack. Threw bones. Read spit and blood. Tea leaves. Whatever. She was quick with a backhand and there were plenty of times I learned something because it was the only way to avoid a beating." Genevieve halted as if her words got stuck and suddenly Darius wished he hadn't pushed because whatever she was about to share had torn her to pieces.

"You don't have to go on," he murmured, and she waved a hand. He smiled a moment. "You don't wear your bracelets to bed, obviously, but it's strange to see you make that movement without the jingling."

Genevieve smiled softly. "I'd trusted her. She taught me many things. I…had no real mother figure at that point so when she told me to take a bundle to the home of an influential man in a nearby village, I obeyed."

"How old were you?" he interrupted, afraid, so very afraid of where this story was going.

"Twelve."

He blew out a breath. Back when she'd been twelve, plenty of girls her age had been in the process of being contracted into marriage. But that's not what happened, or she'd be telling a different story.

"He was on me the moment I got inside. I fended off his advances and ran. He followed me to the shack where I'd retreated. I thought she'd protect me. Tell him to go. But she hit me and shoved me out the door and told me to do what I was told."

He barely breathed, not wanting to interrupt.

"He raped me in the dirt just outside her door. She

knew what was going on and did nothing. Didn't even open her door. So when he turned his back to fasten his trousers, I killed him with the rock he'd used on my face at the start." She touched a spot at her temple. "Again, she never came outside to see what the sound was. When I used my magic to open the door she'd barred against me, I walked inside, covered in blood that was mostly my own, I… I killed her too. Too bad she couldn't have seen that in her fucking bones, eh?" Her laugh was dark and bitter.

*Genevieve was so much more than she appeared at first glance*. A goddess in many ways. One that included vengeance. Something at the core of how he'd come to be who he was that day as well.

Like calling to like.

She continued, "I panicked that he'd gotten me with child, but I hadn't bled yet and fortunately fate had other plans." Her gaze, which had been on a faraway horror, returned to his, clear. "I loved her. I trusted her. She threw me away like I was nothing."

"I'm glad you killed them both. I cannot go back in time to do so myself, you see. Neither of them deserved to take up space here. I'm sorry you were betrayed that way."

Her mouth hardened into a tight line and even then she was breathtaking. "It taught me many important lessons. Mainly that until I was powerful enough in my own right, I would be vulnerable to those who wanted to use me. That experience hardened me in ways that have saved my life more than once since. But that heartbreak, those hours when I was alone and betrayed and on the run? Every once in a while, I dream of it. I'm past it. I've healed emotionally and physically. I've grown into a power great enough that most would never dare to take me on. But that day will be in my mind forever, I think."

Darius took her hand and turned it over, pressing a kiss to her palm. "Thank you for sharing that."

"It was a very long time ago. I just wanted you to know you weren't alone. Those big important memories don't just die forever. Nor should they or how else would you remember your sons and your wife?"

Most women wouldn't so easily bring up a man's old loves. But Genevieve wasn't most women.

"There are times when I wake up panicked I've forgotten them. My oldest son was ten, the youngest barely walking. Even millennia ago they were children. They played and got dirty, harried their mother, quickly learned how to care for our animals and to fish. They wanted to help." He smiled. Gods, those little faces. "But then something will happen. A sound, or a smell, something will trigger those memories and I can see, so clearly, Huy's big brown eyes, his arms folded across his middle as he laughed. Or Nimlot's shaky little steps on his chubby legs, always following his brothers, looking for mischief. Or snacks. He had his mother's nose and lips. Mery, he was our middle. Ferocious. Fearless. Curious about everything. The first thing he did upon waking was tell us something he'd learned. How an insect may have walked the day before, or how the river rose and fell. I think in today's world he would be endlessly pleased by the ability to find out information. Huy was solid, like a little tank, you understand?"

Genevieve nodded, wearing a sweet smile, her hand still in his.

"Mery was the tallest. Long and lean like his mother. His mother. Ah, my Tiya. We knew one another from childhood. From those early years it was simply assumed by our families that we would end up together and they were right. She had the most beautiful hands. I used to simply watch her as she helped me with the nets, or when she cooked. We were friends as well as lovers. I miss her laugh and the exasperated way she said my name when I got the boys excited right before it was time for them to sleep."

He missed the way she'd felt against him as they'd slept. Missed the sound of their small house as no one else was awake but him. He didn't miss the lack of mattresses, running water, or electricity, but he missed the way time moved then. When the world was younger and he was still human.

"I'm glad you remember them all."

He was too. The memories of those sweet people he'd loved so fiercely no longer made him sad. They made him glad he had that time. But he wasn't that man anymore. In the multiple lifetimes he'd led in the millennia since, he'd let go of the guilt that he wasn't home when they'd been attacked. The insanity that had come after, the blood and the ritual, the night he'd made the choice to give up his humanity. Back then it had been about the ability to locate and punish those who'd broken his wife and children. It had taken him a good thousand years to let it go.

Time had made that long-ago humanity feel like a movie he'd seen once. He'd been wrapped up in the Trick and their business and that had insulated him. But nothing could insulate him from the way every moment he spent with Genevieve tempted him further away from that cold isolation and into a chair in the bedroom of a woman he very much wanted to strip naked and pleasure until she said his name in the dark with nothing between them but skin.

"What things do you like most about being here in Las Vegas right now?" he asked, changing the subject because his cock was very interested in that and perked up.

"Pancakes. There's a diner Rowan and I go to regularly. They have pancakes the size of the plate. Fluffy. They're amazing."

"Would you take me there? I haven't had pancakes in a very long time."

Her smile seemed to send a wave of her magic over his skin.

"What are you doing in the morning? Later, after ten or so?"

"Taking you to get pancakes."

"Would you take us on your motorcycle? I would like to ride on it. It looks enjoyable."

The things she said…it was as if she'd read through a list of all the things he wanted from her and then delivered.

"I'd like that," he said. "What are two other things you're enjoying about the city right now?"

"I'm quite pleased with the work I'm doing with Rowan. I think it's that purpose I was talking about earlier. There's this feeling that each step I take I'm supposed to be. It's been a while since I've felt so certain about where I'm supposed to be."

She stood and walked over to the sliders overlooking the yard, peering out.

"Three is this. This house. This land. The Dust Devils." She turned to face where he'd remained sitting because if he stood she'd see his dick because he was so hard. "And you."

* * *

Genevieve could scarcely breathe with the weight of his power hanging in the air around him. Humming with so much sexual energy her own stood at attention.

She wanted him.

"Would you like to go out back with me for a few minutes?"

If he was surprised, he hid it as he came to his feet in one fluid motion, all power and deadly grace. Her mouth watered.

She took his hand and led him out into the yard, away from the pool and into a little spot she'd set her working circle into.

His intake of breath at her back told her she wasn't the only one to feel the raw power all around. It was their land that had unlocked this potential inside her. As if it had been waiting her whole life for that connection so it could fully bloom.

"You've been busy," he murmured, taking the space in. He kept her hand and she strolled with him as he checked everything out.

"I've spent some hours when I could over the last week to set it up. The stillroom is just over there." Marco had shown up with a few others and they'd cut a door into the wall so there would be easy access from that part of the house out here to where she'd be performing workings. "The door they brought is exquisite," she said of the beautiful wood and glass creation covered in detailed woodwork.

"Marco has many talents," Darius said. "It pleases them to help you. Thank you for allowing that."

"You all seem so endlessly competent at everything. Mechanical things, construction. Pip took Lorraine out to wild forage some ingredients. She said he knew many good places and was a good guide who did not sass."

His startled laugh captured every bit of her attention. He lifted his hand to cup her cheek briefly. "Does she bring her wooden spoon with her when she leaves the house?"

He was playing with her. It sent pleasure and happiness reeling through her system.

"No. But she has a walking stick. Longer reach and it's pointed slightly at the tip. The spoon is easier to evade."

"I like her more and more every new thing I learn about her." He dropped his hand. "Pip requested to be on duty to guard her. She's scary, but also maternal in a way we've not had for a very long time."

The moon wasn't quite full but nearly so and it bathed the circle she'd created and then warded in silver. Genevieve stepped in and the power parted around her, sliding against her skin in welcome as she did.

"My circle would recognize your magic. If you wish," she said. They didn't talk very much about his magic. It was clearly there and in rough proportion to hers. It was wildly different, but practitioners were individuals so their power signatures and the way they practiced varied as well. She hadn't seen him perform anything major yet though there was evidence in the way he showed up nearly immediately when she called his name into the air.

Much like the story about his family, Genevieve knew it would take Darius time to reveal the most intimate parts of himself to her. She would do the same. She'd been used to keeping her own counsel for so long and suddenly there'd been Rowan and it had been *natural* to open up to her friend. And now Darius. He was something entirely different. Sharing with him, giving him bits of herself, made her vulnerable. She took a leap every time she did it. And every time he smiled or laughed or asked her to take him to pancakes was him doing the same. Pulling them closer and closer.

"I don't know how your magical practice works," she went on when he remained standing a few feet away. "You don't have to perform a working here. Or you can on your own, if you prefer, whenever you like. I thought that since I'm your priestess it might be helpful. Or something like that."

He remained standing outside her circle, and she let it go because it wasn't about her. It was about individual practice.

"I'm grateful you created this. The others will be as well," he said quietly.

"I just need to finish this spell," she told him. "I've had these tinctures here in the circle under the sky. They've been curing for the last day." She bent to retrieve one of the tall clear bottles holding different colored liquids and held it up, looking at the moon through it. She repeated the steps with the other bottles until they were all finished.

She placed them around the circle at the innermost edge. Then she opened herself up and let the power free. Unleashed it like she'd thrown off a cloak. Genevieve knew from long experience that patience at this step was necessary. There was so much magic inside her that if she didn't let it all run free like a bunch of kittens when she first opened herself up, all she did was fight against herself to get it under control.

And it was more time to fight herself. Dulled her results.

After two or three minutes, she drew in a deep breath

and let it free on a count of five, reversed and drew another in on the same slow five count. All her facets, as Darius called them, lined up and cooperated, eager to help. The words to the song she sang were in a language no one but witches had spoken for at least four hundred years or so. An opening of the way. Then she added claps and hand movements to go with the slow, shuffling steps she took in a meandering pattern within the circle.

Wisps of energy floated around her and then knitted together, slowly drifting down, covering the bottles. The spells she worked would bind the ingredients in the bottles with the magic. Amplifying their effects.

Genevieve was the conduit. Not just for the magic to imbue the tinctures with the final bindings, but for that energy to flow into the Trick as a whole. All over their ground, Devils would have felt a rush of her working. It would nourish them in the same way their rides down the Strip did.

Better. Because the magic she performed was life magic. Healing magic. The greenest of her talent, and that would be cleaner and more direct than their normal diet of jilted boyfriends and gamblers on highs or lows. This was filtered energy, similar to the way water filters pulled away impurities.

Invigorated and energized, Genevieve clapped three times and the spell ignited fully, seeping into the tinctures and leaving behind nothing but a slight misting of power.

That done, she broke the circle and tasted salt on the air. Another new aspect to her magical power was that she'd discovered—via the Dust Devils—she was a salt witch. Veins of it ran through the land, eagerly rushing to her call, pleased to weave itself into her workings.

Just a few feet away, Darius remained where he'd been before, but his eyes had gone impossibly darker.

"You're delicious," he said, words rough as if he'd been sleeping. "Devils for miles and miles have just been showered with so much energy and power they'll probably start a shrine to you." He reached above his head and clasped his hands, stretching.

Genevieve wanted to kiss whoever had installed the lights that had been strung through the trees and bushes because it enabled her to catch that slice of bare belly when the hem of his T-shirt rode up.

He helped her with the bottles, and she took him into the stillroom where they were stored.

Once back in her bedroom—and she did so like the sight of him there—he said, "I have not seen the like of such a space in many years. A prior priestess—not here, a Trick I was in while in Lebanon—had a stillroom I remember smelling far worse than this."

"The nice part of having that working space outside is I can perform the smelliest spells out there. I'll try to give everyone a warning to stay upwind during those times."

He took two steps and her back bumped against the door to the adjoining bathroom. Her hands ended up on his very warm, very firm chest. Not to stop him. Her fingers curled into his muscles, the heat of him bringing a gasp to her lips.

"You make me laugh," he told her, smiling briefly and frankly, she wasn't sure what else he could have said that would have thrilled her the same way. It was rather delightful the way he'd begun to show a lighter-hearted side of himself to her.

"Laughter is important," she said, aiming at being

teasing, but the truth of that statement cut through the haze of desire enough that she knew she wanted more.

He bent and when they were so close she only needed take a deep breath to touch him, he said, "I've been thinking about your taste since I kissed you yesterday."

Then he was kissing her again. His mouth on hers, his arms wrapped around her shoulders as she clung to his chest and back. She fit against him shockingly well. Like she was made for it.

Shoving that thought aside, she let herself sink into the moment. His tongue slid against hers and she squeezed her inner thighs against the near painful need.

His taste was rich with power and sex. It gamboled through her, setting off little earthquakes of sensation, especially after he tightened his embrace and only clothes separated them.

When his mouth lifted, she noted somewhere in the back of her mind the disappointed and grumpy sound she gave and when she opened her eyes it was to catch the sight of a wicked grin full of intent.

Then those endless midnight eyes slid halfway shut and that teasing light turned low into barely banked heat.

"Don't fret. I'm not going anywhere," he murmured and lowered his mouth to her throat, his lips leaving a heated path in their wake. He slid his palms down her arms, capturing her wrists a breathless moment.

When he freed her, it was to cradle her neck, kissing and stroking his fingers afterward. Each sweep of his touch seemed to ripple outward.

A phantom breeze, stirred by their combined power, sent the flames from the candles dancing, making shadows against her closed eyelids.

He swept an arm around her waist and hauled her

close once more, his face buried in her hair. Heart beating wildly, desire liquid in her veins, she dragged in a breath that was full of him.

Neither moved for a minute or two and then she was back against the door and his hands were at the buttons of her pajama top and there was a question in his gaze. Did she want to go further?

She put her hands over his and guided them to pop that first button. He kissed across the line of her collarbone and then down over the exposed skin at the center of her chest. Then her hands helped him with the second and last button and the fabric had parted, exposing her breasts to his view.

Again he captured her wrists but this time he pulled her arms up above her head and pushed slightly. *Don't move.* As if she wanted to!

He murmured words too soft to hear clearly, but she understood them, nonetheless.

Fingertips traced up her ribs and then circled her breastbone and down until he took her breasts in his hands, twisting his wrist so he could pinch her nipples between his thumbs and forefingers.

She bowed her back, arching into his touch, and then his mouth replaced his fingers, sending licks of flame straight to her clit.

His hands slid down to her hips and caught the waist of her pants, pulling them down as he dropped to his knees in front of her, pressing his cheek to her through her panties.

Genevieve nearly trembled, nearly panted with anticipation as he turned his face and breathed warm air over her pussy.

"I want you. I want this," he said as he flicked his gaze up to hers. "Do you want this?"

"Yes," she told him without hesitation.

In one easy movement, he stripped her of her underpants and arranged her so her thigh rested on his shoulder. Genevieve had to rest most of her weight against the door and even then she nearly fell over when he spread her open. "Pretty," he said and took a long lick.

She didn't even recognize the sound she made as her own at first. It took a few moments for the sound and sensation to connect and then boom, he did something with his tongue that hauled her right to the edge of climax.

Then he did it over and over and over again until she came in what felt like an endless rush that knocked her world sideways.

His hands nearly shook.

Darius fisted them to steady himself as he pressed a kiss to her inner thigh.

He hadn't been prepared for things to be so intense.

It felt as if a crack had developed in the shell that had naturally hardened around his heart. The taste of her on his lips, her scent on his hands seemed to rain down on him, dissolving his reserve until he was standing, cradling her face.

He needed to go. Needed to create some space between them so he could get hold of himself once more, but then she wrapped her arms around his shoulders and he never wanted to move again.

"You're by far the best neighbor I've ever had," she murmured. "Since I'm unsure if my legs are working, I'll need your assistance to get to my bed and into me."

And how could he resist such an invitation? Especially because he'd imagined her asking him to fuck her more than once but probably less than a hundred thousand times.

One arm banded about her waist, he picked her up, swung them toward the bed and though he'd planned to lay her on it gently, she kept her grip on him and pulled him to the mattress with her.

It had been an epoch since he'd laughed in bed with a partner and though it had been gone from his life for so long he'd forgotten how wonderful it felt, now that he had it again, he grabbed it with both hands.

"Why are all your clothes on?" she asked lazily.

"Why indeed?" he asked as he managed to get free of his shirt, pants, and shorts. The shoes he'd left at home anyway.

It was the way she looked at him, her gaze sliding over him from his feet to the top of his head, that had him back on the bed, kneeling over her body.

"What a gift you are," she murmured, running her hands over his upper body before she grabbed two handsful of his ass to pull him closer. "So beautiful."

"I was thinking the same of you," he said, kissing her again. Because he could. Because she wanted him to.

He rolled to his back, bringing her with him. Her hair, unbound, curtained around her face as she looked down at him.

She raked her nails down his chest and over his belly, halting and reversing course until all he could feel was that sensation, sharp and soft, sensual and provocative all at once.

Her weight on him was perfect. The softness of her, that smooth skin stretched over fire and power the likes of which he rarely saw much less wanted to possess more than he cared to examine deeply.

Her lips against his neck felt so good he arched, needing to be closer. Wanting more. The constant since he'd watched her walk into their bar a handful of months before. The flashes he had considered fantasy weren't.

He slid his palms up her thighs, over her hips and ribs. In a quick set of moves she'd removed the pajama shirt and rose, grabbing his cock in her fist and slowly pulling it up and off and down again. Semen beaded at the tip, and she ran her thumb through it before bringing it to her lips to lick, her gaze locked on his.

The naked sensuality in that act sent a shock through him. That she would be a graceful, sexual being wasn't a surprise. That she sought it openly and with relish was deeply satisfying. He, too, could be who he was with her on this level.

Words came but he held them. That hazy pleasure in her gaze sharpened.

She paid attention. Another irresistible quality.

A question in her gaze along with passion and knowledge. Solidarity, he supposed, in this deep wanting between them.

"Ride me," he managed to say instead of begging.

Her concern was gone, replaced with more want. Reflecting his.

He reached down and held the root of his dick as she rose up. All the rest faded as all he could do was snarl at the sensation of her tight, wet pussy surrounding his cock. Pleasure shot up his spine, so sharp it sliced, right on that edge of too much and never enough.

Flames danced as this queen—his queen—moved over him while he nearly lost his mind at the intensity of connection and sensation between them. He gripped her hips as her muscles played against his palms.

A quick shift of his weight and he'd flipped them. Yes. Having her spread out below him, her hair like a corona around her head as she looked up into his face, incited him further as he deepened his thrusts.

He had to get to his knees, desperate to be deeper, and then she added a swivel of her hips and he was lost.

Her hips had been tipped up and Darius grabbed her then with one hand, stilling her at that angle. Served up just how he wanted.

"Perfect," he said and then as he continued to thrust, he pressed the pad of his thumb over her clit, keeping that pressure as he circled.

Her pussy superheated and went molten as she tightened around him. Enough to drag him over that edge with her.

He'd always known he could see the future. But he'd never seen her coming and wasn't that fascinating?

# *Chapter Sixteen*

Fleur was full of pleasant memories for Rowan that stretched back to the early—and admittedly turbulent—days of her relationship with Clive. Back then she'd delighted at scaring them all, but in the years since they'd become part of her family. Even the grumpiest of servers and the temperamental chef.

She shook that free. She was there for all of them. And the others she'd gathered along the way. There at Genevieve's side for this meeting to be sure these magic fuckheads didn't try to mess with anyone.

At the two-story glass entry, the house manager waited. He didn't smile when he recognized Rowan, but his gaze warmed. He bowed to her and then nodded at the others.

"It's good to see you, Ms. Summerwaite," he said. "I've set the small private dining room for this meeting. Coffee, water, tea, juice will be brought out when you're ready. You said no food, but the chef has prepared some little bites for you, should you change your mind."

"We don't want them to get comfortable enough to stay," Rowan admitted before she indicated Genevieve. "This is Genevieve Aubert. She'll be heading this meeting. Genevieve, this is Gioberto."

Genevieve fluttered her lashes and said complimentary things in that way of hers. Had Gioberto stammering and blushing within moments.

David had shown up at Fleur via their underground service corridor so even if the Procellas were watching the front and side door to see who was coming and going, they wouldn't see him. And of course they were surveilling the place, they'd be fools not to. At least three Devils had been stationed around the area as well.

"They'll be here soon so let's get ourselves seated," Rowan told Genevieve. She liked to have first pick of such things. "On the way, let me show you where David is."

Gioberto led them through the open dining room. The Portnoy Glass chandeliers suspended over the tables sent slices of red over the furniture and floors as the light caught the glass just right. Through the double doors and into the kitchen where staff was already prepping for that night's service. The fresh green scent of herbs hung in the air with the sound of slicing, grating, chopping, and cook banter, which Rowan sometimes got mixed up and thought it was a fight, but it was really just semi-affectionate teasing. They headed up a flight of stairs and took a turn down a narrow hallway used to ferry the food back and forth quietly and efficiently into the banquet-type rooms beyond.

Being a place run by Vampires, there were what Rowan termed spy stations notched into that hallway at the corners of each of the three private dining rooms. David was already set up, multiple screens running, as they approached.

Genevieve made an approving sound as she stood behind him, looking at his screens over his shoulders.

"Nothing as crude as him looking through the eye

holes of a portrait in the other room," Rowan said and to her surprise, Genevieve laughed.

"Like in Scooby-Doo! I love that show." She launched into French as she happily detailed her three favorite episodes.

"You have layers," Rowan said, smiling.

"Is that a nice way of saying I'm old?" Genevieve teased.

"I would never," Rowan said, neatly avoiding that. "Vampires are very good at spycraft. These rooms are wired with multiple cameras and listening devices. But will they work if Hugo or Grandpa Procella work some privacy spell?" Rowan asked Genevieve.

"I should be able to null any spells in that room but mine. I'll set that in place before they arrive. I'll know if they try a spell. Unless the Procellas bring a witch who is better than they are, none of them will even know I've neutered them."

A burst of warmth seemed to roll through Rowan. She looked at the clock on a nearby wall. It was twenty-five minutes to sunset and Clive had just risen to consciousness. He'd be there looming over David the moment he could leave the house. In the meantime, everything in that room would be recorded so he could watch it back at his leisure.

Within herself, Rowan got the sense Brigid was as amused by that flash of Clive watching the video while munching on popcorn as Rowan had been.

Once in the private dining room, Genevieve did her magic thing while Rowan and David tested their equipment.

"Don't chitchat about anything you don't want Clive

to know," Rowan told Genevieve quietly, half an hour later when Gioberto had come up to let them know their guests had arrived.

They'd worked out a plan. Genevieve would lead and Rowan would follow when necessary. In the back of her consciousness just a few short minutes later, she knew Clive had just entered the restaurant. Probably heading up to check in with David and watch the monitors.

He must have been dressed and ready to rush over to Fleur the moment the sun was down.

Just a heartbeat later, Gioberto led the other witches into the room where Genevieve and Rowan were standing. "Ms. Aubert, your guests, Mr. Sergio Procella, Mr. Hugo Procella, and Ms. Antonia Procella."

The other witches breezed past Gioberto like he didn't exist, except for Antonia, who paused to thank him and then stepped inside.

It said a lot about a person to watch how they treated anyone in the service industry. Rowan liked Antonia more for it and creepy Hugo and Grandpa less.

"Before we start, I have an official complaint to lodge," Sergio said. Both his grandchildren winced, and Rowan simply pulled her chair out and sat because it hadn't been two minutes and she already wanted to punch these assholes.

He stopped speaking to stare at Rowan, incredulous. As if that would do anything other than annoy her?

"Can I help you?" she asked.

"Let's get on with this," Genevieve said before Sergio could speak. "I assume you're mad, or sad, offended, something similar. The about what part isn't that big a mystery. It could be that I left after your appalling lack of hospitality. It could be that I refused to return to your home after that display of rudeness. It could be that I have Rowan here and she's not a witch. It might even be all of them. Noted. You're sad or mad or offended." Genevieve sat and indicated the other chairs around the table.

Rowan really wanted to start a fan club for Genevieve. Especially when Grandpa Sergio's face darkened, and he started to go on a tirade.

Genevieve held up a hand. "You have two options and only two options, Sergio. You can sit down and answer my questions civilly and truthfully, or you can leave now and consider this rule adjustment a lost cause. That is how this will work. You have no say otherwise."

Antonia looked down quickly but not before Rowan noted the quirk of a smile at the corner of her mouth.

Hugo put his hands up. "I'm sure we can all sit and come to an understanding," he said, holding the chair out for his grandfather, who paused for just a moment but did relent and take a seat.

"I don't see why we can't have this meeting at my home instead of this…place," Sergio said like he wasn't standing in one of the most consistently high-rated and in-demand restaurants in the state.

Genevieve sat and looked Sergio up and down. At his side, Antonia took her seat and sent a hopeful look her grandfather's way.

Hugo took a deep breath, and in that, Rowan saw the cracks in his facade. He was as annoyed with his grandfather as everyone else was. But he had a role to play so he tucked that away and indicated the chair.

"Grandfather, please. This is our opportunity to explain

ourselves to Genevieve. Once she understands our motives, she'll sign and we'll be able to move forward," Hugo said.

"Bah!"

Genevieve knew one of them had attempted to place a security spell over the room. She also knew it didn't work because her counterspell was far more effective. Still, she was glad of it because it allowed her to test the magic of a potential enemy and while all three Procellas were talented witches, none had even a shadow of Genevieve's power.

She'd been watching the interplay between Hugo and Sergio when he said, "Bah!" Rowan's right eyebrow slowly rose. Genevieve thanked her long experience with keeping a bland expression or she'd have laughed at the way Sergio saw it and his spine stiffened as he jumped to his feet with Hugo at his heels.

"What's she doing here?" Sergio demanded of Rowan's presence.

"You're too old to be this rude in the presence of a Senator you need something from," Genevieve said. "You embarrass all witches when you behave in such a fashion to our honored guests." They had no idea what Rowan could be stirred to should they provoke her once too often. That she remained quiet and seated was because of her loyalty to Genevieve. Genevieve would not forget it.

"He's very direct," Hugo rushed to say. "He doesn't mean to offend. We're merely curious as to why an outsider to the Conclave process has been included."

"Imagine a world wherein you address others in the way your grandson just did instead of your approach," Genevieve told Sergio. "And where you make your own apologies for your inexcusable behavior. As for Ms. Summerwaite, you were informed she'd be attending both the meeting at your home yesterday and today's second chance. You've had the opportunity to ask the question civilly but have only responded with the sort of unmannered behavior I expect from children still in short pants and not supposed successful captains of industry."

Sergio's mouth worked as if he was processing all his responses to decide on the best.

"We very much appreciate this opportunity and your time, which I know is precious and in demand," Antonia said.

"Begging your pardon, Genevieve," Hugo said in silky tones that made her skin crawl.

Genevieve looked down at the watch on her wrist and then over to them again. "You can address me as Ms. Aubert, or Senator Aubert." This tendency Hugo had of speaking to her as if they were acquainted and close was unacceptable and she needed to underline that. "You have one minute to sit down or get out," she added to Sergio.

Sergio's gaze narrowed. He wanted to turn on his pretentious heel and storm off, but he couldn't because they needed her. He knew it and best of all, they had to understand Genevieve knew it too.

Genevieve rather hoped she was the reason Sergio had to eat antacids night and day. It was what he deserved. Eternal heartburn.

Meanwhile, Hugo took a seat and turned those beseeching eyes to Sergio. Sergio, who had to see beneath the mask of adoration Hugo wore. And Antonia, waiting, watching. *Calculating.*

Finally, Sergio hauled himself into a chair.

"Thank you for agreeing to see us today," Hugo said to Genevieve.

"Again, our apologies for your reception yesterday. It was inexcusably rude," Antonia told them.

Sergio grunted but gave a quasi-sincere nod of agreement.

Genevieve looked at Rowan. The rudeness was toward the Hunter directly but only Antonia had included Rowan in her gaze as she spoke. Rowan's slight nod told Genevieve she'd noted the same. She nearly felt sorry for Sergio and whatever punishment was to come from Rowan for this behavior toward her.

"I'll get right to the point," Genevieve said.

"I don't talk business with humans in the room," Sergio interrupted as he flicked his gaze to Rowan briefly and then away. "No offense. This doesn't concern her."

Rowan said nothing, but continued to stare at Sergio, unspeaking.

Genevieve narrowed her gaze at him. "I'll decide what concerns who, Procella. All *you've* done since I've made your acquaintance is give offense. Let me disabuse you of these ill-fated ideas you seem to have. You're not in charge here. I don't like what you're asking permission to do. I wanted some more information and every step since I've asked for clarification has been filled with outright rudeness. I have no idea how you prospered in business *without* manipulating humans against their will, if I'm being honest. Because you don't seem to understand how to deal with other people. Especially when you need them."

"We don't want to manipulate humans against their will," Hugo said quickly before his grandfather could speak. "It seems that way, but it's really just temporary and limited only to the audience participation during these shows."

"It seems that way because that's what you're asking to do. The language you're proposing is very vague. That leaves you with a great deal of leeway to do all sorts of things. I cannot support it in its current state," Genevieve explained.

"Would—" Antonia began when her grandfather interrupted her.

"Humans are irrelevant," Sergio said. "We're Genetic witches. I do not seek permission from my inferiors. They want to be entertained. They buy a ticket. We give them a show but you're asking us to be sure they can consent when they can't handle even the most basic of tasks. They don't know what's best for them because they're fools."

Rowan stared at him in such a delightfully unsettling way. Genevieve really did adore her friend.

"Ms. Summerwaite, care to tell them what Hunter Corp. might have to say about such a thing?" Genevieve asked.

"The Treaty doesn't bar being a small-minded fool. Sadly, you're not very rare." Rowan shrugged and continued, raising her voice slightly to continue over Sergio's sputtering. "It does, however, require being sure humans consent, be that to take blood or to be hypnotized by a witch. The Treaty binds *you* to this as it does Vampires. Hunter Corp. is charged with the enforcement of the Treaty."

"She's our competitor and you let her sit at this table. Your position is to represent the interests of witches. Your loyalty should be to us first and last." Sergio sat back in his seat, crossing his arms over his chest. Then he pointed at Rowan. "You can't tell me how to run my business."

Rowan didn't snort, but she did lift a brow again as if to tell Sergio no one told her how to do her job. "Don't flatter yourself. None of you could even dream of rising to be my competition for anything."

"Pay attention now." Genevieve leaned in a little as she spoke. She'd had enough of these witches. "You wouldn't be here if you could go around me. You must know the Senators you've contacted have informed me of that contact. So, to avoid any misunderstandings, let me be plain. I know you discovered they all had the same concerns I do. I also know they informed you none of them would sign on to any changes you proposed without me."

Genevieve found herself delighted by the way Sergio's face got tighter and tighter as her truths rained down on his head.

"Let's discuss those concerns," Antonia began as she caught Hugo's attention and jerked her head as if to tell her brother to get their grandfather calmed down before things got worse.

"I should have known when we heard the rumors about you running off to join those freaks out in the desert," Sergio said.

Hugo turned quickly to his grandfather. "We need to take a few breaths to get ourselves back on track. This is unraveling rather quickly, and we wouldn't want to waste Senator Aubert's time with fighting. She's asking for some clarifying changes. We can accommodate that."

"What is it you're saying about the Dust Devils?" Genevieve asked, ignoring Hugo entirely.

At her side, Rowan shifted slightly, making ready to do whatever it was she needed to protect Genevieve.

Genevieve pulled magic from the Trick and added to her own and let it free. Let them see the error of their ways for coming at her and anyone she protected. Sergio's eyes widened. Hugo got to his feet and Antonia stared, waiting.

"I am the Priestess to a Trick of Dust Devils. Is that what you alluded to?" Genevieve asked, letting all those voices filter through her own. "You don't have any inkling of their true power. Of *my* true power. Know this, old man, I'm stronger than you are in every way. I have more connections, more political clout, more favors owed me than you could ever dream of. Think *you* to challenge my magical gifts? My training? Do try, Sergio Procella. Try me and see what happens to you as a result. I would love to show you."

"Sincere apologies, Genevieve," Hugo said, using her first name again. He attempted to help his grandfather up, but Sergio slapped his hands away.

Antonia met Genevieve's gaze from across the table. "I appreciate your time and apologize yet again for our appalling rudeness. We will work on new wording and get it back to you via proper channels." She stood and went to the door before stepping back, her face gone pale as Clive Stewart, every inch the Scion of North America, glided into the room. The angry energy of him stung like tiny needles.

"You're consorting with Vampires too?" Sergio asked.

"Get this garbage out of my establishment and clean this room thoroughly before guests are allowed in," Clive said to another Vampire who'd appeared out of thin air and Gioberto at his side.

Like a madman, Sergio attempted to use magic to attack Clive. The Scion was far faster and managed to avoid the spell hurled his way. Genevieve reached in and yanked on Sergio's magic, pulling it to herself and disabling it. Clive, very angry after the attempted attack, cuffed Sergio's head hard enough to knock it back and sent the older witch stumbling into a nearby wall.

Before Genevieve could say another word, Rowan

flowed to stand next to her husband and her sword cleared its sheath. The sound rang out and froze everyone in place and that was before she'd brought the edge to Sergio's throat.

Sergio squeaked and Rowan pressed the edge of her blade into his skin until a thin red line beaded up.

"You dare attempt to harm my spouse?" Rowan demanded, her goddess present in the moment in the flow of Rowan's eyes and the echoey nature of her voice.

The energy in the room built steadily.

Then the *throb-throb-throb* of Darius's power flowed down the hall and into the room seconds before he stepped through the door. He crossed the space to stand at Genevieve's back and despite the seriousness of the moment, it left her giddy.

"Surely you must stop her from harming my grandfather," Hugo said to Genevieve, his tone thready with fear.

Genevieve didn't hide the curl of her lip. "Sergio Procella has just used magic to attempt to harm the Scion of North America. In the presence of his wife. In the restaurant the Nation owns and runs. Be grateful you still breathe because Rowan is charged with enforcing the Treaty, *which you have broken.* After you detailed your beliefs that humans are so stupid, they aren't worth free will. Surely even you can see how much trouble you're in at this moment."

"It is my right and obligation to handle such lawlessness," Rowan said, not moving in the slightest. Genevieve wasn't sure if she hoped Rowan would stand down or not and she decided not to say anything either way about it. It was up to the Hunter to decide. "You attacked my husband at a meeting *I* arranged your safe passage to and from. I'm no witch, but I know enough that in all our worlds, a violation of safe passage and harbor is a grave dishonor to the perpetrator. *You* have no honor, Grandpa."

"Self-defense," Sergio shot back, reaching up as if to wipe the blood from his split lip but lightning fast, Rowan knocked it down hard enough she might have broken a bone if Sergio's yelp of pain was any indication. "That Vampire attacked me!"

Genevieve made a cutting motion with the side of her hand. "*No.* You struck first. We all saw it. Scion Stewart would be within his rights to beat you until your bones were dust."

Clive smirked and raised his shoulders as if to say he was still considering it.

"Senator Aubert, perhaps if we could just take our leave. Things will cool down and then we can address this," Antonia said.

"No." Genevieve really liked that word. "It strikes me that your grandfather not only broke our laws, but did so rather casually. Almost as if he does it regularly. It does leave one wondering just how regular an occurrence such a thing is."

"He's an old man frustrated by not being able to run a company he built from the ground up," Hugo said, turning on the humility, trying to draw her into sympathy. "He didn't mean to hurt anyone."

"Or, he's a monster who always wants his own way no matter the cost. Then others have to deal with the carnage in his wake. That's not success, Hugo. We all saw this unfold. Yesterday that scene with Lotte. Then this relentless rudeness since. Despite the fact I was doing your family a favor in giving you a second opportunity to discuss your project. All very odd. But, as Rowan pointed out, not so very rare in a certain type of person. And then on top of all that, he used magic to harm and *not in self-defense* in the full view of a Senator and a partner of Hunter Corp. If he can't control *himself* then I have a great deal of hesitation believing he could ethically handle the manipulation of humans and their consent."

Clive said Rowan's name softly. Not a demand. Just her name. A shiver ran through Genevieve's friend and then Rowan pushed herself back, shoving Sergio toward the door. Clive handed her a handkerchief and Rowan blushed before using it to wipe the blood from her sword and then tucking the snowy-white linen away.

Zara stepped to the doorway, David at her side. Genevieve hoped for Sergio's sake that he kept his magic away from David or Rowan might kill him on the spot.

"Get out of my sight," Genevieve told them.

"She can't do this!" Sergio said heatedly, holding a linen napkin to his throat where Rowan's blade had been.

"I just did. And I'll do it again, old man, if you come at me and mine. Your money and power mean absolutely nothing to me. You can't scare me with it or influence me to let you continue stomping around like a rabid raccoon."

Zara, trying to stifle a smirk at Rowan's remarks, managed to herd Sergio on one side with Hugo and Antonia on the other and soon enough they were all gone.

"Well. That was a thing," Rowan said slowly when they were alone again.

"I'll return in a moment," Darius said and followed the others out.

Clive had to satisfy himself with a look that told his wife just how much he enjoyed that little bit of violence on his behalf.

"We'd made it an entire week without violence," he murmured, brushing a tendril of her hair from her face.

"I'll never get that world record at this rate," she told him.

He grinned at her quickly and then shifted his attention to Genevieve. "Are you all right?" he asked.

"I should be the one saying that to you, don't you think?" Genevieve snapped and then took a deep breath. "Forgive my fit of temper. It's not you. Please allow me to extend an apology on behalf of the Conclave and me personally."

"The air stunk of evasion," he said. "Not outright lies." Those were bitter.

"Grandpa has a whole lot of feelings about himself and his superiority," Rowan said. "His eruptions came directly after his authority was challenged in any way. I bet he's ill acquainted with being told no and you told him so repeatedly in a short span of time. If I could get fifteen minutes at his front door again, I could unravel him and leave him a sobbing mess. That sounds like so much fun."

Clive laughed. He knew that for a fact. She was excellent at finding someone's buttons and weak points and then hammering at them until they broke apart.

"They're fools to have let him come to this meeting," Darius said as he came back in. "The witch and the Hunter's assistant are shadowing the witches to be sure they go home."

"I'm done with the Procellas. They can keep doing their little shows with the rules they have now, along with everyone else of that type," Genevieve said.

"The Procellas aren't done with you though," Darius said.

Clive noted none of them were meeting anyone else's gaze for longer than a second or two. Four very powerful beings in one room meant they all needed to be careful, and he was glad to see they were doing just fine at it.

"Especially not Hugo." Rowan shook her head and then lowered her voice slightly. "Genevieve, I'm bothered by the way he looks at you. He talks to you like you're intimates. Not sex intimates, but like he's on the way."

His wife rarely spoke this way and Clive was relieved to see Genevieve take her words seriously.

Genevieve made a rude noise. "He apparently tried to have that handbag redelivered to my offices at the Conclave. He's been forbidden from sending anything to anyone there now. I certainly will inform the others on my committee of my decision not to sign this change request and to be on the alert for more of this type of ask. I know the others on the committee so I've also mentioned the rumors of perhaps a new movement of these witches trying to loosen our laws and my concern, especially at this point, that it's a slippery slope. I do love that term."

"That's good to hear. If it's cool with you, I'd like to have Hunter Corp. updated and also on the watch for any such moves by practitioners worldwide," Rowan said. "This is Conclave business, and I won't step on that part. But I'm uneasy. There's something happening here we can only see the outline of."

"That *you* see the outline of," Darius said as he came back into the room. "Their reaction to Rowan is far too severe to just be elitism. They want to keep her out of the process and it's getting in the way of their meetings with you, which they need to get this change."

Genevieve appeared to consider it and found herself leaning toward agreement. "I'll need to think on why they're so averse to Rowan."

Rowan laughed at that. "You're going to find lots of people are averse to me."

"Because you can see through bullshit," David said. "It's very difficult to hide from a truth teller."

That was a very good point.

"I have no doubt they're going to file a complaint about Rowan and Clive. We're not going to let them know we have video of the meeting until they claim it was self-defense and accuse me of lying." Genevieve grabbed her handbag. "I'm going to call Samaya now to file my own damned complaint."

"You always deliver a good time," Rowan said. "I need to get back to the office. Clive is reading our other new Vampire hire."

"I'll ride with Darius and meet you there. I can do the read after Clive finishes."

David and Zara also headed out.

When it was just Clive and Rowan, he pulled her close and laid a long, deep kiss on her. When he set her back from him, her eyes remained a little blurry for a bit. "Thank you for protecting me," he told her.

"You're the one who came in here because he was insulting me," she said, answering his question about whether or not she'd known he was watching the feed with David. Rowan grabbed his hand. "Come on. Gioberto said the chef made me a bunch of yummy stuff to take with me after the meeting. I'll eat it while you read Katya. Don't worry, I'll save you some."

"Or you could have a meal with me here," he suggested though he knew she wanted to be in her office where she could speak freely without a bunch of Vampires in her business.

"Normally I'd say yes. It means you take care of yourself, and I can watch," Rowan told him as she gathered her things. "But I want to take care of Katya's readings before we leave for Prague. Then she can get started training and it won't be hanging over my head. And, it gives her extra protection because once she's gone through the full process, she'll be an official employee and that comes with more protection just in case these shitlords of yours decide to make a go at these extrajudicial killings they promised."

He certainly couldn't argue with that. She was right. It would protect Katya and that was important to him as well because Katya was an affiliated Vampire living in his territory. Far from seeing her as betraying the Nation, Clive saw it as the sort of PR one couldn't pay for. A Vampire would have access to Hunter Corp. in ways even he didn't, and he was married to Rowan!

He could help steer the Nation through this very rough patch. A big maybe, but one he felt he could manage because Nadir backed him, as did Paola and Warren. The situation with Tahar and Takahiro was fluid and changing by the hour, but they were beleaguered enough they didn't pose any real threat to the other Scions.

"As you say," he told her as he placed his palm at her left elbow. Normally he might touch the small of her back, but she wore a sword along her spine, so he avoided that.

By the time they got back down to the host stand, Gioberto was there with several insulated tote bags containing their food.

"I'm sorry the witches were so rude to you," Rowan told Gioberto. "They're the ones with poor manners. You were quite perfect the whole time. I know Clive appreciates you and your service. And so do I."

Clive was flooded with pleasure—and pride—at her words. At the way she sought to comfort and lift up one of his people. It was precisely what the partner of a powerful person was supposed to do but Rowan had been born to it. A lot of her so-called training from her father combined with the gifts from the goddess who lived within her had given Rowan a sort of ease that the recipient could see was genuine.

And this particular recipient was a human in service to the Vampire Nation. Not always a place full of acceptance from any direction. Clive made a mental note to check on the salary numbers for the humans in his direct employ. Gioberto deserved a raise and doubtless, others did as well.

Gioberto blushed as he smiled at Rowan with open affection. "I'm pleased to know I was useful to you in such a difficult situation. There's no need for you to take responsibility for those others. That sort of rudeness is more of a reflection on them than on me."

"There's extra security here tonight. If there's a problem or any magic users come in and seem intent on causing a problem, report it immediately," Clive told him on their way out.

"I can't fucking believe that asshole came at you," Rowan snarled once they'd driven away from the valet stand and were on the way back to her office. "If it had been anything but Genevieve's meeting I'd have beat the shit out of his ass."

"You did slice into his neck," Clive purred at her.

She gave him an exasperated look. "Barely. I wanted to lop his head off. He used magic on you. To hurt you. In your own place. And I was the one who made it happen. What if he'd have attacked Gioberto? What if they now think they can come at me through Fleur and those who work there? I was so stupid to bring them there."

"It was incredibly clever to bring them there, as it happens. As flattered and turned on as I am that you defended me so ably, of all the people he could have attacked, I was the perfect target. The entire room is loaded with spy gear so you can watch it all over and over to figure out all the weak spots with these three. You couldn't have done that at your offices. They wouldn't have relaxed the way they did today. You know more now than you did before they came through the door."

Traffic snarled as it often did at this time of day, but he was with Rowan so that was fine with him. Clive wasn't pleased she was blaming herself, so he'd be paying close attention for any repeat so he could nip it in the bud right at the start. She had an impossible job, and she did it to protect other beings. He would not tolerate anyone degrading her path even and especially Rowan herself.

"As for targeting Fleur? I've increased our security. But they won't come for me or mine because he knows I would retaliate until there was nothing left but ashes. And after your reaction to his attack? He'll know you'd be striking the match at my side. They needed to understand that. I watched you in that room. You were calm and remote. Perfection. Until someone under your protection was assaulted. Then you reacted swiftly and violently. Now they know."

# Chapter Seventeen

Rowan waltzed into work the following morning, waving as she caught sight of Genevieve. They hadn't been able to chat much the night before after the meeting at Fleur. There'd been a quick debrief but they'd all gone off in different directions to do other things.

"I was hoping you'd be in soon," Genevieve told her. "Madam made you a batch of muffins. They're still warm."

"Now that's how a gal likes to be greeted when she comes into work," Rowan said. "I need to check in on a few things, but are you free in twenty minutes or so? We can eat muffins, have coffee, and you can let me know what's going on in Conclave land."

After that was handled, she began to go through all her messages. Most were administrative. Those she happily forwarded to David and Vihan.

From Nadir she read, "The parties in question have been located and/or presented themselves to be questioned officially. The Vampire Nation wishes to repudiate, once again, the unsanctioned actions of a small group of lawbreakers and underline its willingness to discuss the ways in which Hunter Corp. and the Nation can work together on issues going forward. My office will be in contact with your assistant to work some meetings regarding the employment issue, into your upcoming Joint Tribunal meetings."

Yadda yadda. But it got the job done and that's really all Rowan cared about. Essentially, they were back at square one, before these lords put themselves in the middle of the process. Rowan had made her hires and the Nation's ability to be part of that was past. But a good clearing of the air and the establishment of some ground rules for the future would be important.

Twenty minutes later, Genevieve and Rowan decided to take some muffins down to the first floor where several of the new employees were receiving their paperwork, getting codes, keys, and assigned workspaces. David moved efficiently through the space, pausing to give directions or answer questions.

"My little man is all grown up," she said to Genevieve, who laughed.

"He's very good at this. You chose well."

"He chose me, as it happens. He assures me it was on purpose. By the way, he left me a note that he had some more data for me on the missing humans situation. I'll make sure he keeps you updated too."

Genevieve's phone rang and when she picked up, Rowan overhead Darius saying something about someone coming toward the building and that Marco was watching.

"He is?" Genevieve asked. "Well, I can't imagine why, but he's no threat to me."

Whatever Darius said was too low for Rowan to hear.

"What's up?" Rowan asked.

Genevieve tipped her chin toward the reception area where Hugo Procella stood holding a giant spray of roses.

"Want me to handle it?"

"Yes. But I need to do it." Genevieve stood taller and headed toward where Malin was telling Hugo to wait while she contacted Genevieve.

"Genevieve," Hugo said while thrusting the flowers at her.

"Senator Aubert. I'm sure I don't know why you're here," Genevieve said, avoiding the vase as he repeatedly thrust them in her direction. Clearly frustrated, he finally put them on the counter of the reception area.

Hugo's gaze cut to Rowan, who simply stared back.

"I was thinking...can we speak privately?" Hugo asked.

Rowan looked to Genevieve, not bothering to give any attention to Hugo. Genevieve nodded slightly that it was okay.

"I'm just going to be over there speaking with David," Rowan said. "Watching in case something needs to be handled." Then she made one of those fingers to the eyes moves before she pointed the same fingers at Hugo.

She stepped just a few feet away and David stood at her side, both with their attention on Genevieve.

How this sense of family and connection had found itself in her life, so at home and deeply comforting, she wasn't sure. But she was too selfish to let it go and head back into a place she felt like she was on her own all the time.

Feeling the need to get away from those damned roses, Genevieve indicated Hugo follow her to a place near the doors. There they'd be in full view of the parking lot where Marco was. Somewhere. In some form. No doubt Darius was either there or on his way after he made that call to tell her Hugo was on the way into the building.

"Here?" he asked, disappointment in his tone. "I thought perhaps your office. Or I can take you to lunch."

"You don't have clearance to leave this area. What do you want?"

"I do hope you won't hold my grandfather's zeal to run his business his way against me personally," Hugo said.

Genevieve had been alive long enough to know what he was doing, and she most fervently did not want anything to do with it.

"I told you everything you need to know yesterday at the conclusion of a meeting you then went home and filed an official complaint about with the Conclave. I will ask once more. Why are you here?"

"I don't think I'm imagining this heat between us. So much chemistry. I'd very much like to get to know you better. We can refuse to discuss business."

"You *are* imagining it, yes. I've told you no multiple times. *I'm not interested.* It's absolutely unacceptable for you not to back off at this point. Though I'm fine refusing to discuss business with you. Please leave and take those flowers with you."

"We got off on the wrong foot. Let me take you out so you can get to know me better."

"I said no." Genevieve kept her expression as bland as she could. "You need to leave. I'm not going to discuss business or personal matters with you."

"Is there someone else? You just moved here. How could you be with anyone yet?"

"I told you the first time I said no to your invitation to dinner. Yes, there's someone else," Genevieve said because she would have felt wrong denying it. The answer wasn't so much about Hugo as it was about herself.

"However, let me make clear that even if there wasn't anyone else the answer would be no."

His magical energy began to coil up and she flicked two fingers his way, freezing him in place and draining the energy from his spell that dissolved all around him.

"What are you doing?" he demanded.

"What are *you* doing? You can't possibly imagine I didn't know the instant you began to build a spell. You come *here* to Hunter Corp. after your performance yesterday? After claiming your grandfather was attacked? After you violated the laws of safe harbor? Then you try to work a spell?"

"I was only going make the rosebuds open fully."

That's when Darius walked in and Hugo's gaze flicked between him and Genevieve, leaving his mouth in a hard, flat line.

"You've been told to go more than once," Darius told him in that very cold and remote way the Devils had with most outsiders.

"You can't possibly choose him over me," Hugo hissed at her.

"Stop this. You're embarrassing yourself."

Rowan bustled over and without pause, grabbed Hugo by the back of his tailored sport coat and dragged him to the doors David held open.

"You've abused my hospitality the last time. You are banned from this building, this parking lot, this area of Las Vegas, and before you tell me I can't do that, I just did. Try me, you ratfucker. *She said no.* Respect that."

"Again, you manhandle me!" Hugo screeched.

"I'm ratfuckerhandling you. Be glad I'm delivering the non-bloody version." Rowan tossed him out onto the sidewalk. "You can report that too." She flipped him off and he scampered away.

"You'll be sorry for meddling, you stupid bitch," he yelled out before getting into his car and zooming out of the lot.

"Sorry for taking that out of your hands, Darius," Rowan told him when she came back over. "But he deserved so much more."

"He says he was only trying to open the roses fully, and that could be true. But I don't trust his word," Genevieve told them.

Darius picked the roses up and strode from the building.

"Okay, then," Rowan said and then looked Genevieve over closely. "You okay?"

"He's very fervent in his affections. It's always unsettling when they're like that."

Rowan nodded with a shudder. "Yeah. I'll have David be sure to get his photo out in all the appropriate places so he can't come back. It's not as if he can get to your home without getting through a few dozen Devils, so that's good to know."

That was blessedly true. Powerful connected witches or not, not a single Procella would get two steps past the very first level of security the Devils had up around the outer edge of their subdivision. Would they try? That remained to be seen. Genevieve would bring it up with Darius to see what he wanted to do.

"So grandpa assface filed a complaint?" Rowan asked.

Genevieve laughed, releasing some of her pent-up tension after that exchange. "He did. It's as we thought it would be. I imagine you have surveillance here?"

"We do. I'll have it pulled and a copy made of the

whole thing, including audio, and sent to you. I really hate tattletales. Especially entitled ones who constantly start shit they can't end but still cry about it and act like they're the victim."

"It's always far more satisfying though when they eventually come up against a stronger opponent. And that's me. And you. I rather find myself quite excited for the moment when I can give over the video evidence to prove them both liars."

Darius came back inside and as he appeared to be unharmed, she hoped that meant there'd been no drama with the roses.

"Those flowers had bad magic in them," he said.

Genevieve started. How could she have missed that? "Explain."

"Obsession and focus magic. When he opened those buds, he'd have triggered it."

Suddenly she very much felt like taking a shower for about an hour to scrub that entire exchange off her skin.

"I still don't understand how I missed it. I felt him start the spell, so I saw that. But if there was a trigger embedded in those roses, I should have seen it."

"If I can interject here?" Rowan asked. "He kept trying to hand you the flowers and you avoided him every time. Finally, he had to put them on the counter. I think maybe it was that you were trying not to focus on them so he wouldn't get any ideas. And also? You did know on some level, right?"

Genevieve considered that and agreed it was very likely.

Rowan said, "And that's why he tried to set the spell off when he did. When he asked if there was someone and you said there was, that's when he decided to just pop it off to coerce you into wanting to go out with him. Which means he's used that spell before because come on, that was very smooth."

"It certainly puts his claims to not want to actually coerce humans to a lie, does it not? If he'd do that to a witch, what would he do to a human? Or any other being he wanted?" Genevieve curled her lip.

"He needs to stop existing," Darius growled so low she barely heard him.

"Let's hold off on that unless there are no other options," Genevieve told him, admittedly fascinated by the way he was reacting.

He harrumphed but didn't say anything, so she had to hope he'd hold off on the killing and such for the foreseeable future.

"I'm quite hungry," she told him. "You should take me to pancakes if you're available right now."

He nodded once at Rowan and then swept out an arm for Genevieve to leave with him.

"I'll be back in an hour or so."

Rowan shrugged. "Your schedule is your own. Have a good lunch. See you later."

Darius had taken the flowers out to the parking lot and destroyed them after noting the dark smudge of obsession magic all over them.

The urge to run Hugo Procella to ground and feed on him until there was nothing left filled his system with adrenaline-fueled aggression. That meatsack had tried to steal Genevieve's will. *Tried to take her.*

"Thank you for coming today," she said quietly. And because she was so quiet, he needed to turn the anger down to hear her.

"Hugo Procella is dangerous. Sergio Procella is dangerous. They are both reckless fools and this distresses me. What will they do next? Now that Hugo seems to consider you something he wants as much as this change to your rules."

"He won't get *anything* he wants. Never me. Not this change. Certainly not now. No matter what wording they propose I won't support it. They can't be trusted. I'm petitioning Konrad to let me investigate their family and businesses."

"I already ordered round-the-clock surveillance on all four Procellas and the house." Truth was, Darius had started the process of investigating the Procellas after that mess the day before, so he'd start tugging a lot more lines of inquiry. "The Trick doesn't need Conclave permission, nor do we need to follow anyone else's rules," he told her before she could mention it herself. Witches—especially his witch—loved rules. He knew that.

But he served chaos, not the Senate. Sergio and Hugo Procella were up to something, and he'd find out just exactly what. Because it involved Genevieve and the way Hugo acted was reckless and unhinged.

It wasn't jealousy.

Yes, he wanted Genevieve with a greed it had been some time since he'd felt the like. But she wanted him with the same openness. What Hugo brought out in him was protectiveness. This asshole posed a threat to Darius's witch.

He took her to the diner she'd introduced him to the prior morning where she settled into a booth. "This is just the thing after such a distressing experience. I'm famished." She smiled at him, so fucking pretty. Her hair had been pulled back from her face, but curls had escaped here and there to frame her features like she was a painting come to life.

Clearly she was a regular because immediately the server brought them both coffee and Genevieve a large glass of orange juice as well.

It was a good thing he liked pancakes, because if that's what made her happy, he'd feed them to her every day.

When the food arrived she ate steadily but he didn't fail to notice a fine tremor in her hands more than once. Finally he reached out and took one of her hands in his. It was ice cold.

"What is it?" he asked.

"Not here," was all she'd say.

They finished up and instead of taking her back to the Hunter Corp. building, he drove them out to the open desert, knowing on some level she needed that.

Just that morning before he'd left home, Marco had handed him a folded-up blanket and told Darius to put it in the trunk just in case he needed it. Darius had done as he'd been told because Marco knew things.

And, as Darius spread it out so they could both sit on an outcropping of rocks, he knew this was what Marco had meant.

"You don't have to tell me anything," he said as she settled at his side. "I just want you to be able to unburden yourself. That's all."

She put her head on his shoulder a moment, leaning into him, and he wrapped an arm around her as she did. The day wasn't cold, but she shivered and snuggled in closer, so he squeezed her tighter until she seemed to calm.

"The coercion spell just brought up an old memory."

He stiffened and she hesitated. The last thing she

needed was his response right then. He shoved it away and slowly ran a hand up and down her back until she relaxed again.

"Before I married Tristan, there was another I was engaged to. Our families were pleased at the way to unite their houses. I'd been trained all over the world even at that point. I was about two hundred or so and thought I could make my space within a marriage and be satisfied with that. He often treated me like I was a spoiled child with no real idea of how the world worked when in truth I was by far the more widely traveled of us. I'd learned more disciplines than he had. I was more gifted. Then he began to blame my father for entertaining such ideas of independence. I hadn't lived in the same home as my father since I was a very small child. I'd had to fight and claw my way to have enough power to make my own choices and as we got closer to signing the wedding contract I became certain I would be a prisoner. My light dimmed so his could glow brightest.

"I'd written a letter to my father telling him all this. We weren't close, as you know, but I knew if I told him, he'd be on my side when I broke things off. But when he arrived a month later, I… I'd forgotten. My fiancé pretended it had been a forgery and my father pretended to believe him but several hours later he sent people to my rooms to pack everything and told me we'd be leaving within the hour."

Darius had a feeling he knew where this was headed and more of that color seeped into his life when a throb of heartache filled his chest.

He swallowed hard against a knot of emotion.

"I didn't even ask questions. I just grabbed a few important things, and we rode away. He told me some hours afterward when we'd stopped to change horses that my fiancé had used a similar spell to the one Hugo did. No one but my maid knew of that letter I'd sent to my father. If he hadn't come or hadn't seen something was off in my behavior, I'd have married and never known why I was so desperately unhappy."

Darius would deal with Hugo Procella for this. For bringing these memories to the surface. For attempting to harm Genevieve physically. But first he needed to comfort her. Put her before everything else.

"I'm sorry. And I'm sorry today stirred all that up."

"You saved me," she murmured.

"I think Rowan was correct when she said your avoidance of the flowers at the start was because you knew on some level something was wrong. Moreover, you are not the same Genevieve you were five hundred years ago. You would have fought through it this time."

"But I didn't have to. Thank you. I just had a flash. It happened a long time ago."

"You didn't have to, no. I've got you. Not just because you're our priestess." He said things to her he hadn't planned to say out loud all the time. "The Procellas will not harm you."

They stayed there on the blanket, Genevieve tucked into his side, for another hour until she finally stood, stretching.

"You need to tell Konrad about this," he said. Though he wanted to handle it himself, Darius knew it was important the leader of the Conclave Senate—and Genevieve's father—needed to be informed and allowed to address this breach.

Darius would still deal with Hugo after all was said

and done. The witch needed to understand where he was in the larger scheme of things.

"You're right. I'll call him when I get back to work. He might want to talk to you about the spell."

"Understandable. I'd want all the information possible in his place as well." Darius realized too, she might need a little more reassurance after she'd been shaken. "I took everything. Every last bit of energy. There's nothing left of the flowers, the vase, the water, or the spell. I give you my word."

"I trust you," she said and then grinned for a moment, utterly beautiful. "But I also can't deny I'm very curious about Dust Devils and how your magic works."

Pleased, he hugged her to him quickly, kissing the top of her head. Though he wanted to take her home where she'd be surrounded by so many layers of safety and security nothing could harm her, he didn't want to clip her wings. She needed to be her normal confident and self-assured Genevieve. He understood that.

"You'll learn as you go. Being our priestess will mean your officiating at rites and ceremonies of all types."

"You're teasing me," she said, shaking out the blanket before folding it and handing it over.

On the way back to work, she called her father.

"I need to speak with you about something," she told Konrad.

"Something to do with the Procella family?" he asked. "What's happened?"

"I'm unharmed. But earlier today Hugo Procella attempted to set off a coercion spell he'd put into some flowers he was trying to give me. The flowers and the spell have been destroyed. If he could so easily use such a spell on me, how can we allow the rule change they want? They clearly have no intention of being responsible and no problems taking whatever they want whether they're offered it or not."

She told him about the video and audio from the HC lobby and that she'd send it his way.

"You will file an official complaint. That's what you're doing right now," her father told her. "I needed the Medicis. Before," he said, meaning the powerful family of her ex-fiancé who had been helping fund the armies defending magic users. "Things are different now. There will be an investigation. You can't do it, you're too close now. But there are others who are more than qualified. Are you safe?"

"The Dust Devils have a guard on me twenty-four hours a day. I can't explain my living situation over the phone, but suffice it to say I'm very secure at home. Rowan was already in the process of tightening security and dealing with the Hunter Corp. response to Hugo's behavior so I've no doubt she's already got things in place or about to be."

"He won't let you come to harm," Konrad said. Not a question.

"No. I will not," Darius said, obviously overhearing the whole call.

"Good. I'm going to get this complaint process started when we end this call. Send me everything you think will help. I plan to let the Procellas know they are to stay away from you. If you see them, contact me or my office immediately."

"If I see any of them trying to get access to Genevieve you should hope your witches can get to them before I can. Fair warning," Darius said.

Konrad was silent for several moments before clearing his throat. "I'm sure I didn't hear that last part. Take care of yourself."

"I have not met the father of my…sweetheart since I was a very young man," Darius said after Genevieve disconnected the call, making her laugh.

Telling him about her past had taken the weight of it from her. Not entirely. Even five centuries later the thought of how powerless she'd been and hadn't even known it still sent panic through her system. But it had created another deep tie to him. A moment of shared confidence and vulnerability.

She reached out to cup his wrist for a few moments. Just a touch because she'd needed it. He turned his hand then and tangled their fingers together, kissing her knuckles.

Genevieve leaned back in the seat, and despite all the things going on in her life, satisfaction settled into her bones.

And she let it.

# *Chapter Eighteen*

The next afternoon after she and David had left a lunch meeting with some of the new employees, Rowan dropped David off at the office. "I need to run home to grab a file I left behind. Be back in half an hour or so."

"I can go get it if you'd rather," he said, always helpful. "Or Elisabeth would be happy to bring it over."

She knew Elisabeth would do that without blinking. Or that she could have sent David in her stead. But she wanted a few minutes on her own to think over all the puzzles in her head and she told him so.

David nodded and jumped out. "Got it. See you in a bit."

Rowan had had another dream. One she was still puzzling over. She'd talk to Clive about it when he woke for the day. If Genevieve was around—and Rowan wasn't sure if she was or not because there'd been some back-and-forth to Los Angeles to deal with official Senate stuff—she'd be helpful too if for nothing more than listening while Rowan broke it all down.

Ships. Storms. Then empty places. Empty parks. Deserted grocery stores and malls. Some of the same imagery from the first dream but it seemed more…nuanced.

And the empty places, that chilled her more than anything else.

She should have written it down in the dream journal, but there'd been so much to do and she figured she'd work it out and then write it down when she got home for the papers she needed. The problem of working out of several places was she ended up leaving stuff invariably in the office space she was not. Rowan needed to train herself out of that. Maybe she'd get two decent-sized baskets she could leave at the door to her office to put all the necessaries she'd need in to carry back and forth?

The light went red, and she sat in the left-turn lane, thinking. That's when she did a double take at the sight of Carl, her own personal sage, standing on the sidewalk with about a million others.

She rolled her window down to look more closely. The light turned green, so she inched up to wait for a spot in traffic. Rowan waved at Carl, and he looked straight at her and mouthed, *watch out.*

Then the sound seemed to slow and speed up just a second later and that's when she saw the big armored SUV in oncoming traffic, veering into her lane. Too fast. It was going to blow through the red light.

Rowan looked in multiple directions to find herself an avenue to get out of the way without hitting anyone else and that's when she noted a similar SUV coming from the opposite direction—her passenger side—speeding toward the intersection.

No. Not the intersection. At her.

She hadn't even noticed the one that hit her first, against the driver's side door, but then in rapid succession, she was hit on her passenger side and head-on. The airbag blew with a strange sound, pinning Rowan to her seat as the contents of the car flew in the air. Pens, a lipstick from her handbag, the Mike & Ike's she'd been eating pelted multicolored missiles against her arm and the side of her face.

Though it felt as if ten minutes had passed, it had only been seconds and Rowan knew if she was going to survive, she had to move.

Ears ringing as the seconds ticked by and she tried to get her limbs to move, Brigid rose to the surface hard and fast enough to bring a gasp to her lips. Get moving. Live. The panic ebbed, adrenaline pumping into her system with the heat of the Goddess's magic.

"Okay," she managed to say when she got herself turned enough to squeeze between the driver's seat and the ruined passenger side where David might have been sitting.

Rowan dropped into the footwell of the back seat, panting with the pain that threatened to steal her consciousness. Brigid beat at her ears, ordering her to stay awake. To fight back.

"Okay," she told herself as she managed to make her fingers work and dug her miraculously unbroken phone from her back pocket. She hit redial on whoever she'd called last, which was thankfully Genevieve.

"Rowan?"

"Help," she said and gave the cross streets. Then the bullets began to hit the car. Thank goddess for the extra armor plating. Most of what Rowan thought of as a hail of bullets pinged off, but that would only last so long.

Genevieve told her to leave the line open so she could listen along and help if needed so Rowan tucked the phone in her bra and got herself over the second bench of seating and into the trunk space. There was a weapons locker back there but her keys had flown through the car along with everything else and the thumbprint scanner had been damaged.

She gave a look around the area, trying to find something to use to break it open, and a bullet pierced through the back where she'd been crouched, tearing through her calf. It had gone through but no doubt it would slow her down.

It was broad daylight on the fucking Las Vegas Strip! Cameras everywhere! Who the fuck was taking such a bold chance?

Another bullet broke through, this one lodging in her left shoulder and the pain got her moving.

The rear liftgate was stuck so she managed to shift herself around, bleeding all over the damned place to kick it open with her right—unwounded—leg.

All the while the sound of weapons being discharged and bullets hitting metal, asphalt, and glass rendered her nearly deaf and the stench of cordite stung her lungs.

*They could have killed David.*

That was the thought that gave her strength to push past the pain and continue until the damned liftgate finally released, dropping her to the ground at the rear of her SUV. The fall jolted all her aches, but it also spurred her forward as the battle took over her entire focus.

The sounds and the smell all faded as she crouched and duckwalked around the backs of the other vehicles to sneak up on the two massive dudes wearing ski masks and shooting high-caliber ammo from weapons on full auto.

She paused to take in as much of the scene as she could. It looked like three armored SUVs had crashed into hers and none of them would be driving away from the scene.

But she did see similarly dressed figures running toward a waiting car that barely paused long enough for them to get in before tearing off. Rowan didn't see anyone else but the two shooting so she needed to focus and take them out.

Complicating matters—meaning she couldn't just walk up and shoot these dudes in the back of the head—was the public nature of the situation because it would be on camera and the sidewalks all around were full of onlookers filming with their cameras.

Rowan took a deep breath and it hurt so bad her vision went gray a moment. Too late for crying over it, she had a duty to protect the secrets of the paranormal world from discovery and so instead of shooting them in the head with the rifle she'd take from one of them, she grabbed the tire iron in a baseball bat hold and used all her strength to hit a triple against the back of the first one's head. When he crumpled into a boneless heap she snarled and felt the wound on her split lip open again.

The other shooter spun, his weapon still discharging and hitting her at least two more times. It was now or never. This dude would kill her first if she wasn't smart. He tried to knock her down, punching her in the face, sending her stumbling, jostling new hurts to the surface.

It just made her angrier.

He tried to knock her down again, but she was slick with blood and glass and he wasn't full of rage like she was. She bared her teeth, screaming at him as she jumped up onto his chest and used her weight to topple him to the road. She ignored the screaming pain in her leg as she clamped her thighs around him to hold her position as she then set to pummeling his face.

The sound came rushing back as he finally lost consciousness and she sagged off his body, trying to breathe around daggers of pain in her chest.

People from the sidewalk began to run at them, dragging the bad guys away from where she'd gotten to her knees.

Bystanders tried to talk to her, holding out their hands to help, and she shook her head, shrinking back.

An ambulance arrived and she managed to get herself into a position to lean against it so she wouldn't collapse or take a nap right there in the street.

Carl hurried in her direction, Star at his side.

*Star?*

Rowan looked down at herself and realized she'd been shot more than those two or three times. Blood rushed from her with each beat of her heart, leaving her faint.

"Oh. I've been shot a lot. That rhymes," she mumbled.

"Rowan, you're safe now," Carl said and then she passed out.

Clive came to consciousness quickly, sitting up on a gasp. The buzzer connected to the automatic locks on the door and windows to his bedchamber droned on until he managed to stumble to his feet to check the camera.

He unlocked immediately when he saw it was Genevieve.

"What?" he demanded.

"It's Rowan," she said.

He grabbed her upper arms, and the Dust Devil must have been in the connecting room between his and Rowan's bedchambers because he heard a snarl. Clive's incisors lengthened as his consciousness rose and he realized something was very wrong with Rowan. She was alive. He could tell that much through the bond. But unconscious.

Genevieve said, “Stop this. Both of you. Darius, please wait in the living room. Your presence is only going to make things worse.” Then to Clive again, gently. “You have twenty-eight more minutes until sundown. Betchamp is organizing things now so we can move once that happens.”

“Where is my fucking wife?” Why was she unconscious?

“I’ll allow that loss of composure because you’re afraid. She’s alive. There was an accident. No. An ambush. Rowan was driving back here to pick something up. Three cars from different directions slammed into her at once from multiple sides. There’s video, that’s part of what Betchamp is doing. Getting that handled so you can see it and know what to do. *She is alive*,” Genevieve repeated.

“Scion, I have your portable computer with the traffic video queued up,” Betchamp said as he entered the room. He’d closed off the sitting room as well so they moved out there because even though it was an emergency, anyone being in a Vampire’s bedchamber while the sun was up sent that Vampire into fight or flight and they didn’t need any more complications than they already had.

Clive’s head spun. He needed to know so much more. Needed to go to his wife but until the sun finally went down, he was stuck.

Betchamp led him to a chair and then before he hit start, he looked Clive in the eyes. “As Ms. Aubert said,

Ms. Rowan is alive. This video is upsetting. Hold yourself together. She needs that."

On the screen Clive watched the traffic feed. Rowan at the wheel of her car, waiting to make a left turn. Because he knew what was coming based on what Genevieve had said, he caught sight of the three oncoming vehicles, big, beefy SUVs that appeared to have been armored. They struck Rowan's—thankfully also armored—SUV from the front and two sides.

Rowan's airbag went off so he couldn't see much more than the mass of the bag itself. Steam rose from the wreck as one of the SUVs opened up at the back and two people in ski masks carrying weapons got out and began shooting at the front driver's side of Rowan's vehicle.

People had begun to stop and gather on the roadway, pointing. Phones to ears as they hopefully were calling an ambulance instead of the media. A few people tried to run toward Rowan's wreck but had to retreat as the bullets peppered the whole area.

Clive held his breath the whole time he watched the ski-masked people continuing to shoot Rowan's SUV. The other two attackers burst from their wrecked vehicles and headed in opposite directions.

That's when the back doors of Rowan's SUV opened and his wife, covered in blood, tumbled out to the pavement with a thunk he felt to his bones. Then, out of the view of her shooters, she skirted the wreck and ended up behind them.

She glanced up at the traffic camera and instead of shooting the attackers in the face like he could see she really wanted to, she had tested the weight of the tire iron in her hand before she wound up like she was playing baseball and hit one in the back of the head so hard he immediately hit the pavement. The other turned and tried to beat her into submission but clearly the man had no real idea who Rowan Summerwaite was because she'd writhed and spun as they rolled around on the roadway, the tire iron clattering away.

Clive held his breath, watching his wife scramble atop her attacker's chest, gripping with her thighs like she was riding a horse without a saddle. Her face was a mask of vicious concentration as she used her fists until her opponent's head flopped to the side in a way to indicate he was unconscious.

When that happened, some of the crowd rushed in to help.

There was a fracas but shortly, Rowan was hauled from the fray.

She pulled herself to stand, nearly fell again, and then shifted her weight. Broken leg most likely. An ambulance showed up and Clive could tell at a glance given the way the EMTs moved, they weren't human. Which was good because it meant their people had shown up to help before human authorities could take her to one of their hospitals.

Before the EMTs could reach her though, Rowan took two steps toward…fuck, Carl? And then crumpled into the sage's arms before she could hit the ground.

Everyone went into hyper speed then and before long, she'd been loaded into the back of the ambulance and it had sped away but Clive couldn't see the point where Carl appeared or disappeared. He was there and then not. Chances were though, he'd stepped in somehow to save Rowan. The next time that crazy old sage kidnapped them for a prophetic taxi drive, Clive planned to thank him.

"Where is she?" he managed to ask, surprised he didn't sound as worried as he felt.

"At a local private hospital. There's a wing we control," Genevieve said. "She's under guard. There were some broken bones. She's been shot fourteen times. There was a great deal of blood loss. That's why she collapsed. They operated and she's in recovery."

Hearing it all listed filled him with dread and an intense need to see Rowan, know she was still in the world.

Genevieve touched his wrist, just a light, reassuring brush of her fingertips. "There's no question she'll recover, Clive. I'll take you directly there now the sun's down."

"Sir," Betchamp said once Genevieve had left to speak with Darius. "Please feed from me and Elisabeth before you go. You'll need to give Rowan your blood at some point and you might need to fight or otherwise burn through a great deal of power."

Though most Vampire families—the Stewarts included—fed from their closest household staff to create bonds and give their human staff the extra protections that came with it, Clive had a select group of humans he employed to give him their blood. All male now as he knew Rowan was uncomfortable enough as it was, with the intimacy of sharing blood. All a certain type of human many of his brethren—the asshole ones—referred to as blood servants. Essentially they had genetic markers that made them into the creators of blood that was the best possible for a Vampire.

They could easily survive with the blood from humans who didn't have those markers. But it was a difference in how much one needed to take and how many benefits came to the Vampire who fed from them.

All that aside though, his usual donors were roughly a ten-minute flight from the house, and it was still daylight for another twenty-one minutes. And, Elisabeth and Betchamp both were among those he paid to take blood from when necessary.

"Thank you. I'm going to get dressed. Give me ten minutes and I'll meet you back here."

Everything hurt.

Rowan tried to open her eyes, but it was hard. She might have dropped back into that safe, dark space a few times but finally she caught the scent of book leather and expensive whiskey with a whisper of peat.

Clive was nearby and he'd be worried, so she needed to reassure him. And maybe she needed some reassurance too.

"Rowan, I really must protest. Wake up this instant or I shall be very cross," he said. Even her muddled brain heard the anxiety in his tone.

"Trying," she mumbled. The tightness as she tried to move told Rowan she'd been stitched up in several places. She managed to wiggle her toes and twitched her fingers slightly. Not all of them, she realized. There was a splint on her left hand and three of her fingers were bound.

"There you are," he said, his voice right up against her ear. "Open your eyes, darling."

Nothing happened when she tried to reach up to pry her eyelids open with her right hand. Her limbs were heavy and numb.

"She's regaining consciousness. Please get someone," Clive said to someone on the other side of her closed eyes.

David answered and relief coursed through Rowan that he was all right.

Rowan managed to get one eye open. "Can't work the other one yet," she said.

"It's swollen shut. I'm going to give you my blood."

"Wait," Genevieve said as she came into the room. "The police are here. They want to talk to Rowan. Right now, she looks like she was hit by three giant SUVs and shot fourteen times. If you give her blood, she'll start healing far faster."

Rowan managed to squeeze his hand a little. "Gonna be fine. Let's do this part. Want to leave soon as possible." It took far longer than she'd expected to finish those three sentences, but her brain was working a little better every minute she was awake. Cops had to be dealt with after that scene in the middle of the street. And Genevieve was right. Let them see her all mangled up and then she could take Clive's blood.

"I'm not leaving the room," he said in a tone that threatened violence if anyone argued.

Someone new spoke, "You don't have to. You're her spouse. Rowan, I'm Dr. Jenkins. I'm going to be here when they speak to you as well. First, let's look you over. They're not coming in until I know you're up to very gentle questions."

Rowan managed to focus her eye enough to take the doctor in. Basic white coat thing. Slate gray sweater beneath that did something for her light brown eyes and skin. Threads of silver shot through her short curls. Rowan liked the way Dr. Jenkins stood. Ready to punch someone if they caused trouble.

"Love scary women," she said and blamed the damned drugs.

Thank the Goddess there'd been drugs that worked. Being a Vessel meant most drugs used for sedation didn't fit with her metabolism. She burned through them too fast. A great feature when it came to things like poison. Fortunately, there were a few medications that managed to do the job, which meant they'd known who—and what—she was.

Dr. Jenkins smiled. "Good to hear. Eight of the fourteen bullets remained lodged in your body so we needed to get you into surgery to repair the damage to your left kidney and lung. Your eye should be fine once the swelling goes down. You've got a broken tibia, three broken fingers, severe bruising, and some muscle tearing in your chest, but your ribs are miraculously unbroken."

At Rowan's other side, Clive had gone into that silent, still place Vampires went when they were murderous.

"After some Vampire blood you'll be more comfortable. Your husband is correct," Dr. Jenkins said as an appeal to Clive. "I think you're up to a ten-minute *maximum* interview with the police. The sooner that happens, the sooner you can get on up out of here and at home where everyone will feel safer."

"Okay," Rowan said. The quicker they could get her away from all the patients there and into a more well-guarded place, the better.

Two police officers came in and one of them physically recoiled when she saw the state Rowan was in.

The other cop with her took a quick look around the room, noting Clive and the doctor.

"If you can step outside while we speak to her. We won't be very long," the male officer said. He had teeny-tiny eyes, like a bird without the charm.

"I'm her husband. I'll be staying. As will her doctor," Clive told them, all cultured and shit. Rowan ignored the compulsion he used.

"Just to establish some basics. You're Rowan Summerwaite and you were involved in a traffic incident earlier today?" Tiny Eyes asked.

"Yeah," Rowan told him.

"Traffic incident is an interesting term for what happened," Clive said dangerously.

"And you're a...private investigator here in Las Vegas?"

It made her dizzy to nod so Rowan answered in the affirmative.

"Your address on file is an office building."

Clive interrupted. "That's not a question. It's a statement. You can make statements when my wife isn't in the recovery room after nearly dying. My turn to ask questions. Where did you take the men Rowan disabled? And did you find the ones who fled? Who are these people?"

"They're both in the hospital. One is in a coma from the head injury you gave him. The other is under sedation."

"Wait for me to cry over it with my one good eye," Rowan managed.

"Do you know why anyone would want to hurt you like that?" the other officer asked.

"I deal with scumbags sometimes. Not usually scumbags who come at me like mercenaries." Rowan winced as she tried to move to a more comfortable position and her stitches tightened. Things in her belly hurt. "What does the video show? I know there had to be a feed at that intersection."

"Awfully convenient," Tiny Eyes said.

"I love it when surgeons dig bullets out of my body and fix my torn-up internal organs. Lucky me. What's your fucking problem?" Rowan snarled at him, annoyed she didn't sound as scary as normal when her face was a swollen mess.

Clive stood, getting himself between the police and the bed. He was beyond livid. His outrage rushed through their bond, cold and fast, and she was in no condition to deescalate or give him backup. *Oh shit.*

"I was of the understanding you wanted to speak to Rowan about her attempted murder. In the middle of the afternoon. Complete with an audience because—which is also why there are cameras—it's a busy tourist intersection with three of the four major casino hotels. If you're not here to do your job and interview a crime victim, get out. You can speak to her via our attorneys from now on while I call the governor about this."

"You're upsetting the patient," Dr. Jenkins said. "Time to go."

"Wait just a minute," Tiny Eyes said.

"Officer Rankin, ease back," the other one told him quietly. "We have absolutely no reason to believe she's anything other than a victim of a rather unusual violent crime."

And there was nothing they could pin on Rowan for that attack because she sure as fuck had nothing to do with it. Since everyone was being calm-ish, she figured there wasn't anything supernatural on camera.

Tiny Eyes could eat a bag of cold, unsalted dicks.

"He has to leave," Rowan said carefully through swollen lips. He had bad energy, and she didn't want him anywhere near her.

Clive didn't move until Tiny Eyes left.

"He's a transfer and super eager to prove he's brilliant so he can be promoted," the other officer said, clearly annoyed. "Hope that's soon so I can work with someone else."

Clive grunted but sat back at Rowan's side again. He looked her over carefully, wincing when he paused at her neck and chest.

The questions were a lot more relevant after that. Rowan was certain David was at work on their sources within the police department to get more answers than they'd ever give her during an ongoing investigation.

"If you think of anything else, please give me a call." The officer held up a business card and placed it on the nearby bedside table. "This is early days, but if anything major develops, I'll reach out."

After a few more questions, she finally left.

"When can we give her Vampire blood?" Clive demanded once they were all alone once more. "When can I take her home?"

Dr. Jenkins poked and prodded a few minutes longer before saying, "My recommendation is that you give her a very small amount. She's already supercharged. Her system is healing itself at an exponential rate."

"Not fast enough," Clive said.

"If the cops come back or need to speak to me again and I look dramatically recovered in too short a time it could be problematic," Rowan said, trying to be diplomatic.

"I don't bloody care about problematic. You're lying there struggling to breathe, trying not to move because you're in pain. That's my concern."

"I know. Thank you. But even a sip or two will help. I'll feel way better tomorrow. I can take more after the threat of having to be interviewed again has passed. Just like a day or two at the most."

He leaned in and spoke in her ear. "I will be helpless and unconscious for part of tomorrow. I will not have you here unless it's medically necessary. And if it's medically necessary you will take my blood until it's not."

"Give me a sip, for fuck's sake," she said. "Then we see where I am in an hour."

He growled but stood to remove his suit coat and roll up his sleeve so he could offer his wrist after slicing it open for her.

Clive wanted to rip someone apart.

After taking a few small sips of his blood, Rowan had closed her eye and fallen into sleep.

"Let her rest. Give the blood an hour or two to work. Let's assess then to gauge when she can go home," Dr. Jenkins told him.

Genevieve came back into the room with David.

"I need to deal with my people. I'm just stepping next door into the lounge. I don't want her to wake up without me here and not know where I am," Clive said.

David nodded. "I'm not going anywhere. I can get work done here. Vihan is holding the office together just fine. I won't leave her alone." He paused. "You should know her father has called multiple times."

Clive pinched the bridge of his nose. He'd had Alice inform Nadir of Rowan's attack not too long after he'd arrived at the hospital, but he knew they couldn't hold off dealing with the First forever. The sun would be rising there soon enough. "Thank you for letting me know. I'll handle it."

Genevieve patted his arm on his way past. "I'm here as well. Darius is in the waiting room. No harm will come to her. We're all here now. She's going to be okay."

He wasn't there when she'd been attacked. But that extra armor he'd had custom plated for her vehicle had helped save her life.

Clive held on to that and knew he'd use this as an argument for every single security measure he insisted on for the rest of her life.

He didn't need to call Alice because when he walked out into the hallway she was there, Patience at her side.

"They said we could use this lounge," Clive said as he led the way and closed the door behind them.

"First, is she all right?" Alice asked.

"She'll recover." He ran through the list of injuries. He didn't say he'd given blood or that she'd have absolutely died if the attack had happened two years before. Rowan would hate for Patience to have too many details of any possible weakness. "They're keeping her under observation for the next few hours to see if she can be transferred to the house."

"You'll tell us what you need," Alice said and then pulled an insulated cup from her bag and handed it to him. "Tea."

"Thank you. Update," he said to Patience.

"We've got copies of the surveillance footage. Got a partial plate on the car that picked up two of the runners. The third we're still tracking. Gathering more information and video angles trying to follow him. They can't be Vampires because it was full daylight, but they moved like paras," the head of his security said.

"Agreed. Witches. Maybe Weres." The shooters were beefy, broad shouldered. Like tanks. That indicated a shifter but there were witches who were linebackers too.

"The SUVs used weren't stock. They were custom," Patience added. "Seth is on that. He and David have connected. Hunter Corp. has some contacts in that world too."

"I want security on the house. Triple the guard but keep it discreet." If Rowan saw three times as many guards as usual his wife would not be pleased. He also didn't want to wave a giant red flag indicating someone important was inside.

"There was a police officer today. Last name Rankin. I want to know everything there is to know about him." The manner with which he'd treated Rowan was simply outrageous and he would not tolerate it. He just needed to understand more before he decided how he'd deal with it.

"Just because it was daylight doesn't mean it wasn't a Vampire who organized the attack," Clive said. "Could be witches as we said. There's something happening with them, though I have no idea exactly what. But Rowan has been working with Genevieve on it and there've been a few problems over the last day or two especially."

"I will continue to coordinate with David," Alice said carefully, reminding him his wife would not be pleased if she felt they were doing things without her or around her. This was most definitely a Hunter Corp. issue and as soon as she could stay conscious for longer than a few minutes, she'd tell him that herself. Repeatedly.

Clive couldn't wait until she was well enough to harangue him once more.

His phone rang. Nadir. He held it up to quiet the other two and then answered without preamble. "She's out of surgery and healing." He detailed the list of injuries and what the surgery had addressed. "I gave her some blood. They're observing her for the next two hours or so to see if she can come home tonight. To be frank with you, she's hard to look at right now without wanting to burn something down. You've seen the camera footage so you'll understand she's bruised from the accident and then the fight afterward. There are myriad stitched-up wounds. She's swollen." He had to swallow back his emotion for a moment. "I'm not sure it's a good idea for any sort of video chats with her and anyone else at least for a day or two." Like her father. "I've got people on the surveillance video and tracking the attackers who escaped. I need to get someone into that hospital where they're holding the two Rowan took down. One is in a coma." It was easier for Clive if the guy stayed that way. He could take those memories without a struggle. It was a matter of getting the information and eliminating the suspects before they could reveal the existence of paranormal beings to humans.

Nadir blew out a breath. "You have access to Nation resources to make that happen. Is this connected to Vampires?"

"I do not know. It's very coincidental that it happened right after this situation with the lords. But Rowan busily makes mortal enemies of powerful beings on a regular basis. It comes to her as easy as breathing."

"Her father is unsettled and worried. I have convinced him, after lengthy discussion, to remain here at the Keep rather than traveling to Las Vegas to see her himself. I take your point about a video call, but a call of some sort after sunset for us would be a good thing," Nadir said very carefully.

In other words, the First was worked up because his child was hurt, and he was too far away to do much of anything other than worry. And Clive understood that part. Rowan was not in any shape to manage her father's emotional state, but Nadir was telling him that a call was necessary or things would escalate. He didn't want the First in his guest room.

"Any update on the lords situation?" he asked. If Rowan had to deal with her father while Clive was at daytime rest, he'd at least be sure she knew what was going on so she wouldn't be making that call cold.

"Andros managed to find the stragglers after an enterprising Scion or two managed to locate their hiding place. They're all here now. Below. The First is leaving them there a few days, but I've had a chat with them. There are things I would speak to you about when you're not at the hospital on a cellular phone. They can all wait for the time being. Go tend to Rowan."

"I'll have David work with her to set a time to have a brief call with him. She'll be healing still." *So please try to keep the First in line.* He couldn't say that part out loud, but he hoped she heard it anyway.

## *Chapter Nineteen*

Genevieve took a deep breath, letting it out slowly. It wasn't the time to lose her composure. There was a lot to do. She needed to give an update on Rowan's condition and find out if there'd been any news from the searches they'd been running through Genevieve's office at the Senate.

Zara had a contact in the Las Vegas PD, so she and David had combined those resources and were expecting some more information by midnight or so when their person was off shift and could meet them.

The Vampires apparently had a plan for dealing with the two attackers currently in custody. David had called some sort of special threat level for Hunter Corp. All across the world wherever Hunters were, they'd take extra care. They all wanted to know who it was that had attacked Rowan. And why.

Many parts were moving, all searching for answers. So many smart people looking there was no doubt they'd eventually find them.

Genevieve wanted the answers too, though she was worried it would be connected to the magical community. She was the one who'd brought Rowan into their world.

*This* was why she held herself back from getting attached to anyone new. Being in Genevieve's world was dangerous. Immortality was a gift, but not without a price. To walk among those whose pace could never equal hers was bittersweet. Still, Rowan wasn't human. Her life burned bright and steady within her, and Genevieve believed it would continue to do so for centuries if she managed not to get killed in the interim.

She wasn't going to think about that part. Instead, she reported what she knew thus far to Samaya and then Konrad, dashing off several texts and emails after that.

The moment she slowed down all she could think about was how Rowan had sounded when she'd called for help. How Genevieve had listened to groaning metal, the slap of bullets hitting the armored parts of the car, Rowan's breathing as she'd moved, the grunts of pain, the intake of breath and at one point, a sob.

Shoving her fear away, Genevieve went cold as she'd gone to her backyard, opened the slider, and called Darius's name. He'd come immediately. As he always had.

Rowan wheezed out the intersection her car had been wrecked at. Genevieve heard herself calmly tell her friend she was getting help and to keep the line open so she could follow along.

It had been muffled then, but clear enough to get the horror of it all.

Genevieve had her cellular device to one ear when Lorraine had rushed in, thrusting her phone at Genevieve. Urging her to use it. She did, arranging an ambulance and a medical team to be waiting at the hospital for Rowan. Then she had to call David and that had been…a lot. Darius too had been giving orders in the background. Darius had driven Genevieve to the hospital to wait though there'd been a terse argument as she'd wanted to go to the scene, but he didn't want to endanger her or to present another target that would only complicate matters when the focus needed to be on Rowan.

But David had arranged for Hunter-style backup to be sent. There was only so much they could risk in public, but she knew without a doubt they'd break every law they had to if it meant saving Rowan's life.

Her friend being the power she was hadn't needed the help, as it happened. True to form, she'd single-handedly taken out the two remaining shooters before passing out from blood loss.

They'd remained at the hospital while Rowan had been in surgery. Genevieve had been there to lend some power to her friend. Even at the worst moments, Genevieve hadn't doubted Rowan would recover but, as sundown crept closer, she and Darius left David at the hospital and headed to the house to tell Clive his wife had nearly died while he'd been at rest.

She grimaced at the memory. But he'd been strong and unwavering by the time Rowan had regained consciousness. His dangerous side had risen, and Genevieve approved mightily.

It played through her mind over and over. Well, she didn't want to do it alone, so she headed to the kitchen and found Lorraine there with Darius, making a meal.

When she'd first met him, Genevieve wouldn't have imagined this domestic scene. His locs tied back from his face, feet bare as usual as he padded over to her and gave her a close look before brushing his lips over hers in greeting.

"I'm teaching Madame how to make kung pao with fried tofu," he said with a smile in his eyes.

"Tofu," Lorraine said with a sigh that made Genevieve smile for the first time in hours. "How is the girl?"

"They allowed her to go home not too long ago. I'll stop over there tomorrow afternoon when she's awake."

"I made her a package with some teas and honey. You take them when you go." Lorraine pointed at a pretty little basket with several glass jars holding teas and tisanes to aid in healing and rebuilding stamina. "You should sit."

"I can't sit right now. All I did at the hospital was sit." Her voice wavered slightly.

"It was all you could do," Lorraine said in her matter-of-fact way.

"I don't know about that. But it was all I knew I could do."

"That sounds like guilt," Darius murmured.

"It isn't. Well. So. Maybe a little bit. If this was witches, I brought it to her door."

Darius shook his head slightly and went back to turning over the tofu cooking in the oil. "She brought you to her door. She sought you out on another case. You've worked with her. She knows her world and you know yours. To say you brought it to her door, when in all truth, Genevieve, the two of you being friends and partners strengthens each of you by an order of magnitude. This would have come to her in one way or another with or without you. This is the life she leads. But you can lend her magic when she's in surgery and you did. You're the one she called. She needed help and you gave it to her."

Genevieve poured herself a glass of wine and then another for Lorraine. "I've got other things to drink as well," she said to Darius. "Vodka in the freezer, gin of course. White wine if you prefer it to red."

He reached to take her glass and took a sip, nodding after. Then he kept it and said, “Thank you.”

Smirking at him, Genevieve poured herself a glass as well and perched on a stool on the other side of the kitchen island, deciding to let herself be happy with the things in her life—in her kitchen—that held fast through the bad times.

“Carl was there,” Rowan said before taking a sip of water. Clive gave her a look, but tucked the blankets around her better and fluffed the pillows.

“He’s on the footage. At the end of the attack. I tried to see when he arrived and left but there’s so much going on I can’t see it.”

“I was in the left-turn lane, and he was just there on the sidewalk. Like he’d been waiting for the light to change. He mouthed *watch out* at me. Star was there too for a while, but I don’t know if that was real, or I dreamed it. I need you to get David.”

Ignoring that entirely, Clive said, “Star was at the hospital. That was a surprise, but no one seemed to mind she was there, or maybe they didn’t even notice her. One never knows with Star.” There was a slight smile on his lips, and she loved him for it.

Star was a supernatural-type dog and she seemed to go wherever she pleased by some sort of magic Rowan didn’t have any real understanding of but accepted, nonetheless. Far more than a pet or a familiar. She was Rowan’s family and took that very seriously.

Then Rowan sat up so fast she couldn’t stop the yelp of pain. Clive was on his feet immediately. “What? Lay down. You’re going to hurt yourself.”

“Today. That intersection. I need to see the footage.”

"I don't know if that's a good idea just yet. It's quite… shocking."

She heard it then. The thin thread of fear in his voice.

She forced herself to focus on him a moment. "I'm sorry. You must have been really scared."

He shook his head at her and bent to kiss her forehead as he gently urged her to lie back. "When I woke up and Genevieve was here, I knew it was you. I knew you were alive because the bond was there. But you were unconscious. In surgery." He ran his hands through his hair. "I have seen you in far, far worse straits. But it is never easy to see you hurting or vulnerable. And it's impossible for me not to want to fix everything to protect you."

"I understand that. I love you for that," she said. "I need David. And to see the video. There's something there I need to check."

"Rowan, it's time to rest. There's plenty of opportunity later to give him items for his to-do list when you aren't recovering from being shot fourteen times and then refusing to take the blood of a fecking Scion to speed your healing."

"I'm already healing at a superhuman speed." She was! It was easy to forget just how fucked-up she'd been when she'd first arrived at the hospital. It wasn't wise to remind him about how badly she'd been injured, so she didn't say anything more on that.

Instead, she said, "When you wake up tomorrow night you can give me more blood. That tiny-eyed cop is a dick who has wood for getting promoted so I wouldn't put it past him to figure out where I live and roll up to the gates for another interview."

"Even if by some means he found this house, unless he has a warrant, the guards won't open the gate and Betchamp wouldn't open the door. There'll be half a dozen Hunters out there. Genevieve will certainly park herself in our living room and smoke cannabis, keep an eye on you and defend you if need be. He can call to make an appointment and we will control the particulars of that. It can be done over the phone or even a video call. But because of all that," he held up a hand to silence her, "I accept the offer to take my blood when I rise at sunset. You will be safe until then. Frankly, I do wish you'd reconsider sleeping with me in my bedchamber. Once it's locked, you'd be secure with me."

Rowan probably hit her head a few times that day. That was why she was all gooey for him and that worry in his tone. The desperation to protect her. To know she was safe when he couldn't do anything.

Probably all the drugs too. The painkillers were top-notch.

"That's probably all true except for me being locked in with you. We'd both hate that. Plus the doctor is coming over in the morning to check on me and if she came into your bedchamber while you were at rest there'd be a whole thing and everyone would be anxious and nervous. So. I'll sleep in my bed though I do like snuggling with you. *Oops* said that out loud. Anyway, as you can tell, the drugs are doing their job. So. Back to you needing to get David and the footage so I can look at it."

With a sigh he left the room and returned shortly with his notebook with the traffic camera footage of the attack.

David tapped on the door and came into the room. His expression softened when he caught sight of her, and relief flooded through her once more that she'd been alone in the SUV.

He gave her hand a very gentle pat before taking the chair Clive had vacated.

Clive climbed into bed so she could snuggle on him. Before she could do something stupid like cry, Rowan leaned on him a little as six and a half minutes that had felt like forty-seven years played before her eyes.

The angle wasn't perfect, but she could see everything she needed to between the three SUVs that had hit her, and then the shooters. The sidewalks weren't visible except right at the corners at the stoplights. Carl could have been two feet to the right and he'd have been out of the shot.

"The Tempest," she told him after she'd watched herself get beat all to shit and still manage a win at the very end. The losing consciousness that happened shortly after deducted a point or two, but she tried not to be too disappointed by that. She also tried not to think about what it had felt like to watch it happen to herself. It was too much to examine so she didn't. Fuck self-reflection.

The Tempest was one of Las Vegas's trendiest casino resorts and it sat directly to her left at that intersection. The entire center of the hotel was built around a massive shipwreck. There were pools and aquariums full of sirens with perky tits and blue hair.

Ships.

A tempest was a storm. A churning sea. Waves and water.

"My prophecy dream. That's the connection."

"Are you certain?" Clive asked.

"Well, this stuff is all very woo-woo and so I'm learning as I go, but I think yes. And Carl was standing on that corner, right in front of it. That's like prophecy-Inception-type shit."

Her lips were still swollen so all her S sounds were messed up and he snickered at her before sobering.

"Who owns it, Clive?"

"Consortium of some sort. I've only met a few of those who managed the build or have some part in running it now." He pulled his phone free. "Let me speak to Alice about it. She'll get us the information."

"While he's talking to Alice, tell me what's going on," Rowan said to David.

"We're working with Patience and Seth on tracking the attackers who fled the scene. There's a partial plate so Vanessa is hard at work at that. She and Alice have teamed up to create a timeline with the camera feeds we have to follow the other attacker. It's just a matter of a lot of staring at the screen seeing nothing important for hours at a time. But we've made progress. Vanessa says probably by midday tomorrow." He held up a manila envelope. "Our lovely friend at the PD has come through. We have the info on where the prisoners are being kept. One is in a coma and the other has given a name but it's a fake. Identity is super shallow. Vanessa is unraveling it as we speak. So we don't know who either is at this point but it won't be long."

"I may be able to help with that," Clive interrupted after ending his call to Alice. "We managed to obtain blood and DNA from each of them. Patience is having them run through all known databases. Since David is here to keep you company and talk business, I'm going to nip out. We're working on creating a window of time where I can have access to them. We don't know what they'll say to the human authorities. We can't risk being exposed and I don't want them to die before I can try to read them. After that would be fine."

"I can't snort because it'll hurt," she told Clive. "But know I wanted to."

"Of course."

"You're taking a big risk," she added.

"It's hardly the heist of a lifetime. I'm a *Scion*. The surveillance cameras are already taken care of. I have a small bit of talent with others, especially humans, or so I'm told. By everyone." His hauteur over her concern was so delightfully Clive it was as good as medicine.

"I'm obviously not questioning your abilities," she muttered. "It's still risky. Lots of cops with guns in one place." She worried about him for goddess's sake!

He kissed the top of her head like David wasn't right there and she pretended to be annoyed, but really it was very nice when he kissed her like that.

"I never underestimate weapons. I give you my word. Trust the process. Isn't that what you barked at me just a few days ago when I questioned you about something or other? You're not the only one who can put together a sneaky plan with lots of moving parts."

"What did Alice say about the Tempest?" she asked, trying to smother a yawn because her jaw hurt.

Clive's gaze narrowed and she realized he'd taken note of her flagging energy. That meant she only had five minutes before he started poking at her to sleep. Probably less.

"Consortium as I'd said. Alice related that she's heard the investors were Russians, Chinese, English, Italian, and-slash-or Argentinean. She's already started to dig deeper. Between her and Vanessa, we should find some answers soon enough. Your eyelids keep drooping."

"Let me just finish talking to David," she said.

David held up a hand. "I'll check with Vanessa on

the Tempest connections. I'll also work with Alice on the identities of the prisoners once we find that out. I'll update you on the search for the ones who ran from the scene when you wake up. I'm going to take a run through the police information and bounce ideas off Pru, who came in from LA to provide backup."

"Good idea," Rowan said. Pru was the Hunter Rowan had recently promoted to head up the chapterhouse in Southern California. She'd been a great ally during the last struggle they'd had against the Fae who'd been trying to tear a hole into another world and killing lots of humans to get there.

Speaking of that. "Wait. I had another prophecy dream. Storms again. And empty places. Malls and restaurants, parks, all empty. I think it's connected to the missing humans."

David nodded, making a quick note in his phone. "It sounds like that's a pretty safe bet, yes. I'm going to add in some search terms to see what sorts of connections we might find. It's blunt, scattershot even, but worth a try."

Scattershot. "Yes. Do it. Whatever terms you're thinking of, do the search. Another image-type thing was confetti, but now that you say scattershot I think that's it. It was a concept I didn't know how to describe yet. It just feels right."

"He'll get right on it once you rest," Clive said as he moved from the bed.

"I'll be right outside in your sitting room. Star was here earlier but she's disappeared for the moment. I'll leave the door open slightly so she can get in." David stood and then he bent to kiss her forehead and she was horrified and touched so deeply she nearly burst into tears. All things indicating she needed sleep.

Once David'd left, Clive refilled her water and left it within easy reach. "I won't be gone very long. Everyone will check on you. Accept that now. Let them. They care about you and you gave us all a scare today."

"You're being very nice to me," she said. Or tried to anyway, she wasn't sure if she got all the words out or not.

"There now," he told her as her eyes slid shut. "I adore you." His murmur ended on a surprised sound. "Ah! There you are."

She managed to open her eyes as Star jumped up on the bed and settled in between where Rowan lay and the door.

Star whined a little and Rowan softened.

"I know. I'm okay now. I saw you there."

Star sighed softly and stretched, slowly and gently until those fluffy paws nearly touched Rowan. As if she wanted to be close but didn't want to touch anything injured. And since between the airbag, getting shot, and all the glass, pretty much every bit of Rowan's body was bruised, lacerated, stitched up, in a sling or a cast, or otherwise injured in some way, she was grateful for Star's care.

Clive ran a hand over Star's head, pausing to scratch behind her ears. The big old softie.

"Rest or Star will bite you."

"Nuh uh. I'm her bacon connection," Rowan said drowsily.

Clive played with the end of the loose braid trailing over her uninjured shoulder. "Rest well. Let your body and your Goddess do its work."

Her eyes drifted closed again and this time, a deep, healing sleep pulled her under quickly.

# *Chapter Twenty*

"I appreciate your staying out here while I'm away," Clive told David quietly once they were out in the sitting room.

"Don't insult me. I can just as easily work from here and if she needs anything, I'm available immediately."

Relieved that David had things in hand, Clive searched for a way to say the rest. "I spoke with Nadir right before sunup at the Keep to update her. The First wants a video call but I discouraged that idea and said you'd set up a *brief* phone call for right after sunset their time. Then he can be assured she's all right but not take so long it's a burden on Rowan's health and well-being." Clive didn't think she was up to a face-to-face with her father. Even if it was from an ocean away. Especially from an ocean away when her father got a look at her face and decided nothing was going to stop him from coming.

Certainly, she shouldn't *have to be* up to it. There was enough going on with this whole lords situation and he didn't want the First to try to manipulate it when she was weak even if the reasons behind it were driven by wanting her attention rather than wanting to harm her.

There was no way around connecting Rowan and the First so they needed to plan it to protect her.

David nodded. "All right. But so you understand, I will find a way to disconnect that call if he upsets her."

Clive skirted criticizing too much out loud, but in his head he'd committed ten kinds of treason in the last several days.

"I wish he would consent to wait until after I'm awake." He could help manage her father that way.

David said, "He'll want to speak with her as soon as he can. And, to be frank, if you were there he couldn't have all her attention. He loves her. Powerfully so. I've seen it for myself more than once. He approves of her marriage to you. You're well placed in the Nation. Strong enough to protect her. Wealthy enough to keep her. Connected enough to open doors wherever she went. And you make her happy. But he doesn't like to share her. And he doesn't always love her the way she needs to be loved."

"That's what we're for, David," Clive said.

Twenty minutes later, Clive found himself standing in a little-used breakroom on the secure floor of the hospital the prisoners were in. He waited four minutes exactly before flipping a switch on the little box he'd carried along with him. After blinking red several times, it switched to a steady blue. The signal that the interior cameras on that part of the floor had been handled to hide evidence he was there.

There were two armed officers on that level, one posted directly in the elevator lobby and the other outside the door of the suspect they'd questioned earlier that evening. He'd told them nothing. Given them a fake name. Said he'd been paid to do a job, but it was an anonymous process.

Clive certainly wasn't prepared to believe such a thing. Not until he'd had an opportunity to ask the questions himself. And he bet a smart cop wouldn't be either. They'd be back to ask questions again and who knew what would happen then. It would be totally out of their hands and that was too dangerous a reality to let come to pass.

Keeping track of the time, Clive slipped from the room and eased down the long hallway to the west of where he'd come out. Moments later, one of Clive's Vampires appeared. Viola had been a nurse at that hospital for fourteen years, but Clive had known her for at least two centuries. She had a knack for persuasion but a preference for living a quiet life outside the court of a Scion, even one she liked. But when he'd approached her for anything he'd needed over the years, she'd always shown up and done everything within her abilities to assist.

Even in the low lights, he knew she'd caught sight of him when she nodded slightly and then strolled past, turning at the next line of patient rooms. It was under two minutes when she'd given the signal.

Despite the gravity of his mission, Clive enjoyed the challenge each step presented. Such things kept his mind sharp, and his body engaged. He backtracked to the prisoner's door where the guard stood staring off into a corner at the opposite end of the corridor as if nothing else existed. Viola had left the door unlocked and he made sure to use the key he'd been given to relock up, giving himself a few more seconds to escape should he need to do so.

The room was not quite darkened, though the curtains on the window had been pulled to shut out the electric lights from the parking lot outside. There was noise from outside. The hum of the HVAC system for the building, electric lights, traffic even at three in the morning grumbled along on a nearby street.

The man on the bed pretended to be asleep but his heart rate kicked up because he'd just scented a Vampire. Hopefully he'd simply assume it was Viola.

Clive pulled the curtain around them both and then sat right next to the bed. "They don't know wolf shifters exist," he said softly, threading his words with compulsion so subtle they were the merest whisper. "But I know."

In one smooth move, Clive tore his thumb open and shoved it into the shifter's mouth, willing compulsion into the blood. Next, he bent close, his eyes just inches from the shifter's as he pushed compliance with his gaze at the same time. Binding him to Clive's will before he could evade the attempt.

Clive poured his magic into the man on the bed until his eyes glazed and his mouth slackened. He'd created a bond between them. Not like the one he shared with Rowan, but a master vampire to a servant.

"What's your real name?" he asked the shifter.

A softball question. Easy to answer so he wouldn't fight it. He'd want to please Clive by telling him. Each time he gave in and obeyed it would be easier to get compliance in the future.

"Oliver Shank."

"Where do you live, Oliver?"

"Seattle."

"Is your pack there?"

"Some of them."

Clive continued in that pace. Asking easy, general questions that enabled him to figure out more of who this Oliver was and who he worked for.

Soon enough Oliver had tipped under Clive's total

control. This shifter might be able to resist a human police officer, but someone with Clive's skill could roll him right over. Which he'd done.

Clive bet Oliver was supposed to self-terminate rather than get arrested. He was a gold mine of secrets, this wolf shifter handcuffed and chained to the bed. At first glance his biology would look human and maybe the authorities would never figure it out. But there was also a chance someone would look more closely and figure out Oliver wasn't anything close to human. There were shifter gangs within the human prison system so chances were he'd have some sort of protection if he made it through a trial and sentencing. But Oliver wasn't the smart one. Eventually he'd crack. Either to brag or to trade for personal gain. Whoever hired him had thrown him at Rowan, fully expecting him to die or escape with the others.

And whoever hired them had underestimated Rowan greatly. Had Clive's wife taken Oliver, she'd have tortured the truth out of him and then tracked her way back to whoever hired him. No bad guy wanted Rowan in his television room breaking his glassware and exposing all his secrets, so Oliver's bosses were stupid, or ego had led them to make incorrect assumptions about the Hunter they'd paid money to kill.

"Tell me the story of how today's attack on the Hunter came to be," Clive said at last.

"Shank's family business is muscle. Patrick got a contact four days ago. A request for a hit on some human chick in Las Vegas. Chick is wicked hard to pin down and is guarded half the time so we gotta be smart in the how. So we showed up in town to plan. But then day before yesterday Patrick gets contacted again and this time, they want the chick dead right then. Pat told them given the way the woman traveled and her weird hours, to get at her so fast was risky and potentially public. Originally the contact says he wants it kept quiet, you know, when he first called Patrick. But he's big mad at the woman for something or other and wants it done within twenty-four. Wants it done extra hard. Wants her to suffer. Contact says it can look like an assassination but just not by werewolves. Patrick hates it when anyone says werewolf instead of Were or shifter but he didn't argue. Patrick likes money.

"We got a call from our spotter that she was alone in her vehicle and in less than ten minutes we were heading to her. There was another car that should have rear-ended her but they got caught up in traffic and bugged out. The three teams left hit her pretty much at the same time. Patrick was impressed."

Clive shoved the rage far, far away, keeping his face impassive as this man described the attack on Rowan. He'd let that rage free when it was time.

"I said we should go. There was no way this human could have survived being crushed by three of us at once. But Patrick said for me and Eustace to go forward with the rest of the plan. So we grabbed weapons, jumped out the back, and started shooting into her SUV. That's when we saw it was armored. Patrick and Angus told us to keep shooting and then to get on up out of there before the cops arrived and they booked it to where Angel was waiting with a car.

"The other teams shot at the car for a while, and they ran too when sirens got closer. Me and Eustace were about to do the same when that bitch ambushed us from behind. She looked like that chick in the movie with the prom where they dump blood on her? Anyway, she was fucked-up but had that look, you know, the battle face where everything that makes them a person is gone, leaving only the need to kill. I've never seen a scarier face in my whole life. She hit Eustace so hard he didn't get back up. I managed to shoot her two more times but she just kept coming. Beat my face to a pulp. Then she finally knocked me out and I woke up here."

Clive had been at Rowan's side in more than one fight. He'd seen her give over to the warrior within, let that aspect of her Goddess rise. But the look Oliver described was one he'd only seen a single time and that had been when she was desperately trying to kill the other being before she got killed. Clive had seen it and like every other aspect of his wife, he loved it, but Oliver was totally correct to have been frightened. That Rowan would do whatever it took to win. He'd yet to see anyone who could stand in the full force of it and remain standing.

"Where are they now? The rest of your teams?"

"They'd have blown town by now."

"Back to Seattle?"

"Not for a while. It's too hot and they can't risk bringing the law back to the den. Probably headed to the ranch we been using. Near Goldfield. On the way back up to Seattle. Pretty desolate out there so we can see anyone approaching for miles in every direction."

Clive thought about that and bet he could find a way to approach unseen.

"Will they try to free you? Or will you take all the blame, do your prison time, and then return home?" Clive asked.

Oliver's sigh was sad. "They'll kill me if they can. Too big a risk I'll tell on them. Like I am now. But that's just you. You're a Vampire. You won't tell. I'll take my blame and I'll prepare to do my time. Cops wouldn't say if she died or not, but I heard the one outside the door here saying she had gone into hiding. So not even a murder case. I can do the time. We got family inside. But I don't know if Patrick will trust me. I think he won't take that risk and I'll be dead before the trial is over."

He would most assuredly be dead before the trial, Clive thought.

Clive chatted with Oliver for a few minutes more and then Viola returned, checked vitals, made notes, and then went back out giving him three fingers, indicating he wait three minutes before leaving.

Once she'd gone, instead of giving blood, Clive took it. He bashed his way through Oliver's brain, taking every memory he could and destroyed anything that would cause harm to the supernatural community or Rowan.

Oliver was beyond pain by that point. Clive hadn't avoided killing him out of mercy. There was a nonlethal way to eliminate the danger he posed. Killing him would raise alarms and create more risks. Oliver already had a serious head injury. When they checked on him next they'd assume the damage was due to that and there'd be no connection to Rowan at all.

Time up, Clive slid past the guard and headed the opposite way.

This time he headed to Eustace's room. No guard outside because the shifter was in a coma, but he was still shackled to the bed by his ankle.

This one would never regain consciousness again. Despite Clive's rage at what this pitiful creature had done to Rowan, she'd most assuredly gotten her own back. A shifter's skull was hard as hell, and she'd done so much damage he'd never recover, and wasn't that fitting? Clive dipped his mouth to Eustace's neck and struck quickly. He didn't much care for shifter blood, but this creature didn't have any of the normal defenses against being read so completely by a Vampire. There was nothing there but a pool of memories Clive would have to piece together. He took them all, drawing his tongue over the wounds to close them totally and erase any evidence he'd been there.

Twenty minutes later he'd landed in the backyard of his home. With some answers and several more questions.

David looked up as Clive entered the sitting room.

"She's sleeping still. Betchamp checked her vitals and they're improving. He was quite pleased about that. He wrote up a report of sorts for you. I sent him to bed. Elisabeth will take over for me in two hours."

He wanted to discuss what he'd learned with Rowan, but Clive had no plans to disturb her rest. She rarely slept enough as it was. Her body needed the rest.

"I'll take over here. You should sleep. You'll have her work on your shoulders until she's more recovered. Sunrise isn't for two and a half more hours. When Elisabeth arrives, I'll head to daytime rest." He'd never really examined what he lost by not being awake during the sunlight. He was born a Vampire. The only thing he couldn't hold were those hours of the day and when he'd weighed that against the things his birthright had given him instead, he didn't mourn.

But once Rowan had streaked into his world, he'd resented those hours he couldn't reach her. Worried about her inability to reach him while he was unconscious. He knew what could happen to her during the daylight. Knew he might wake up one evening to find she'd been in a tussle and maybe the news wouldn't be hopeful.

He resented the sunshine because it kept him from her when she might need him the most.

"I won't mess up," David said as he stood to stretch his muscles.

"That never crossed my mind."

David's confusion tugged at Clive's conscience.

"Well, she's a tough act to follow."

Clive said, "You don't need to be Rowan. She already does that just fine. And Rowan believes in your ability, David. If she didn't, you would not be running things while she was down. She'd have called in someone else. She relies on you now more than ever before. Because she trusts you. I'm sure you understand trust is something Rowan gives very rarely and not without a great deal of struggle. All you can do is your best. I've yet to see you give anything but."

David blushed a little. "I just want to be worthy of that trust."

"So say we all. All of us who love her and see her for who she is just want to be worthy of her."

"I used to think you were a haughty asshole," David said.

That made Clive laugh. "And now?"

David gave one of those *either/or* movements of his hand, but he grinned a moment as he did it. "I think you're still a haughty asshole, but I know there's more to you. Especially when it comes to Rowan. So. I like that. And thanks, for the pep talk. I needed it, I guess. She's just so strong and in charge that seeing her helpless has been messing with my head. If she can't solve a problem, how can any of us hope to?"

"She does have that effect on people. But she did solve the problem. Not how she set out to, but this attack and her strength and stubbornness not to pass out until she'd taken down her attackers made a difference."

"Can you tell me about what you learned?" David asked. "Normally I would understand if you wanted to inform Rowan before anyone else. She'd be very upset in another circumstance. But I don't think this would be one of them. This is ongoing and time is of the essence."

"She's trained you well," Clive said.

"I'll never be as good at being pushy as Rowan, but I will never stop trying," David said with a smirk.

"Let me change clothes. I'll be back out shortly and I'll give you an overview of what I discovered."

# *Chapter Twenty-One*

Rowan woke to her dog licking her nose and the low sounds of a discussion taking place in the sitting room on the other side of her slightly open bedroom door.

She poked the bond she shared with Clive. He was unconscious but healthy otherwise. Relieved, she did a quick inventory of her body. Generalized soreness, especially her chest and ribs where she'd taken a hit from the airbag and the crash.

When she realized she was looking at Star's adorable face, Rowan figured her wounded eye had healed itself.

Star yipped and the discussion halted. Seconds later there was a tap on the door before it was pushed open to reveal David, Genevieve, and Betchamp.

"Right," Betchamp said, hefting a bag Rowan knew carried medical supplies. "I need to check on Ms. Rowan and that means you two need to wait out there. Except you, Star. You can stay as my assistant."

Rowan's face didn't hurt when she smiled, so that was something else for the plus column.

When they were alone, Betchamp gently took her temperature and blood pressure. "How are you feeling?"

"Better than I did yesterday. My eye doesn't hurt. Seems to be working fine."

Betchamp nodded. "Your vitals are back to your normal range. Scion Stewart told us your Goddess wouldn't allow infection, and your temperature seems to prove that correct. It never hurts to double-check. Your wounds are healing at an accelerated rate."

"Handy, right?" she teased.

"Just so," he allowed with a small smile. "I'm going to have a call with Dr. Jenkins. Elisabeth started some bone broth last night. Once I get permission, I'll bring you some."

David and Genevieve rejoined her when Betchamp went to contact Dr. Jenkins.

"What were you arguing about just before you came in here? Don't deny it because my ears are working just fine."

"It wasn't a disagreement between young David and me," Genevieve said. "Your father wants to speak to you. David and I were attempting to find a way to give him what he needs with the least amount of pressure on you."

"We're both annoyed it has to happen," David told her.

"If wishes were fishes and all that." Rowan rolled her eyes.

"An eye roll means you really are recovering well. You look a far sight better than you did when we brought you home from the hospital last night," David said, attempting nonchalance it was clear he didn't feel.

Rowan said, "First, give me an update on whatever Clive found out. Then what I think I should do is call him directly in his suite. He'll be surprised, which will keep him from manipulating me too much at the start. It'll only take him two, maybe three minutes to get himself together though. He's crafty. So I'll disconnect after no more than five minutes." She was too weak to fend him off for more than that.

David heaved a sigh.

"You," she pointed at David, "get to updating."

"The surest sign she's recovering," Genevieve muttered and settled herself at the foot of Rowan's bed.

"Your very enterprising husband was very useful while you were sleeping," David said. "We've got the names of the two you took down at the scene. They're wolf shifters."

"I knew they weren't human," Rowan said.

"They're from Seattle but I think they're part of a larger pack that's located in the northern Cascades. We're working on that now." David told her the rest.

"Okay, so we still don't know who hired them yet, but we have a way to find someone who does know. I can deal with that for now."

"Clive was also able to get the location of their probable safe house so he sent out some surveillance before he went to daytime rest. The car with the partial plates has been found. Total wreck. Burned at a very high heat. Reported stolen yesterday morning," David said. "The ones they used to crash into you were stolen a month ago from a custom-build shop in Ventura. No fingerprints, hair, or fiber evidence."

"These Weres are professionals. Except for the weak links in the hospital. I bet the pack is pretty frantic to eliminate those two dicks." Rowan was relieved Clive had handled that problem. "I also bet this Patrick Shank guy has a boss, and whoever *that* is will be even more frantic to stanch the wound. These two Weres will be dead by the end of the week. There's no way they can leave loose ends with the DNA proof of animals who can shift into humans and vice versa. There are too many opportunities for exposure on multiple levels for these Shanks. They're going to close ranks, but before that happens entirely, let's find out all we can about them and wolf shifters in general. I know the basics, but I want to know everything."

"Working on a quick guide to Weres for you. Vanessa has been working on trying to track the other group of attackers who fled. We have their names already, but more information is better. It'll help us find them all eventually," David added.

"The doctor is recommending you not travel for at least the next two weeks," Betchamp said as he came in. "She's making me tell you so you can't be mean. That's what she said. Imagine."

Rowan sighed heavily. She couldn't be mean to Betchamp. Dr. Jenkins was very clever indeed. "This is ridiculous. Who else is going to handle the Joint Tribunal? I'm the liaison. I've got all the background research handled but it took two months to get up to speed. It's not to Hunter Corp.'s advantage to have me absent."

"Well of course it isn't!" Genevieve waved a hand and that jingling soothed Rowan's agitated nerves. "The entire thing needs to be postponed for at least two weeks. I'd say three just to give yourself that extra time."

"Two *weeks*? The Vampires are going to refuse just because they're contrary like that," Rowan said.

"I don't think so," David said. "They're dealing with this lord situation right now. Having some breathing room so they can come to the Joint Tribunal with a stronger position will benefit them. And your father will be feeling guilty. As he should. Use it to get this delay. *You* be the one to manipulate *him* this time."

"I can totally go to Prague in two days." Clive could

give her blood when they left Las Vegas, and she wouldn't have to hide how much she'd improved so quickly. She'd still be healing, but she'd have mobility.

"Tomorrow, you mean. Not two days. As for whether you could get on a plane while recovering from surgery, gunshot wounds, and broken bones? You could. Should you? And, let me add something extremely relevant to this," Genevieve said. "Your husband is going to wake up and find out your physician told you no travel for two weeks and you decided to travel anyway. I predict a fight. And he'll be right. I'll be on his side, Rowan. That is very unfair of you to do to me."

That was a real thing. He'd be super mad and probably hurt because she made an important decision without him. A decision that would cause her injury even if she could lessen it with his blood.

"Are you in a place where you can have an in-person meeting with the First? Negotiate with him?" David asked.

Theo didn't have to attend the Joint Tribunals at all. But ever since Rowan had been named liaison—by him—he'd made sure to attend. It wasn't as if he attended meetings or negotiation sessions. He just wanted to be in her orbit after years of estrangement.

And despite the scars and pain he was her father. She could admit—to herself and herself only—that it made a difference. Loving him was like loving a hurricane. Damage came just from being around him. Mostly the damage he left in his wake wasn't malicious, but if you got close enough, eventually a house fell on you.

So if he saw her at the Joint Tribunal in the shape she was currently in, even after Vampire blood, he'd sense her weakness and pounce. She already couldn't let down her guard for a second. It would be exhausting to fend him off and deal with six days full of fourteen hours of meetings and more meetings where she had to keep sharp on top of that.

Damn it. David and Genevieve both were right.

Rowan growled at her inability to just do whatever she needed to do whenever she wanted. “Fine. Give me the phone.” She got herself comfortable and tapped his name in her contacts. Once, she'd had *Vlad*, as a joke, but then she ended up knowing like nine of them, so she just changed it to Theo.

“Petal, are you well?” he said as he answered, raw emotion in his voice.

He was the first of Vampirekind and more often than not, he was coolly remote. If one was lucky. Other times he was ice cold and murderous. But with her at moments like this one, when he was her father instead of the First, his tone was open, warm, and teasing, or taut with concern as it was right then.

Their relationship was fraught. Complicated by years of blood and pain. He walked the razor's edge of sanity. But she seemed to keep him on the right side of that edge.

He was thousands upon thousands of years old and he'd never ever see the world as Rowan did. As she deserved him to. He was her father, and he might manipulate her to get all her attention, but he didn't want her to be harmed.

And because she loved him too, she said, “I'm alive. Recovering. They said I could make a five-minute call so I thought to let you know I'm okay.”

Rowan didn't know why, but the backs of her eyes burned with unshed tears.

“I wanted to come to you immediately, but Nadir

talked me out of it. I do so dislike not being right there to see for myself that you are whole and hale. I was also told no camera calls."

Rowan ignored that last bit. If he saw how she looked, even though it was better than the day before, he'd be there no matter who told him not to.

"Not so hale, but I'm in one piece." Clive had told her what information Theo had been given about the attack, so she didn't need to lie. "I'm going to find the ones still alive by the time I'm on my feet once more. Speaking of that, I've been told by the doctor that I can't travel for two weeks so David will work with the Nation and the Conclave Senate to reschedule for after that passes."

Rowan felt it was better to simply assume control of most situations rather than ask questions when she didn't need anyone else's opinion to make a choice. It was one of those do a thing and apologize after type situations.

David nodded his head approvingly.

Theo went quiet for long seconds. "I don't like that. I've planned to travel to Prague tomorrow after sunset."

"I could send someone else I guess," she said, taking a chance.

He grumbled, and she knew she'd scored a direct hit with that.

"Four minutes," Betchamp said in the background, though he flattened out his voice to sound like an American.

"Only a minute left and I don't want to waste it arguing with you about this. I hate to reschedule. You know that. But if I take a chance with my recovery, Clive will be very angry, and we'll argue. And my doctor will take his side. They'll say, why doesn't your father want you to get better?"

That last might have been too much, but she rode with it.

He blew out a breath. "Fine. I will inform Nadir. She will be in touch with your David. Who is responsible for the attack on you? Do you know that much yet?"

"Not yet. But we're looking. Or, they're looking and I'm laying in a bed with a dog who growls at me when I try to do too much."

He laughed and it lightened her heart.

There was much to love about Theo.

"I'm certain Scion Stewart is helping you with that. You will update Nadir when you get more information," he ordered.

"Sure. And you can update me on the Vampire lords who put an execution order on my Hunters." She coughed and the pain of it was so sharp she struggled, holding her breath, trying not to cough again.

"I insist you stop this instant!" Theo demanded over the line. "You will rest and heal, or I will come to see to it myself. You can be angry at these ridiculous lords when you're better. They'll be here below when that happens."

By *below*, he meant the actual dungeon beneath the Keep.

Like Tupperware but with Vampire dinguses who called themselves lords. Probably with torture, but she couldn't think about that.

After sipping some water she was able to speak again. "I'm fine. I need to go so I can rest. I'll have David contact Nadir about rescheduling."

"I do so hate to travel." He huffed and she realized he was starting to get himself together. Soon enough he'd be trying to exploit her weakness to get whatever he wanted from her. More visits. Attendance at endless parties she'd hate, and Clive would wet himself over.

"I will check in again tomorrow at this time. Be well, *Vater*," she told him, meaning it. It was good to hear his voice. He was holding up just fine, no shadows of the darker aspects of his personality, which was good for everyone.

"Five minutes is up," Betchamp said and took the phone, ending the call.

"I'll get right on the reschedule issue. Coordinate with London. Then we'll reach out to the Senate liaison," David said, looking at Genevieve, the liaison between the magic users and the Joint Tribunal.

"We're fine with moving things. There's a lot going on right now so I'm glad we don't have to leave the country," Genevieve said and then looked very carefully at Rowan's face. "Let me help you with the pain and stiffness."

Rowan agreed. Her friend did her witchy mojo, her hands moving in graceful turns and arcs as she sang under her breath. Pins and needles made her gasp a moment, but soon enough the pain receded enough that Rowan could move without wincing.

They left her to rest and Star trotted back into the room, settling at the foot of the bed, still between Rowan and the door. Ever a protector.

# Chapter Twenty-Two

When Genevieve pulled down the private road leading toward the front gate of the private residential complex her home was in, she saw Darius standing not too far from the guard shack. Anger roiled from him, like heat off a pavement.

Startled and wary, she pulled over and turned the engine off.

He turned when she opened her car door.

She knew she wasn't going to like whatever he was about to say.

"Have you heard from your father today?" he asked, blocking her view of whatever it was he'd been examining.

"I have a call with him in a few minutes. Why?"

"I'm going to tell you everything at once so save your questions for the end," he said.

She put a hand on her hip and nodded for him to continue.

"There was a delivery for you today. Here. Private delivery service. They had your street address. Wanted you to come out or to be let in but left it after we refused entry. They called me out to look at the stuff. There's magic all over it. Trap spells. Confusion spells. Obsession and love workings."

"Well." Genevieve thought for a while but that was all she could come up with for long moments. "Show me," she said at last.

"I believe you're the trigger, so I'd prefer for you to go no closer than where we are," he murmured and stepped to the side.

It looked to be an obscene amount of money spent to try to impress someone who has already told you in multiple ways she is not interested in you. With heart balloons attached. Hugo was, as Rowan would say, bananapants.

She didn't see the magic at first glance but eventually she caught a glimpse in one of the bags. Mindful to keep her distance, she moved a little and caught another. Shadows where none should be. If she got closer Genevieve figured she'd be able to see more. Changes in texture or variations in color that would indicate the presence of a spell were hard to spot from a distance.

"There's even something inside the balloons," Darius told her. "Look at the ribbon, about six or seven inches up from where they're tied to the handle of the bag."

"I can't see that at all," she said after she'd tried from various angles and remained frustrated by her inability.

"You probably could if you were closer," he said. "What do you want to do? I can destroy the spells like I did the one on the roses, but I figured you'd want to speak with your father, and I didn't want to do anything so final until we'd spoken."

"Why is he so stupid? His name is all over this! Everything about this comes straight to him. It's madness," Genevieve said, throwing her hands up, frustrated.

"Has the Procella family as a unit responded to your complaint about the roses?"

"I think that's what Konrad wanted to talk about. Let me call him now. I want to use the camera to show him. Then we can destroy it."

Her phone rang before she could touch her father's number to call him.

"Rowan? Is everything all right? You should be sleeping."

"Put it in a circle first," Rowan said.

"What?"

"I just had a *knowing*. I can't tell you what it's about or anything more specific. Just if you're dealing with something dangerous, put it in a circle."

Genevieve looked at Darius and then to the bags.

"All right. Rest. I'll update you as to what all this is about when I can." Genevieve disconnected and headed to her car. "My kit is in the trunk. I need to change. I look too cute to get this outfit dirty. Then I'll connect with my father."

Darius's mouth trembled just a bit and then he smiled.

She left the back of her trunk open while she pulled on pants and swapped out a plain white shirt for the dress.

Darius approached, leaning against the car while she traded her pretty heels for flats and then pulled her hair into a high tail.

She waited for him to say whatever it was he had to tell her as she pulled her work bag free and then faced him completely.

Darius took her in. "You wear white a lot when you practice."

"Not always, but when I'm dealing with something

that might be dangerous or malicious I might. Many scales together make armor. It's one tool."

He brushed his fingertips over her cheek. Just a butterfly of a touch before he said, "She didn't say it had to be you. Only that it needed to be in a circle."

"I'm not being vain when I tell you I'm far more powerful than every witch in the Procella family combined. That spell can't penetrate my personal wards," she argued. "You said so yourself. The Genevieve I am today would fight through it."

The hard line of his mouth softened and his spine relaxed slightly as he pulled her into a hug and let her go, keeping her hand. "Why would you want to have to fight it off? Yes, I believe you can. And yes, I believe you're absolutely powerful enough to set the circle. But if you're the trigger and it binds and the spells release, that's malevolent energies in the air. Even if the spells didn't hurt you, they might hurt others and I know you don't want that."

With a sigh, she put the bag down and pulled two glass jars free. "Salt and ash."

He took them from her and with a jolt she realized she got to watch him perform a working and that was far more interesting than setting the circle herself.

Darius approached the bags, and when he tipped the salt into his palm and then onto the ground, a concussive echo of the power he wielded rolled through her. And then, he…blurred. She couldn't tell if he was moving too fast to see clearly or if it was a shift to another state of being, or any one of a million things. Time slowed around them.

Darius's magic was beautiful. The blur was midnight, darkest night and deepest ocean. Shafts of gold and bronze shimmered and glittered within. As the circle neared completion, his power rose around them, swirling, stealing her breath until there was another *boom* of light and noise and energy and he stood there again, the same Darius he was five minutes before only slightly smudged at the edges with that same midnight and bronze.

"It's done," he told her.

And now that a circle had been cast around the delivery, she felt a great deal better. She could think clearer even as she replayed how magnificent he was doing something as simple as laying a circle.

"Thank you," she said softly, and then called her father.

Her father didn't bother trying to hide the annoyance in his tone when she told him about the latest thing Hugo had done.

"Your street address is in your personnel file," he said, looking back at the phone's camera after some keystrokes at his computer. "I'm ordering everything locked down. This is unacceptable and not just because you're my child. This after the same thing was done to all those witches who were taken? Unacceptable," he repeated.

"There are missing humans now," she said. "Let me come to you to report. There's much happening but I don't want to say all this over the phone." It had been unthinkable that anyone should come to the gates from the outside world that way but now it had happened. There was a sense of being watched, an itch between her shoulder blades she did not like.

"I will come to you," her father said. "These things from Hugo need to be destroyed. I'd like to examine them myself, but it's too long to leave it."

Darius rumbled in the background.

"Darius is going to do that right now. I just wanted you to see it first while I made this report."

"I'm going to call Hugo Procella in for questioning while I'm there in Las Vegas with you. Since I'll be in the city, it makes sense. And I don't want to leave it because he'll take that as permission to do more," Konrad assured her.

They disconnected and Genevieve tipped her chin to Darius. "I am grateful for your assistance," she told him.

"A moment," he said before turning a full circle and then he was *other* again. That blur of obsidian glinting with ambers and iridescent blooms. This time that blur churned in place as a concussive *wom-wom-wom* of energy filled the air.

The sage and sand rose, the salt unifying with him. The tug in her belly was a signal and she opened, serving as a conduit, both to the Trick and to Darius in particular. How very easy it was to share that connection with him.

Her intent rose and twined with his, the pale blues and purples of her magical energy threading through the blur.

The boxes and balloons within the circle seemed to glow brighter and brighter and suddenly it reversed. Dimming until there'd been a pop in the air and everything that'd been in the circle was gone.

Then as before, the blur became solid between one breath and the next and Darius stalked to the edge of the circle, breaking it.

"It's done. Come on, let me take you home," he said. He held out his elbow and Genevieve took it, letting him lead her to the vehicle.

Something inside Genevieve seemed to wrench out of place and a flood of tenderness rushed through her.

Genevieve placed a hand on his arm once they were back in her home.

"I want to thank you again. And to apologize for bringing this here to you. I know you try to stay neutral." Genevieve knew if she'd offered to leave, he'd shut down and she found she very much didn't want that.

He picked up the hand she'd placed on his arm and brought her knuckles to his lips to kiss. It was remarkably old-fashioned and sexy at the same time.

"We've talked about this, Genevieve."

The way he said her name sent flickers of pleasure through her. He said it like he tasted every sound of her name. Like she was delicious.

"You're one of us. So, to threaten you is to threaten every single Dust Devil on this territory," he told her. "To threaten you is to threaten me, because by all that is holding this world together you are mine to protect."

Genevieve swallowed hard. The words were a portent. They were an oath and a magic spell. What use would it have been to deny it? To play coy with this being who was brutally honest seemed a cruelty. And cowardice.

"It's true that in general we do not take sides in issues between other groups of supernaturals. But we *always* pick our own side, yes? We don't get involved in other people's business unless it's about us and defending what is ours. You are ours. This land is ours. In bringing this *here*? To our hive? He's issued a challenge I'll happily accept." He crossed his arms over his chest and she found her gaze returning over and over to the muscles of his biceps straining over the wide expanse. She'd seen that chest utterly naked. Had cruised over that hard, rippled skin with her lips and her fingertips.

Suddenly the room seemed a great deal smaller than

it had moments before. And as if he'd physically grabbed her, she found herself standing so close to him she could nearly taste him.

He cupped her cheeks in his palms, the heat—oh the heat—of his skin against hers was glorious. She looked her fill at the features of his face. The blade of his nose, the slight dimple to the left of his mouth, the endless wonder of his eyes. His lips curved as he smiled and the ground she stood upon seemed to wisp away so that it was he that held her to the earth.

"I should be concerned by that smile," he murmured, his lips against hers.

"Should you?" She reached up to wrap her arms around his neck as his hands left her cheeks and came to rest at her hips with no small hint of possessiveness.

"Whatever it is, I'm sure I'll like it," he breathed into her mouth, and that sweet teasing kiss became something else.

The fingers at her hips dug in as he hauled her impossibly closer, sending a ribbon of pleasure through her veins.

His tongue slid against hers, flirting and tasting, but when she made a soft sound of pleasure he groaned, biting her bottom lip, and sucking into his mouth.

Though Genevieve should stop the kiss and save the rest for later that night, she tugged *his* bottom lip between *her* teeth. Wanting to incite him as he did her.

Waves of heat rolled through her as she held on, his taste making itself at home, chasing everyone else who'd been before him.

As if there could be anyone like him.

Marco called out from the front door as he came into

the house and it was Darius who ended the kiss with a reluctant sigh.

He put a finger against lips still tingling. Repeating, "We'll protect you. I'll protect you. You're capable of doing it yourself," he said as she was about to interrupt. "But you don't have to." He kissed the tip of her nose and with a little bit of a limp for a few beats, followed the sounds of Marco and Lorraine.

Warm with the weight of what he'd just given her, she trailed at his back so she could get herself together again even as she knew on a deeper level she'd been forever changed by him.

# *Chapter Twenty-Three*

"We've identified the others who fled from the scene," David said as Clive entered the sitting room.

The sun had only set five minutes before. He hadn't even had blood or a cup of tea yet. And there his wife was sitting at a couch instead of resting in her bed, her casted leg propped up on an ottoman. "Should you be sitting up?" he asked, and it apparently was the right thing to say because Rowan's smile softened and a delicate pink stained her cheeks for just a moment.

"Dr. Jenkins says I can sit up for a bit as long as it doesn't hurt. You should go feed, and then David and I will give you an update on everything that happened while you were at rest," Rowan said.

Betchamp showed up just then with a tea tray, Elisabeth at his side, ready to pour out after a quick look in Rowan's direction. A reminder most likely from Elisabeth that she could handle the pouring out as Rowan healed.

"I imagine you'd like a cup of tea as you catch up with Ms. Rowan," Elisabeth said, placing some simple tea sandwiches on a plate and handing it Rowan's way. "These are bland, and the doctor says you can have them. I thought you might be getting bored of broth."

"Thank you, Elisabeth," Rowan said.

"I don't need to feed today. I'm fine," he told Rowan in an undertone as he settled next to her on the couch.

"Well. Hold that in reserve until after we get you caught up on everything. Let's see. The Joint Tribunal has been rescheduled for three weeks from tomorrow because Dr. Jenkins didn't want me to travel for two weeks. I told Theo the same during a phone call earlier, so that was handled. I only gave him five minutes. It's fine."

"I don't know whether to be grateful you obeyed medical advice or concerned you're complying so easily because you're not as healthy as you need to be," Clive said.

"Genevieve and David bullied me into seeing the situation more clearly. Mainly they pointed out I'd be at a disadvantage because Theo would know I was weak and would manipulate me. And, to be honest, he thought about arguing. So I suggested sending someone else and he backed right down. Anyway. Everyone has responded to the proposed schedule change except you and Paola. Witches are fine with it."

"I'm quite happy to accommodate whatever your doctor says you need to get better. What else?"

"It was an okay call," she said quietly. "He's worried. Threatened to come here if he had to. Told me he had all the shitlords below. Ready when I was recovered enough to deal with the situation."

Clive was pleased the call left her in good spirits. She and her father both would be calmer after a positive interaction.

"Apparently the non-comatose prisoner had some sort of episode last night and he's conscious but nonresponsive," Rowan said. "The nice officer video-called to tell me about it. Probably also to verify I was still too fucked-up to go breaking into jails on killing sprees. Didn't hurt that David had to hold the phone and the light hit the bruising on my face and chest to heighten the drama. Our inside source says they're chalking it up to gang violence and they don't much care to expend the resources. They'll say they're looking, but I'm recovering and the only other people who got hurt were the bad guys and so who cares in the long run?"

"It'd be for the best but it infuriates me nonetheless," Clive said. "I'm afraid to ask what else."

Rowan told him about the things sent to Genevieve's home address from Hugo Procella.

"Her street address right in the middle of Dust Devil village. And wouldn't you know it? These beings who don't normally take sides can—and do—defend themselves," she said with a shrug.

"So Hugo has now created an adversary in a Trick of Dust Devils? I imagine he can't be very smart to have made that choice but a boon to Genevieve." And Rowan, because she and Genevieve were close, though he didn't say that out loud.

"The call with Theo was fine, as I said. That's pretty much everything. Oh, Konrad Aubert is here to speak to Genevieve in person regarding this Procella situation," Rowan said.

"And how are you feeling?" Clive looked her over closely. Her eye was no longer swollen and most of the red had receded, but her bruising had settled in and she looked like a Monet, all yellows, blues, and purples.

He swallowed back the fear because there she was, after being rammed into by three separate armored vehicles at the same time, riddled with bullets, and assaulted during some hand to hand where she'd taken down two fully armed wolf shifters. Looking mildly annoyed at the current restrictions on her movements, including the sling holding her arm in place while her torn muscles and the gunshot wounds in her chest and shoulder healed.

"Better. I've slept a lot. Elisabeth brings me juice and tea and broth and Genevieve brought over some sort of healing tea that smells like a cough drop and tastes like the bottom of someone's handbag."

He leaned close to kiss her temple in an unbruised spot. "I prefer all this to the alternative."

"Well, for Goddess' sake, me too. Anyway, I'll keep getting better and now I don't have to go to Prague so I can handle all these pressing problems here in Las Vegas first."

"For the next few days let's say you let other people handle most of those pressing problems? You can tell everyone just how you want things done. But stay still long enough for your lacerated insides to heal before you and your sword go out on a jaunt. For my nerves if nothing else. My hair will begin to fall out at this rate," he teased.

She flicked her glance up and smirked. "I doubt that. Even I can't do damage to that mane of yours."

Ridiculously flattered and not giving a fig if anyone else saw, he leaned in and kissed her again. "I'll instruct Alice to respond to the request to reschedule the Joint Tribunal. What of the attackers you've identified?"

"Like the others, they live in the Seattle area. Genevieve's assistant, Samaya, connected Vanessa with someone within the Conclave they call the Archivist."

"Oh, very mysteriously official," Clive said.

"She's brilliant," David added. "Helps that the witches are sharing a great deal of their information about wolf shifters. And within Hunter Corp. I've been able to put together some basics about this Shank family. They're mercenaries for hire. Mainly for muscle and body work."

"Drugs too, right? I'm remembering something about them cooking meth and not being poisoned?" Rowan asked.

"Yes, but this particular family likes to hurt people."

"Delightful," Clive said.

"This is our own fault," Rowan muttered. "They fly under the radar and Hunter Corp. generally leaves them be. Not because we like it. But because we've focused on Vampires and magical practitioners." She blew out a breath. "David, can you see about setting up a meeting with some of the others in Hunter Corp. on this issue? This sort of thing absolutely impacts humans and that falls under the Treaty. The drug thing, well, that's something we might find a way to toss to locals. But mercenary shifter hit teams roaming around trying to kill people in broad daylight the way they did? The risk of it all—to everyone—is simply too grave to ignore."

"I'll have Vihan get to work on creating a pool of possible Hunters to tap for this new approach to shifters," David told her. "And I'll coordinate with Alice, of course."

Clive inclined his head in appreciation.

"Sounds like we need to go to Seattle," Rowan said.

He didn't bother to stifle his indignant reply. "I cannot say I heard that at all," Clive told her. "You just moved an entire Joint Tribunal because your doctor said no travel for two weeks. As we don't currently live in Seattle, getting there would fall under the travel descriptor. In any case, we already know from Oliver Shank they're hiding out at a ranch here in Nevada anyway. We don't need to go to Seattle at this stage."

"I propose we connect with the Hunters in the Northwest before heading to Seattle anyway. Let them continue looking into the Shank family as we do from here," David said, smoothly interjecting. "Once you're recovered and we're ready to proceed, we can travel there and be prepared."

"That's a fine idea, David." Clive kept his gaze from Rowan's for a few moments, the two of them not wanting to inadvertently restart this struggle for dominance between them.

"Yeah, it's a good one. Make it happen. I'm going to want to talk with the Hunters up there anyway. I do need to head to Seattle, Portland, and Vancouver to assess their situation. What they need from HC to strengthen their profile in the Northwest. Obviously after I'm recovered," she added just for Clive, and he let it mollify him. "I know a few of the people up there. Don't ask me last names but all that information is in my files."

"On it." David stood. "I'll return shortly."

Once he'd gone, Rowan took his hand in hers, which was lovely but worrisome.

"I've come to a decision. There's a lot going on right now. Way too much for me to be weaker than I have to be. I'm done being slow and in pain because someone might want to talk to me. It's not like I'll be healed instantly anyway, but I think I should take your blood. If you're still offering, that is."

Stunned he hadn't had to argue or cajole her into it, words escaped him for a few beats. Not wanting to give her any time to overthink and change her mind, he tore his wrist open and held it for her to feed.

He wrapped the other arm around her uninjured shoulder and cradled her to his body. The weight of her there was perfect. She held his arm in her hands, her mouth open against his skin, her hair, a river of sunset reds and golds, slid over them both. Each pull she took was like an invisible cord to his gut. To his heart and lower places. Seeing her, knowing she turned to him to help, knowing she trusted him enough to be vulnerable and admit weakness did something to him. Settled his unease.

Normally she took a few sips, but she drank fully and without hesitation.

Finally she lifted her head and he eased her back to the cushions as her color pinkened. His blood would be soaking into her system, healing the gravest internal injuries before the more superficial wounds and bruises that her body was already healing anyway. "Thank you," she said before allowing her eyelids to slide shut.

"There's not a single millisecond of any day when I would not offer you my very life," he murmured. "Whatever it is you should want or need I will provide. It is my pleasure and my responsibility."

"You spoil me." This was said while her eyes were closed, and a smile marked her mouth.

He scoffed. "Darling Hunter. If there's someone who deserves spoiling in the world, it's you. It pleases me to find ways around your general disapproval of presents." He had to surprise her into accepting a gift or be so clever or romantic she couldn't refuse. Or bloodthirsty. She always accepted weapons.

"I need to call Genevieve," Rowan told him after a few minutes of companionable silence as he'd held her.

"Tell me about werewolves," Rowan said simply when Genevieve answered her phone.

Genevieve paused a moment as she gathered her

thoughts. "I think they prefer wolf shifter, though they all fall under the Were descriptor. Something about being able to shift at will instead of being tied to the moon. What do you want to know? Asta, the Archivist, said your David had requested information. I gave permission."

"Yes, thank you for that. It's helped a lot. David says this Asta is *brilliant* and it does seem like the information she sent along is a great deal of help. I want to know something specific, and I think you're a better person to answer. What do *witches* hire *wolf shifters* to do?"

"You believe it was witches who hired these Shank wolves to harm you," Genevieve said what she'd already been thinking and was sure Rowan had from the start.

"Do you hire them for muscle?"

Genevieve looked toward her father, who sat not too far from her. He'd be hearing every word and that was fine. It was why she hadn't left the room.

He shrugged very slightly.

"It's a known thing that some witches hire wolf shifters for this sort of thing. They hire shifters for bodyguard work, or security in a corporate setting. Generally, I prefer highly trained witches or Vampires. There's a great deal of conflict within the world of wolf shifter packs, so dealing with them means that could bubble over at any time."

"Yes, I think a Procella, I'm not entirely certain which one, hired these wolves to kill me. It was a reckless move because I know who these shifters are and what family they belong to. And now that I know, I'll backtrack to find who hired them."

"Konrad has called Hugo in to be interviewed over the latest delivery," Genevieve said. "You already knew about the other complaints they filed. But I forgot to tell you Hugo complained you threw him out of the Motherhouse."

"Surely not in your house!" Rowan exclaimed. "Don't let him past the front gate."

Darius drew in a breath at the Hunter's emotion, and it was his gaze she was meeting this time as an entire conversation happened without a single word.

"Not here, no," Genevieve said, and once she had, all the anxiety she'd been holding in her muscles seemed to ease. "We've arranged a tightly warded space."

"Guarded?" Rowan demanded to know.

Konrad's mouth trembled a little as he fought being charmed by Rowan. Genevieve would have told him it was useless. Rowan was impossible not to admire at the very least and like a great deal because there was no one quite like her in all of existence. Her fire was in defense of Genevieve even though just twenty-four hours prior she'd been in the hospital due to a deadly attack that Rowan rightly assumed led back to witches.

"Yes. Guarded. Darius will be there as well as my father. Neither is exactly helpless. I can make do in a pinch if need arises," Genevieve teased. In truth, her father had a property he'd sent his own personal guard to cleanse and add wards to the ones he'd already laid. Dust Devils had been in a perpetual state of readiness since that delivery had been made. Her normal guard had swollen to over a dozen with Marco in charge. Darius insisted on being inside with her and Konrad had backed him up.

If Hugo or anyone involved with him thought to overcome that sort of power, they deserved whatever happened to them.

"I can't wait to hear how this whole thing goes. Would you like some Hunter Corp. backup? Oh for fuck's sake,

Clive, of course I know I can't be backup even though I really want to. They don't want me around for some reason. Maybe more than one reason and that's a weapon."

"I think you make a good point. However," Genevieve added quickly, "they might have hired wolves to murder you. I don't want to risk your safety." As powerful as Rowan was in her own right, as canny and unrelenting, she simply wasn't at the same level as she, Darius, and Konrad were. "I have enough guilt, Rowan. Please don't push the issue."

"Guilt? For what?"

"We both think it was the Procellas. They wouldn't have spared you a second look if you hadn't been with me. If you hadn't interceded to protect me." Genevieve hated that part.

"Don't underestimate my ability to piss people off, Genevieve," she said, dry. "You have nothing to feel guilty over so please don't."

Darius had left the room moments before but came back in, stopping next to Genevieve's chair and kneeling.

"I spoke with Marco. He says if Rowan and Clive wish to watch back at one of the relay points, they can view the video feed. As they'd be within our obfuscation spell, no one would know she was there. Marco says he's got a wheelchair he can bring if Rowan would like so she won't tax herself."

Genevieve knew she blushed. Knew too that her smile was silly and sentimental, but she didn't care.

"That's…very nice of him," Rowan said. "Clive agrees."

Genevieve gave them the information on time and place and disconnected.

Darius and her father had clicked nearly immediately, both clearly comfortable with protecting and leading.

Neither seemed to feel threatened, even though Konrad was used to being the oldest and most powerful witch in the room.

When Marco had come in and they'd all planned the security for their meeting, they'd all traded ideas easily. It was—oddly enough—the most comfortable she'd been with her father in centuries.

"You should meet Rowan and Clive," Genevieve told her father. "With so much more interaction between the Senate and Hunter Corp. it's necessary. And she's my friend."

"She seems very provocative." Konrad meant it in a nonsexual way.

"Rowan is, simply by nature, a very plainspoken person. Impatient on many levels but when it comes to stalking prey, she's endlessly patient. When she wants to be utterly controlled and businesslike, she will be, and she'll perform flawlessly, but she's also capable of stunning insight and driving people to madness so she can break them. It's quite striking. You'll like her, I think."

They were alike, Rowan and Konrad. Driven by a fire to defend while retaining their sense of independence. A deep respect for loyalty and honor. On the surface they couldn't be more different, but a person wasn't the wrapping, but what was inside.

"The Procellas have indicated they're bringing their attorney to our meeting," Konrad said.

"It's cute they think that will make a difference." Genevieve waved a hand. "Will he write us a memorandum of understanding then? Use a series of five-syllable Latin words to…show us the error of our ways? They don't seem to comprehend the depth of their trouble. Is it willful ignorance or naivete?"

"Genevieve," her father began, "there are a type of people in the world who behave as if rules only apply to other people. It's not naivete. It's entitlement. In a boardroom I have no doubt their attorney is quite useful. But they can't scare me with that. It's no threat. Sometimes it's a delight to teach people a new lesson."

"These Procellas have stepped into our world," Darius told Konrad. "Woe be to them."

# *Chapter Twenty-Four*

When they pulled up to the GPS coordinates sent to them, Rowan put a staying hand on Clive's thigh.

"Let's wait for them to approach."

Thankfully that happened rather quickly as she caught sight of someone bringing a wheelchair to her door.

"Do not open that door," Clive said. "I'm going around to help you out of the car. After I look this Devil over."

Rowan peered at the side mirror and nearly guffawed. "Don't worry. It's Carl and Star is with him."

"Still." He slipped from the front seat and though she wanted to leap out, she waited, knowing he needed to exert some control over something. Oh and that she wasn't in leaping condition.

Soon enough the door was open, and Star leaned in to give Rowan a good sniffing before she backed up and barked at Carl, who bowed deeply and waved an arm at the chair.

"Hiya, Agnes! You look like you slapped a brick wall with your face."

Carl calling her some random name was precisely the sort of bizarre normal her life had become. It centered her in ways she couldn't contemplate deeply just then.

Clive growled and though Carl wheezed a laugh, he

locked the wheels and got out of the way as Rowan's husband stalked over, picked her up ever so gently, and put her in the wheelchair.

"What's up, Carl?" Rowan asked.

"I'd planned to tell you to take blood from your man, but you've done that already and good for you."

It was positive to have that decision reinforced. "I wanted law enforcement to see me at my worst so they wouldn't turn it around and say I was the offender. Once that was done, I gratefully accepted the help offered by Scion Stewart."

After a grin at the latter, Carl frowned. "Sometimes people are terrible, Jenny. You're okay to accelerate your healing," was all he said, but it made her feel a great deal better.

Okay, then. "I remember you at the attack," she told Carl.

"I was two minutes behind schedule. Lots of chaos in the air these days when I'm in Las Vegas," Carl said, absolutely talking about the Dust Devils. "I wish I'd been just a little earlier."

Everyone had guilt it seemed.

"I would wave away your apology, but one arm is still healing and the other isn't my waving apologies away hand," she told him.

Carl's craggy face broke into a smile.

"I've had dreams. I don't know how to decipher them." Rowan didn't do well with not knowing how to deal with important things like these dreams.

He cocked his head. "I think you're learning just fine."

"I didn't figure out that I was going to be nearly killed while waiting to make a left turn. That doesn't seem *fine* to me." It frustrated her to no end that she'd dreamed of storms and empty places and all that, but nothing about an ambush.

"Not everything is a portent. Sometimes? Shit happens. You're sailing in the right direction." Carl stepped aside and indicated Clive take care of the wheelchair pushing.

Unexpectedly, Carl took Rowan's hand. "There will be a time when the first answer is on your tongue, but you try to talk yourself out of it. Don't." Straightening, he pointed to a shimmering spot a few feet away. "They're just right there."

"That was pretty straightforward. No poetry or stories about camping." Carl was a sage and like all sages, he had his own way of revealing knowledge or prophecy and all that stuff. Her fairy godsage was a kooky outdoorsman who usually did his thing via wild stories featuring unpredictable wildlife and/or offending humans.

When Rowan looked back to ask him another question he was gone.

"Where did he go?" She tried to twist around farther, but Vampire blood or not, it wasn't such a comfortable thing to do so she stopped immediately.

Star just barked and trotted over to the blurry spot as if to tell them to hurry up.

Genevieve said to her father, "Up until now, Rowan has been generally unaware of just how active witches are here in Las Vegas. She won't care if it doesn't hurt humans. But she's paying attention now. Take care."

They'd arrived in a room set up tribunal style with seating behind an imposing table facing three chairs. Darius approved of the way guards had been stationed throughout the building as they'd approached. Konrad knew how to run a security team.

Darius didn't know Rowan as well as Genevieve did of course, but he tended to agree that any unsavory business wasn't going to go unnoticed by the Hunter.

She and the goddess she carried within.

He was developing a soft spot for the fiery-haired Vessel Genevieve trusted so deeply. Her fate had aligned with Genevieve's and it was a good thing.

He wasn't needed to do anything other than protect Genevieve, so that's what he did, moving to stand at her back, his arms crossed over his chest once they'd gotten word the Procellas had arrived. Darius didn't need weapons. And if he did, he'd conjure them with a thought.

Two of Konrad's people escorted Sergio and Antonia Procella and a third witch Darius hadn't seen before. None of them were Hugo.

"This is our attorney, Felix Procella," Antonia said as they were pointed to seats.

"Where is Hugo?" Konrad asked.

"He will not be attending this meeting," Felix said.

"The summons was not optional," Konrad said. "The allegations against him and your family are very grave. Inform him to present himself immediately."

"That won't be happening. I'm not going to let you railroad my grandson because your daughter wants what she can't have," Sergio said.

Genevieve maintained her control, but Darius knew she'd be seething inside.

Konrad sniffed with utter disdain before continuing, "Hugo Procella has on multiple occasions harassed Genevieve Aubert. On two of those occasions, coercion spells were set to be triggered by Genevieve and hidden within romantic totems. First in roses and then in multiple pieces of a delivery sent to her home just hours ago."

"Bullshit! She's a liar. He doesn't need to stoop to such behavior. She wants him, plain and simple," Sergio said.

"Grandfather, please," Antonia said and then turned to Konrad. "I know my brother can be enthusiastic and sometimes that gets misinterpreted."

"We could far more easily interpret his supposed *enthusiasm* if he were not evading questioning on the matter," Konrad repeated. "Why don't I see a phone in someone's hand?" This was a demand from a man used to absolute obedience in certain things.

Darius saw echoes in Genevieve's mannerisms.

"As I've said, he's not going to attend," Felix began.

Konrad turned to one of the guards at the door. "Issue an arrest warrant for Hugo Procella and bring him in immediately."

Sergio stood and leaned over to raise his voice at Konrad, who stood as well and stalked around the table he'd just commanded. The guards at the door didn't move to intervene and Darius admired the control Konrad had over them. They believed without a doubt their benefactor could handle anything Sergio Procella tossed his way.

Konrad stared down his nose at Sergio, their bodies close enough that even a deep breath would bring contact. The power rolled from him, filling the room with magic that tasted of him alone. Sergio's was the merest whisper in comparison.

"Did you have something to say other than accusing Genevieve of lying about something multiple witnesses and surveillance video can corroborate? Your son was stalking her and attempted to use magic to steal her choice. That's rape. And I'm absolutely positive she's not the only one he's done this to."

"You can't arrest him!" Sergio declared.

"I can. I will. I've presented you with opportunities to intercede here and get him in to talk with me. You've refused. Officially. All right, I'll take you at your word, then. You wanted to take a chance to see how much power you really have in our world and I'll be pleased to educate you. He'll be arrested. And if he continues to run like a coward, we'll try him in absentia. He can't hide forever. I have an information network that spans every corner of the planet. He can't leave the country as his face is on a terrorist watch list now and his bank accounts have been frozen. There's nowhere to hide where I cannot find him."

Darius wanted to nod his approval of this sort of bloodthirsty response, but he kept it all inside. Giving nothing but silence and menace to the Procellas gathered before them.

"Moreover, you'll both be taken into custody as well. Not just for aiding a fugitive. There's also the matter of a recent murder attempt on Rowan Summerwaite in broad daylight just yesterday," Konrad continued.

"What are you talking about?" Antonia asked.

"A team of wolf shifters ambushed Rowan in her vehicle as she was waiting to make a left turn. In full view of traffic cameras and no fewer than a dozen tourists who filmed it with their phones and uploaded to social media. She was shot fourteen times. Her car was rammed into from three different directions," Genevieve said. "I find it difficult to understand how this is news to you. It's been on the human news shows ever since."

Antonia's features shadowed under her eyes as she paled. "I don't watch television and given the state of the politics in the world, I avoid it all. I did not know. Is Rowan going to be all right?"

"Eventually."

"What could Hugo have to do with wanting to hurt her?" Antonia whispered.

"It's all lies, you stupid girl!" Sergio yelled. Konrad made a little flick of his wrist and Sergio's knees buckled and he ended up in his chair again in a boneless heap.

"Do shut up as we answer the question," Konrad told him.

Genevieve said, "Hugo showed up at Hunter Corp. here in town. He's on video from the parking lot into the first floor and then interior cameras picked him up. He wouldn't leave so Rowan physically threw him out."

"That was when you showed up at his front door," Sergio said. "He told me all about it!"

"He lied. Or you're lying. Regardless. We have footage, as I said. Please roll it," Genevieve said and one of the guards brought a laptop and queued up the footage and hit play.

Darius watched the Procellas as they took in the video image of Hugo doing exactly what they said he'd done, including Rowan tossing him out into the parking lot and him tearing off.

Konrad looked over to Felix. "You're going to want to rework your strategy."

"He's been so anxious about the rule change," Antonia began.

Konrad said, "That's not a problem. There'll be no rule change. In fact, there'll be a full-scale investigation into the types of entertainment you provide to both witches and humans. The nature of these compulsion spells is too dangerous to ignore."

Sergio struggled to stand up but let it go when it was clear whatever Konrad had done wasn't something anyone of his power could undo.

He did manage a disgruntled, "You can't do that! That's abuse of power."

"I can do whatever the fuck I want. Even if it was an abuse of power. Don't you forget it," Konrad growled out. "The Conclave is dealing with levels of betrayal from witches against other witches the likes of which we haven't seen in centuries, and you want to play games? Who will you complain to, Sergio? You can tell me where Hugo is or spend the night in a cell. Both of you." He looked over to Antonia.

"I didn't know he'd been stalking you like this," Antonia said. "He's fascinated by you."

"Obsessed."

Antonia winced at Genevieve's correction, but then nodded. "Obsessed. But I didn't…the coercion spells… I wouldn't allow that. Even if he is my brother, I would not have remained silent if I had known. I don't know where he is. I swear it."

"Where's your father?" Genevieve asked.

"He's in San Diego. That's where our offices are for our cruise entertainment business," Antonia said. "He and Hugo are estranged. My brother won't go to him."

"Just because a father is estranged from a child doesn't mean he wouldn't still move heaven and earth to help if asked," Konrad said. "If you know, if either of you know where Hugo is, it's better to say so now. Better for him to give himself up before my people run him to ground."

"I don't know," Antonia repeated.

Both Procellas were taken into custody. Their attorney was allowed along until they were secured properly, and soon enough, the room was empty of everyone but Darius, Genevieve, and Konrad.

They'd been listening via the microphones placed in the room with the Procellas and Genevieve. Rowan was quite honestly near speechless at the ridiculousness of the whole thing.

"Hugo is a creep. A stalker. He couldn't have just developed this behavior recently when he saw Genevieve for the first time. Yes, she's pretty fucking gorgeous and all, but he seems to have a routine, which indicates a history, they're going to find out she's not the first woman he's obsessed on. Probably not the first he tried coercion on either."

"Darius won't allow him to remain at large," Marco muttered. Rowan liked Genevieve's lead guard. He was more human than many of the others and though he was still scary, he was also more accessible.

"Let's hope he doesn't get smuggled onto a ship or whatever," Rowan said.

"No ship is leaving their dock without being searched for him. I guess with that name this should be expected," Marco said with a sigh.

"Hugo?"

Marco shook his head with a chuckle. "No, Procella. In Latin if I remember correctly, it means uh, like a big storm."

Holy balls.

Twenty minutes later, Rowan was being rolled into a private meeting room at *Die Mitte*. They'd left the area around Fremont Street but needed a place to meet and talk through all the things they'd discovered.

And since Rowan was hungry and Clive's staff seemed

to crave making her food, she agreed when Clive made the offer of a very late dinner.

Clive had then waylaid her in a small office and made her take his blood again. And when Dr. Jenkins showed up and pretended it was a coincidence, she'd examined Rowan and said she was recovering so well she could eat some cacio e pepe and a little bread.

Rowan wasn't going to be running a marathon anytime soon, but her ribs and shoulder were healed enough she didn't have to wear the sling except when she was sleeping, and her calf didn't throb so severely though it would remain casted for a while longer. Since a human would have to deal with four or six months' worth of recovery and it looked like Rowan only had to tolerate weeks at most, she kept it in perspective. She was lucky.

Once food had been delivered and everyone had been introduced, Rowan said, "I learned something new an hour ago. The Latin meaning of Procella."

She watched as Genevieve, Darius, and Konrad ran it through their memories and everyone but Konrad understood.

Genevieve explained Rowan's prophecy dreams and knowings to Konrad and then he too got the reference.

Clive had risen to go deal with something and when he returned, she knew he had something else to add.

"Two things. First, we've identified the property the wolves who escaped the scene are hiding out at. We'll get back to that in a bit. Second, the Tempest is owned by a witch-owned-and-operated consortium of investors, as I had remembered," Clive began. "There were fronts and fronts after that, a few different offshores. As you might imagine, this made me and by extension, my assistant, ever more curious as to who would hide their involvement that deeply and why. Sergio Procella is one of the principals."

David quickly typed things into his phone with a speed people his age had naturally. His age. For fuck's sake, he wasn't quite ten years younger than she was. Still.

"Just letting Vanessa know," he said as his thumbs flew.

Rowan slowly made her way through her pasta.

Clive watched her carefully, assessing her health and her appetite. Regularly, he reached out to touch some part of her. Her elbow, the back of her hand, whatever. As if to assure himself she was really there and all right. And, she thought, to make a brand of ownership in the way of powerful beings.

"So we've got connections to the Procellas in a few ways. As for ways we can act on? Konrad and the Senate can handle Hugo as it pertains to his stalking and attempted assault on Genevieve. But the rest is tenuous," Rowan said.

"Perhaps not tenuous as much as we don't have all the pieces yet. We've got the who, but not the what." Genevieve grabbed another piece of bread.

That was easier to bear than the way she'd approached it. "Okay, I can see that. We need to lay it all out. David, you're on whiteboard duty."

He jumped up, his sandwich in one hand as he grabbed a marker and began to write down the symbols from her dreams and knowings. And on another line, he wrote out the various incidents they were dealing with. Vampire lords, missing humans, the attack on Rowan, and Hugo's stalking.

"I think you should add the rule change," Konrad said. "That's connected to the Procellas."

When David stepped back, Rowan took it all in, letting her subconscious mind begin to unravel it all.

"We need to take these wolves who escaped the scene. If we can find that connection between them and the Procellas, that's a huge step forward," Clive said, studiously avoiding Rowan's gaze.

"Are they in the Goldfield area?" Rowan asked.

Clive nodded. "Yes. There's no other house for miles. The area is already fairly deserted. We can't get close by vehicle without being spotted. But my people were able to verify there are four shifters there. No others. No animals. We don't know yet where the other three went."

"That's not even a three-hour drive. I can totally go," Rowan said.

As a group, they all turned to her and said, "No."

"What? Why? It's not on another continent. It's not in another state. I'm not saying I'll be out there kicking wolf shifter ass or anything. But I should get to go. This all connects to my dreams." She really wanted to cross her arms over her chest but that would have hurt, so she didn't.

"Because the way Oliver described it, any approach by vehicle would be seen. Which means it'll take some Vampires to fly in and handle their apprehension. You can wait here. *Safely.* And when we bring them into town, you can definitely interrogate them," Clive offered.

As bribes went, it was pretty decent given her physical state.

"We've got four hours before sunrise. My team is researching and planning now should the Dust Devils or Senate wish to take part," Clive said. "The tentative plan is to move tonight after sunset. We have modes of transportation shifters won't see until it's too late for them."

"They won't see Devils. Not if we don't want them to." Then Darius turned to Genevieve and stared at her so intensely Rowan blushed. He briefly put a finger against her lips. "Your side is our side. We've gone over this. We'll provide overwatch for the Vampires and give an escort back. If anyone runs, we'll catch them."

Genevieve nodded and said faintly, "As you wish."

"The Procellas work with cruise ships," Rowan murmured. A way to smuggle someone out of the country.

Genevieve said, "Antonia said her father is in San Diego where that part of their business is located near the cruise terminals. She claims the father is estranged and Hugo wouldn't go to him."

"Bullshit. Of course that's where he's headed. He can't get on a plane. Major bus lines and trains are being watched. Where's he going to go otherwise? His family is going to cut him loose like dead weight because he so openly broke your laws with Genevieve. If the dad can get him out of the way now, they can avoid total ruin."

"Speaking of that," Konrad interjected, holding his phone aloft a moment. "I had someone look through our files. There were two other women who made an official request for assistance from the Conclave regarding stalking and obsessive behavior from Hugo Procella. Neither woman wanted any further involvement once the family stepped in and called him off. One is married. With two kids and a wife. Their family moved out of the country. The other woman sold her house and now lives in a high-security building with a doorman. The Procellas made large cash payouts to both and from what information we have so far, Hugo left them alone afterward."

"I wonder if Sergio accused them of lying too?" Genevieve murmured.

Rowan growled. “You know he did. Hugo is a devious, perverted little shit, and his family seems to have enabled him to continue. I could kick him with my casted leg. It would hurt me, but it’d be worth it.”

“Sergio or Hugo?”

“Both. And look, Antonia acts one way, but let’s be real, he’s done this before, and she has to have known and she still made excuses. I don’t trust anyone in that family at this point,” Rowan said.

“She’s in custody for the night but I probably won’t hold them for longer than forty-eight hours. We’re searching their home here in Las Vegas right now, but I’ve also sent out one of my teams to surveil Alfonso Procella, as well as the ships they deal with. I agree it makes sense to think Hugo will go to his father for help,” Konrad said.

Rowan bristled. “We’ve been very forthcoming with you on several delicate matters. Mounting a search without involving Hunter Corp., even just to inform us, is not a move I’m pleased with.”

“This has nothing to do with Hunter Corp. This is an internal matter,” he said, and it was arrogant as fuck and not sexy like when Clive did it.

“That’s bullshit.”

Konrad Aubert was clearly not used to being spoken to in such a manner. He stiffened, and at her side, Clive sat taller, leaning slightly closer to Rowan to signal his allegiance.

“Who do you think hired those wolves to try and kill me? Witches did. Whose office building did Hugo have to be removed from when he tried the roses stunt? Who physically threw him out? Whose prophetic gifts have guided you to the guilty parties? It’s not like I can go running up and down stairs, kicking in doors to see if they're hollow. But I most certainly deserved to know a search was happening long before now."

"I did inform you. Just not on your timeline. And I have every intention of sharing what we find if any of it is pertinent to your investigation."

"Jesus on a pogo stick, what were you thinking about just now when I was speaking? All those things done by me and Hunter Corp. means I have pertinent information that would have been useful during a search. It's sloppy to have ignored that."

Genevieve looked over to her father and cocked her head.

"We all have our own concerns. I cannot be expected to do Hunter Corp.'s job as well as my own," Konrad said, exasperated.

"Please." Rowan rolled her eyes with a snort. "When *I* do a job, it gets done right." She probably shouldn't have said that, but Rowan had had her fill of entitled powerful people acting as if everyone else in the world was just an accessory to whatever they wanted to do.

And since it had already been said, Rowan continued, "I have zero interest in the vast majority of witch business. Yes, yes, all you big powerful beings tend to forget the existence of pretty much everyone else on Earth, but I don't have that luxury, Konrad. I'm not a thousand-year-old warlock, but I'm also not a punk. You'll take my intel, no hesitation, but I can't expect the same? That's far from a working relationship I'd pursue in the future, if you take my meaning."

"As I said, plainspoken," Genevieve said to Konrad. "You're correct, Rowan. I apologize this didn't come up at the beginning of our conversation. There is no ill intent. We have long been on our own to defend ourselves.

It has made us insular in many ways. I'll endeavor to improve on this matter."

"I promise to let you kick a door in when you recover fully," Clive said in her ear, making her smile.

Konrad leaned forward, his elbows on the table. "Genevieve is correct to apologize and to say there's no ill intent. I have protected my people century after century. So long I forget we are not entirely alone. Your intelligence did indeed save countless lives and that you so freely shared it matters." He inclined his chin.

Rowan didn't want to be crosswise with witches, but like any other alpha predator, they had to learn she wasn't weak or easy to overlook or manipulate. She'd earn their respect but wouldn't tolerate their high-handedness. "I should add, you have, in return, helped Hunter Corp. and me personally on more than one occasion. I do not wish to sound ungrateful. Merely to point out the importance of reciprocity."

Sometimes you had to sucker punch an apex predator in the junk a few times before they finally respected you. Or feared you. But careful so they didn't kill you before they got to the respect part.

Quickly from that point they agreed to share information and to meet back just after sunset for the raid on the ranch the wolves were at. Rowan would toss anything back that wasn't relevant. She had enough of her own secrets to keep, she wasn't interested in borrowing trouble.

"Now, as there's not much else we can do and my wife very much needs her rest, I bid you all good night." Clive stood and they all headed downstairs.

"Well done," Genevieve whispered in Rowan's ear when she bent to deliver cheek kisses. "I'll check in with you later."

## *Chapter Twenty-Five*

Genevieve walked through her backyard and found herself tapping on his sliding glass doors. It was an hour shy of sunrise and already the blanket of darkness had begun to lift.

She was tired, but for the first time in days she wasn't afraid someone she cared about was going to die. It might be the eye of the storm, but in that respite, she reached out to Darius.

He opened a nearby door, poking his head out. "Through here," he said softly.

Golden light drew her in as she found herself in what Rowan called a mudroom. It held laundry machines and various types of outerwear hung on pegs, along with racks near the floor that held boots of all types.

"I was in the garage," he said and then she was in his arms, not even remembering moving. Burying her face in his neck, she breathed him in.

"Here now. Is everything all right?" he asked, his hands running up and down her spine, soothing her jangled nerves.

"It is now," she said, finding herself on the verge of tears.

He made a low, inarticulate sound that meant nothing

but to comfort and she held on, taking that warmth and steady strength he always presented.

"Do I need to beat someone's face in?" he asked, teasing.

Restless after the last several days of one threat after the next, Darius had made sure Genevieve was settled next door and he'd headed to the garage to tinker with an engine he was rebuilding.

Over the eons, as the world had changed and machines of all sorts could be found everywhere, he'd found a simple sort of satisfaction in learning how to build them. How to repair them.

It was a fascination many of his fellows shared and many Tricks—including his—ran repair businesses to pay the bills and keep busy. Most of them did shifts at the shop either as mechanics or doing the books and that sort of thing. It kept them all anchored to one another, even those who stayed to the outer reaches of their territory came in at regular intervals.

Immortality was a gift and a curse. It became easy over the years to lose touch with the human you'd once been. You forgot human frailty as anything but a weakness to be ignored or exploited. Sometimes, those very old ones simply stopped existing. There one moment and gone the next.

Darius had been there. Had drifted from place to place in perpetual gray where he began to let go of his life. And each time he'd been on that precipice, something or someone had come along to haul him back into the land of the living.

Which is why he was elbow deep in an engine when he felt Genevieve approach.

When he'd opened the door and she came to him so easily, when she'd walked into his embrace and…fit perfectly, the last of the gray washed away, replaced by the vivid hues she brought into his life.

An actual life. With a person he shared meals with. Inside jokes with. A woman who trusted him to be her safe harbor.

There were no half measures with this witch who'd brought him and his Devils so much power and light.

She trembled. Little waves of pent-up energy. He drew them into himself. Away from her where they stole her rest and calm.

"Give me a tour. I want to be nosy and poke through your things," she said, her face still against his throat.

Easily, he turned her, still tucked to his side, and took her through to the kitchen beyond.

She wandered past his bookshelves, peered closely at the bits and pieces of his life scattered on surfaces here and there but did not touch them.

She'd reach out and then clasp her hand into a fist before dropping it to her side.

"Unless you're going to throw something to the ground and stomp on it, you can touch things, Genevieve." He brutally repressed a laugh, not wanting her to feel mocked.

Her features lit. "I just wanted to be respectful."

She picked up a carving of an ibis done in malachite, smoothing her fingertips along the edges and curves.

"You have an amazing collection of these carvings," she told him as she looked over another, a far older one, a fish done in lapis.

"For a long time I never settled in one place for long. But the carvings found a way to me. They were small enough that I could take them to my next home whenever I wanted. They're a reminder of the places I've been."

"I like that. I love the similarities between carvings across cultures but also, how they begin to differ and create something that is uniquely their own. The imprint of thousands of years of human endeavor seems to flow from them."

There was no way to avoid the way she seemed to peer into his thoughts and speak them. To be understood like that was something he couldn't protect himself from.

"Will you tell me what's bothering you?" he asked.

She turned. "Earlier, when we were at *Die Mitte*, you told me you'd protect me and then you looked at me so deeply I felt it in my bones. And I believe you. You just gave me a home in a way. I've always done things for myself. I'm proud of that, please do not misunderstand. It's important to me that I can manage all the things I need to. But no one else but me has ever seen me and valued me the way you do."

She moved to examine some of the art on the walls and he forced himself to stay in place, knowing she had more to say.

"I was in my house. Everyone was asleep and I had all these words and feelings racing through my brain and it seemed cowardly not to tell you. I know you have duties and responsibilities and I never want to put you in a place where you feel you have to choose. I respect your position and all you and the others have done for me. I do not like bringing trouble into your world."

Darius shook his head as he took her hand and drew her down the hall to his bedroom.

"We're bikers. You know that, right? You've seen us and been around us enough to know there's constant trouble and blood in our world. You speak as if you do not flood this Trick with energy. We're fat and satisfied with it. That makes us more stable, not less. Though still troublesome because that's who we are."

He cupped her cheek, tipping her face up so he could kiss her.

"You bring us not just more power, but color. You smell good and you're so fucking pretty it makes me feel better just looking at you. Madame makes food for everyone all the time. Genevieve, you make everyone happy just by being around. You brought this Trick back to life.

"As for our neutrality and you making me choose," he shook his head, "it's not something you need to worry about. There are rules, as you know. We obey them. But we don't have to obey rules that don't apply. And when it comes to protecting our own, as I said, we absolutely have the right to defend ourselves. You're a Dust Devil Priestess. You're our conduit. You bet your very delightful French ass we will defend you."

Her mouth curved up into a very Genevieve smile. Mysterious. Supremely feminine and powerful. Sexy.

Darius believed very few people in Genevieve's life chose her. So few she found it hard to understand when someone did. He hated that.

"Have you poked in my things enough?" he murmured against her temple.

"No. But I can be nosy later. I *will* be nosy later," she corrected with a laugh. "I'm very interested in you." Her words were a little shy at the end.

"How fortunate I am," he said, meaning it. "I come to your door when I know you're in there, clothed in something silky, your hair down. Beautiful and vulnerable and so Talented you could power a nuclear reactor." He slid his fingertip down the front of her pajama shirt, swirling around each button. "That is to say, I'm very interested in your interest."

His lips met hers once more before he put his hands above her hips and lifted her. She helped, wrapping her legs around his waist while he braced an arm under her ass to balance her weight.

He spun, stumbling to the bed where he managed to take them both to the mattress without crushing her.

Her eyes had taken on a slumberous glaze, eyelids half shut. Her skin was flushed, hands quick as she pulled his shirt off and hummed her pleasure.

"You speak of beauty while this is here, taunting me day and night. So handsome and strong, capable, it renders me a little weak," she admitted.

What a wonder it was, then, to not be alone in the face of such tremendous emotion.

She rolled to straddle his waist, looking down at him with a smile on her mouth still swollen from his kisses.

Sometimes age seemed to press down on him so heavily it was hard to breathe, but she made him lighter, younger.

Still, age and experience were his gifts when it came to removing her top, tossing it somewhere in the darkness of his bedroom.

For all her feminine ways, makeup, and pretty clothing, she was a warrior. Bare to the waist, he could imagine her on a battlefield of long ago, breasts painted, bloodlust in her gaze.

That was what ate away at his reserve. Her inner core of strength left him helpless to do anything but fall for her.

She bent and licked a line down his chest, shimmying farther to remove his jeans. While she perused his cock—no small compliment—he took advantage of her divided attention and divested her of her pants and the tiny scrap of lace she'd had beneath.

Laughing, he flipped her to her back and covered her body with his own. Her laughter in response loosened something, a stopper he'd placed to bottle up his joy.

"In me," she whispered. An incitement. An invitation. Neither he'd pass up.

"I can manage some actual foreplay first," he chided before taking one of her nipples between his teeth.

"You're hard. I'm wet. Fuck me," she said on an arch of her back. Her nails scored a path down his spine as she urged him upward.

The struggle was lost completely when she shifted her weight to bring her knees up, wrapping her calves around his ass. Opening her fully.

"Please," she said and that was it.

The heat and wet was irresistible as he sank into her body. Pleasure arced up his spine and then down, settling in the pit of his gut.

Her body pulled him in, inner muscles clutching and fluttering as she accommodated his cock. He never wanted anything but this. The pleasure and the weight of it, the trust to be this laid bare by one another.

This was worth decades of gray. This connection, heat to heat, hard to soft, this was what he'd been waiting for but had no idea. He was glad of that part. Waiting for *this*, knowing that someday he'd look up to find a pretty witch in a minidress stalk into his bar, order shots, and open up a parley with him would be the key, the brush to spread life into his heart again, would have been utterly miserable.

Patience had always served him. And she was his reward. And the inspiration to never walk into the gray again.

He'd keep her safe and ensure she'd never have any cause to leave his side.

He'd never be a human man again. But he'd damned well be a man who was worthy of this witch.

*His* witch below him, the chocolate and caramel of her hair spread out over the pillow. Her gaze settled on his, glossy with desire, and he bent to kiss her over and over as he rolled his hips, taking her in deep thrusts.

Leaning so his weight rested on one elbow, he managed to reach between them to find her clit, circling it with the pad of his middle finger in time.

She turned her head and sank her teeth into his shoulder as her climax began to shudder through her. That pleasure limned with pain grabbed him with claws and dragged him closer and closer. He closed his eyes, trying to hold back, but there was nothing but that headlong fall into orgasm in powerful, all-consuming waves.

She turned onto her side and watched as he left the room and returned shortly with a warm, wet cloth, but she didn't move once she'd cleaned up.

He licked his lips and said what he'd wanted to say for some time now. "Stay."

## *Chapter Twenty-Six*

Not more than an hour after sunset, Clive, Patience, and three more of his security team who could fly dropped to rooftops and tree branches at a collection of squat, single-story buildings that made up a small compound in the desert twenty minutes or so outside Goldfield, which was already fairly desolate to start with.

They'd been able to collect satellite images to add to the flyover some of his Vampires had done the night before. Several miles away, behind some sort of obfuscation spell the Dust Devils put up, two armored prisoner transport vehicles waited to be called to the scene once the shifters had been incapacitated. Genevieve and Darius were there, along with David and Konrad, who volunteered his magic should they need it. It was a way to apologize to Rowan, Clive thought, for not informing her of the searches being conducted on the Procella property.

Alice was back at *Die Mitte* with Rowan, who he'd convinced to rest in his old apartment until it was time for her to interrogate the prisoners.

The so-called ranch sat at the top of a rise and was surrounded by barbed-wire-topped fencing. A windmill spun lazily but there was an empty lookout post near the top.

All the Vampires had gone preternaturally still as they opened their senses fully.

Muted conversation floated in the air, along with the sound of a television show with a laughter track. The main house had four wolf shifters in it. One of the outbuildings held a late model midsize SUV and two dirt bikes. No animals he could sense, no humans for miles.

Silently, Clive touched down near the door to the building holding the vehicles. The space stank of shifters but no one else. He hoped that continued to hold up. Four shifters they could handle. More, they could handle. But if one added humans or animals, it complicated matters considerably.

Patience used a small device to cut the security system so Clive popped the hood and disabled the engine thoroughly before he slashed the tires of the car and motorcycles. No one would be running, at least not that way.

Once that was handled, they edged back outside. Two of his Vampires were on the roof of the main house, near the entry points. Via hand signals they reported no one had been outside.

What was the purpose of having a property positioned the way it was as your hideout and not bothering with a watch or guards? Lazy. But it worked for Clive's purposes quite well.

He met up with the others and then fanned out and on his go, they entered the main house, sticking to the plan they'd made. Patience stayed at his back as they headed toward the living room where the television was on.

There was a bedroom where a female had been sleeping. She was quickly subdued, gagged, and bound. Three more to go. Another male was in the kitchen and Clive watched as two of his Vampires flowed into the room, getting to the shifter before he could arm himself. In that struggle, a jar was knocked off the counter.

The television snapped off and one of the males from the living room called out a name but didn't wait for an answer. In a burst of speed and violence, two very large shifter males *charged* into the hallway where Patience stood with Clive, their hands partially shifted with deadly claws ready to rip an enemy to shreds.

Clive didn't have the brawn the shifters possessed, but he had better balance and speed, so he managed to jump up, making his way up the wall, using his momentum to turn and land on the back of one of the wolves. Patience had managed a similar move and when she dropped, she latched herself onto the head of the other, biting, scratching, and repeatedly boxing the shifter's ears.

Clive clung to the shifter's back, digging his own claws into muscle and flesh with one hand while he managed to grab two gleaming silver stilettos with the other. Relieved he'd worn the special nitrile gloves to protect his skin, Clive climbed higher on the shifter's back, even as the wolf tried to shake him free.

Maneuvering, Clive drew his hands—a stiletto in each—back and then used all his strength to plunge one to either side of the shifter's throat all the way to the hilt.

With an agonized roar of pain, the shifter tried to buck Clive free. Clive held on, using the blades deep in the shifter's skin as handles.

Two more Vampires came into the hall and helped Patience securely bind the other male, but Clive didn't want any assistance.

"You tried to kill my wife," he snarled in the ear of the wolf he was pretty sure was Patrick Shank. Clive tore into the back of Patrick's neck, staying clear of the blades, blood flying everywhere, sending a red haze over his vision.

Patrick sank to his knees, screaming in pain.

"She was shot fourteen times. You broke more than one of her bones," Clive said through a mouth full of blood and teeth.

"Fuck you!" Patrick sobbed as the silver in his neck, piercing lymph nodes, began to slowly, painfully, poison him.

Using the weight of his body and a knee, Clive rammed Patrick's face into the wall three times and scrambled to the shifter's back, all the while keeping the blades in place.

With one last surprised squawk of indignation and pain, Patrick's body hit the floor in a pool of his own blood, unconscious.

"Do not remove the stilettos until he's bound," Clive ordered as the others took over.

"Transports just pulled up," John, one of the team, called out.

"I'll drive back with them," he told Patience. "Stay here. Search every blade of grass. I want to know everything we can. There are three other shifters who escaped who aren't here. Keep John and Amal with you. Konrad Aubert will remain as well, helping in case you find something magic related."

He was also a warrior, so if it came down to that, if they were attacked, he'd be useful there as well.

Ten minutes later, they were on the road back to Las Vegas where Rowan would be getting herself ready to interrogate the prisoners.

Rowan had cleaned herself up, putting her hair back in a braid. She didn't often wear a full face of makeup, but today she chose red lips. On a redhead, she found it made even more impact when she was trying to intimidate someone. Intimidating people was one of her favorite things.

Thanks to Clive pouring his blood down her throat every time he could, she no longer had to use the sling, which made getting a shirt on and off far easier. The snowy white linen was tucked into black pants, though Elisabeth had to help her cut the bottom of the right leg so it would fit over the cast, laughing as she told Rowan Clive had already bought her a dozen pairs to replace the one she was having to destroy.

Fucking stupid, is what the whole thing was. Without these asshole shifters, she could be up, pacing and kicking things. Now she was down a pair of pants and stuck with crutches or a wheelchair, which severely curtailed her kicking.

She wanted to twist someone's balls off like the stem of an apple. Filled with satisfaction, she considered how to make that happen.

Fortunately she had great upper-body strength and could still punch. Plus, she'd been practicing all day with using her crutches as a weapon in various ways. She'd gotten very good and certainly looked forward to using her new tricks with the prisoners she was going to interrogate.

Instead of David showing up to let her know they'd arrived—she'd known the moment her spouse had entered the building—it was Clive who came through the door looking dangerous and rather bloody in all black.

"My. You look like you've had a busy day," she said, joking to get past the knot of fear she'd just let go of when she'd seen with her own eyes he was alive and well.

"Give me ten minutes to shower and change. They've been brought in and put in safe holding cells." He lifted a hand as if to touch her and she leaned forward. But he remembered himself and closed his fingers into a fist. "Apologies. I'm a bit of a mess and I don't want it on you. I'll be right back."

She wanted to follow him, wanted to help him get clean. Shower sex always made them both feel much better. But she'd have to put her cast in a garbage bag first, even if she could stand up on her own.

So, she waited, looking over her notes, and texted back and forth with David, who was downstairs handling the setup for her.

"Now, then," Clive said as he came back, dressed in a new suit, his hair perfect once more. He pulled her into his arms and held her gently. "You aren't wearing the sling?"

"Dr. Jenkins gave me a once-over. I even went to get X-rays. Your blood healed up all that damage. The one on my hip and on the leg that's casted are a little slower but still doing well."

"I wanted to go to that appointment with you," he said with a frown. "I don't like that you had to go by yourself."

"You were busy. I knew you'd want to be sure I was up to the stress of an interrogation, and I didn't want to have to argue and con you into it. I knew she'd be a good authority figure on the matter. I wasn't alone. Betchamp went with me, and a guard drove." That made her very grumpy, but she knew it was necessary, so she sucked it up.

"And if she'd said you weren't well enough?" he asked, dropping a kiss to her lips quickly.

Then Rowan would have not mentioned visiting the doctor at all.

All she said was, "But Dr. Jenkins didn't say that. I even made her write it up so you could have official verification."

That made him smile. "Trust but verify? Isn't that the saying?"

"She emailed it to you, but I had her print it out and I handed it to Alice earlier. She said she'd have believed me without having to prove it."

He raised his brows and smothered a laugh. "She doesn't know you as well as I do." He paused, searching her features. "You're really okay?"

She gave him a quick kiss of reassurance. "I am. I promise. I mean, I have a broken leg. That sucks. And I couldn't be there when you were prowling around all in black looking—and acting if the gore on your clothes was any indicator—dangerous. I couldn't punch anyone. Not a single person. Life can really serve up some bullshit. But, on the bright side, I'm healing lightning fast and now I can terrorize some prisoners. Not as good as my usual, but better than being in a coma." She smiled brightly.

He made a derisive sound at the mention of comas but shook it off.

"I fed earlier. I'm only telling you this because I promised you I'd take care of myself on that front. I'm going to ask you to take more of my blood and you'll know I have plenty to share without it weakening me in any way."

She'd gotten to a point where taking his blood wasn't something that filled her with unease and guilt. But she'd just taken some before he'd left for the ranch. And if she did it daily, she'd be…dependent on that. Maybe.

He cocked his head and sighed softly. Reading her perfectly.

"It would never be that between us. To do so would break our bond. Break you. My greatest, deepest love. You're recovering from severe injuries that occurred just three days ago and my blood will ease your pain and speed your healing. You offer your strength to me all the time. Let me do the same. And really," he added, "if it was my cock you'd have no trouble accepting."

"I really do love us," she told him through laughter that wanted to be tears of sentiment too. "I trust you. It's just sometimes my past gets in the way. I really do think it'd be cool if you could give me the benefits of Vampire blood but through your dick and sexing instead." She took his hand and kissed his knuckles. "Thank you. I love you too."

After she fed and was feeling absolutely no pain, she let him push her in the wheelchair until they reached the floor where the interrogation rooms were.

"Crutches from here on. Not because I can't be commanding in a wheelchair, Carinna Lesva is one of the most badass Hunters I've ever met, and she uses her chair as an extension of herself. It's fucking scary and I adore it. But I like the idea of having the extra reach of the crutches. I've practiced with them all day to hit stuff. Got used to the weight and the reach. I think the first time there'll be a great surprise factor. Eventually I'll break them and it'll be fear. They'll never see a crutch again without wetting their pants."

"You are the most fascinating creature I've ever known," he told her, opening the doors so she could go through first.

Genevieve was there already, as was David.

"Thought you were staying at the scene for the search?" Rowan asked him.

"Vihan and Vanessa are there now. I felt it was more important to be here to take notes and assist during the questioning."

Look at him all grown up and being the boss of other people!

"Sounds good."

"Darius stayed at the ranch," Genevieve explained. "My father is there as well. They've located some rudimentary spells. First aid and that sort of thing. But also two canvas duffel bags full of cash, but it wasn't actually cash. It has been spelled. Darius says the magic feels similar to Hugo's, but it could be a Procella signature. We'll find out."

Rowan felt her heart swell like the Grinch's had. "Hugo fucked them over?" She snorted. "How effective was the spell? Like could they spend it and everyone else saw it as real money too? Or like it turned into paper when the sun came up?"

"Good question. Let me ask." Genevieve pulled her phone out, so Rowan gave her privacy and turned to Clive where he stood with Alice.

"Did that blood all over you come from multiple wolves or did one or two get the bulk of the beatdown?" she asked him as she perched her butt on a desk to rest her leg.

"It's Patrick Shank's blood. He's a bloody giant, but I used those stilettos you suggested," he told Rowan. "The gloves worked great to protect me from the silver. Once the lymph nodes were pierced he went down."

"Are they still in? The blades?"

"Didn't want to kill him before you spoke to him, so I

removed them but he's in silver cuffs and leg irons. He's working on healing a significant injury to the muscles of his back and shoulders." That little smirk on his lips said he'd been the one to deliver those injuries.

"Really bummed to have missed that," she murmured. He was ridiculously hot when he went into that nearly feral place. He fought like a man who'd been trained to fight since he was in short pants and was really good at it. A natural predator. Mmmm.

"Stop that, darling Hunter," he said softly.

"I'll let you reprimand me later," she said in his ear.

"Konrad says the money spell would have worn off over time. Two to three weeks," Genevieve told them as she approached.

"I assume Patrick is the most injured of the four?" Rowan asked and Clive nodded. "Let's talk with him first. Can he shift? Should we be worried about that? They can't tell me all I need to know if they're a wolf."

"I took care of it," Genevieve said. "A spell that breaks their connection to the magic controlling the shift. I made some calls after you asked me about why witches hired wolves and between me and Samaya, we connected with a very old witch whose family are what you'd call organized crime. Not magical organized crime, but money laundering and the like."

Rowan couldn't get mad about it. She had too much to handle as it was. She understood the Senate faced similar issues. There were only so many hours in a day.

"She claims the spell is really used for self-defense. And like the money magic, it wears off if it's not removed. I'm not entirely convinced of the former." Genevieve raised a single shoulder slightly. "But in this case, that is true. It wears off in twenty-four hours so I can renew it if necessary."

"Okay, here's how this will go. I'm going to take Patrick first. He'll be smarting from Clive dogwalking him. Ha! Dogwalking. Werewolf. You all can't be in the room. It's too much. All that power in the air, all the scents, it'll overwhelm him to the point where he's not useful." She needed him focused on her. "David will be with me. He'll record the interview although I'm sure the Nation has the room mic'd up and full of cameras. He also has access to whatever I might need as I go. I'm explaining this so no one gets upset when they can't come in. Clive, not this one. I have to terrify him now. You'll mess with my scary Rowan mojo because he'll have to divide it with yours."

"I can't believe I understood all that. But I agree. Not to the other three. We'll revisit when you've finished. Genevieve can join us in the viewing room."

"Let's go, then."

Rowan entered the room and didn't stop her smile at the sight of Patrick Shank. Bloody runnels marked the side of his neck on both sides where Clive had used the stilettos. His face was bruised and bloody, like the entire back of what little shirt he had left. The skin had been shredded by another paranormal, and because he hadn't shifted, he'd be hurting.

*Good.*

She sat out of arm's reach but not out of crutch reach.

"You have no right to keep me here," Patrick said.

"You shot me fourteen times, Patrick. Also, broke four of my bones. You came into my city and you tried to kill me. And then you abandoned your dumbass brothers and ran off, leaving them holding the bag. Now, why did you do that? I don't even know you. I don't deny being able to drive people into a killing mood, but that's just rude."

"I don't know what you're talking about."

Rowan sighed. There used to be a speech about telling the truth to avoid what would be a great deal of pain and they'd still tell her the truth. But they never listened. So she was going to try something else.

"You had to know what a risk you were taking with this attack. Broad daylight? Cameras everywhere. Dude! This is Las Vegas. You can't pick your nose without it being filmed. Plus there's the whole oh-my-god-no-one-knows-about-the-existence-of supernatural-beings so we're all supposed to avoid doing things that would expose Diane in accounting to the existence of people who can turn into animals."

"I don't know what you're talking about."

The blood she'd recently taken from Clive made her even faster when she twisted to grab the crossbar in the handle of one of her crutches, lifted, swung it right into Patrick's thick fucking neck exactly where that blade had been. He bellowed in pain, and she yanked back and shot her arm forward again, hitting him with the rubber tip right in his Adam's apple, making him gag through his cries of pain.

"That was quite vigorous," David said. "Well done."

"Something new in the repertoire. Seems effective."

"You fucking bitch!" Patrick yelled.

Brigid rose hard and fast and a sense of deep outrage drowned Rowan. "You dare speak in such a manner? A faithless coward who has brought dishonor on his family. I know who you are, Patrick Shank. Nothing." As she'd spoken through Rowan, the energy in the room had risen. Tingles ran over the surface of her skin.

Patrick knew he wasn't only speaking to a Hunter. Rowan noted the moment when he understood he was in way over his head.

"Now, then," Rowan said after Brigid had slowly faded, warmth still in her belly. "I know you're a wolf shifter. I know you and your brothers and cousin were hired to kill me. I know it was you. I know you were paid half a million dollars and really, half a million dollars for all that? How much money could you possibly have made after the overhead on such a production? You had nine people at the scene and another SUV that didn't make it. Ammo. Weapons you probably already had but it's still a cost. Travel here. Lodging. That profit margin sucks. Also, did you know the money you were paid, the cash you had stored at the ranch house I mean, did you know it was bespelled? It's all paper. It'll wear off in two or three weeks I'm told."

"That's a lie," Patrick said.

There was a knock on the door and Alice brought two duffel bags in, placing them on the table. "Marco brought these up, thought you might like them."

"Perfect. Thank you."

"No," Patrick said.

Alice left and Rowan stood, leaning slightly as she unzipped first one and then the other bag. Neatly wrapped stacks of paper. She held up several stacks and then shoved the bags closer to him, making her way closer, liking the wary glance he gave the crutch.

"Wolf shifters have a very sensitive sense of smell. So you know these stacks are what you thought was cash. Oh, I bet you flipped through them, working yourself up into a frenzy thinking about it. You didn't have to share with Eustace and Oliver. More cash for you. And the other three who escaped but never turned up at the ranch. Wonder what happened to them. Did *you* happen to them, Patrick? Loose ends tied. Your fuckup brothers and cousins handled. More money for you again." She'd been spitballing, but damn if that didn't fit perfectly.

He glared at her, lips clamped tight.

"Who hired you, Patrick?"

No answer.

Faster than he could track her, Rowan had pulled one of the silver stilettos Clive had returned to her and slammed it into his upper thigh. Close enough to the femoral artery for him to panic slightly. Definitely close enough the silver would quickly reach his bloodstream and fill him with fiery pain.

Patrick screamed.

"I know where your family is in Seattle," she said in a tone he had to stop screaming to hear. "I bet your uncle and your dad are going to be positively upset when they discover you've not only bungled a job you never should have taken, several sons and daughters won't be coming home. Oh, and four of you have been taken into custody by three different supernatural parties. All those years they spent building the Shank empire and you're fucking it up for half a million dollars that was just fucking paper with a magic spell on it." She paused to laugh at what a stupid cock he was. "What a dingus you are. I'll have all your accounts by this time tomorrow and I'll drain them. Even if you could escape—and you can't—where would you go? You've got no money. All your connections are blown. Your family doesn't want any of the trouble you're bringing with you. You've killed members of your pack and brought the heat down on their heads. You're radioactive now."

Those were the right buttons to push. Pack was deeper than most human understanding of family. They needed that community and connection to thrive and he'd acted so selfishly all the protection of that pack would be gone.

Sweat beaded on his temples as pain wracked him.

"Why protect someone who betrayed you? I'll take the blade out when you answer the question. You have no other reasonable option. Who. Hired. You."

"We've done work for the Procellas in the past. The old one called first," Patrick said. "Sergio said he wanted a hit on a target quickly. We started to put the plan in place but then all of a sudden the grandson gets in touch. Says he wants it right away. You're a high-profile target and hard to get alone so I say we can't do it that fast. We negotiated a bit and in the process I figured out who he was. Hugo Procella. Guy's all wrapped up in some pussy he can't have and you got in his way."

"The first one who called wasn't Hugo?"

"No. The patriarch. Sergio."

That motherfucker. Both of them? For different reasons but clearly Hugo knew what pop-pop was up to since he called direct to change his assassination order. These fucking people!

Rowan headed to the door but then paused, turning to face Patrick again. "What else do you do for the Procellas?" she asked, and Brigid burned so intensely from within she knew it was the right question.

Clive watched his wife obliterate a werewolf in under an hour.

The whole room had erupted with surprised sounds when Rowan had used her crutch.

"She's a beautiful nightmare," Marco said.

"Isn't she?" Clive said. "Magnificent."

The money bit had been done perfectly. The Dust Devil had walked back in with the bag after only being gone twenty minutes. They traveled in their own ways Clive wasn't privy to. But it had worked.

"I'll contact Konrad to let him know we've got a positive identification of Hugo and Sergio as being responsible for this assassination attempt," Genevieve said with a sigh.

Marco patted her shoulder. "This isn't on you, Butterfly."

Genevieve breathed out before she shrugged. "Some of it is."

"No more than rests on Rowan. Or me. The Vampire Nation surely." Clive shook his head. "One thing I've found since my wife exploded into my world is this is all of us. You didn't make these shifters take this job. Or the Procellas do whatever they do. To stop all this, blood gets spilled. Regularly. But without it, more would be spilled, yes? Our world gets unveiled and the humans will panic. That puts us all in danger too. All the carefully crafted rules to keep humanity safe from us will fall apart. And humanity will turn on us. None of it can happen. So we do what we can."

Clive watched Rowan finish up with Patrick on the other side of the glass. She was back in the zone, clearly pleased with herself, which never ceased to incite him. Beautiful nightmare indeed.

## *Chapter Twenty-Seven*

It was about two and a half hours before sunrise when they finally finished up for the night. Rowan had questioned all four shifters and had allowed Clive to sit in on the woman and the guy from the kitchen. Genevieve had assisted when she'd interrogated Angus. He'd gotten all caught up in the witch and her beauty and had spilled as much as Patrick had, though without Rowan having to slam a blade into him a single time.

That made her a little sad, but also relieved they'd been able to get so much information about all the errands the Procellas had hired the Shanks to perform over the last two years.

"Do you want to get pancakes?" Genevieve asked her once they'd gotten down to the parking garage of *Die Mitte*.

Clive was dealing with a bunch of Vampire shit before the sun rose and Rowan didn't envy him that at all. But, a stack of fluffy carbs sounded like exactly what she needed.

Rowan texted Clive where she was headed and he told her he'd see her at home and admonished her to be careful. As Darius was with them, she wasn't too worried, but she assured Clive she was safe as houses.

The city was relatively quiet, though never abandoned, even at that time of the morning, as Darius drove the short distance to Rowan and Genevieve's favorite pancake house. Like he knew exactly where it was.

"She got you hooked on the pancake train?" Rowan teased before she realized who she was teasing. She was too tired to take it back.

Darius made a sound, a cross between a snort and a growl. "Turns out I'd forgotten how a stack of fried dough really hits the spot when you've been out all night."

Genevieve looked at him, a sweet expression on her face, and Rowan was simply so relieved, so pleased her friend had someone who made her feel that way.

"Bacon doesn't hurt it either," Rowan added.

Genevieve quite often ordered a milkshake with hers, so she never looked twice when Rowan got a double side of bacon to go with her short stack.

The parking lot of the diner was pretty full, but they found a spot easily and she managed to scoot herself out to where Genevieve stood, ready, holding Rowan's crutches for her.

They set off toward the door, Rowan slower than usual but it wasn't such a big deal because Darius and Gen slowed for her and carbs were about to enter the chat. She didn't even think she'd be able to eat solids for a week and there she was, mouth watering over pancakes.

Score.

Then something hit her square in the back. So hard she stumbled and hit the pavement in a heap.

Genevieve turned, surprise on her face. "Rowan!"

"Something hit me," she said as a wave of cold began to open over her skin, making her shiver and her teeth chatter.

"Magic," Genevieve said with deadly calm. She touched Rowan's shoulder and cursed.

Darius peered around the area. "We need to get out of the middle of the lot," he said quietly.

"A moment," Genevieve said and began to mutter under her breath. The fingers she'd had on Rowan's shoulder tightened painfully but the cold began to ebb until the weight of it was gone entirely.

Darius picked her up, one-armed, and Rowan tried not to squirm to make it worse as they backed up, looking around to see where the spell had come from.

They couldn't go inside because dozens of humans were in there and they weren't going to bring that danger to them.

Genevieve continued that quiet muttering and singing and the light posts around where they stood went out.

Darius set Rowan to her feet carefully as he handed the crutches over. He looked to Genevieve. "This magic is the same as what was on the delivery."

Hugo couldn't possibly be there! He'd escaped with his life already, why would he be back, facing beings he couldn't possibly overcome?

"Hugo," Genevieve called out, "you can't win. We already know you were behind the assassination attempt on Rowan. And the deliveries you sent to my home." She didn't mention what they knew about his grandfather and Rowan was glad about it. They didn't know if he'd been in contact with Sergio or not, but it wasn't wise to give away all they knew at that point.

Darius, who'd been standing at their side, simply went…insubstantial. A dark swirl of power that reminded Rowan of the dust devils she saw out in the open desert. Mini tornadoes of energy.

Genevieve squared her shoulders as Hugo Procella stepped out between two cars. Even from where they stood in the dark, Rowan could see the madness on his face.

Genevieve drew in a surprised breath that told Rowan she'd seen the same thing.

"You're mine," he said to Genevieve. "They tried to take you from me and I will not allow it. I've been watching since the wolves failed. Tried to get into the hospital but couldn't," he said bitterly. "I can't go home because my family is looking for me. Vampires are looking for me because of her!" He pointed at Rowan. "I can't get on a ship because my father won't help and there are Vampires and Hunters sniffing around the cruise dock. But you and I, Genevieve, we'll find a way to be together. No one can stop us."

Rowan shook her head at this creep. "Shifters will be looking for you too. Witches as well," she replied.

"Why won't you die?" he screamed and raised his hands, clearly about to throw magic at her. But Genevieve flicked her wrist and with the other hand, made a sharp cutting motion. Hugo's hands fell to his sides as he cried out in pain.

"You first, fucko," Rowan said.

"He's…" Genevieve started to speak and then quieted a moment. "He's covered in coercive magic. I neutered his Talent. He's no magical threat at this point."

"How could that happen? Is someone using him to mess with you?" Rowan asked.

"It's his own magic," Darius said as he once again stood with them.

Rowan shook her head. "He deliberately spelled himself? That doesn't make sense."

Darius said, "No. He's contaminated himself with his own spellwork. This is what he wanted to turn *Genevieve* into."

"I wouldn't weep salty tears if you killed him right now for this," Rowan said, "but being able to interrogate him might be very helpful."

Clive approached at a high rate of speed.

"By the way, super-angry Scion incoming," she whispered to Darius and not more than half a minute later he touched down in between them and Hugo.

"Don't kill him," Rowan said quickly, touching his back to break through the killing haze buzzing around him like pissed-off insects.

"Why not? I smell his magic on you. He tried to hurt you. Again."

"He did. And Genevieve stopped it. Rowan is not influenced by Hugo's magic," Darius said calmly. "Your wife has reminded me it would be helpful to take him in alive for questioning before we kill him."

She hadn't said *before*, but whatever. If Hugo disappeared from existence after they were able to wring the truth out of him it'd be no skin off her nose.

"She is mine!" Hugo screamed again, coming closer.

Darius strode up to him as they were all frozen, waiting to see what would happen, Clive included.

"She is mine," Darius said so quietly Rowan wondered if she'd imagined it. But Hugo's reaction, well, that told Rowan it had been real and designed to poke at Hugo exactly that way.

"She'll be mine tomorrow and a hundred years from now."

Hugo raised his hands, apparently not knowing Genevieve had done whatever she had to take his magic.

Darius simply waited for the moment when Hugo figured it out. Then he punched Hugo's face so hard he fell over like a tree.

"Sometimes the simplest ways are the best." Darius tied Hugo up before hefting him from the ground and tossing him into the trunk of Genevieve's car.

They headed back to *Die Mitte* and brought Hugo to a holding cell. Genevieve did something to keep Hugo's magic null until they were ready to deal with him. If ever. Rowan planned to propose—if Hugo was alive at the end—he never get his magic back because he'd used it for harm so many times.

"He'll be unconscious for some time," Genevieve said after looking Hugo over.

"Will you wait for after sunset to revive him? I'd very much like to be there when he's questioned," Clive said around a mouth full of teeth. Still worked up. Rowan took his hand, squeezing. Reminding him she was fine.

"I'm fine with that," Rowan said.

"Me as well. It'll give us more time to collect more evidence in the interim. I don't think he'll be that hard to break," Genevieve said. "We'll let Rowan question him too. She's very good at it."

"He'll hate it even more if it's me. I love that. Let's coordinate with Konrad too. See what the search turned up," Rowan said. "His little obsession with you was the crack in their plans. Got all sorts of negative attention thrown on them when they needed to keep their heads down. I love it when people think they're revolutionaries and shit but they're just narcissistic fucks who will stop at nothing to make a dollar. What a dingus. His grandpa will be so pissed off. Oh gosh, I can't wait to question him too. It's like my birthday and Yule at the same time."

Clive turned to her and kissed her forehead. Teeth back to normal. "Darling, you do know how to celebrate the positives. Can we please go home after we get this arsehole in a cell?"

"Definitely. You'll have to be better than pancakes." She waggled her eyebrows at him. "I have every confidence you'll be up for the task."

Genevieve waited for them to be finished flirting before speaking again. "Thank you both for all your assistance on this."

"Pshaw," Rowan teased. "We all managed to make this happen. I'll see you tomorrow at the office? We'll work on a plan, be sure we ask all the right questions since I don't know all the relevant magic stuff. Maybe your father can be there too. Though he's very bossy and you need to let him know I have trouble with authority and therefore will be handling the questioning and he'd be assisting."

Darius chuckled, making them all pause a moment. "He knows, little goddess."

Recht, one of the Five, also called Rowan little goddess. In much the same affectionate and admiring way.

It edged out the fear at the crushing weight of Darius's age and power. Pushed more like into their relationship.

She grinned at him and he smiled back before looking at Genevieve, who looked at him with so much open pleasure Rowan was a little embarrassed. Clive wasn't going to be the only one convincing his partner he was better than a stack of pancakes.

"See you tomorrow," Genevieve said.

* * * * *

# *Glossary*

Adaeze: Human. Runs the Hunter Corp. Motherhouse in Nigeria.

Alice: Clive's personal assistant. A powerful Vampire in her own right.

Andros: Vampire. One of the Five. Silent Death. He's the tracker and the one who metes discipline of Vampires on behalf of the First when they break laws.

Bastien: Witch. Son of Lorraine. Works for the Aubert family.

Betchamp: Human. One of the couple who run Rowan and Clive's household. Have been in service to the Stewart family their whole lives.

Blood Front: Vampire organization centered on the idea that humans are little more than walking meals and daytime service for Vampires. Was nearly wiped out entirely. Remaining Vampires have gone underground to avoid detection and discipline by the First or Hunter Corp.

Brigid: Celtic triple goddess representing poetry/inspiration, the hearth and forge, and healing. Love and war rolled into one. Brigid is a goddess worshipped across time and religion, and it fuels her strength. Her various powers manifest in Rowan and each year, they grow stronger.

Carey: (d) Human. Employee of Hunter Corp. Very close with Rowan. Was killed by Blood Front Vampires.

Carl: Sage who uses various modes of transportation to reveal himself in Rowan's life. Often shows up with several taxidermy animals. Never calls Rowan by her correct name.

Cataline: Human. The house manager at the Keep.

Celesse: Human. Runs the Paris Motherhouse of Hunter Corp. Rowan's first trainer.

Clive Stewart: Vampire. Scion of North America for the Vampire Nation. Husband to Rowan Summerwaite. His family is one of the oldest and most powerful in the Nation. His title is House Stewart of Two, which indicates he's next in line to run House Stewart if his father steps aside.

The Conclave: The governing body for magical practitioners. Led by Konrad Aubert.

The Conclave Senate: Legislative group ruled by Genetic witches from powerful families within the Conclave.

Conclave Witches: Belong to and participate in a local

magical organization like a coven overseen by the Conclave. Many are humans with magical gifts of a specific discipline (air, water, etc.). Similar or slightly longer life span than other humans.

Darius: Leader of a Trick of Dust Devils in Las Vegas. Four-thousand-year-old chaos demigod. Genevieve's romantic partner.

David: Human. Rowan's valet and the manager of the U.S. Hunter Corp. operations.

Dina: Human. The cook at the Keep.

Dust Devils: Chaos demigods organized in groups called Tricks. Darius leads one in Las Vegas. There are multiple Tricks worldwide and each pulls in the life energies it needs to feed all the members in various ways from body disposal to settling in cities with high levels of emotion (like Las Vegas) and absorbing it that way.

Elisabeth: Human. One of the couple who run Rowan and Clive's household. Have been in service to the Stewart family their whole lives.

Enyo: (d) An ancient, magic-using Vampire with ties to the Blood Front. Ambushed Rowan, nearly killing her. Rowan killed her after a hunt.

The First: The first of all Vampires and the title he carries. (see also, Theo)

The Five: The First's personal guard. Made up of five

very old and powerful Vampires who operate on Theo's orders. Only one ever speaks in public.

Genetic Witches: A totally different species than humans. Like Vampires, their life spans can extend centuries or longer. They're able to practice multiple disciplines and types of magic. They rule the magical world via the Conclave Senate. These family lines have spent centuries accruing wealth and power.

Genevieve Aubert: Genetic witch. Conclave Senator. Romantically partnered with Darius. Priestess for a Trick of Dust Devils.

Gregor: Vampire. One of the Five. A master spy and assassin. Intelligence gathering.

Guy: (d) Faerie. The bad guy at the very top of the conspiracy to kidnap and drain witches and other Vampires using spells that redirected all their excess power to him. Had been exiled from Faerie and was using the stolen power to attempt to break back in. Was killed by Genevieve in Blood and Blade.

Hunter Corporation: The organization made up to enforce the Treaty signed by magic users, Hunters, and Vampires at the end of the Treaty Wars. Hunters monitor and carry out the Treaty's rules meant to protect humanity from powers they have no ability to match or even know about.

Independent Witches: Don't belong to a coven or other sort of organization. Still required to operate under their basic rules regarding harm to others.

Ivan: Human. Runs the Hunter Corp. Motherhouse in Russia.

Joint Tribunal: Quarterly workgroup meetings for all signers of the Treaty.

The Keep: The castle in the Wetterstein Mountains in Germany where Theo lives and Rowan grew up.

Konrad Aubert: Witch Warlock who leads the Conclave. Genevieve's father.

Lorraine: Genevieve's personal assistant. Cook. House manager and witch wrangler. She's a kitchen witch and her family has served the Auberts for centuries. Her daughter, Samaya, is Genevieve's assistant at the Conclave and her son, Bastien, is a green witch who grows Genevieve's specific marijuana strain. (see also, Madame)

Madame: What Lorraine is often called by Genevieve and Darius. (see also, Lorraine)

Malin: Human. Receptionist at the Las Vegas Hunter Corp. Motherhouse.

Nadir: Vampire. One of the Five. Called the Voice. She's the official voice and representative for the First to the Nation and other organizations.

Niklaus: Vampire. One of the Five. Works with Recht as chief of security. Works with the Scions and their personal security to be sure they're using the most up-to-date training and technology.

Patience: Vampire. One of Clive's top lieutenants. Was known as China for many years until Rowan convinces her to go back to Patience, her given name.

Paola: Vampire. Sción of South America.

Recht: Vampire. One of the Five. The First's weapons master and the person who trained Rowan with blades.

Rowan Summerwaite: Human vessel of the Celtic triple goddess, Brigid. Runs the United States' operations for Hunter Corp. Married to Clive Stewart, Vampire Scion of North America. Foster-daughter of Theo, the First, leader of the Vampire Nation. Has gift of prophecy dreams. Over the last several years has ingested large amounts of ancient Vampire blood, which has left her with a version of their speed and strength.

Samaya: Conclave witch. Genevieve's personal assistant at the Conclave. Fiercely protective of Genevieve and Samaya's mother, Lorraine.

Scions: Vampires who are considered next in line to the First to lead the Vampire Nation should they be called upon. The strongest and best politically. There are five total, and each holds a specific part of the globe and are responsible for the Vampires in their territory.

Seth: Vampire. One of Clive's top lieutenants.

Star: Magical dog. Rowan's familiar and guide.

Susan: Human. Runs the Hunter Corp. Motherhouse in London. Rowan's former trainer.

Tahar: Vampire. Scion of Africa and the Middle East.

Takahiro: Vampire. Scion of Russia, Asia, Eastern Europe.

Theo: The First, and oldest of all Vampires. Undisputed leader of the Vampire Nation. Rowan's father. Not always stable. (see also, the First)

The Treaty: The document that created the modern rules for how Vampires and magic users interact with humans and one another.

Trick: The name of a grouping of Dust Devils.

The Vampire Nation: The governing body for Vampires worldwide. Led by Theo (the First) and his five Scions.

Vanessa: Human. Tech expert at Las Vegas Hunter Corp. Hired after Carey's death.

Vassalus: The title of a person in service to a Vampire. Rowan's former title when she lived in the Keep and served Theo.

Warren: Vampire. Scion of Europe.

## *Acknowledgments*

Thanks to Kerri Buckley for the excellent edits!

My appreciation to the entire Carina team responsible for getting this book out into the world.

To Ray, thank you for all you do. For shouldering the heavy stuff. For believing in me. For being my hype man since we were eighteen.

## *About the Author*

Lauren Dane is the *USA TODAY* and *NYT* Bestselling author of more than seventy-five novels and novellas in the romance and urban fantasy genre. She lives in the Pacific Northwest among the trees with her spouse and children.

You can check out her latest releases, backlist, and upcoming books at her website, www.LaurenDane.com, or you can write her at LaurenDane@LaurenDane.com or via her PO Box: PO Box 45175, Seattle, WA 98145.